# Sanctuary in Time

# Phil Walker

<u>Sanctuary in Time</u>

ISBN 13: 978-1-887982-06-1
ASIN 10: 1537700596

# **<u>Dedication</u>**

**To my wife, Verna.
My constant companion
My perfect partner
Standing with me when the
rest of the world fell away**

## _Acknowledgements_

This portion of a book is usually about the last thing you do before sending it off for publication. Mostly I've been trying to decide what else I should say before launching you into the book. The answer is... nothing. Anything else would only be more story previews.

This book took longer to write than my last six books combined. A good thing. I rewrote and re-edited the work because of the continuous and relentless attention to every word I wrote. I enjoyed the wisdom of a corps of dedicated writers who help each other write better. You should know them.

David Bishop  
Christie Boeke  
Barry Greenawald  
Darlene Greenawald  
Beverly Johnson  

Bob Konig  
John Mallon  
Carrie Murgittroyd  
Mark Pryor  
Katherine Schumm

There are others, but this list is of people who poured out pages of critiques for me since page 1, chapter 1.

To all my literary friends, Thank You.

Sanctuary in Time is a good story. Because of you, it sings like a bird.

# Contents

Chapter 1    *Squaring Off*

Chapter 2    *Hauser's Decision*

Chapter 3    *Insight*

Chapter 4    *Cause and Effect*

Chapter 5    *Planning and Conclusions*

Chapter 6    *Exploring the Timestream*

Chapter 7    *Sanctuary*

Chapter 8    *Welcoming the Academy*

Chapter 9    *Into the West*

Chapter 10   *The Unmasked Conspiracy*

Chapter 11   *Assault on the Gateway*

Chapter 12   *Marooned*

Chapter 13   *Breaking the News*

Chapter 14   *Together or Nothing*

Chapter 15   *Setting the Pace*

Chapter 16   *Another Revolutionary Idea*

Chapter 17   *Assembling the Plan*

Chapter 18   *Reconnaissance*

Chapter 19   *Locking Down*

Chapter 20   *Into the Future*

Chapter 21   Taming the Toltecs

Chapter 22   *Midway*

Chapter 23   *Stirring the Pot*

Chapter 24   *Cocking the Trigger*

Chapter 25   *Defiance*

Chapter 26   *Setting the Trap*

Chapter 27   *The Final Battle*

Chapter 28   *Mission Accomplished*

Chapter 29   *Timequake*

Chapter 30   *The New, Old World*

# Chapter 1
## Squaring Off

Admiral Jonas Cisco's face pinched in annoyance. "What do you mean I'm not authorized to be read in on any information regarding your project? I'm the commanding officer of this entire Joint Operations facility, and I have a top-secret clearance. You're a civilian operation, and it's taken three months to meet you face to face."

Doctor Scott Hauser fidgeted uncomfortably in his chair. He was a middle-aged man with broad shoulders and despite a slightly expanded waist had an athletic look to him. He had a round, placid face beneath a hairline growing thin. His intense green eyes, glistened with intelligence, countering Cisco's first impression of him being ordinary.

"I'm truly sorry, Admiral. I argued with the Academy, the group who provides our financial and political backing, to withhold nothing from you for exactly the reasons you just mentioned. However, they are determined to keep everything limited to the smallest possible number of people. Even our teams of elite scientists, the best in the world, are compartmentalized. Only three of us, in charge here in Charleston, have the full story. What are your superiors telling you?"

"Nothing. They're as much in the dark as I am. They gave me orders to make an entire warehouse available and house a group of thirty people for whom I only had names. It was supposed to be a temporary situation.

"Since then, truckload after truckload of freight, all properly manifested, arrived. Our inspection of your equipment reveals you have more computers than we have on this base, plus all kinds of other mysterious equipment. It vanished into my warehouse. Suddenly, the Navy informs me, every bit as upset as

I was, you are bringing in your own security, and the building sprouts armed guards. The number of people I'm housing has risen to over a hundred. I understand the security restrictions. We have other secret operations underway here where I have no access because I don't have a need to know. However, we have practical matters regarding general base operations for which I am responsible. In your case, I don't know anything."

"Again, Admiral, I'm sorry. This is frustrating for you. Perhaps worse, I'm afraid our stay in Charleston will not end anytime soon."

"Terrific. In a general way, can you tell me anything? Let's start with you. I don't even have a clue what kind of a doctor you are."

"I have a Ph.D. in Computer Science. Most of my colleagues have doctorates in other fields, such as high energy physics, quantum mechanics, and electro-engineering."

"And what are these eggheads doing in my warehouse?"

"I can only tell you we're conducting experiments into advanced new technology."

"No kidding. My electric bill has doubled since you guys started puttering around. Can I expect more of the same?"

"Significantly more, if we keep advancing our research."

Cisco pushed things around on his desk. "This is getting better by the second."

"We're making remarkable progress building on the initial experiments in our first laboratory. This is the main reason I came to visit you. Our electrical needs will indeed grow. However, we expect to cover the additional power drain with the installation of several SMRs, small modular reactors."

"You intend to bring nuclear power reactors onto my base? How many?"

"The plan is for three. They're safe and reliable. Best of all, the excess output they generate, beyond our expected needs

2

should power your entire facility. So, instead of costing you more, your electric bill will become zero."

Cisco snapped back at him. "Nuclear reactors are serious business."

"My team regrets the intrusion, inconvenience, and secrecy we've brought you. We want to be model guests at your base and do what we can to limit the disruption."

"I can't say your model standing improved much today. Not only have you avoided meeting me since you got here, but you introduce yourself now by making an outrageous demand."

"Just as you," acknowledged Hauser, "we all follow orders."

Cisco knew what it meant to carry out directives without any explanation or apparent reason, so he moderated his tone. "Look, Doctor, there's a real limit on how much the Navy will tolerate being pushed around. When I report your latest requirement to Washington, it won't go down easily."

"I can imagine. Nevertheless, our orders come from the highest authority." Hauser stood and stuck out his hand to Cisco. "I'm sorry about not coming by earlier, Admiral. Mostly that's my fault. Getting settled has kept me busy. I'll continue to urge the Academy to bring you more into the loop."

Cisco shook Hauser's hand. "I suppose it's good to put a face to a name, despite the fact I don't know any more about your work than I did before."

The Admiral got up from his desk and escorted Hauser to the door.

As the door closed, Cisco sat back down and picked up the phone. "Molly," he said to his longtime secretary and office manager, "I need a couple things. First, contact Admiral Clarkson, the Chief of Naval Operations, at the Pentagon and tell him I need to speak with him on a secure line ASAP. Then contact the command team and tell them to be here at 1600 today."

"Right away, Admiral. I'll call you back."

Admiral Cisco sat back in his chair and tried to relax. At 58, he still had a full head of hair with a few strands of gray. Tall, trim and fit, he tried to lead by example with regular runs and racquetball at the gym. A Roman nose and strong chin complimented his angular face. Dark brown eyes glowed with awareness and intelligence.

Cisco finished a half an hour of processing routine work on his computer before Molly called him back on the office intercom. "Your secure call from Admiral Clarkson will be incoming in a few minutes, and I've contacted the command team."

He drummed his fingers as he waited, thinking what to say. The phone rang. "Is this none other than the Cisco Kid?" asked a deep voice at the other end of the line.

"Howdy, Andy. How's the weather in Washington?"

"Mostly cold and crappy. I can't wait for spring. Of course, you already have sunny skies and warm days in Charleston. But I guess you didn't call to talk about the weather."

"What are you going to do about that bunch of scientists you dumped on me?"

"Anything new from your mysterious guests?"

"Zippity-do-da. They haven't or won't share anything about the work they're doing. However, I had my first face-to-face meeting with the man running the operation this morning. He informed me they intend to install three small modular nuclear reactors to generate more power."

"Holy shit is that going to cause shock waves around here. You can't wave a wand and make that happen. There are all kinds of rules and restrictions from a dozen government departments."

"I'm sure that's true, but Doctor Hauser acted like it's a done deal and will happen tomorrow. He even tried to sweeten me up by saying all the excess megawatts generated will supply electricity for the whole base."

4

"What did you say?"

"I said bringing in nuclear reactors is a big deal and warned him the Navy would not easily permit such an intrusion. Really, I thought their adding armed security was over the top. Tell me something I can do about this super-secret operation over which we have no control and no idea what's going on."

"I think we can grab a better handle on it with this new demand. I'm going to drop in and talk with the Chairman of the Joint Chiefs. He's already annoyed a bunch of civilians have so much influence at one of our military bases. When I tell him the latest, he'll go into orbit. I'll get back to you."

"Thanks, I'll wait for your call." Cisco rang off, thought about it for a few minutes, and decided to work on other business needing his attention. He'd waded through about half the list in his inbox before his secure phone rang again.

"Well," said the CNO, "it didn't go quite as I expected. The chairman had already heard about the plans to put SMRs in Charleston. Apparently, the command and control of our mutual pain in the ass are so far up the chain they're out of reach even for him. The Navy is filing an official objection with the Secretary of Defense."

"What am I supposed to do?"

"Until the ruling comes back, you can reasonably refuse to allow the introduction of these reactors on grounds of safety, environmental concerns, and public input. That's what we want you to do."

"Lucky me."

"Do the best you can, Jonas. I'm sure your creative mind will think of something."

Molly buzzed him just past four. "The team is here. I put them in the conference room."

"On my way."

When Cisco entered the room, five men rose to their feet.

The officers represented the commanders of the combined services of the Charleston Joint Operation, Army, Navy, Air Force, Marine Corps, and Coast Guard. All were veteran career officers with many years of experience, including deployments to Iraq and Afghanistan. Cisco had never served with better men.

"Take your seats," waved Cisco. He went to the head of the table and sat down.

"The supervisor of our mysterious warehouse, Dr. Hauser, finally dropped in for a visit today and told me they plan to bring in small modular nuclear reactors, three of them. Apparently, we aren't supplying enough electricity to run all the electronics in their laboratory."

Colonel Wyatt Duval, a West Point graduate without an ounce of fat, second in command, and commander of Army forces on the base, spoke up. "I can't say I like the idea of having nuclear reactors located so close to our operations. They may be the next step in energy independence from oil, but they are intended for isolated areas with populations without access to electricity."

"Pardon my ignorance," interjected Commander Ben Crenshaw, the head of the Coast Guard contingent at the base. "I guess I don't understand much about these baby nuclear reactors."

Crenshaw achieved his rank at a young age. A tan and fit bachelor, Cisco knew him to be highly competent, fluent in several languages, and bound for a brilliant future in the upper ranks of the Coast Guard.

"I didn't know zip about them either," said Navy Captain Wilton Judd, "until we decided to investigate using them to power surface ships. They're not like our nuclear-powered submarines. With a submarine, they build the entire ship around the reactor. These SMRs are manufactured in a factory and shipped out on trucks. They're easy to install, can be hooked into a municipal power grid or attached to other modules to provide additional power."

"They're about as safe as anything with 'nuclear' attached to it," added Colonel Duval. "SMRs produce up to 300 megawatts, enough to power 200,000 homes. The actual technology for them is over fifty years old. Lately, a number of countries are building improved systems, and the IAEA is relaxing the regulations and licensing for them to encourage more production."

Cisco looked off into space. "You fellows seem to have a lot more information about these SMRs, than me. I had to research it on the internet. Still, this preoccupation with bringing in more electricity is as big a mystery to me as our off-limits warehouse. With three SMRs, the power output could be close to one gigawatt. Most large cities don't need that much. I spoke to the CNO at the Pentagon today about Hauser's demand. It shocked him so much he took the matter to the Chairman of the Joint Chiefs. When he called back this afternoon, he said the Chairman already got briefed about the plans to install the SMRs, had filed a strenuous objection with the secretary of defense, and told Admiral Clarkson to tell me to think of a way to slow them down."

"How do you intend to do that?" asked Captain Judd.

Cisco waved his arms in frustration. "That's why I called this meeting. I thought you guys could help me."

Air Force Colonel Robert (Chips) Gallant ran his hand through his thinning hair. His years as a stealth fighter pilot were over. He commanded the air wing of the Joint Operation. These days, he played a mean game of poker, the origin of his nickname, and did terrific card tricks for friends and school kids. "So, here's something so secret the Pentagon is in the dark. More than likely the people working in the warehouse are under strict orders to disclose nothing to anyone. We need to think of another way to approach this."

"Here's a thought," said Colonel Duval. "Since these people put such a high premium on energy, we might try a different approach to give us some leverage."

"Go ahead, Wyatt. I'm ready to try almost anything."

"Bringing in these modular reactors means hooking them up to our power grid, nothing about that is going to be secret. When the press gets wind of what's going on, the spotlight is going to shine directly on those warehouse operations."

Captain Judd brightened up. "That means you can bring up other issues relating to routine base operations, Admiral. It might cause the people in charge of this project to rethink their position."

"The most likely outcome will be Dr. Hauser calls up whoever is running this operation, and they send 'comply immediately' orders down through the chain of command," said Colonel Gallant.

Cisco sat back in his chair. "Maybe, and maybe not. Dr. Hauser is clearly not in favor of all this secrecy. He said so today. If we apply pressure and tell him we won't expose the personnel of the base to any risks, without knowing more about what's going on, he might find a way to open the door a crack."

The command team talked for another hour, exploring the full range of issues that might raise.

As they finished up, Colonel Duval jiggled Cisco's elbow. "I'd like to be there when you drop the hammer."

"I wonder if I can get Hauser to the officer's club tomorrow night for happy hour." Cisco picked up a phone and fumbled in his pocket for the number he had to contact the scientist.

A minute later Hauser came on the phone. Cisco put it on speaker. "Dr. Hauser, this is Admiral Cisco. I wonder if you could spare some time tomorrow evening for a little gathering with my command team. We'd like to discuss the modular reactors you intend to bring on the base."

"This is all routine, Admiral. We have nothing to discuss."

"Nothing about this or anything else about your activities is routine," growled Cisco, more harshly than he intended. He glanced around the table and then continued more mildly. "Look, I think we should all become better acquainted with more relaxed surroundings. Bring along your own staff if you like."

"Very well, Admiral. Where would you like to meet?"

"How about the officers' club? It has a private lounge. Say about 6:30?"

"We'll be there." Hauser hung up abruptly.

"It looks like we'll meet somebody besides Dr. Hauser. I suppose we could consider that progress."

The command team filed out of the conference room. Duval lagged behind, "Let me do the yelling and screaming tomorrow night, Jonas, I'm better at it than you."

"My thought, exactly. Tell the others to not be shy about chiming in."

"I hope we learn something."

"If they don't walk off in a huff, after we tell them we need a better reason to cave on their reactor installation demands other than them just saying so."

# Chapter 2
# Hauser's Decision

Scott Hauser sat behind his desk while Doctor Lino Arnett paced the floor. Doctor Missy Long lounged in a chair.

Arnett stopped pacing. "Come on, Scott, we've got tests and trials running all over the lab. No time to waste on a bunch of military men."

Arnett functioned as Dr. Hauser's nominal second in command, although the scientific stratosphere, in which both men operated made the term almost meaningless. Arnett was short and so thin it made him look even smaller. Yet his energy level spiked higher than all the seventy or so scientists laboring at the pinnacle of advanced technology in the warehouse. He didn't possess the steady temper of his colleague and easily qualified as the man to avoid the most when a critical test failed, or someone botched an experiment. His groundbreaking work on quantum chromodynamics put him in a select group of fewer than a dozen people in the world who understood his concepts.

Doctor Missy Long served as the theoretician in physics. She was one of the people who understood Arnett's technology. She had an eidetic memory, valuable for the research work. She also had an interest in history regurgitating dates and facts like a walking Google. Although over fifty, she retained a trim figure. Her sparkling blue eyes set off long auburn hair tied back in a ponytail. She had cushy lips and a smile that lit her pretty face.

"We're on thin ice with the military since we shoved our way in and appropriated one of their big warehouses. When the Academy made us add armed security, it got worse. Now we're saying we need small nuclear reactors. Admiral Cisco didn't wait to bring the matter up with his superiors after I met with him yesterday. I spoke about it to some people at the Academy today. The Navy is making a strong case with the Defense Department to keep the reactors out."

"We gotta have the extra power, Scott."

"All the more reason to find ways to get along with these people. I've been on the phone half the day with some of the senior staff at the Academy, asking again for clearance to bring the commanding officer of the base into the fundamentals of what we're doing. Before, they turned me down flat, but this new development is forcing them to reassess the situation. There are mixed feelings and an obvious debate is underway."

"That's because what we're messing around with terrifies everyone, me included," said Arnett. "Can you imagine how an outsider would go ballistic if they sniffed even the basics of our unexpected discovery?"

"I believe Admiral Cisco is a rational, intelligent man. I read up on him when we got to Charleston. He was a Rhodes Scholar, has advanced degrees in engineering and economics, enjoys a spotless career in the Navy, is a combat veteran, and was the commanding officer of an aircraft carrier. I think he would understand the magnitude of our breakthrough better than almost anyone. If I can bring him onboard with clearance from the Academy to tuck him into our security envelope, I think he will work with us as we power up for a full-blown test. In any case, he's found a soft spot with the SMRs. If he's capable of exploiting it, we'll find ourselves in real trouble."

Arnett shrugged his shoulders in submission. "Okay, okay, don't expect me to like it. The military always turns our significant achievements into weapons. You can't trust them."

"Thanks, Lino. At least put on a clean shirt."

After Arnett and Long left his office. Hauser puffed his cheeks and picked up the phone to make another call. Shortly, he spoke to Cameron Fisk, Chairman of the Academy.

"Well, Hauser, they say you've been burning up the lines talking with the staff today. Tell me, what the fuck is so goddamned important this time?"

Hauser resolved to ignore the abuse and attempt to reason with the arrogant man. "Mr. Fisk, I called because we are facing a crisis here in Charleston. We need to acquire more power to conduct our final tests. Now the commanding officer has filed a protest with the Navy. The same man I told you a number of times should be briefed on our work."

"I know all about their fucking protests. Forget about them. Start paying more attention to delivering some fucking results on the work we keep shelling out our money to support."

"Mr. Fisk," continued Hauser, struggling to control his anger, "this issue is directly related to our ability to produce the results you continuously pressure me to deliver. I have told you—several times in recent weeks—we cannot conduct a full test of our system without additional power. If we overrule the officers at this base and install the SMRs, we will have no cover whatsoever with the press and the public who will want to know if the military didn't authorize this, who did. We will have no answer."

Fisk said nothing for a minute, then blared explosively. "Well shit, Hauser. What kind of a fucking mess have you gotten yourself into?"

All Hauser's reserve and calm melted away. He almost yelled into the phone, "We are in this fix because of you, Mr. Fisk. Your irrational preoccupation with security has alienated the military and created this current crisis. For years you drove away extremely valuable members of our scientific and research team because they were constantly badgered about security by your corporate goons. Our work would have proceeded much more smoothly if you had not insisted on compartmentalizing the research so severely our senior department heads can't even speak to one another."

Impervious to Hauser's outburst, Fisk shot back. "Doctor,

we have all this horseshit security because you people stumbled onto a much bigger discovery. Now you spend all your fucking time and our money trying to turn it into something we can use."

"You aren't listening to me, Mr. Fisk. We can't give you anything without more power. We can't generate more power without the SMRs. We can't install and activate the SMRs unless the military can smooth over public concerns. At the present time, they have absolutely no reason to do this because they have no idea what we are doing. Unless we provide, at least the commanding officer of this base, a more comprehensive insight into our project we will go nowhere, and you will have wasted your money and our time."

"Now you listen to me. You do whatever you have to do to put this fucking project back on track. But I want some results. If the story of what you balloon brained bastards are doing gets out into the open, you'll be holding the fucking bag!"

A loud click sounded in Hauser's ear. "Guess the conversation is over," he said to the wall in his office.

Doctors Scott Hauser, Lino Arnett, and Missy Long arrived at the private lounge of the officers' club a few minutes late. Admiral Cisco and his command team were already sipping drinks.

A cigarette dangled from Arnett's lips.

"This is a no-smoking building," said Cisco mildly.

"Is that right?" Arnett flicked ashes on the table. "Well, I do smoke, Navy, and if you don't like it, tough shit. I'll be happy to leave. I didn't want to come in the first place."

Dr. Hauser chuckled a little. " Honestly Admiral, we didn't cook up a 'good-cop/bad-cop scenario' in advance. Lino is a royal pain in the ass, and you should be glad you don't have to put up with him every day. However, Dr. Arnett has one of the best minds on the planet, and we would not be in Charleston, annoying you, if it weren't for him."

"It's still have a no-smoking building."

Arnett glanced at Hauser and crushed out the cigarette on his heel, "Score one for you."

Hauser smiled and turned back to Cisco. "May I also introduce Doctor Missy Long. She's our theoretical, abstract and metaphysical expert on the rather exotic technology we are investigating. Don't tell her anything you don't want her to remember because she never forgets anything."

"An eidetic memory Doctor?"

Long cocked her head in mild surprise over Cisco so quickly putting the pieces together. "More or less," she said with a smile shaking Cisco's hand. The Admiral took Long down the table introducing her to his staff. They all jumped up politely and shook her hand. Arnett followed along, half mumbling greetings to the officers as they shook his hand.

With the formalities over, a waiter came in. Cisco made a hospitable gesture. "Drinks are on me tonight."

Hauser ordered a plain Coke, while Arnett quizzed the waiter and settled on an expensive single malt Scotch. Long ordered a glass of white wine. When the drinks were served, Hauser said, "Your meeting, your agenda."

Cisco nodded to Colonel Duval.

Duval got to his feet. He spoke to all three scientists, but his massive frame loomed over Arnett.

"This is a little uncomfortable, so let me make this as clear to you as I can. Despite the fact you newcomers either don't understand or don't care about our business, we do conduct critical, sensitive work here.

"The Charleston Joint Command supports every branch of the services. We have a large base, encompassing more than 48 square miles. We have a high-tech nuclear school, a deep-water harbor, multiple air and sea operations, and ongoing

14

engagements with dozens of military commands and federal agencies.

"Now you are squatted on our base. You have commandeered an entire warehouse and surrounded it with armed guards even though we run top-secret operations on a daily basis. Your warehouse is embarrassing and disruptive to this command."

Hauser conceded, "As I told Admiral Cisco yesterday, I didn't want such strict security. In fact, I don't like it any more than you since I have to check in and out of my own facility."

"We come now to your latest demand. You are proposing to introduce three small modular nuclear reactors. I'm surprised your superiors don't recognize the mountains of regulations associated with nuclear reactors. You say this is routine, but we believe these reactors represent a clear risk to the safety and security of this command. What about the question of how to provide cooling for the reactors. Then we have the considerable issue of dealing with the nuclear waste."

Colonel Gallant added. "If we announce nuclear reactors will be installed, with no other explanation, you can be sure the press will demand to be told why we are endangering the lives of families. There are no answers for them except to point at your laboratory."

"Unless," barked Arnett. "There's always an unless."

"No unless, Dr. Arnett," said Duval sharply. We strongly oppose the installation of these reactors. We've already pushed our objection up the chain of command as I'm sure Doctor Hauser has told you. Unless we find out more about your operation, we could hardly support you."

"This is serious," intervened Captain Judd. "On one hand we work to do our jobs with the least amount of friction. On the other hand, your group arrives locks everyone else out and succeeds in scrambling routines all over the base in addition to making everyone nervous."

"So much for the social niceties and congenial ice-breaking," interjected Arnett.

"Is that your official position, Admiral?" asked Hauser.

"Apart from the considerable issue of the reactors, there are other, more fundamental matters for which I'm responsible."

"What if you have a fire?" asked Colonel Judd "Do you have a single fire extinguisher?"

"What if you have a medical emergency?" inquired Colonel Gallant.

"Are you using or storing hazardous materials, which could be a danger to others?" added Commander Crenshaw.

"I don't have answers to those questions, and we still don't have a single clue about any of your operations."

Even Arnett said nothing to this and an uncomfortable silence filled the room.

At last, Hauser stirred. "Your objections and concerns are completely valid. Before this meeting, I spoke with my own higher command and repeated my previous opposition to bullying our way onto this military base without any explanations to anyone, including the commanding officer. I then brought up the matter of the reactors voicing your expected opposition. Moreover, I added the likelihood this conflict could cause people to ask questions we can't answer."

"What did they say?"

"Mostly the responses are not repeatable. However, after thinking about it, the chairman of The Academy admitted there could be a significant public relations problem and entirely too much publicity over the reactors. I reminded him we are unable to move forward with our project without additional power."

"Just who is this Academy?"

"They are the venture capital group who pay for our research as well as the political firepower whose influence you've seen."

"That influence must come from very high up to be able to order the Joint Chiefs of Staff around."

"You have no idea."

"Thanks for the insight. Go ahead with your train of thought."

"Here we are stuck between a glacier and a mountain. Their so-called solution was predictable. The chairman reminded me I'm responsible for producing results. If I must disclose sensitive information to achieve this, I'll also be held responsible for any resulting negative outcomes."

"That sounds like a lose-lose situation to me," said Cisco. "Your people are dumping the whole load on you."

"That is essentially correct."

"Have you decided how to handle this?" asked Colonel Duval.

"Yes. I intend to bring Admiral Cisco into our laboratory and show him exactly what we're attempting to achieve. After you've seen everything, Admiral, it will be up to you to decide whether or not our work justifies the additional power we require to take the next step."

Both Doctors Arnett and Long looked surprised at Hauser's decision.

Arnett rose halfway to his feet. "You can't do this, Scott. This guy will find out what we're doing and go into orbit. All you're going to do is bring an outsider into the lab and give him an excuse to object to the reactors. We'll be stopped cold."

"Excuse me, Doctor Arnett," said Cisco with a grim face. "Do you really believe a military officer is incapable of recognizing the value of advanced technology?"

"The technology we're working on is not just advanced; it's revolutionary. So far beyond your scale of understanding it will terrify you to the core. All you'll want to do is shut us down."

"If that's the case," said Duval, "you have to tell us what's going on."

Cisco nodded. "I would second that."

"Frankly, I can't think of any other way to break this impasse. Lino is right about our work being revolutionary. Getting your head around the concepts won't be easy."

Missy Long leaned across the table toward Cisco. "Scott didn't mention any of this before we got here tonight. He probably wanted to find out how determined you and your staff were before deciding to proceed. I don't think we have any choice, but I would ask you, Admiral, to keep an open mind.

"I most certainly will."

"Very well," concluded Hauser. "It will take some time to prepare a presentation of our technology. Plus, I have some other matters to resolve. I'll contact you when we're ready."

"This is unbelievable! We're cutting our own throats."

Cisco sat up straight and looked directly at Arnett. He said quietly, "Doctor, clearly you strenuously object to allowing anyone to peek at your project. I'd like to understand your concerns about this. Can you help us out here?"

Arnett blinked, then sat back in his chair, crossed his arms and looked at the ceiling for a moment. Cisco could see the little man was in deep thought. At last, Arnett put his hands on the table and said, "In 1945, after three years and several billions of dollars, a group of scientists created a nuclear weapon, which they detonated in New Mexico. Everyone who witnessed this staggering explosion came away awed and dismayed by what they saw. After that, Albert Einstein, along with at least fifty other scientists working on the Manhattan Project, wrote a letter to the President urging him not to use this weapon on the people of Japan.

"We all remember what happened. The United States did drop the atomic bomb, twice, resulting in the deaths of half a million people. President Truman said it served the greater good, but the result changed the world forever.

"Our project is on the same order of magnitude. It will change everything. The possibilities are simply beyond our ability to comprehend."

# Chapter 3
## Insight

Four days later, Admiral Cisco parked his car and walked to the warehouse. Two armed guards blocked the entrance. Dr. Hauser stood waiting.

Hauser shook Cisco's hand. "Next time we'll give you a pass to wear."

"Assuming there is a next time."

"I'm more confident in you than that. Come on in and welcome to Wonderland."

Cisco couldn't remember if he had ever been in this particular warehouse before the arrival of the scientific team. He knew from checking the inventory log the building was two hundred feet long, a hundred feet wide and stored a couple of trucks, spare machinery, and replacement parts. None of that remained. In their place, a wall-to-wall overhaul made it look like a warehouse only from the outside.

As they walked through the entry doors, a corridor ten-feet in width went straight ahead two-thirds of the way to the rear of the building where a floor-to-ceiling wall stood with a pair of solid doors in the center. The central corridor had no doors or windows, but hallways went off in both directions in several places along the corridor.

Hauser walked to the first hallway and pointed in one direction. "Down there are the administrative offices, including mine. Going the other way is our lounge, break rooms, and conference room. We even have a couple rooms with beds for people to sleep. Our folks work very long hours.

"At the end of the halls are doors leading to the racks of computer servers. They run the length of the building on both sides and are isolated on raised supports to let the air-conditioning flow up through ventilator vents to keep them cool."

Cisco glanced down the central corridor. Other hallways branched off, presumably leading to many more offices and enclosed workstations. "How many people work here?"

"Our scientific, engineering and tech complement is about seventy."

"Quite a few people crammed into this warehouse, despite it being so big, but I suppose they all enjoy collaborating together on this project of yours."

Hauser turned away for a few seconds and then faced back to Cisco. "Not exactly. In fact, hardly at all."

"How do you manage to get anything done if you don't talk to each other?"

"You must understand, Admiral, our work is incredibly complex with many components leading toward the final objective we hope to achieve. All these people worked in separate teams with offices and laboratories all over the country for several years. Each team engaged in a different part of the end goal. Only Lino, Missy and I saw the data and results from all the teams. At last, everyone is assembled here, because the work is reaching completion. However, we still maintain a strict compartmentalization of the teams."

"To what end, Dr. Hauser? It seems to me this would be the time to bring everyone together as one team."

"On a ship don't you have separate groups to run the engines, man the guns, plot the navigation and so forth?"

"Of course, but we don't keep it a secret. We work hard to cross-train our crews in as many areas as possible. That's how to ensure the safety of the entire crew. If we ran a ship as you're running this operation of yours, we would end up with rival groups, friction, and general disharmony everywhere. When the time came for the ship to go into action in a hostile situation, it would be the first one sunk because it didn't function as a team."

"I agree with you, Admiral. The problems you mention are

an unresolved issue for us, and I've struggled with it some time."

"Why haven't you brought them all together and told them what's going on?"

"Because the Academy doesn't want too many people knowing the full picture fearing one or more of them will take what they know and sell the information to the highest bidder."

"If you keep going the way you are you can bet that's exactly what will happen. If you aren't willing to trust the men and women who are generating this wonder of yours, why should they be loyal?" Cisco rubbed his forehead in deep thought for a moment. "Why is your Academy driving all this secrecy?"

Hauser paused for a moment. "When Lino, Missy and I took our initial research to a venture capital group in hopes of them funding our work, things got complicated very quickly. We found ourselves surrounded by a small, but powerful, group of people who had money, and tremendous influence. This group was code-named Academy, with oversight directly from the White House.

"We got the funding we wanted—in an enormous flood. But we were also saddled with a collar of secrecy so strict, we had to break our research into different workgroups and restrict information between them to no more than they needed to take new steps to complete their work. That was almost ten years ago. When our research progressed far enough to begin testing, we put many of our scientists, still mostly working in the dark, into a laboratory in Denver. The success of those tests led us to realize we needed a secure facility such as a military base, which already had secret programs and in-place security, where we could expand the testing to its full potential. We selected the Charleston Joint Command."

Cisco nodded. "I suppose your Academy expected you to keep the same compartmentalization and secrecy here?"

"I pleaded with them through the assembly and installation

of this expanded laboratory to let me bring our researchers, all excellent people, inside the security envelope. I got nowhere. It was you, Admiral, who gave me a way to break the logjam."

"We threatened to go public on the installation of the SMRs. So, your Academy told you to do what you had to do and said the blame would fall on you if it all went south."

"Correct. If I'm going to take the fall for everything, I'm going to do what I thought was right in the first place. Today I'm going to use your being here as an opportunity to bring our entire scientific team together and unload the whole story. I'm going let them have it, both barrels, right between the eyes."

Cisco chuckled a little and then smiled at Hauser, patting him on the back. "I've had to make a few difficult decisions in my life, so I sympathize with your trouble making this one. In any case, I think you're doing the right thing."

"Lino and Missy stuffed everyone into our conference room. I'd like you to join us."

"Let's go."

Cisco followed Hauser down the side corridor and into the conference room. Clearly not planned to hold so many people, the men and women were shoulder to shoulder in chairs with only a few feet of space in front with chairs for Hauser, Arnett, Long, and Cisco. Hauser held his hands up for quiet. The group went silent immediately. He smiled at his audience and spoke in a calm and measured voice, "I would like to introduce Admiral Jonas Cisco, the Commanding Officer of the Charleston Joint Command."

Cisco stood up and received polite applause. Tall, with a poised command presence, he presented an aura of dignity and authority in his starched and perfectly creased whites, with the rows of awards over his left pocket, and the two silver stars on each collar. He stood in stark contrast to the casually dressed and somewhat untidy people he faced. Nevertheless, he was certain he stood before some of the most capable minds anywhere in the world. He smiled. "It is my pleasure and honor to be here today. My hope is, with this beginning, all our lives will become more comfortable as we enjoy mutual cooperation with each other."

This drew a more enthusiastic round of applause. Hauser, Arnett, and Long joined them. Cisco sat down quietly. He recognized his aura of personal charisma. It had served him well in times of mortal danger, panic, and fear when all his crews had—was his steady grip. He'd never exploited this quality for personal gain.

He turned his attention to Scott Hauser. Although they had only met together twice, Cisco recognized some of the same unique mannerisms in this brilliant scientist. He sensed the two of them were on the same side and determined to help him in any way he could.

Hauser now stood to speak. "Meetings like this are pretty rare. In fact, I think today marks the first time all of us have ever been in the same place at the same time. In my view, that's the problem. We've all been working in a kind of fog for years, not knowing what others are doing. The choking smoke of secrecy and security stifled our efforts, drove many good men and women away, and robbed us of creativity and imagination. That ends now. I intend to break all the security protocols and give you the answers to the many questions you have been asking for so long."

Cries of "about time" and "took long enough" echoed through the room along with smatterings of applause. A general undercurrent of hubbub flowed off the walls. Hauser let it go on for a minute and then put his hands up for quiet.

"For the past ten years, we worked industriously to perfect a means in which matter can be transferred from one place to another. Even the topic of this investigation was highly classified. Different groups worked on different aspects of the problem. As we found new and promising lines of investigation we concentrated on them, giving you all new avenues to pursue."

"We weren't getting anywhere until you brought Doctor Arnett aboard," said Missy.

"True enough. The addition of Lino with his groundbreaking theories on quantum chromodynamics proved to be the difference."

"Yay Lino," came a cry from the back of the room.

Arnett lit another cigarette and smiled, a little self-consciously, Cisco thought.

Hauser continued. "Dr. Arnett's research gave us the ability to transfer matter from one place to another. During the past several years, quantum physicists worked at the sub-atomic level. They learned how to transmit electrons and protons, but never the nucleus of an atom. Lino found a way to do that."

Cisco shook his head in confusion. "Excuse me for interrupting, Doctor, but for the benefit of us lesser minds let me make sure I understand what you mean by matter transference. Is that where you move people and objects over long distances like in Star Trek?"

"Exactly," Arnett replied. "The number of people in the United States who would not recognize the phrase 'Beam me up, Scotty' is roughly comparable to the number of people who have never heard of ketchup."

"Have you accomplished this?" asked an astonished Cisco.

"Yes," said Hauser. "We started with elements and inanimate objects and then moved to amoebas, single-cell organisms. The physics says the electromagnetic pulse of the power source we are employing will fry all brain waves, heartbeats, everything in organisms more complex. It didn't happen. We have no idea why. Everybody says it isn't supposed to be even theoretically possible. Our current experimentation is with Rhesus monkeys, which we are successfully transporting."

Cisco shook his head in amazement. "Remarkable. I can't imagine anything, which would change the world more profoundly. No wonder your Academy imposed such secrecy."

Arnett pontificated. "They expected to be wealthy beyond the dreams of avarice." Missy Long giggled.

"The security they imposed on us was stifling," said Hauser. "However, as we continued to work we discovered something else which altered the entire subject of matter transference. This is the line we have followed for the past several years. None of you were allowed to know what this new discovery was. All you got were increasingly more difficult and seemingly unassociated experiments to conduct. Furthermore, all you thought you knew about Project Horizon is a lie."

This time the outburst loudly filled the room. Hauser stood placidly. Cisco had to admit the good doctor certainly could sink a hook. After several minutes Hauser raised his hands for order once more. "By happenstance, it is as a result of our interaction with the military officers here in Charleston we've come to this turn of events. Lino, can you explain?"

Arnett crushed out his cigarette and stood up. "You know we moved to this base because of its existing security and relatively small number of people moving around the more sensitive areas. We also came here because we needed a larger facility to conduct more advanced experiments and provide suitable housing for you all. We've built a much more substantial broadcast platform from the one we had in Denver. Our experiments were successful but limited. We need significantly more power to test the full capabilities of our equipment.

"We planned to install several small modular nuclear reactors. These would give us more than the necessary power to run our expanded system. However, Admiral Cisco objected to bringing nuclear reactors onto his base. We need the power but couldn't tell him why. The Academy was ponderously unsympathetic. They have the political power to force the reactors on the military. However, they failed to consider the inevitable public outcry if they did. Doctor Hauser gave the chairman of the Academy a choice. Either tell Admiral Cisco the whole story or pack up our bags and mothball the entire project. He chose to let our fearless leader make the call and said he was responsible for anything bad that happens. I didn't help the situation. I made a scene at the officer's club ranting and raving about how military people were too stupid to grasp the fundamentals of our science."

Hauser picked up the conversation. "After the meeting, Lino, Missy and I got together and went through everything that happened. I pointed out how difficult it is for you to work in this way, and how frustrating it is to filter everything through us instead of collaborating with each other like real scientists. The decision I made was to go all the way bringing, not only Admiral Cisco into the information loop, but including you folks as well."

"The more I thought about it," said Arnett, "the better I liked it. Not only do we get to stop keeping stuff from you, but we also get to tell the Academy to shove it."

Arnett turned and faced Cisco. "I don't know whether the military can or will help us out, but I owe you an apology for being such a jerk, Admiral."

"Since we are putting everything out in the open," said Hauser. "Time for you all to have a look at the Gateway, as we call it. Only a few people are permitted access to enter this part of the laboratory. No more of that. Come along, Admiral, and everyone else. Let me show you what's so important we can order four-star generals around."

Cisco, the three seniors of the project, and seventy others, who represented some of the finest minds in the world, left the conference room and walked down the central corridor.

The corridor ended at a pair of heavy doors. Hauser swiped

a card through a terminal. When it blinked green, he pulled it open and waved Cisco and the eager scientists into the substantial open space. In the middle of the big chamber, a round, raised platform spread out thirty feet in diameter. A short staircase circled the platform. In the center, a six-inch red line marked a twelve-foot circle in the middle of the platform. Twenty feet above the ring, an array of fluted cones, almost like the base of a multi-engine rocket, were anchored in a steel frame with thick power lines flowing into each of the cones. Inside the left edge of the circle, a three-foot-high metal pole supported a two-foot square clear, plastic box mounted on a stand. An identical arrangement stood on the right edge.

"Take a seat," said Arnett waving Cisco to a chair as he went up onto the platform, "We'll attempt to make this simple."

"I'll try to keep up."

Dr. Hauser took a chair next to Cisco and Long. Meanwhile, the entire contingent of researchers, scientists, engineers, and techs spread out in the room, standing, sitting in chairs or on the floor, filling all the space in front of the platform.

Arnett expounded. "As so often happens in scientific experimentation, the results turn out to be much different from your original intention. Such is the case with our work. Everything you'll see today is a significant departure from our expectations. We began with the belief we had achieved a breakthrough in matter transference, except for one annoying twist. After running the system in our smaller laboratory, we measured the time interval of the delivery of matter from one place, to another, and discovered they weren't the same."

"Why is that important?"

"Because there should be no interval; the transfer should be simultaneous. In the other laboratory, the plastic boxes sat side by side, yet the subject monkey arrived on the receiving platform a micro-second before it left the sending platform."

28

Cisco looked puzzled. "Meaning?"

"Meaning," said Arnett, "in addition to transporting matter, we also tapped the fourth dimension of the space-time continuum. Our monkey is moving in time."

"Does that mean the monkey is going forward in time?"

"Not forward, Admiral, backward. Otherwise, it could not arrive earlier than it left. What we want to do now is demonstrate the system."

Hauser picked up the narrative. "Our equipment requires a significant amount of power, more than we had available earlier. This is one of the reasons we moved to Charleston. Here, we separated the boxes trying to learn if the distance between them made any difference. We've also increased the energy delivered to the transmission cones. We've learned how to calibrate the interval. For this demonstration, I set it for fifteen seconds."

A tech came forward with a Rhesus monkey in a cage. The monkey had a red ribbon around its neck and a metal bracelet around its wrist. The tech placed it inside the plastic box. Hauser went to a control panel near the stage and powered up the system. An intense blue column, crackling with energy, appeared from the base of the cones, filling the circle outlined with the red band, and the two boxes. A less intense but significant blue glow spread through the entire Gateway.

"Watch the far stand," said Hauser as he pushed a red button.

Instantly, Cisco saw another monkey, with the ribbon and bracelet still in place, appear inside the cubicle. By all he could tell, the monkey looked the same and behaved normally. Then he turned back to the sending platform, astonished to see the same monkey still in its box.

The seconds on the clock clicked slowly away. When the timer reached fifteen seconds, Cisco jumped when the monkey in the sending cubicle vanished. He shook his head attempting to process what he'd just seen.

Arnett stepped off the platform and plopped into a chair next to Cisco. "I know how you feel, Admiral. All of us felt the same, wondering if we'd released a monster."

"I have a few dozen questions," said Cisco. "The first one is, did I just see you send a living animal back in time?"

"You did," said Hauser.

"Can you bring it back to the present?"

"Why, gee, we never thought of that!" cackled Arnett. He wiped the silly smile off his face. "Sorry, my crude stab at humor. The answer is, yes we can."

"How?"

"Evidently, the energy used to send the monkey back in time is somehow stored at the molecular level. We can activate the Gateway, and the recall bracelet sends a signal from the original power source, and the process is reversed."

Hauser pushed a few more buttons, and the blue energy beam crackled on the floor of the empty cubicle. This time there was no delay. The monkey in the far cubicle vanished and reappeared in the sending cube.

Cisco looked around the room. The blue energy field glowed again, casting a kind of cerulean light on everything, people included.

"If your energy field is spreading out beyond your main transmission area, why isn't it affecting the people inside the room?"

Arnett gave Cisco a curious look. "My, my, aren't we the insightful one? I think I misjudged you, Admiral, we have a brain in there after all."

Cisco waved away the jab with a flip of his hand. "So, what's the answer?"

"We wondered the same thing," replied Hauser. "The transmission cones produce an intense field inside the Gateway.

We've come to think of it as a power dome concentrated on the sending platform."

"There's a secondary power dome," said Arnett. "You saw it radiating out, turning us all into 'blue people'. The impact it has is to freeze time within the secondary power field while it's functioning. We know this because we had people with watches outside the warehouse with the field operating, and others inside the field. We measured a difference."

"Okay," said Cisco, "what do you intend to do with this Pandora's Box?"

Hauser crossed his legs and speculated. "The most obvious and benign application is to use our tool as an observer of history. Imagine all the questions we could answer if we could actually observe events as they unfolded."

"Think of being on a ship watching the Titanic sinking," said Arnett.

"What a terrible example," sighed Cisco. "My first impulse would be to rush in and save as many survivors as I could."

"The exact reason he used it," said Doctor Long, joining the conversation "Rescuing people would be anyone's first impulse. That's the problem. If you saved people who otherwise would have died, what change would there be in the fabric of time? In other words, interfering with history might produce a profound effect on our lives today."

"An age-old paradox," said Hauser. "You go back in history and meet your father, long before he marries your mother. You get into an argument and kill him. If that is so, how could you ever have been born?"

"There are two distinctive schools of thought," said Arnett. "The first one is the Universe has made up its mind on this. Time, in cosmic terms, never changes. Everything that did happen will happen and continue to happen."

Long picked up a notepad and a felt pen. "The other view is

31

called the 'branching universe' theory."

She drew a curving line across the paper and continued. "In this theory, we see time as a river flowing from the past to the future. However, if you introduce a significant enough change at any point in the river you create a new branch, still flowing toward the future, but along a different route." She drew a second line about halfway along the original

"What happens to the old river?"

"It might continue parallel to the new branch." Then she drew a scribble through the old branch with her pen. "Most likely it ceases to exist."

"Which means we cease to exist, at least in this version of history," said Arnett pursing his lips.

Cisco sat thinking for a moment, then looked sharply at the two scientists. "But you said a while ago the second field freezes time. If that's true, it would be a safety net. Any changes to the time stream would not affect people inside the dome."

"That is exactly what we said," declared Long. "We reported our alternative theories to the Academy. After considerable discussion, and our insistence, they admitted we needed to do everything we could to minimize the effects of major historical interruptions. Since we stumbled on a secondary energy dome which apparently freezes time in the immediate vicinity of the primary field, we want to increase the size of this field."

Hauser continued. "The general idea is to make the safety zone extensive enough to deal with a catastrophic event which alters the present so radically it wipes out our contemporary twenty-first-century world. It will be possible for humanity to begin again."

"You must have already figured out that won't work under the present circumstances," said Cisco.

"I don't know how to create a new world with a gene pool of seventy people inside a warehouse with only two bathrooms," said Long wryly.

"Which is why you want to bring in the SMRs," said Cisco with dawning understanding.

"Correct, Admiral," said Hauser. "We won't conduct any real jumps back in time until we've established this survival beachhead, and that means more power."

Arnett added, "This technology scares us to death, and we've finally gotten the Academy providing the funding and the influence with the government, to recognize the grave nature of our concern."

"Assuming you did install the extra power generators," asked Cisco "How large a secondary dome could you produce?"

"We think adding something like one gigawatt would increase the diameter to about twelve miles."

"What additional steps and preparation does the Academy say you should be taking?"

"They haven't mentioned anything else," said Hauser.

"Then they are deliberately keeping things from you or are incredibly naïve."

"I guess I don't understand."

"If all you have in your 'survival beachhead' is a way to keep the servers running and the lights on, I can tell you everyone inside your twelve-mile secondary dome will be dead in less than a year."

"Now I really don't understand," repeated Hauser.

"The trouble with the people calling your shots, and maybe you guys, is you don't have a lot of experience in what it takes to maintain a functioning infrastructure. We military officers, whom you seem to dismiss so quickly, spend our lives thinking about what it takes to keep such a system working. For example, has anyone thought about how we would keep our vehicles, ships, or airplanes running without fuel? Has it occurred to you our food supplies wouldn't come from the shelves of grocery stores if there were no infrastructure to resupply them? How would you house, educate, or provide other services to a population who suddenly found themselves cut off and isolated? How about treating the sick or injured? Where are you going to find doctors, drugs, and medical facilities?"

Hauser's face turned almost white as Cisco delivered these assessments of additional requirements he hadn't considered.

Arnett exploded in anger. "Those sons of a bitch are trying to give us a false sense of security so they can forge ahead with their plans to use time travel for whatever purpose they want. They obviously don't believe we can alter current events by changing the past, or they think whatever the odds are, is an acceptable risk."

"That would be my guess." Cisco looking around. Most of the scientists and techs were on their feet crowding closer to the platform, the deep concern on their faces unmistakable. "You already a problem right here. I think these folks are wondering how they would survive. Pushing your team forward toward the same goal is now going to be more difficult."

The admiral stood up and faced the men and women. "I'm sorry for painting such a bleak picture, and for frightening you. The good news is there are solutions to every issue I raised. It won't be easy or finished overnight, but I can promise you if we end up stranded on some grim survival beachhead we will be ready. Frankly, there are worse situations than this. There probably won't be anyone shooting at us. The solution to our puzzle will come from proper planning and detailed organization."

Hauser, Arnett, and Long smiled at the smooth and effortless way in which the tall Navy admiral calmed and relaxed the anxious crowd.

Cisco walked among them shaking hands, exchanging greetings, smiling, and receiving little hugs from many of the women as he interacted with the brilliant minds who had created this wonder of science but were overwhelmed with the prospect of not being able to buy a loaf of bread.

Hauser turned to Arnett. "Still think bringing the military into our inner circle is a bad idea?"

"He does have a way of identifying a problem and instilling confidence for finding solutions."

Cisco smiled at the sudden endorsement. Doctor Missy Long stifled a laugh with her hand over her mouth.

# Chapter 4
## Cause and Effect

Half an hour later, Cisco waved goodbye to a smiling crowd of people and stepped out of the warehouse with the leaders of the Horizon Project. When they were alone, Cisco turned to the three scientists. "The next time you plan a demonstration without knowing the outcome, I suggest you conduct it in a somewhat more private setting. Like a lawyer, never ask a question to which you don't already know the answer. We put a lid on the immediate problems with your team for today, but you can bet they'll be back with some pointed demands for more information on how we intend to proceed. When they do, we'd better have a solid plan."

"What do you suggest, Admiral?" asked Hauser.

"The first thing we need to do is bring in my command team, and they will have to be told everything. Next, we need an appraisal of what it will take to turn our military base into a self-sufficient city capable of existing independently of any outside assistance. I assume you have big money backing your program?"

"I don't think money will be a problem."

"I wouldn't say that if I were you. What we'll have to do will cost billions. Even if money is not a problem, time is. Your Academy won't be pleased with long delays before they can start using the technology."

Arnett shook his head. "Well, Admiral, I didn't expect—"

"Excuse me," interrupted Cisco, "my guess is we're going to be working with each other every day from now on, and you must realize we're in this together. I think it's time we dropped the titles in private. My name is Jonas."

"I'm Scott," said Hauser, "and this is Lino."

"And I'm Missy."

The four shook hands.

"As I was about to say, Jonas, I didn't expect you to think first of how we can survive a catastrophic collapse of our timestream."

"After what you told us about dropping atomic bombs the other night, I'm not surprised. No military officer approaches wars, or any crisis or emergency, without beginning with the welfare of the men and women he commands. My primary job is to minimize risks, which is why I picked up on your worst-case scenario and started thinking of ways to prevent it. I think you're going to find the members of my command team feel the same."

"You didn't even ask what we're going to do to refine our technology, so time travel becomes routine," said Hauser.

"I'm interested, of course, but I've no doubt you'll be able to work it out. After all, Scott, what you've accomplished to this point is exactly what Lino said—revolutionary. This whole thing is like an avalanche coming down a mountain. There's nothing you can do to stop it. We only need to know how to move out of the way and keep it from killing us all. By the way, about how long will it take for you to get your finished system up and running?"

"Best guess is at least a year and a half after we have the additional power online," said Long. "Add two or three months for that. Say, about two years."

I'm glad to know that. Rebuilding the Charleston Joint Operations Command will take at least that long."

Cameron Fisk stormed around the conference room. The other senior members of the Academy looked equally upset.

"Those shit-ass scientists are now telling us we have to fund an enormously expensive project to build, what they call a 'survival beachhead' in the event something goes wrong with our time travel expeditions, and we change the past in a way that affects the present."

Fisk turned to the lone scientist in the room and said, "Tell me again the prevailing ideas about such a possibility among all your fucking, big-brained colleagues.

The scientist, distinguished in his field, nevertheless fidgeted nervously in the face of the volcanic chairman of the Academy. "As I've told you, Mr. Fisk, the preponderance of opinion among leading physicists and other experts in associated disciplines agree with the Russian physicist Igor Novikov who developed a theory called the Self-Consistency Principle under which the odds of any action you might take, creating a time paradox, is basically zero. Changing the past is essentially physically impossible. Somehow, the universe balances the scales to keep the timeline in order."

"So, if I go back in time and kill Hitler before he gains power, World War II would still happen?"

"According to the consistency conjecture, any complex interpersonal interactions must work themselves out self-consistently, so there is no paradox."

"I've no idea what you just said. I wish you motherfuckers would speak plain English once in a while."

The scientist struggled to make the science simpler. "Take the often repeated 'Grandfather Paradox' in which a man travels back in time, meets his grandfather, and kills him. If this happens how could he ever be born? It would be the same if you went back in time and met yourself. You cannot will yourself to kill your younger self. You can coexist, take yourself out for a beer, celebrate your birthday together, but somehow circumstances will dictate you cannot behave in a way that leads to a paradox in time."

"Then where the hell are these people in Charleston coming up with their bullshit ideas?"

"I've no way of knowing. The very fact they have apparently worked out a practical means of traveling into the past is beyond any known technology. I should add, Mr. Fisk, with that brain trust they've assembled, led by Lino Arnett, Scott Hauser, and Missy Long, if such a thing is possible, they would be the ones to do it."

"Yeah, well we only work with the best, even if they are opinionated assholes."

The scientist remained tactfully silent.

"Okay, that's all I need from you. If you should come up with anything else, contact my secretary."

The scientist made a hasty retreat.

When the Academy directors were alone, Fisk gave his conclusion. "We funded this project and have put out millions every year for ten years in the belief the Project Horizon boys would deliver a means of matter transference. The possibilities were staggering. We imagined a world where all means of transportation were rendered obsolete, with us holding the golden key. It would have meant billions, maybe trillions of dollars. That's how we got the current President onboard, promising him a generous partnership when he left office. He cleared the way with all the government agencies, including the Department of Defense.

"Now we have no matter transference and get time travel in return. From a consumer point of view, we might make substantial money selling trips to the past to people, organizations, and businesses, but nothing like we expected to earn.

"The latest demand from Charleston is that we fund a new project to build some kind of a special city, which is supposed to be immune to any drastic changes in history. I haven't seen the details yet, but they tell me it will take two more years to perfect the time travel system, and at least as long to build this city. I'm afraid to guess how much this will cost. I think this is the time to bail out and cut our loses."

Fisk looked around the table and saw general agreement. He was about to adjourn the meeting and begin the process of disengaging from everything related to time travel when one of the directors held up his hand.

"Yes, Mr. Aswira, you have something to add?"

Ahmed Al Aswira came by his billions from Middle Eastern oil. He had collaborated with Fisk and the others in different projects, all of which proved to be highly profitable. A slender man with darker skin and a neatly trimmed full beard, he always dressed formally in a three-piece suit. He rose to his feet now to address the other directors.

"Gentlemen, I wonder if we haven't missed some elements of this situation. I would like to think through this again from a different perspective."

"Okay, Ahmed," said Fisk. "Tell me what you think."

"We might not be able to realize the substantial return on our investment from matter transference, but there is a sizeable profit we can acquire by exploiting the opportunities in time travel."

"Like what?" asked Fred Williams

Aswira began ticking off his points. "Think how much we could make if we were to get our hands on Solomon's treasury, or any other of the caches of gold, silver, precious jewels in ancient ruler's coffers. What if we were to loot the treasures of the Inca or Aztec Empires? How much would we make if we were the first to recover diamonds from South Africa? How much gold did Hitler have stored in all his underground bunkers? The list of places we could search is endless."

"Say," said Fisk, "I hadn't thought of all that. We could bring back billions of dollars in gold alone."

"Here's another avenue we haven't considered. How many precious artifacts, works of art, beautiful statues, and similar relics could we recover, in their original condition? For example, what if we brought back the Venus de Milo as she first looked? How much could we realize by selling such things to museums and collectors?"

"Holy shit, I think I like this better the more I hear it," said Fisk.

"Since the majority of scientists, and physicists are telling us we can invade the past with impunity, with no worries of changing the present by any action we take, why not recover a few tons of gold, diamonds, emeralds, sapphires, rubies, and anything else we can imagine for ourselves?"

"What about the scientists who discovered the means of traveling in time down in Charleston," asked Frank Williams?

"At the present time, the Project Horizon researchers are preoccupied with their own belief the present must be protected from alterations in history. They believe they have the means to do this because of the unique secondary energy field produced when the primary field is in operation. They truly believe the secondary field embargos the effects of any changes in history inside their energy dome. Why don't we accommodate them? Let them build whatever survival city they wish. When they are finished, we simply move in with our own people and commandeer their systems."

"The downside to doing that, Ahmed, is the cost of building this city of theirs in the first place. They haven't come up with any plans or proposals for that yet, but you can bet this enterprise is going to cost a shitload of fucking money."

"I am prepared to bear the financial burden of such an undertaking. I believe the benefits will far outweigh the costs. Bear in mind, Doctor Hauser and the other heads of the project are already refusing to proceed in perfecting the time gateway unless we accede to their demands. They have us at a disadvantage. Where else can we go to find a means of traveling in time?"

41

Aswira could see the consensus of the directors turning in his favor. *Fools,* he thought, *they are seduced by the opinions of their own experts, just because they are in the majority. All they see are dollars, where I see destiny.*

# Chapter 5
# Planning and Conclusions

At his very heart, Chips Gallant was a builder. He thrilled at seeing houses, buildings, whole neighborhoods go from the drawing board to reality. He loved the education and the degree in engineering he received at the Air Force Academy. If he hadn't turned out to be such a hotshot pilot with the courage to take fly his plane into dangers of all kinds and come out—not only alive, but celebrated, and subsequently assigned as a commander of flight squadrons—things might have been different.

"I've spent a month going through the specs on this monumental project of yours, Jonas. Do you have any idea what a colossal undertaking like this is going to be, or what the price will be?"

"Not really. That's why I gave you all those project parameters. To find out. So, give me the total picture and the price tag."

"Never mind I'm not qualified to engineer this project. Nobody is qualified because nobody has ever had to design on this scale."

"You're whining."

"Sorry." Chips pulled out his iPad and set it on the Admiral's desk. "Here are the basics. You want to build an entire city twelve-miles across, inside a circle with a perimeter of thirty-eight miles. Your arbitrary population for this city is 30,000 people. I've no idea why you were specific about that, care to tell me?"

"I asked the computer what the minimum population had to be to live and work independently of anything outside the city. That's the number she said."

"Right. I understand the reason for that. Okay, I've done some computer modeling of my own. The city should be built as a single design, a single project. Most of the buildings inside the perimeter will have to be leveled. Let me show you."

Chips went on to show the Admiral his design for the city. He mixed every revolutionary concept in architecture, he could imagine into a totally futuristic city melting together with parks, pools, ponds, landscaping, a vast central plaza and all connected with a network of public transportation to whisk the population easily and quickly anywhere in the city they wanted to go. He waited while Cisco went through the computer renderings showing how the project would progress through all its stages.

Finally, Cisco looked up. "This is excellent. It fits the picture in my head perfectly. You've captured my thoughts and come up with a first-rate plan. I love your design."

Now, fortified with approval, Chips forged ahead. "Once you have the go-ahead, I can bring in crews to keep what we can and bulldoze everything else."

"You're going to have to go with me to New York and sell this to the Academy."

"I figured as much. Yours is the tougher job. Do you really think your diversionary plan will work?"

"Best way to keep a secret. Hide the secret in plain sight and tell people you have something else. Now, tell me the bad news. How much is this going to cost?"

"I'm going to use some high-tech, radical, construction methods, specifically 3D printing to build the buildings. Costs go down significantly. More important, I need this technology to build such a revolutionary city in under two years. Factoring in everything I can imagine, here are the numbers."

Chips clicked to a different file, and the numbers began to roll. Each phase of the work had an estimated cost. When he got to the end, and the final total came up, he looked to see Cisco's reaction. He didn't react at all, as far as Chips could see.

The Admiral cleared his voice. "Looks like a lot. How would

I know? These numbers are meaningless to me. I think in terms of thousands, or millions of dollars."

"I suppose they are meaningless to me too when you frame the picture like that. However, just think how well these high-tech building elements will fit into your base cover story."

"Helpful for sure. Maybe these heavy money guys will see these numbers and think they're getting a bargain for a brand new, prototype...a city of tomorrow; they can clone all over the world."

"Are you practicing your speech?"

Cisco didn't say anything. Chips watched the Admiral stare up, absorbing everything he'd presented. Now his overloaded leader had to add all he'd told him to a growing list of enormous demands. He waited patiently for an answer.

Cisco seemed to finish organizing his thoughts because he looked down again and said mildly, "Get all this stuff together into a finished presentation. The command team is going to New York with the Horizon team in two weeks."

Aye-aye, Sir."

Scott looked away from the window in the jet. "How well do you know New York, Jonas?"

"I've been here enough to know this isn't my favorite major city in the world."

"Yeah, you either love it or hate it. I did both. I taught classes and did research at Columbia University for quite a few years before Horizon."

A flight attendant stood up at the front of the Gulfstream 550. "We'll be landing in a few minutes. Please buckle your seatbelts."

Two limousines waited for the jet. Cisco and his command team, plus the three seniors of Horizon, divided up. Cisco got into a limo with Scott, Missy, and Ben Crenshaw.

As they drove into the city, Cisco said, "We've spent a lot of time coming up with our plan for the city and the diversion to conceal the existence of time travel. I think we ought to talk about the directors of the Academy, especially the chairman, Cameron Fisk. Tell me about him."

"He's an ugly and profane man," said Scott. "I don't think he has any morals at all. However, in his own field, he's brilliant. Every bit as smart as you and me. He'll question everything and throw in healthy doses of personal abuse."

"Well, I can be abusive myself, if somebody wants to trade punches."

During the rest of the ride, Scott told Cisco and Ben about his previous encounters with the Academy and their mercurial chairman. Missy added her observations. She hadn't had as many as Scott, but her opinion of Fisk put him at the bottom of the barrel in courtesy, understanding, and civility.

The limousines delivered them to a tall office building in downtown Manhattan. As Scott warned, staff members of the Academy were there to greet them. The command team was led off to separate rooms to begin briefings in each of their areas of expertise.

Two days later, the meetings were still going on.

On the second night, after another day of conferences, which were more like interrogations, Cisco got everyone together in their hotel for a private dinner. The meal matched the sumptuous rooms the group had in elegance and taste, but nobody seemed very interested in eating and picked away at their food.

"I don't think any of us has much appetite. I suppose the grilling we've been put through these last two days has soured everybody."

"That's for sure," grumbled Chips. "Those people act like we should be building Quonset huts to house the population of the city, instead of real housing where families can live comfortably. I'll bet I've had to explain twenty times why my construction standards are not so lavish, according to their minimal thinking."

"How are they reacting to your plan to use advanced 3D printing to build the majority of the new buildings?"

"When I showed the technology yesterday, only one guy knew what I was talking about. Then today I found everyone studied the subject overnight and came in with all the reasons they thought the concepts wouldn't work. I talked all day to convince them this type of construction was cheaper, and faster. I think we're now on the same page."

Cisco turned to Will, his officer in charge of amassing the vast inventory of everything needed to ensure the sustainability of the city over many years. "How about you, Will? What's the staff telling you about our extensive reserve planning?"

"Their entire focus is to limit the scope of our preparations. Their motivation is different. They want to reduce our inventory supplies to cut corners and save money. We want to ensure we have enough stored away, or in system redundancies to actually be independent of anything outside the city."

"I've encountered the same stingy attitudes with hiring people to fill all the positions our free-standing city will need," added Ben. "The staff seems to have a mandate from their superiors to employ minimum wage personnel for all the routine and menial work. They can't imagine why we want a much higher standard of workers for everything including the maintenance jobs."

"Most of the heavy guns from the senior staff have concentrated on Scott and me," said Cisco. "They want to know two things. How long will it take to refine the Gateway to a point where time travel is routine, and how much will it cost to build the 'beachhead' community we insist on having."

"That sounds to me like they intend to proceed with the

Horizon project despite the additional time, or the money to build our city," said Wyatt.

"I might be relieved if they decided to cancel the project," said Missy. "Perhaps, we shouldn't be messing around with time travel at all."

"After all the years we've spent getting to this point?" exclaimed Lino.

"Even so," said Missy.

"Do you get the impression the Academy is ready to throw in the towel?" asked Cisco.

"Clearly a debate is going on up and down the entire organization," said Scott. "However, I don't think cancellation of the enterprise is in the board's mind."

"Then why are we going through all these staff meetings?" clamored Will.

"Any number of reasons. Could be they are testing our resolve, trying to find out how serious we are about our convictions. Or it could be nothing more than getting by for the least cost. In any case, tomorrow you can sit back while Scott and I square off with the board of directors."

"Lucky you."

The conference room of the Academy had the same overstated opulence as everything else associated with the elite group. The elegant conference table filled the center of the room. Carafes of water and glasses sat in front of each place.

At one end, Scott sat in the center, flanked by Cisco and Lino. The others, Missy, Wyatt, Chips, Will, Riley and Ben, were seated around the sides.

At the other end, were the directors of the Academy. On the sides were Frank Williams, Harold Kingsley, and Ahmed Al Aswira, all dressed in expensive suits. In the center, stood Cameron Fisk. He waited while everyone took their seats. When all settled into their broad-armed chairs, Fisk sat down and glared down the table. "Alright, let's get started. First, I want to ask you, Doctor Hauser, are you still determined to go ahead with this hair-brained scheme of yours?"

Scott gave a little shrug. "As I have told you, Mr. Fisk, more than once, apart from your fleet of experts telling you travel in time will not affect future events regardless of what actions we may take in the past, we respectfully disagree.

"Perhaps the use of Gateway will happen just as you say. However, we believe changes to the past may alter the present day. In our work developing the Gateway, we have also learned whatever is within the circumference of the field will be unaffected by any changes in the time stream."

"Let me try to say it differently, Mr. Fisk," said Missy. "Think of the energy of the Gateway as a waterfall coming from a high cliff. All the water is concentrated as a single flow, but when the cascade reaches the bottom, the water spreads out into a pool. The properties of the water, or the energy, are the same, but the results when the water ceases to fall are much different. The pool created by the waterfall is smooth, quiet and placid."

"The waterfall and pool are nevertheless a singularity," said Arnett. "Whatever was under the pool before the waterfall, is covered up. The pool of water becomes the principal fact of the land being covered."

"We know of no other way to establish equilibrium and guard against any alterations in time," continued Scott. "Therefore, since this is the only way to prevent any changes to the present by an invasion into the past, an outpost with all the elements of life as we know them, has to be built. Moreover, this survival beachhead, as we have come to call it, must be capable of sustaining itself independently despite any conditions beyond its perimeter."

"I'm in favor of ignoring your request and proceeding

immediately to full use of the technology," declared Harold Kingsley.

"All our scientific experts say no such risk, as you describe, exists," said Fred Williams.

Lino slammed his hands on the table, and half rose from his seat. "I'm sick of you people pushing us around! Let me spell this out for you. This is not a request. If you want to travel in time, you'll damn well give us what we need to survive the timequakes you're going to make or shut down the whole operation and go your merry way."

Now Kingsley was angry. "There are other ways for us to deliver a reliable time machine without you."

"Yeah? Who are you gonna get to build it for you? The seventy best minds in this field, anywhere in the world, are in Charleston today working on the system we have. Go ahead and start from scratch, if you can. I figure you'll work it out in about fifty years."

Fisk shouted over all of them. "Goddamn, that's enough! We are not going to walk away from this opportunity, or our considerable investment. We will consider your demand a closed issue and move on to the matter of building this...outpost."

Fisk turned in his seat and stared directly down the table at Cisco. "Admiral, I opposed bringing you into this. However, circumstances seem to have created the necessity to do so. I understand, you are the principal architect of this oversized building project. Is that right?"

"I suppose, Mr. Fisk, you mean did I evaluate the minimum requirements for constructing a city large enough to function as a self-sustaining human system? If so, that is correct."

Fisk narrowed his eyes and spoke loudly enough to make the room vibrate. "Okay, do you have any idea what this motherfucking boondoggle of yours is going to cost? He snatched a piece of paper from the table and shouted. "Look at all these fucking zeros. And you expect us to pay for all this?"

Cisco sat quietly as the seconds passed. Finally, a red-faced Fisk, blared again. "Do I have your fucking attention, Admiral?"

"Of course. you have my attention. After that outburst, I think you have everyone's attention." He went on before Fisk could say more. "The answer to your question is yes. We do expect you to pay for all this. Where else would we find the money? To be entirely frank, I've no conception of the magnitude of these numbers. My motivation is to build a city able to function effectively and survive independently in the event a major disturbance occurs in the timestream. As I said, these are the minimum requirements to do the job."

"If I may add something," said Scott. "While the city is being built, the Horizon Team will continue to advance our work. I can assure you, by the time they finish building, the Gateway will be fully operational. You will then have the means to conduct routine journeys into the past."

Cisco continued. "I did not mean to imply we do not recognize the substantial financial commitment the Academy will have to make for this project. We appreciate your support. In light of that, we've spent a good deal of time considering how you might benefit from our project. We have a plan we think will significantly improve your bottom line. With your permission, we would like to show you our idea."

"Sure," said a more composed Fisk. He sat back in his chair. "Let's hear what you have."

"Colonel Gallant is the man who's designed our new city. He has a presentation for you."

Chips stood up and turned on the main screen across the back wall, "Everyone has heard of Walt Disney's EPCOT Center. Their idea was to show what a city of the future might look like. This project takes the next step. There's nothing experimental about our town, nor is it a city of tomorrow, but rather a prototype of a truly unique city for today. We believe the country, even the world, will see what we are building and want similar developments in other places. Let me show you how we envision our city to look and function."

The screen lit up and began showing the extraordinary and unprecedented characteristics of this remarkable new community. Chips provided a running narration as each element of design, construction, and ultimate use flashed on the screen in brilliant computer-generated graphics.

At one point, Cisco glanced at his watch, and then down the table. He smiled. Chips had spoken for nearly an hour, and none of the directors of the Academy had moved. None of them had seen how the finished city would look or function. All they'd heard were fragments of the total plan. Now they saw how all the parts became a whole. Altogether, the plans were impressive.

Chips concluded. "You've seen what an incredible place we'll build, and now I give you the final triumph of our planning. How, you can reasonably ask, are you going to manage and control all these interconnected systems? The answer is with the most advanced voice-activated and interactive computer system in the world.

"Compliments of Doctor Hauser and some of his whiz kids at Horizon, our entire city will be overseen, managed and coordinated by a city-wide master computer. We will be able to access the mainframe from anyplace in the city, giving commands and knowing it can understand the nuances of our motives as well as what we ask it to do. This is the secret of how we expect to have such a smooth flow of data from men to machines. Once the rest of the country sees what we've accomplished, they're going to want the same for themselves. Using our prototype, you will be able to market and build similar projects everywhere."

"Son of a bitch," said Fisk, "that's slick. We've been so busy thinking about...other things, we hadn't considered the value of building the city itself."

Riley spoke up. "Thus far you've surrounded this entire project with blankets of security, scared to death somebody would leak time travel secrets. How about this? Go back to the original goal of matter transference and stop keeping that a secret. Say the purpose of the city is to support the infrastructure to achieve this goal. You would still need tight security for the Gateway Center, but public interest will be misdirected away from the true purpose you conceal, and not driven to a fever pitch because of the tantalizing prospect of traveling in time."

"You can make quite a thing of both the research being done, as well as the considerable star-power of the city under construction," added Cisco. "In the end, all that free publicity will play right into your plans to find big-time customers to build cities of their own."

"Maybe I should hire you to run my marketing department, Admiral," said Fisk, now considerably mellower.

"Thanks, but I expect to be pretty busy for the next couple of years. Besides, most of this 'marketing' I cribbed from some of the other people at the base."

"Speaking of the base," said Frank Williams, "this is still a military facility. How do you intend to get all this by the Pentagon?"

"We don't," said Cisco. "You've been able to force the armed services to comply with everything up to now. I'm certain you'll find a way to handle them."

"Because we're still a military base," said Riley, "we will be able to restrict the flow of 'tourists', wanting to see what we're doing."

"I think you will learn, Mr. Fisk, all our planning is equally as detailed and comprehensive," said Cisco tying the whole presentation into a neat bundle.

"Very well," said Fisk, glancing at Ahmed Aswira who had not spoken at all.

Aswira gave Fisk a tiny nod. "I think we can give the go-ahead on your project. By the way, Admiral, have you chosen a name for our new city?"

"We've given that a lot of thought. We've decided to name it Sanctuary."

# Chapter 6
## Exploring the Timestream

***Two years later***

Lino wandered around Scott's office thinking and talking at the same time.

"Are you absolutely sure you want to do this?" asked Lino for the third time in the last ten minutes.

"Jonas had it right, standing outside the old warehouse almost two years ago. You can't ask your people to do something you aren't willing to do yourself. Besides, I'm the leader of our little band of explorers, I have to go."

"You don't have to prove anything to me. I thought you volunteering to be the first human we transported, inside the lab scored right up there with the bravest thing in history."

"We only repeated what we'd done with the monkeys. The time had come to transport people. Everything went off without a hitch."

"My point exactly. What we did with you happened in the lab just a few feet across the platform. This new undertaking means we actually transport you to another time, another place, and then recall you."

"The obvious next step." Scott looked closely at his colleague, "Is there any doubt in your mind we haven't missed something working up to this?"

"No, there isn't. Installing the SMRs gave us the power we needed to generate a wider secondary power dome. We've spent another year and a half fine-tuning the bigger field to calibrate exact moments in time and set GPS coordinates to precise locations anywhere on the planet. Whatever we send will arrive in the right place at the correct time."

"We've worked flat out, month after month, and driven everyone to almost complete exhaustion. Don't you think it's time to conduct a practical exercise of what we've achieved? Aren't you the least bit excited?"

"What you're going to do scares *me*."

"Yeah, me too."

"Are you gonna bring in the Sanctuary command team to send you off?"

"Hell no. In the first place, there won't be anything for them to see. In the second place, I'm not going to put an ounce of additional pressure on those guys. They've worked harder than we have, turning Sanctuary into a self-contained city against considerable more public opposition and crabbing by the Pentagon. If Jonas, and the others, knew how far out we've pushed, it could put them into a panic mode to finish building the city before we start regular time jumps."

"No question they're a tough, hard-working outfit. Jonas is a gifted leader. I doubt there's a single detail he hasn't considered. You have to admire him and his team for doing so much. I hardly recognize the place."

"Me either. The old Charleston Joint Command military base is now a compact, circular city, twelve miles across. Jonas bulldozed most of the military buildings to make way for all the new ones in his master plan."

"Including our old warehouse, and we got this new Gateway Center, custom-made to our specifications, right at the exact center of Sanctuary."

"It was the first project. We moved the center of the Gateway's secondary energy field four miles north to a better location enclosing all the government-owned land. The whole of Sanctuary is inside its operational perimeter."

"I sure do enjoy all the other new city innovations."

"The real innovation is the connection of everything to a sophisticated computer system that automates so much of the infrastructure and gives us voice-command access to the mainframe. It tells us anything we want to know from anywhere inside Sanctuary. Talk about having a Smart City."

"That too. It's real convenient to be able to speak 'computer' into the air and ask any question I like."

"Remember Lino, the command team has thrown away their careers over this. The Academy might still have the juice to override objections by the Pentagon, but their higher command won't forget being told what to do by junior officers. Jonas spoke the plain truth when the three of us stood outside the old warehouse in what seems like a lifetime ago. He said the first thing a leader does is consider the welfare of the men and women under his command and reduce the risks. Jonas chose that option instead of thinking of the personal price he would pay. All his officers did the same. We owe them a lot."

"I was wrong in believing military men couldn't think creatively or in ways that can dramatically improve the lives of people. I'm not afraid to admit it. But I tell Wyatt all the time I've decided our military is the exception, and the rest of the Pentagon Poohbahs are still a bunch of jerks. What's more I..." Lino paused and smiled at his friend and colleague and then sighed. "Now that you've managed to change the subject entirely, for a whole two minutes, and since I can't talk you out of this, when are you planning to jump?"

"The day after tomorrow. I still have a few details to work out with Missy."

Missy continued as the principal theoretician on all components of time travel, from paradoxes to branching universes for Project Horizon. Her extraordinary knowledge of historical events served as a guide for planning the first-time jump.

Currently, she stood in Scott's office, facing a table with assorted items neatly arranged across it.

Missy shoved her glasses back in place on her nose. "Let's go through this one more time. Your destination is New York City, ten years ago, May 11, 2018. We selected it because you know the city from living there, and the crowds of people will ensure anonymity.

"You will arrive at four a.m. at the edge of Central Park. We couldn't think of any time or place to make your arrival more inconspicuous. After you leave the park on Central Avenue West, you'll be in front of the Museum of Natural history. The Hotel Excelsior is a short walk down 81st Street. We want you to rent a room.

She picked up a pile of money from the table. "All this currency is older than ten years."

He shoved the thick wad of bills into his pocket.

"All your transactions will be in cash. We obviously can't create a paper trail using credit cards. Here's a ten-year-old driver's license with your picture on it. This is your primary identification. You will probably need it to rent a room. It says you live in Los Angeles. We've added other types of identification including a library card, and membership cards in some organizations and clubs." Missy put everything in a small wallet and handed it to Scott.

"Guess I'd better hold on to this," he said, stuffing the wallet in a zippered side pocket of his pants.

Missy went to the next item on the table. "You'll have a camera hidden inside this pair of glasses. It'll record both video and audio of everything you look at. It doubles as sunglasses. We also want you to take this camera as a backup and shoot pictures everywhere you go, like a tourist."

Scott tried on the glasses and dangled the camera from his shoulder.

Missy handed him the recall bracelet. "Put this on and don't give it up for any reason. This is your way back. The system is set to recall you in exactly 24 hours. Should you find a need to initiate a recall before then push the button on the side. Your signal will automatically activate the Gateway.

"I don't need a briefing on the recall bracelet. The way you're talking you'd think I wasn't around for all this."

Missy smiled. "Then relax. You're way too tense. The whole idea is not to attract attention. Act normally, read the morning paper like its real news and familiarize yourself with what's happening there today. You may engage in conversations with people, but make sure you say nothing which might reveal you know anything about future events."

"Can't I even buy a lottery ticket?"

"You're joking?"

"Yeah, I was, kind of."

"Doctor Hauser, it's precisely that sort of thing which could have huge effects."

"I'm sorry. You don't have to explain it to me."

Missy went on as if she did. "Let's say you do buy a lottery ticket and it turns out to have a thousand-dollar payoff. The person to whom time intended the ticket might have used the money for a purpose resulting in a change in their life, or the life of others. If you deny that, you will have changed the present. If there is any truth at all to the theory of branching universes, this is a sure way of proving it."

"I apologize, Missy. You're right, of course. I shouldn't have made light of it. My plan for the largest single day of my life is to not leave a single fingerprint."

"Now you're talkin', Scott. I haven't called you Doctor in a dozen years."

Both of them laughed.

"According to the weather forecast of ten years ago, it will be 82 degrees today, so you won't need the coat. Take along the sweater for the early morning and overnight. Stay off the subway from Grand Central to Central Park. There will be a derailment at one o'clock, blocking the track for the rest of the day. One last thing, Scott, our goal is to find out if we can move in and out of time. You going there and coming back will accomplish that. This is not a sprint. If you get hungry, eat. If you get sleepy, sleep. That's the only reason we're risking renting a hotel room with no luggage and paying cash. We couldn't think of another way to get you off the street for part of the twenty-four hours. Make sure you tell the hotel clerk your luggage is in a locker at the airport."

"If I do sleep. I'll be sure to set the alarm to make it to the recall point."

"Okay, time to go. Try to hold on to one of your ways of documenting all this. The glasses are the best."

They left Scott's office, walked down the central corridor, into the Gateway Center, and up to the gleaming platform. Lino greeted them. All the other members of the Horizon team broke into applause as Scott stepped onto the platform. He hugged Missy and walked into the twelve-foot-wide circle, beneath the array of transmission cones anchored twenty feet above. He stood calmly as Lino went to the control panel, setting it for May 11, 2018, calibrating it for a pre-selected location, fifty feet inside Central Park in a grove of tall bushes. He engaged the system.

The transmission cones burned brightly and shot an intense blue energy field onto the platform. For a moment, Scott could be seen standing inside the field. Then, he disappeared. Lino cut the transmission, stepped up onto the platform and counseled his colleagues. "Twenty-four hours. If you're of a mind, you might say a little prayer for the safe return of our teammate. We've worked hard to arrive at this moment. All of you should go home and get some sleep."

One second Scott stood on the platform looking at Lino, the next he found himself standing on soft grass, amidst bushes. In an instant, he'd transferred from the Gateway Center to Central Park in New York City. He experienced nothing physical about the transfer. He turned his head in all directions hoping the blue flash of his arrival had not attracted any attention. It was still dark, and from all he could tell, quiet.

He brought his arm closer so he could see the time. When he pushed a button, the display showed 23:59:50, then 49, 48. The countdown had begun. The recall bracelet on his other wrist comforted him. He needed to be back at this spot in 24 hours. Until then he had the freedom to go where he wanted.

As he made his way out of the foliage and onto a pathway, adjusting the camera on his shoulder, it occurred to him he hadn't thought at all about how to spend the time. In fact, the idea of having a day to himself, with no pressure, no deadlines, made it feel like a vacation. He smiled at the prospect as he strolled out to the sidewalk along Central Avenue West.

Scott glanced again, to check the local time, just past four a.m.. *Scott, you lived in this city for years. How many times did you stand outside Central Park at 4 a.m.? Never. Start moving before you get mugged.*

He walked briskly to the Hotel Excelsior on 81st Street, glad for the sweater in the morning chill. A nodding attendant with wavy hair sat at the front desk.

"I'd like a room"

"Do you have a reservation?"

"Nope, kind of a last-minute trip."

"How many nights?"

"Just one, I have to catch a plane about this time tomorrow morning."

"Then that would be two nights, this one and tomorrow."

"But this is already tomorrow."

"And at eleven a.m. we'll start a new day."

"Oh alright. How much is the room?"

The attendant checked his computer and announced, "Total comes to three hundred sixty dollars. What credit card are you using?"

"None, I'll pay cash."

"We need a credit card to cover incidentals."

Scott shoved four new hundred-dollar bills across the counter, "Keep the change and thanks for your courtesy."

Wavy hair seemed to process this and then said, "You need to fill out the registration and show some ID."

Scott pulled out his driver's license and filled out the hotel registration. His four hundred dollars vanished from the top of the counter. He took his key card and rode the elevator up to his room.

The view from his window overlooked the Museum of Natural History, lit in the dark, with the skyline of Manhattan in the distance. He sat on the bed and glanced at the service guide to find out when they served breakfast. It started in a couple of hours. The bed was seductively comfortable, and he realized how tired he was. Not much sleep in the previous two days, and none at all that night. He set the alarm for six-thirty, kicked off his shoes, pulled the bedspread over him and fell asleep in minutes.

When the alarm went off, he got up and washed his face. He rummaged in his small bag for a hairbrush. When he finished combing his thinning hair, he said to the mirror, "I could have left the brush behind and combed my hair with a washcloth."

He checked his pockets for his money and wallet and took the elevator to the breakfast lounge. The meal made him feel almost normal.

After breakfast, he left the hotel and walked the few blocks to Columbus Circle, where he went down to the subway. Hundreds of people jammed the platform, mostly headed for work. Scott wedged into the subway, coming out at Times Square. He slipped into a Starbucks, ordered a double shot latte and bought a copy of the New York Times. He settled down to read it. Traffic snarled and honked outside, and thousands of people went their way this Tuesday morning.

Missy said to take lots of pictures. She wanted to compare those photos with others from the same time to compare if Scott's presence alone made any difference in the timestream. The best way to take a lot of pictures was on the touring double-deck buses. He tossed his paper and headed outside to take the subway to Grand Central Station where the tours started.

He spent all morning riding the buses taking endless pictures. During the tours, he chatted with tourists. Nothing seemed out of the ordinary. Surprisingly, Scott was a little bored. He wondered how anyone could find the inaugural demonstration of time travel boring.

After leaving the tour bus, Scott ate lunch in a diner. He stopped at an outlet center and bought an overpriced ticket to take in the Broadway show *Wicked* that night. He then retraced his steps, took a non-derailed subway back to 81st Street, and entered the American Museum of Natural History. The visit took all afternoon. He enjoyed it. When the museum closed, he took the subway back downtown to the theater and loved the show.

He glanced at the countdown numbers on his watch. Six hours remained before recall. What better place to pass the time than in one of the many after-theater watering holes along Broadway. A lively bunch hooted away in the place he chose.

He barely got settled at the bar and ordered a drink before he heard, "Scott, Scott, is that you?"

He froze in shock. After a quiet and uneventful day, terror gripped him to his core.

He turned. Headed his way through the crowd, smiling and waving was Linda Lou Hopwood, a colleague and sometimes date from his days at Columbia University. They hadn't been very close but spent enough time together to make the reunion impossible to ignore. Scott waved back, trying to smile.

Linda enfolded Scott in a full embrace. "I can't believe running into you like this. How long has it been?"

"Wonderful to see you again too, Linda. Are you still teaching at Columbia?"

Linda slid on a stool next to him. "Same old, same old. The last I heard you were with that research group in Denver. What brings you to New York?"

"A conference with fellow researchers."

"Will you be in town for a while? I'd love to know all about your research project."

"I'm catching the red eye in a few hours."

"Too bad. At least you have time to buy me a drink."

"Of course." Scott motioned to the bartender.

"So, tell me, are you still working on your Star Trek thing?"

"More or less. These days we've moved into some new areas." He immediately regretted saying anything about the project. Having to come up with an instant cover story flummoxed him.

"What's this new stuff all about?" asked Linda sipping her drink.

"We're still working on matter transference but are trying some different approaches. You should know better than anyone how difficult such an undertaking is."

"Impossible, I would say. Who do you have working with you?"

"The very best, Missy Long and also Lino Arnett.

"Wow. I read Arnett will likely be nominated for a Nobel Prize for his theories in Quantum chromodynamics. You must have something earth-shattering going to attract the likes of him."

"One can only hope."

Scott steered the conversation away from him, toward

Linda's work. She gave details of her current research projects. Scott encouraged her to talk about all the latest gossip and drama at the university. Mostly he listened while the two of them had another round of drinks. He considered himself lucky he started with plain Coke.

After an hour, he slapped the bar. "If I don't get a move on I'll miss my plane."

"Want me to drive you? I have a car."

"That's sweet of you, Linda, but I have some important calls to make. I can do them in the cab. Anyway, it's late, and I expect you have a busy day tomorrow. The next time I'm in town I'll call you, and we'll have dinner."

"Looking forward to it. We've talked so much about my life; I didn't learn much more about yours. I hope next time, you can give me more details."

Scott gave Linda an expansive hug and made an exit from the pub. It was now 10:30. The chance meeting with someone he knew bothered him a lot. What if this single incident altered the timestream in some way? Certainly, something to discuss with Missy and the others as part of his debrief.

Clearly, he'd achieved the principal goal of moving to another time. He decided there was no reason to take any more risks. He hailed a cab and returned to the Excelsior. Once in his room, he switched on the TV to scan the news and found himself getting sleepy again.

This time he stripped down to his underwear, set the alarm for three a.m., and left a wake-up call for the same time at the front desk. Almost as soon as he got under the covers and switched off the light, he fell deeply asleep.

The phone and alarm went off simultaneously, startling Scott. He jumped up, got dressed, and left his room. He took the key card with him curious if something from the past would transfer into the future.

The walk to Central Park took only ten minutes. Scott stayed on the sidewalk, sitting on a bench letting the time slip away. He felt exposed and vulnerable. On an impulse he clicked the memory chip from the camera and shoved it into a zippered pocket

Only minutes remained before the Gateway opened when two very rough looking young men approached him. Scott started to stand up, but the bigger of the two jumped behind the bench and pinned his arms. The other man stepped in front and delivered a hail of fast, hard punches from his gloved hands into Scott's face. His head spun from the blows, and blood gushed from his lips, nose, and eyebrows. His glasses went flying across the sidewalk. His assailant purposely crushed them beneath his heel.

The bigger man pulled Scott to his feet and held him while the other one hit him again in the stomach. He bent over in pain, struggling to catch his breath.

"Check his pockets," said the bigger man.

The man in front of Scott sneered at him and crammed a hand into his pocket. "Why lookie at what we got here," he said as he pulled out the folded cash. He looked at the money and then back to Scott. "Hiding anything else?"

"You got everything."

The man patted his pants, found the billfold and ripped open the zipper. "You forgot about the wallet, sucker."

"You won't find anything in it, but my driver's license."

"We gotta move, Eddie," said his partner.

"I'll just take this camera so I can shoot pretty pictures," grinned Eddie. He backhanded Scott and shoved him back onto the bench. "What about that fancy bracelet?"

Scott knew appeals of sentimentality for the recall bracelet would be ignored. He also knew he faced genuinely mortal danger. What he did in the next few minutes represented life or death. These thoughts flashed through his mind in an instant and propelled him to action. Eddie faced him as he sprawled on the bench.

With a quick flick of his shoe, he kicked Eddie squarely in the crotch. The man bent over in pain. Scott sprang from the bench and ran for the park. The muscular man grabbed at him, and Scott hit him in the stomach with all the strength he could muster. It bought him a few seconds, and he dashed along the walkway headed for the recall point in a grove of bushes. Both enraged men rushed to catch him, more intent on delivering death, than a casual violent robbery.

Scott shook his head as he ran trying to clear his mind. He wiped the blood from his swelling lips and gushing nose. Panic struck him as the air begin to crackle. Only seconds remained before the energy cone cycled. With every ounce of strength, he had, he rushed the twenty feet into the bushes and threw himself to the ground.

Eddie bellowed right behind. "Watch, I'm gonna waste you, motherfucker."

The blue curtain sizzled. Eddie was caught part way into the cone. He screamed in agony as only the top half of his body went with Scott back to the present.

The next thing he saw was Lino's face just outside the transfer circle. Eddie's body spurted blood over Scott and Lino and gushed on the floor of the platform as he shrieked a final tortured squeal.

"Oh my God!" cried Lino, frantically wiping blood from his face.

Scott rolled over on the gory floor, his hands, arms, and face dripping with blood.

"I need help here."

Several techs rushed to the platform. They helped Scott to a sitting position and handed him a towel He wiped his arms and hands, and very gently dabbed at his face.

Lino shuddered in horror as he forced himself to consider the corpse lying obscenely on the platform. He yelled at the techs. "Go find a blanket or a tarp or something to cover this body. You and you, find some more towels, and bring a bucket and a mop."

He looked back. Quite a bit of the blood on Scott's face was his, continuing to stream from his nose and drip from his mouth. Great welts were forming on his cheeks.

"Somebody call 911 and get an ambulance over here. He jumped forward and dropped to his knees to steady his friend, mindless of the blood-soaked platform. "Easy, Scott, help is on the way."

Scott leaned against Lino. Two other techs squatted on either side supporting them both.

"I got mugged waiting for the Gateway to open."

"I told you time travel is dangerous, but you're alive, so I forgive you. Plenty of time to tell the story, later,"

Scott got groggier by the second. "Tell Missy I'm sorry about the glasses." Then, he passed out.

# Chapter 7
# Sanctuary

"I can remember a time when I could empty my entire inbox," bemoaned an exasperated Cisco. "These days I consider myself lucky to get through the top two pages."

"Don't think we've played racquetball in a couple of months," added Wyatt.

"Look at this. Two hours of work, and I don't think we've made a dent."

"To say nothing of all the requests you have for interviews from every news outfit in the world on top of the work we're doing now."

"They do eat into a fellow's free time."

Wyatt laughed loudly. "You were the one who sold the Academy on how they could make a lot of money advertising what an innovative and novel concept Sanctuary would be."

"It didn't take them very long to crank up their public relations program. Almost overnight we became the darlings of social media and the hot topic of conversation around every dinner table in the country. The mainstream media picked it up, and I haven't had a minute of time to myself since."

"Riley would argue with you about that. He had a security problem right off the bat. His people escorted tourists away from construction sites almost hourly. It wasn't easier until you approved his plan to put a ten-foot-high fence around the entire thirty-eight-mile circumference of our perimeter, with guards and barricades at the few entry points."

"This is all very strange to me. Before Sanctuary, we were a relaxed command. You could hardly tell we were a military base. Now we're even less like a military base but have security as tight as Fort Knox."

"Even stranger is the reason we have all this security is because the world loves us so much."

"Well, the Academy is getting what it wants. They've been marketing our advanced construction methods since the beginning, selling pieces of our technology for a fortune. I can't imagine what they'll do when they have a whole high-tech city to sell."

"The upside is they approve and write checks for everything we ask for, without any questions. Strange people. We still don't know much about this super-secret bunch, except they are rich guys in fancy suits.

"Besides that, they have enough juice to impact a multi-service military command, put our careers on hold for the duration, and order our bosses not to ask any questions about what we're doing." Wyatt shook his head in wonder. "Hearing you tell the four-star head of the Joint Chiefs to mind his own business is something I never thought could happen. I hope when this is all over, they don't take their irritation out on us."

"Don't count on it, Wyatt. We'll be lucky to command a supply depot on Guam."

Cisco looked at his watch. "We have a meeting with the command team in fifteen minutes, and after that, we're scheduled to have a monthly progress report meeting with our guys at Horizon."

"At least we have a blood brother relationship with our compatriots. I even took Lino out for his first ever round of golf the other day. He played terrible, but we both had a good time. I enjoyed his company."

"How did you manage to pry him out of the lab?"

"I went over to buy him lunch. He'd finished some exotic project, spent three days working on it. He said he needed something to take his mind off the work, so I suggested golf. He said, 'why not' and away we went."

Cisco grinned. "Talk about the odd couple. You must outweigh him by a hundred pounds and be a foot taller, but you get along with Lino better than anybody."

"That's because I don't have a clue about his work. We can't talk shop, so he talks about his life, and is fascinated by mine. He loves my kids, and they love him. He's been isolated and lonely ever since people discovered his super mind. Underneath all that tough bravado, he's really a sweet, gentle and loving man."

"None of this would have happened if we hadn't found a way to penetrate the fog surrounding the project. It seems like a lifetime ago. So much has happened. At least we have our own lads providing the security around the Gateway Center."

The command team filed noisily into the conference room. All of them shoved the work they had before Horizon burst into their lives onto their subordinates. They were much too busy with the Sanctuary Project. The details regarding the work of Horizon, and the knowledge time travel existed, remained a closely held secret. However, the members of the command team were enfolded, long ago, into the security envelope.

To a person, they agreed with Cisco, whatever could be done to mitigate possible disruptions in the present by changes in the past, should begin immediately. They took that resolve to New York when they confronted the Academy.

The spacious conference room occupied a good part of the top floor of the new six-story headquarters building, along with Cisco's office. The rest of the command team had offices in the building as well. The entire back wall held an almost floor-to-ceiling LED screen. Cisco walked to the screen. "Computer, show the Sanctuary perimeter on this day, two years ago."

The screen lit up and displayed a crystal-clear image of the Charleston Joint Command just before the enormous project Cisco envisioned for Sanctuary, got underway.

"Computer, show changes within the perimeter month by month, from this date to the present, ten-second intervals."

As he stood and watched the image change, Chips came up. Both men watched as the months passed. At first, it appeared the purpose was to make a level plain of the base, tearing down three-quarters of the buildings. That changed as no less than a dozen mammoth construction areas became simultaneously active inside the twelve-mile diameter circle. With each passing ten-second interval, new buildings emerged from the empty land, vastly accelerated with 3D printing technology. The buildings were connected by roads and public transportation. There were new parks, schools, an expanded hospital, and a medium-sized stadium. The deep-water port for the naval ships, and the military aircraft included with the new, expanded airport had been retained. In a little more than two minutes, the picture changed from a blank canvas of open land to the gleaming reality of a nearly completed modern city.

Additionally, permanent smaller screens lined the other walls, each with a component of the many elements involved in transforming the Joint Command into a unique self-contained, self-sufficient refuge. The headings above the screens included: Energy, Housing, Agriculture, Health, Education, Public Transportation, Infrastructure, Manufacturing, and Reserves. The screens showed a portrayal of what the completed element would look like. Overlaid were images of roads, rail lines, supply centers, and completed structures with notes on current progress, and dates of estimated completion.

Cisco installed the system so each person working in each area of responsibility could refer to their jobs easily during the command team meetings. It was also a good morale builder to show real progress and to share the incredible advances when others from Horizon attended the meetings.

When the slideshow finished, Chips patted Cisco's back.

"The first time I saw the specs of how you wanted to build Sanctuary, I thought you were way too ambitious. Now we're so close to matching that picture for real I'm glad you thought big."

Cisco smiled. "Nothing like the combination of money, men, materials, and motivation. I think your idea to convert from cars to golf carts and ATV's as the principal way of getting around and adding the street cars plus some light rail was a stroke of genius."

"Not too original. Compact European cities have used the same kind of mass transit for years. Plus, there are many retirement communities in the country using golf carts extensively. Since we have a city, which doesn't extend more than six miles in any direction from the center, we were able to dump the bigger vehicles for everything except hauling heavy loads. Besides, we can run our golf carts, streetcars and the light rail on our unlimited electrical energy. It greatly simplifies the problem of supplying fuel to our petroleum-based ships, aircraft and the fleet of ground vehicles and machinery."

"To say nothing of the more leisurely pace of getting around. Whenever I have to take a car into Charleston or drive on the freeways and look at all those people rushing around, impatient and uptight to get where they're going, I wonder how I ever bought into such madness. I really like driving my golf cart to work."

"Who said something about a leisurely pace?" said Will, joining Cisco and Chips. "We've had no rest, running full steam ahead building Sanctuary twenty-four hours a day, seven days a week, for twenty-two months and four days. I know the exact time because my wife keeps track and never lets me forget it. Every time I think we're starting to make progress, something else comes up."

"Not that I haven't got problems of my own," said Chips, "but I always like to hear about the other guy's frustrations. What's going on with you?"

"After we brought in the small-scale refinery to process crude oil, I realized our reserves are still very finite. Presently, I'm trying to figure out a way to transport crude to Charleston, since South Carolina has no deposits of oil.

By this time, the rest of the command staff were standing at the primary screen listening in on the conversation. Cisco waved them all to chairs. "Why don't we sit down and we'll start."

"Computer, what is the current population of Sanctuary?"

***"As of today, the population is 24,567 people,"*** said the pleasant female voice with a somewhat low register.

"Add about 5,000 more to that," said Chips. "I grumbled about my problems a minute or so ago, finding places for all these people to live are the worst."

"Tell me."

"Computer, display the master housing plan on the central screen."

The image flashed an illustration of all the housing for the new city. It showed a dozen inner-connected condominium structures surrounding the city center. Additionally, several hundred single-family residences were grouped in residential blocks, sprinkled within the perimeter

Chips pointed to the picture. "We started construction on the complex of all the new condominium buildings at the same time. I found it was more efficient to work through each phase of construction as it comes up. The goal is to house 30,000 people."

"All that sounds right. Where's the hang-up?"

"The problem is I let too many of the construction people go after the buildings were ready for finish work on the interiors of each living unit. I kept five expanded teams for that, and they've been working non-stop. Maybe I should have held on to a few dozen more carpenters because the fly in the buttermilk is not all the condos will be ready for another two months. We're bringing in fifty families a day. I'm running out of places to put them."

Cisco turned to Ben, "You do all the hiring for our personnel spaces, any way to slow the process down a little?"

"Not for the people currently in the pipeline and scheduled to arrive in the next week or so. After that, I think I can buy us some time and spread out the incoming groups."

"I appreciate it, Ben. It'll give me a few weeks to catch my breath."

"Speaking of catching our breath," said Riley, "we've worked around the clock to stay even with the continuing research at Horizon. What's the latest on their work?"

"Lino said he'd be at the O club in half an hour for our monthly review of across the board progress," said Wyatt. "Last month they were still trying to calibrate all the systems to exact times and locations for inserting people into the time stream, and also to make sure the recall bracelets were reliable."

"Maybe they'll have something new to talk about. Heaven knows those people have worked themselves to exhaustion."

The team continued to review new developments in their mission to create a 'survival beachhead' as Cisco outlined on their visit to New York and the Academy. His mind wandered through the pathways bringing them to this moment.

With the installation of the advanced computer system, Cisco uploaded all the requirements for a small city, into the memory banks. As the work continued he measured progress by looking at the percentages each individual project had achieved, and another measurement showing him the overall progress of everything combined. Currently, the Sanctuary model of independence stood at 81%, with the basics of food, shelter, and clothing at 100%. He felt considerably better. If the former Charleston Joint Operations Command had to stand on its own, beginning today, they could do it.

"So, with about 5,000 acres under cultivation, our food supplies are getting bigger," reported Will. He paused and waved his hand in front of Cisco. "Admiral, did we lose you somewhere?"

"Sorry, Will, I got distracted for a minute. Actually, I heard you, I think."

Everyone laughed. "I can barely remember the last time we all laughed at something," said Cisco, patting Will on the shoulder, "we ought to do it more often. I think we've pushed through the underbrush long enough today. Why don't we break and head over to the club?"

"Good meeting," said Chips. "We have a lot of news to report."

The private conference room in the new Officers Club used by both groups had unique features. In addition to the added security to keep conversations private, an over-sized LED screen covered one of the walls linked with the central computer. Not only could the Horizon team review the current status of Sanctuary, but Cisco and the command team could also review the latest developments surrounding the Gateway.

The two groups were different too. After a rocky start, culminating in the ultimatum meeting when the military command dug in its heels over the nuclear power modules, relations improved dramatically after Cisco witnessed what was going on in the mysterious warehouse.

The new Gateway Center remained a top-secret, highly restricted facility, but the concept of traveling in time no longer had such an 'other-worldly' perception. The meetings these days were as relaxed as possible, given the nature of the work of the groups. As a way of ensuring sensitive matters discussed stayed secret from interruptions from the wait staff, Cisco installed an efficient self-serve bar in the lounge and added a snack table.

Lino arrived with Missy. She didn't always attend the meetings, but today had a special reason to be there. The command team stood and shook hands all around, especially welcoming Missy.

"Glad to have a pretty face in the room," said Chips. A widower since the death of his wife to cancer, he and Missy spent some time together.

"Happy to be here. Good to see you, Chips. I know you're super busy building apartment houses, and finding places for people to live, but we ought to go out and play another round of golf."

"Ben told me a little while ago to expect a short pause in the flow of new people, so I think I can find some time to take a break. I'll call you."

Everyone got something to drink and filled their plates with a variety of tasty morsels, gabbing together as they did.

"Is Scott running late?" asked Cisco. "Do we need to wait on him?"

"Uh, Scott's kind of indisposed at the moment," said Lino fumbling his words. "We should go ahead without him."

"Okay," said Cisco with a polite gesture. "If you'll all have a seat, we'll start the meeting. In the month since we last met, many of our projects are nearing completion. Let me give you a general overview."

He turned to the main screen. "Computer, display the present status of our self-sufficiency model."

The screen showed a colorful graph with all the categories listed along the bottom and the percentage of completion in bars up the left side.

Cisco took a laser pointer and began highlighting each area, prompting the computer to display images of them as he went through the list. "Obviously, the first things we needed to address were food, shelter, and clothing. If we can't supply a resident population with these fundamentals, it can't survive. We've finally gone over the top in food. We now have enough land growing everything we might need to make us independent. The same is almost true for housing. We will complete construction of the condominium complex within the next two months. When you add that to our existing housing, we will hit our goal of being able to maintain a stable population of 30,000 people with allowances for growth in our population of two percent a year. We consider these vital components complete."

"Of course, the power to run all our systems and equipment is also at the top of our list," said Will. "We got a huge boost with the installation of the small modular reactors, so electricity is not a problem. We have more than enough to run everything inside the Sanctuary perimeter for the foreseeable future. Not being satisfied with that, we relocated a manufacturer of these reactors to Charleston, either to replace those that wear out, or to construct new ones to supply future needs. We have a hundred years of spare fuel cells.

"However, electricity is not enough. We also needed a way to provide fuel for our vehicles, ships, and planes. The answer turned out to be a small, but efficient, refinery of our own. We've been stockpiling supplies of crude oil for almost a year to give us a healthy reserve."

The briefing went on at length, covering medical and hospital services, education, internal law enforcement, external security, maintenance, manufacturing, and stockpiles of raw materials of every kind.

When the command team finished, Missy sat back in her chair. "None of this would have been possible or come so far without the dedicated work of you gentlemen. Your insight and planning are something in which we can all be proud.

"And besides, all this might turn out to be completely unnecessary. It would take a massive interruption in the timestream to produce the kind of grim world we are imagining."

"Speaking of which," said Wyatt, "I'm sure there are some new things to report from your side of our brave new world. How about we hear from you Horizon people about that?"

"Well," said Lino, "I'm happy to report our two-year effort to calibrate a specific time from the past and then match it against global GPS coordinates giving us precise coordinates has reached a level of accuracy allowing us to employ this technology effectively."

"We also have a hundred percent confidence in our recall system," said Missy, "which makes it possible to return our travelers on a planned schedule or by demand."

"How fantastic," said Wyatt. "When are you planning on trying it out?"

"We already have," said Missy.

Dumb silence filled the room. Eventually, Cisco ventured, "I hope you're going to tell us a few more details."

"The truth is," said Lino, "there was nothing to look at, and also we didn't want to put any more pressure on you than you already have. Scott feared telling you we were bringing the system online would only cause you additional brain damage."

"Excuse me. I can sort of tell when people are not giving me the whole story. How about telling us what's happened?"

"Two days ago," admitted Lino, "Scott made a jump back to New York City, ten years ago. The whole mission lasted twenty-four hours. There was a complication at the end."

"Like what?"

"He got mugged in Central Park. They took his money, his wallet, and his camera, and beat him up pretty badly."

"Is he okay?" Cisco asked with lines of concern on his face.

"He lost a couple teeth, broke his nose, his lips are like hot dogs, and he has two shiners that make him look like the Lone Ranger," said Missy. "But he's recovering now and will be back to work in a few days."

"That's terrible. You should have told me."

"I'm sorry, Jonas," said Lino. "We didn't tell you for the same reason we didn't tell you we were making a real jump with a human being. As it turned out, I'm glad we didn't pile a bunch more on your plate."

"We have a little more. The muggers tried to take Scott's recall bracelet. He fought with them and ran for the Gateway. When the energy field cycled, one of the muggers was partly inside the transmission cone."

"What's that mean?"

"It means that the top half of the mugger came back with Scott. The worst sight I've ever seen. The guy was still alive when he hit the transmission platform. Then he gushed blood all over both Scott and I and died within seconds."

Missy added more. "A new report in the New York Times for the day after is now in history. It says police are questioning a man in connection with a bizarre discovery of the body of half a man in Central Park. The man insists his friend was gobbled up by a blue curtain of energy. There were no other witnesses. Police have no answers to the many questions regarding this incident."

"Isn't this the exact kind of thing you expect to produce changes to the future?"

"Yes, it is. However, we have not been able to detect any changes in the timeline at this time. Apparently, this dead person was of such little importance, his absence is of no consequence."

"What an awful eulogy for anyone. What did you do with the body?"

"One of my colleagues has a boat," said Lino. "He loaded the body aboard and took it out to the ocean and dumped it."

"Boy," said Ben, "and I thought I had a lousy week."

"Did somebody say they had a lousy week? I got that beat."

Everyone turned and found Scott standing in the doorway. He got a couple steps into the room before the crowd overwhelmed him. Even Cisco reached through a couple of people and patted him on the back.

When the tumult died out, Missy put her hands on her hips. "You're supposed to be resting in the hospital."

"I checked myself out. I got tired of being treated like an invalid. I'm stiff and sore, my jaw hurts and I'm probably going to lose another couple of teeth, but I look forward to our monthly get-togethers, and I wasn't going to miss this one."

"Lino and Missy told us the whole grisly story. You're lucky to be alive."

"Boy don't I know it. I sure did catch up on my praying and told the Lord I'm really sorry for not talking with him for so long."

"Since you are spilling the beans on this giant leap of yours. Is there anything else you'd like to tell us?"

"Yeah. In this jump I really did change history."

"Terrific. What's the story on that?"

"While I was in New York, I had a chance meeting with an old friend, entirely coincidental and unexpected. When I returned to the present, I found I had acquired a new memory of this same person calling me ten years ago, saying how nice it was to run into me in New York, and wanting to get together again. Of course, the Scott of ten years ago had no recollection of such a meeting. To make it worse, I told her back then I hadn't been in New York and certainly didn't meet her. She was confused and hurt. The call ended badly."

"We are extremely fortunate the paradox is confined to only two people and had no other consequences," said Missy. "However, it served as a clear example even the most innocent and minor alteration of the timestream changes past events. The fact Scott didn't have a memory of the confrontation until he returned to the present shows how careful we have to be."

"Where do you go from here?" asked Ben.

"We supplied a full report to the Academy, minus the blood and gore. They've been waiting, none too patiently all this time, while we worked all the bugs out of our system. Now they want

81

to rush full speed ahead to begin more extensive operations," said Missy with a frightened shake of her head.

"We were able to put off the arrival of the Academy directors for two weeks," said Scott. "Between now and then, we have to come up with a means of avoiding any ripples in time."

"We've thought of some ways to operate." Missy ticked them off on her fingers. "First, we can't go anywhere or anytime where we might be recognized. Next, where we go can't be so foreign or exotic we draw attention to ourselves. Finally, as we saw so clearly from this jump, it's not safe for us to do any more solo missions. Too much can go wrong. A person by himself could be injured, killed, or worse, trapped in that time because someone took his recall bracelet from him."

"How large of teams are you thinking of sending out?"

"We believe the optimum number is three. And we feel at least one should have training in combat techniques and hand-to-hand fighting."

Lino looked across the table at Wyatt. "Before you say it, Bub, we don't have anybody with those kinds of skills. It looks like we'll have to lean on your goodwill and friendship one more time."

"I don't suppose our guys can carry weapons?" asked Wyatt.

"Introducing high-tech equipment into less advanced cultures could trigger the kind of time ripple we are attempting to avoid. In fact, your experts will have to be extremely careful they don't kill anyone for the same reason."

Cisco closed his eyes and slowly shook his head. "I need another drink." He got up and went to the bar. He wasn't the only one.

When everyone settled down again, Cisco sipped his drink. "Let's me understand if I've got this straight. You want to put my people on a time umbilical and shoot them into sometime in the past. He's got to be a martial arts expert, but can't use the martial part of his talent, only the art. We go unarmed and aren't even allowed to punch a guy in the nose for fear of changing the future."

"A bit overstated, Jonas," reasoned Scott, "but that's the situation. If it's any consolation, this is as frustrating for me as it is you."

"Okay, anything else?"

"If we are going to function in this manner it means at least one member of the team must have extensive knowledge of the destination, either by studying it or by having been there.

"At least we won't have to come begging to you for more help in that regard. Missy here is a veritable walking Google of history. Before she hooked up with us, figuring out the theories of branching universes, she was one of the world's most foremost historians."

"No doubt about it," said Chips. "I've always been a big student of history. Missy and I spend lots of time swapping stories. I thought I knew a lot, especially with my specialization in American Western history, but she leaves me in the dust."

"At least we know who one of the team will be. I suppose the rest will have to wait until at least tomorrow."

# Chapter 8
## Welcoming the Academy

There was a knock at the door, Chips stuck his head inside Cisco's office, "Got a minute for us, Jonas?"

"Sure, come on in."

Chips came in. Missy and Ben were with him.

Cisco got up from his desk and walked over to the conference table; he kept for small meetings, "Since we have a bunch of you, we might as well sit around the table."

He sat down, and the others took their places. "What's up?"

All three took thick folders out of their briefcases and laid them on the table. Cisco looked at the piles. "Should I order lunch?"

"Most of this stuff is for our research," said Missy. "We brought it along to answer any questions you might have in our scheme."

"Okay, I imagine you're going to tell me what this is all about."

"We've been thinking about a way to impress the Academy when they come rolling into town later this week," said Chips.

Missy opened a folder. "It's important they understand the dangers and limitations of how to conduct time travel operations. If we establish some boundaries from the beginning, we think these ventures will be much safer and more predictable for both our teams and for the people on the other end of the timestream."

Chips leafed open his folder. "We've cooked up an impressive example, which we believe will accomplish both. We propose to transport the three of us to the year 1880 in the old western city of Fort Collins, Colorado."

"Why that particular place?"

"Because that's where I grew up. It's how I got my passion for Western American history. I know as much history about that town as anyone. Being a native and growing up there is a bonus because I'm unlikely to get lost."

"I thought you said we couldn't go anywhere people might know us."

"And no one will. Chips family didn't come to town for almost a hundred years after our target date. We will be completely anonymous."

"Fort Collins couldn't have had many people back then. How are you going to keep from being questioned as strangers?"

"It's true the permanent population of the city in 1880 amounted to less than 1,500 people," admitted Chips, who continued triumphantly, "The good news is at this particular time in Fort Collins there were thousands of men in the area working on ditch gangs, railroads, and quarries. The town was full of strangers. The only time when the term 'Wild West' and Fort Collins could be used at the same time, were the six years between 1877 and 1883."

"That sounds like a dangerous time to me."

"Not really. People only think of places with deadly reputations like Dodge City and Deadwood. It wasn't like that in Fort Collins. Mostly the men and even the women had a tremendous amount of fun. The vast majority of the people came from the East, a pretty dull and stuffy world. But *this*, this was Heaven. For once, the people who wanted to throw caution to the wind, and the rules of society out the window, along with their clothes, outnumbered the people who wanted to stop them. Think of it as a modern-day amusement park, with guns."

"You think you'll be safe in such an environment?"

"That's why we want to take Ben along, just in case."

Cisco turned to his young officer and lifted enquiring eyebrows at him.

"Admiral, I don't know if you are aware, but I've been the base martial arts champion the last three years in a row. I might

85

not have the same strength or agility as some of the younger men, but this is one discipline where years of experience are worth more. I can protect our team, and probably not even leave a mark."

"Alright, what's the rest of this connivance?"

Missy turned over some pages. "We plan to arrive early on February 1, 1880, at a place Chips has chosen, which won't attract any attention. We make our way into town and secure rooms at a hotel. Chips and I will be traveling as a married couple, while Ben will be my younger brother."

"For the next three days, we'll socialize with the people. I'll recognize the leading citizens from photographs, and will find ways to interact with them, based on my knowledge of their lives. We chose this time for two reasons. First, it's the middle of winter, and no one will notice the various recording devices under all the heavy clothing. Second, and more importantly, the leading dry goods and general mercantile building in the town catches fire and burns to the ground on the evening of February 3. It will give us a spectacular visual record for the principals of the Academy and will also provide plenty of cover to slip away for recall."

"Very slick. I suppose you've already got the garment factory making you period clothing?"

"Of course."

"What are you going to use for money?"

Missy and Chips looked at each other for a moment. "Well ...umm," stumbled Chips.

Missy smiled her brightest. "We did a flash jump last night. Lino dropped into the vault of the San Francisco Mint and carried off a whole bag of 1876 silver dollars."

"He also spotted a couple of bags of Fifty Dollar Golden Eagles and brought them back with him."

"Quite a load for little Lino."

"Wyatt was there to cheer him on the whole time," said Chips with a happy smile.

"Am I the only one who doesn't know about this plan of yours?"

"We didn't want to tell you until we had all the details worked out," said Ben.

"So, how do you intend to handle the ranking directors of the Academy?"

"Exactly as we did in New York. You found out they're demanding, impatient men with tremendous influence in both business and government. They seem never to let us forget how much money they're spending. Both Scott and Lino think we should put on an impressive demonstration of how the systems work and have our team jump right before their eyes."

"What are we supposed to do with them for three days waiting for the team to jump back?"

"We were hoping, Jonas, you might give them a complete tour of how Sanctuary is organized and how it would operate in the event something catastrophic occurs in the timestream," said Missy. "After all, they've spent billions on a contingency most of them think has a very low probability of occurring. The least we can do is to make them feel they didn't waste their money."

Cisco agreed. "It will likely take most of three days to show them everything,"

"I guess the last item on our agenda is your approval for Ben and me to make this time jump with Missy."

"Everything about all of this, scares me to death. However, I don't know a better way to proceed. Your planning seems to cover all the bases. When do you intend to make the jump?"

"The big bosses of the Academy will be here the day after tomorrow afternoon," said Missy. "We'll go the following morning. It will give me particular pleasure to haul these guys out of bed at o' dark hundred."

The gleaming Gulfstream landed smoothly at the Sanctuary airport and rolled to a stop. Admiral Cisco and his command team were in dress uniforms, standing next to the three principals of the Horizon Mission.

Wyatt leaned over slightly to Scott. "Aren't we glad Lino put on a clean shirt?"

"Hey, Bub, I'm not invisible. You don't need to talk about me like I wasn't here" Lino, stick his tongue out at Wyatt and grinned.

"Cool it, you two. I hope our VIP's didn't spot that."

Apparently, they didn't. The stairway folded out from the plane, and four serious-looking men stepped down. All wore dark sunglasses, and expensive, perfectly tailored suits. Two young women followed them, dressed as if they were heading to the theater on Oscar night.

Cisco stepped forward to greet the men with whom he and the others had met and walked away with their endorsement two years before in New York. He saluted smartly and then put out his hand. "Welcome to Sanctuary, Mr. Fisk, gentlemen, and ladies."

"Nice to see you again, Admiral," said Fisk with only a trace of a smile.

"You know everyone on my command team."

Fisk went down the line, shaking hands with the officers as Cisco named them. He continued to Lino, Missy, and Scott, to whom he said, "Well, Doctor, we can only hope all the time and money spent on your research is about to pay off."

"I can assure you, Mr. Fisk, what you'll see in the next few days will be remarkable."

"Humph," Fisk rumbled, "that remains to be seen. You remember my other colleagues."

Cisco and the others shook hands with Frank Williams,

Harold Kingsley, and Ahmed al Aswira. Fisk introduced his wife Shannon, and Williams presented his wife, Gloria.

The scene resembled a coin toss of multiple captains at a football game with the command team and Horizon scientists mixing and shaking hands with the leaders of the Academy. Lino got so flustered in the confusion he even shook Cisco's hand.

With the greetings completed, Cisco turned to Fisk. "I would have thought, considering your investment, you would have come here during the building of Sanctuary."

"Why bother? All I have to do is turn on the TV and find wall to wall coverage of everything you're doing."

"We have managed to capture the interest of the country. However, I think you will find seeing the real thing is somewhat different from what's on TV. Haven't you realized a lot of new business enterprises because of our work here?"

"Naturally. I'm glad I thought of it when you came to New York."

Cisco didn't bother to correct Fisk. If he wanted to take all the credit for the media storm produced by the enormous project, he couldn't care less.

He pointed to a line of golf carts, "Ladies and Gentlemen, if you'll be seated, we'll take you to your quarters."

"In those?" said Fisk with obvious disdain and surprise. "You must be joking."

"This is as good a time as any to introduce you to the many innovations we have employed in designing and building the most remarkable community in the world." Cisco led the startled visitors to the sleek-looking vehicles, clearly several steps above a traditional golf cart. "This is where you start."

Cisco didn't give them time to think. "These carts will take you to your quarters in the city center." He tapped a metal tab on his chest. "Computer, on my mark, destination Embassy Suites, run descriptive narratives of principal landmarks."

*"Acknowledged."*

"What was that?" said Fisk, his face twisted in surprise and curiosity.

"I was speaking to the Core Computer telling her to take you to your quarters and to play recorded narratives of the sights along the way. If you and your wife will be seated, I'll send you on your way."

Fisk helped his wife into the vehicle. The other speechless Academy officials got in other carts. Cisco gave another smart salute. "Engage."

The doors of the carts closed and a female voice from a grill on the dash spoke, ***"Please secure all personal items, and fasten your seatbelts."*** A few seconds later, the carts took off at a brisk clip, with their astonished passengers.

Cisco turned to the others. "I told the computer beforehand the route I wanted them to take. It will give our guests an impressive overview of some of the highlights of the city. It will also give us a chance to zip ahead of them and be there to greet them when they arrive."

"This vehicle doesn't have a steering wheel," said Shannon Fisk.

"It must be one of those new self-driving cars, or golf carts, or whatever this is."

"It would take a pretty sophisticated computer to know where we're going, and then oversee the controls to drive us there. I'll bet they have surveillance cameras everywhere to monitor traffic and make changes when necessary."

"Presumably, Admiral Cisco has some kind of program."

Shannon put her hand out. "I feel cold air coming in. They've got this little car air-conditioned. I can't hear an engine, so it has to be running on an electrical battery charge. Putting climate controls in these carts is quite advanced technology."

Fisk shrugged his shoulders.

The procession of carts made their way out of the airport grounds and onto a divided roadway. Trees and landscaping on the center island, almost hiding a set of light rail tracks, and more lush landscaping along the side of the road. It was somewhat narrower than a standard road, but there were many golf carts and ATV's, some of which passed the motorcade, driven by smiling people. Other carts were also self-guided with couples and families, some with no passengers at all. Shannon paid close attention as the cart maneuvered through the traffic.

A voice spoke from a dash speaker. ***"This is Outer Band Boulevard. It encircles the entire perimeter of Sanctuary at the outer boundary. Two similar circular thoroughfares are located halfway to the city center and another surrounding the city center. These are Middle Band and Inner Band Boulevards. The design is primarily for use by golf cart and ATV traffic. However, a larger, segregated lane remains in the center of the thoroughfare to accommodate larger vehicles, and trucks as needed."***

Shortly the motorcade turned off the thoroughfare and onto another road. It also had expanses of green with small ponds dotted along the way. People strolled along pathways winding away into groves of trees. Soon they passed by a large school. An enthusiastic crowd cheered a pair of girl soccer teams scampering across the pitch. In the distance, Fisk saw homes built in curving rows. Church bells rang in the distance.

The speaker sounded again. ***"Sanctuary has four primary education centers serving Grades 1 through 12. Although there are separate areas for primary, middle and high school students, our schools encourage the largest interaction of young people. All dining services are common. Our students attend*** *school year-round, including Saturday mornings, which are testing days. Our curriculum is challenging and demanding."*

Shannon admired the pastoral scene, then noticed the buildings changing to more business and industrial uses. Despite some of the buildings obviously being places for office, manufacturing, engineering and other heavier industrial purposes, none of it had a stark, brash or garish appearance. Everything demonstrated good order and organization. She bet her husband wished some of his business operations had the same appearances.

The speaker came to life again. *"The boundaries of Sanctuary measure twelve miles in diameter around a circular perimeter. The 30,000 residents have an excellent public transportation system. Light rail lines loop in three elliptical circles evenly spaced from the perimeter to the city center. Additionally, a system of streetcars augments transportation for short, local travel."* As the narration played, a light rail train went zooming by.

The motorcade passed between two tall condominium buildings. Shannon saw there were many of these built in a ring surrounding the city center. Like a bullseye in a target, the center emerged. Even though there were many buildings concentrated inside the mile-wide circle, the design framed them in a campus with flower gardens, open lawns and trees everywhere.

The carts made a turn onto another street after waiting at a traffic light. They passed the central library, and an extensive hospital before turning into a curved drive with a lighted sign that read, "Embassy Suites." The motorcade came to a stop in front of a six-story building. Cisco and Scott came out of the entrance, as Fisk and the others exited the carts. Shannon resumed her quiet position in the background whenever she was in public with her husband.

"How did you enjoy your tour?"

"Quite impressive," admitted Fisk. "You've built a remarkable city here."

"You've only seen the tip of the iceberg," said Scott. "Sanctuary has surprises for you around every corner. After you're settled, we have an introductory tour planned for you at the Gateway Center. There's quite a lot to take in there too."

"We've seen a few goddamned computer servers before," said Fisk with a nonchalant wave of his hand, as if he felt it necessary to cancel out his just stated endorsement.

"But you've never seen the Gateway Center," continued Scott. "It's unique and certainly one of a kind."

"Whatever. Can we get out of this hot sun and humidity and to our rooms? I'm getting uncomfortable."

Fisk led the way for the others into the building. As soon as they were well inside, they all stopped short and stared.

Scott looked at Cisco and smiled. The Embassy Suites were built to overwhelm and astonish guests.

The elegant building enclosed an extensive garden and lounge. The center was a vast open space. There were trees, flowers, and an actual waterfall, with tables and chairs and comfortable long couches spotted here and there. On each end of the building, a glass-covered lift moved up and down. Each floor of the building had an ornate railing covered with long boxes filled with blooming flowers.

When Cisco thought the visitors had seen enough, he stepped up to the group. "Your luggage is already in your rooms. If you follow your room steward, he will escort you and provide a general briefing on the features of your suite."

Scott added, "In about an hour, we've planned a visit for you to the Gateway Center before the evening meal."

Aside from Fisk's apparent nonchalance, the stern-faced

directors seemed eager to have a look inside the facility. "We'll be happy to take a look at this wonder of yours," admitted Fisk. He took Shannon by the arm and walked off with the room steward to the elevators.

"So far, so good," said Scott after the Academy party left for their rooms.

Cisco nodded. "We need to keep them reacting to the components of our plan, instead of letting them start hatching ideas of their own. Meet you in an hour."

If Cameron Fisk planned to complain about any deficiencies in his accommodations, his wife Shannon, preempted that with a gush of observations, "Admiral, I had no idea how easy it is to talk to a smart computer and had it do all sorts of things. I had her change the temperature in the room, turn the TV on and off, and she remembers all the music I like. I asked her some tough questions, and she knew the answers to every one of them. We have such a spacious suite, and the view from the balcony is fantastic."

Glad you're happy with your arrangements. You'll find the room service, and our restaurant is also first class."

Shannon Fisk was many years younger than her husband. Unlike many trophy wives, she had a presence, which showed a keen mind underneath the makeup. She displayed more of that with her next question, "How many systems does your computer manage?"

"Probably easier to ask what it doesn't manage. You've already seen a number of its capabilities with the self-driving carts, with traffic control through the extensive surveillance cameras, and then the interaction you experienced in your rooms. The computer manages all the power systems in Sanctuary, keeps the light rail trains and streetcars running on a schedule, and still can answer a question presented to it by a third-grader. Residents can speak to the computer anywhere inside the perimeter simply be tapping the comm tab we all wear."

Cameron Fisk scowled at his wife, clearly annoyed she wasn't playing her role as the subservient spouse, "All this bullshit about the operations of your city, may be interesting, but that's not the reason we're here. I'm ready to inspect this scientific breakthrough of yours in operation."

"Yes, indeed," said Scott. "Let's be on our way."

The Academy party filed out to the waiting carts. Thus far, none of the other members of the group had done much speaking. Apparently, content to allow Cameron Fisk, the chairman of the Academy, and the obvious driving force behind it do the talking. In truth, it was much the same for the command team and Lino, who let Cisco and Scott carry the ball.

However, the present moment seemed to be too much for the wife of Frank Williams who turned on her husband. "Frank, you aren't going to make us poke along in these silly little doohickeys again? They're stupid, and this whole town is prehistoric."

"Now Gloria, we agreed I would do this last piece of business before we head for the house in Italy."

"You agreed. I never wanted to come in the first place." She turned to Shannon. "This dump is a drag. I didn't see a single sign anyone knows how to have a good time."

"Come on, Gloria. In case you hadn't noticed this city is featured continuously on every TV station and social media. This is a most remarkable development and is about fourteen steps ahead of every other city in the country."

"Ahead of what. I'll bet you don't have a single night-time hot spot anywhere in this drab modern version of Mayberry."

This was too much for Cisco, who leveled sharp eyes at Gloria Williams. "And no billboards, no garish neon signs, no all-night strip bars, no drug epidemic, no homeless shelters, and

95

almost no crime. What we do have is a well-adjusted community of nearly 10,000 families, who manage to find ways to entertain themselves with a very long list of wholesome activities. We have over five hundred clubs here, catering to almost any diversion you can imagine."

"Enough of this pointless bickering," said Cameron Fisk, speaking more to Frank Williams than any other. "Let's go to the laboratory."

Wyatt shot a pair of raised eyebrows and a tiny wag of his head to Cisco, as the party headed off to the carts.

Cisco and Scott hopped into an open-air ATV with a steering wheel and shot off with the motorcade following behind, and the command team bringing up the rear. Lino rode with Wyatt.

It was a relatively short distance to the heart of the city, with the Gateway Center located in the exact middle of Sanctuary. However, the end of the workday meant people were coming out of offices, manufacturing facilities and work centers on their way home, so traffic boiled up around the motorcade, and it had to make several stops before arriving at the vast plaza surrounding the Gateway Center.

Most people paid very little attention to the high walls wrapped around the super-secret facility. Of much greater interest was Enterprise plaza itself where activities went on all the time. Like slices of a pie, the plaza was broken in four places at the twelve, three, six and nine o'clock positions with gardens, pathways, lush lawns and quiet nooks. The people loved their city center. At the three o'clock position stood a stadium, next to Cooper River. It was a favorite place for sporting events, concerts, and special shows. Cisco had it built for recreational activities, and also as another redundancy in the event, it became necessary to assemble the entire population to present some vital information, which could not be delivered any other way.

The Gateway Center had a single-entry point, a twenty-foot

wide steel gate that slid open to permit vehicular traffic and a smaller gate adjacent to it to admit those who worked inside to pass through the security checkpoint. The entrance was on the far side of the plaza. Fewer people moved through this sector since much of the heaviest industrial uses emanated from this point. This sector contained, all the small nuclear reactors, the oil refinery, garages, rows and rows of warehouses stuffed to the rafters with equipment, spare parts, food, and an endless list of equipment, electronics, and finely manufactured products, which were not easy to replace without a sophisticated infrastructure to provide the critical components.

The motorcade circled the plaza and drove into the thirty-acre campus containing the laboratories, workstations, and offices of the elite team of scientists who had created this marvel. At the rear of the laboratory building, a two-story structure rose. There were no windows, but a complex of antennas and broadcast dishes festooned the roof.

Scott jumped out of the ATV and escorted the members of the Academy, past the guards, and into the building. He didn't spend any time describing the interior of the building and walked straight down the central corridor, through the double doors, and into the room housing the Gateway. There were chairs in front of the platform. When all were seated, Scott climbed the short stairs.

"First, we would like to give you a demonstration of how we knew we'd penetrated the time-space continuum and entered the timestream. You've read this in the classified reports, of course, but no one outside this laboratory has ever seen what I'm about to show you."

The techs prepared the presentation with the Rhesus monkey, which Cisco saw two years before. A single plastic cubicle sat on a stand at the center of the transmission platform in the middle of the circle lined with the broad, red stripe. A monkey with a crimson collar and metal recall bracelet placed sat inside its box.

Scott stepped down and went to the control panel, next to Lino. He activated the transmission cones over the Gateway. They still looked like the ends of rocket engines, but there were now more of them, packed into a tight bundle. A solid shaft of bright blue light filled with sizzling energy engulfed the platform to the edge of the red line. Cisco shook his head in wonder. No matter how many times he'd seen the Gateway in operation, it remained a dazzling display.

With a rapid stroke, Lino punched a red button on the console. The intensity of the transmission cone increased. Suddenly the monkey disappeared from the cubicle, and the column of light dissipated. "For this demonstration," addressed Scott to the wide-eyed chiefs and ladies, "we've set the recall signal to activate in five minutes."

Cisco peeked at the pinstriped men and elegant women, knowing they were likely experiencing the longest five minutes of their lives. They remained calmly seated, but their faces betrayed them with tense looks as they glanced nervously at each other.

With a flair for the dramatic, Scott eventually announced, "thirty seconds." He counted down the final ten seconds. When he reached zero, the blue column flashed brightly, and the monkey reappeared inside the cubicle.

Fisk reacted first, "How do you know the monkey went back in time?"

"Because in our early experiments we discovered an interval of time between sending the monkeys from one cubicle to another. There should be no interval," said Arnett, "if the goal is to transfer matter from one place to another."

For the first time, Ahmed Al Aswira spoke up. In the introductions, Cisco saw a fierce intensity in the man's eyes, behind a perfectly groomed full beard.

"If your monkey went back in time five minutes, why did we not see it as we came in?"

Cisco blinked at Aswira's surprising insight.

"An excellent question," said Scott smoothly. "The reason you saw nothing is because of the secondary power dome expanding out six miles in all directions when the core transmission dome is activated. It suspends time when the Gateway is operating. You saw the monkey disappear in the 'Now' while being inside the secondary dome. When it was recalled, the 'Now' had not changed, only five minutes had passed. During the last two years, we've learned how to filter the secondary dome, so it doesn't cast a blue tint over everything in the field."

Fisk waved his hand in impatience, "All that is interesting, but I want to know about the actual time travel phenomenon."

"That's the reason you're here, Mr. Fisk. We reported to you two weeks ago I had made an actual time jump," said Scott with some exasperation.

"A lone person, spending one shitty day, ten years in the past is hardly a meaningful test."

"It is when the whole purpose of the exercise was to learn whether or not humans could be transported through the timestream and safely recalled."

Lino jumped to Scott's defense. "The bravest thing I've ever seen anyone do. Talk about stepping off the cliff into the unknown."

"Yeah, yeah, real fucking courageous and heroic. When do we see the next step with the expanded time jump you featured in your report?"

"Tomorrow morning," said Scott with a smile. "We are sending a team, 150 years into the past, for three days."

"That sounds like a more comprehensive test, and we will

observe that?"

"Absolutely," said Scott with a grin. "The jump is set for six a.m.."

"You can't be serious," blurted Gloria Williams. "Why can't you do this at a more reasonable hour?"

Lino enjoyed providing the answer. "We can calibrate for an exact location and an exact date anywhere in the world. What we can't do is adjust for local time at the destination. We need to put our team into Colorado before dawn to ensure they aren't spotted. We think four am is the safest. It's two hours earlier in Colorado right now, and it will be two hours earlier 150 years from now. So, we jump at six a.m., our time."

Everyone in the visitor's group, except Ahmed Al Aswira, grumbled. Fisk put an end to the carping. "Oh shit, I guess there's nothing for this except to plan an early morning. What are we supposed to do for three goddamned days waiting for your team to return?"

"You will have a comprehensive look at the final results of our planning and design and every new innovation which has given us Sanctuary. As remarkable as it is, we need to remember it was built assuming a worst-case scenario in which everything we know could be wiped out by an altered past."

"I doubt such extensive planning and preparation is required," broke in Aswira. "I'm still not convinced all you asked is necessary. However, when we consulted with experts in such a survival environment, it became apparent we would have to accede to your demands."

"And we appreciate your support," exclaimed Cisco. "Without it, we could never have accomplished so much in such a short time. Trust me; less than two years is a brutal deadline to produce results and achieve what we have. Some of the practical applications you've already seen. It will be our honor to show you the rest."

"Which is another way of saying our billions of dollars have served a purpose," said Fisk with little enthusiasm.

"We hope so. In any case, three days is barely enough time to show you everything. We think it will keep you busy."

"Well, I'm not going to waste my time looking at a bunch of buildings," groaned Gloria. "What do you say, Shannon, how about we do a little shopping in Charleston and then head for the beach?"

"Tell you the truth, I'm fascinated to learn how all this fits together. You run along, Gloria. I'm sure you can find something to interest you."

"Suit yourself, brown-noser. I can't imagine you doing this except to please your husband."

Shannon tilter her head. "Time will tell."

Scott watched this exchange patiently. He looked at Fisk, who motioned for him to continue, "One last thing, we'd like you to meet our jump team."

The time travelers came forward and stood next to Scott on the platform.

"You know Doctor Missy Long. She's our expert in history and our foremost authority on how to avoid any paradoxes in time.

"Next, we have Colonel Chips Gallant. We chose the location for our jump, Fort Collins, Colorado in February 1880, because Chips grew up there a hundred years after this time and is an expert on Western history and specifically the history of Fort Collins.

"Finally, we have Lt. Commander Ben Crenshaw from the Coast Guard. Ben is the reigning base champion in martial arts and will provide any needed security."

"Handsome too," said Shannon Fisk, to which her husband scowled.

"When you see them next, they'll be wearing period

costumes, so they blend inconspicuously with the local population. We have equipped them with recording devices and money from the time."

"Any weapons?"

"We can't risk having any modern firearms with us. However, we have agreed to let Ben carry a knife."

Ben took the knife out of the sheath he carried. It glistened in the light as a larger version of a Bowie knife, at least a foot and a half long, and razor sharp.

Shannon whistled. "I'd be scared if you pulled that on me." Ben smiled and winked at her. Her husband scowled again.

"That's everything for today. The Admiral has arranged a banquet at seven p.m. in our officers' club."

Cisco stood up. "We thought you might enjoy some hands-on experience working with our systems. It's only a ten-minute ride to the club. When you leave the Embassy Suites, jump in any available cart, say 'Computer, destination officer's club', and then say 'engage'. That's all there is to it. We'll make sure you are escorted back to your quarters now. I'll meet you at the O club."

"Please excuse Lino and me tonight. We have some work to do before the jump. The computer will ring your rooms tomorrow morning at 4:30 a.m.."

# Chapter 9
## Into the West

For at least the third time, Chips rolled over in bed and stared at his clock. The clock said 2:37 a.m.

He sighed and tossed back the covers announcing to his cat, sleeping peacefully at the end of the bed, "Sometimes, Diablo, I wish I could tune out the world like you. Come on; I might as well give it up and start moving."

Chips continued his conversation with the fat, yellow cat after he showered. "I don't suppose you know where I'm going today? It's not so much where, as when. Would you believe it, I'm going back to 1880 to see the history I've read all my life come alive. Pretty amazing, huh?"

He lathered up to shave. "Pretty scary, too. I bet I've flown a hundred combat missions in the Stealth fighters, but this mission has me so spooked I could slip and cut my throat."

After shaving, without a nick, he brushed his teeth and combed his limited hair. Then he sauntered back into his bedroom. Diablo followed dutifully, waiting for the next part of the conversation.

Chips stood looking at the outfit a well-dressed businessman in the 1880s wore. Black pants, a tightly fitted coat with narrow lapels going most of the way to his collar. The jacket was cut away at the bottom to reveal the vest and a gold watch on a chain. He would add a string necktie and a bowler hat.

"I think the clothing factory did an excellent job, don't you?"

Diablo licked his face and hopped onto the bed for a better view. He let out a small meow.

"Glad you approve. I've got a valise here with a change of clothes, and all the things a fellow like me could be expected to carry in 1880. It also has a false bottom with Golden Eagles stored away. For the times, I would be considered wealthy. Ben

103

Crenshaw is coming along to make sure nobody takes this bag away from me."

Diablo bounced off the bed and did several figure eights around Chips' ankles. He picked him up and rubbed under his chin, "Nice of you to listen to me. I know all you really want is something to eat."

Chips fed his cat and got dressed. He picked up the somewhat heavier bag, because of the gold in the bottom and left his house. The golf cart ride to the Gateway Center took only fifteen minutes but seemed longer.

As he passed through security and into the building, he found the place abuzz with people scurrying about, conducting final preparations. He walked down the central corridor and into the two-story structure housing the transmission cones above the circle marked with a broad red line. He found Missy and Ben already there and dressed to visit the 19th century.

"Guess who else couldn't sleep?"

"How long have you been here?"

"A couple of hours. I tossed and turned so much, I got tired of lying in bed and looking at my clock every ten minutes. So, I got dressed and came over here. How do you like my outfit?"

Chips gave Missy a long look. She turned around as he did. Her dress covered her from neck to an inch above the floor. It had long sleeves down to her white gloves, which set off the dark tan of the dress. It was heavily pleated, and extra material swooped up in the back up to her slim waist.

Chips whistled. "I think you're beautiful. I don't know much about women's fashions, but it's a handy thing Ben's with us to keep the guys from trying to be too cozy."

"Thanks a lot. We spent a lot of time getting this right. I need to appear as a refined 19th-century lady, but not so gaudy I attract too much attention. As for Ben, I hope we can keep him awake. He's been here all night."

"I got a few catnaps, here and there, but I'll stay awake. I think I'm on an adrenaline rush. This is exciting."

"Trust the kid to see this as high adventure," said Chips. "I'm scared to death."

"In the first place, I haven't been called a 'kid' since I turned thirty, and in the second place I've got a few dozen butterflies myself."

"Both of you look very authentic. Chips gives the impression of a successful businessman, and Ben is respectable too. Maybe a bit more casual."

Ben wore a tailored black coat with black pants, a bright blue shirt, no tie, and a zippy straw hat.

The three all had valises with extra clothing and a false bottom to hold gold and silver. Ben and Chips had coin holders for pockets inside their suits and Missy carried a handbag with more coins. They were not going to be short of cash.

Scott arrived as they admired each other, "You guys look great. I know how you feel. It was the same for me when I jumped. We have coffee, juice, rolls, and pastries in the break room. It will likely be awhile before you can eat again."

Ben hopped off the platform. "Lead the way, my man. I may not be able to sleep, but I'm sure hungry."

At 5:00 a.m., the Academy directors arrived. They were dressed more casually than the day before and obviously not accustomed to such an early morning start. Cisco and the rest of the command team came with them, looking considerably more alert.

The seniors gobbled down the pastries and sipped noisily on the hot coffee. Cisco poured himself a mug full while listening to complaints about the outrageous middle of the night wake-up call.

The jump team got a thorough looking over.

"So that's what they wore back in the Dark Ages," said Gloria

105

Williams. "How drab and common."

"I don't agree with the drab part, but we sure want to come off as common. The last thing we want is to stick out."

"Trust me, honey, you aren't going to get a second look."

Chips rallied to Missy's defense. "I think she looks like a million bucks. That dress doesn't make her lose any of her figure."

"Whatever. You wouldn't catch me wearing such a rag."

Scott stirred from his chair. "I think we should head to the Gateway. We need to run some final checks."

The group went down the central corridor and through the doors to the transmission center. The visiting dignitaries took the same seats as the day before, Cisco and his team sat behind, the jump team went to a table close to the central console.

"You can leave these heavy overcoats off until just before you jump. They have body cams built into them to record everything. Whenever you're inside, the cams in your suits and your dress will keep on recording. There are extra batteries hidden inside cigar tubes, don't forget to change them every day."

He turned to Ben. "Got your knife?"

Ben reached behind the inside of his coat and pulled out the long, thick, knife, "Don't worry about it being sharp. I had to do something while I paced the floor all night."

"Try not to cut off a finger."

Lino came walking in from inside the server racks with a couple of techs. "We've run triple checks on all the systems. Everything is working properly."

Scott glanced at the bank of clocks mounted off the side of the central console. It showed the current time at places around the world. The one for Mountain Time said 3:51 a.m., "I guess it's time to gather your gear and get onto the transmission platform."

Cisco and his other officers came over and shook hands with Chips and Ben. They all gave Missy hugs. "I can't say I know how

106

you feel, but I know how I feel ... goosebumps everywhere. God's speed to you all. We'll pray for your safe return. See you in three days."

"Thanks, Jonas, I'll bring 'em back alive."

The three climbed the stairs and stood in the center of the Gateway circle. They sat their valises down while they put on their overcoats and gloves. Then they picked up their bags and stood quietly, facing the console, and the intense looking staff of scientists and techs gathered behind the chairs of the VIPs.

The clock ticked away slowly. Scott and Lino took their places at the console and activated the transmission system. When the clock clicked to 4:00 a.m. in Colorado, Scott pushed the red button. The Gateway glowed with energy. A bright, blue, sizzling column filled the circle. There was a flash, and the three time travelers disappeared.

Chips found himself standing in a grove of cottonwoods. The sudden shift from the laboratory confused him. All he could make out was it was still quite dark and extremely cold.

"Everybody okay?"

"I'm all right, except for hardly being able to see my hand in front of my face. This is one black night."

"We're used to having light all around us, all the time. Our eyes will adjust to the dark in a few minutes.

"Have you ever seen so many stars?" exclaimed Ben.

Chips didn't answer, straining to orient himself. He heard the sound of water off to his left. "That has to be the Poudre River. Fort Collins is away from the river."

Do you think we can chance a little light to help us move in the right direction?"

"I don't think anyone's around. Probably nobody saw the flash as we passed through the Gateway. Have you got your compass, Ben?"

"Right here. I also have our flashlight."

After considerable debate, the team determined they should risk bringing a flashlight with them. This one was no bigger than a cigar but had powerful LED lights.

"Give them to me." He took the compass and the flashlight and opened up his overcoat, hoping to orient himself while shielding the light with his coat. When the light came on, it seemed exceptionally bright. Holding the compass, Chips found north and then turned around to face southwest, the direction of the town from the river. He clicked off the flashlight. "I've just wiped out any adjustment I had to the dark by turning on the flashlight. Both of you, stand next to me and stare straight ahead. Tell me if you can see anything."

Missy and Ben peered in the direction Chips stood. After a couple of minutes, Ben stepped away and looked through the trees. "Still can't see anything, but the slope ahead is rising. I think we have to climb up to level ground."

"The place I chose for our arrival is near the river and at the bottom of a small bluff. If my planning is right, we should come out close to a bridge with a road heading into town."

Even though it was still dark, the three could now make out the shapes of trees and the general rise of the ground. Slowly they made their way up the slope. When they came out of the dark shadows of the trees, they could see much better. Off to their right, a bridge crossed the river, and a dirt road spread before them.

"I know where I am. This is Linden Street. Straight ahead a couple of blocks and on the right, will be the Tedmon House Hotel. It's brand new. There won't be anyone at the desk at this hour, and we have no plausible explanation of how we got here. We'll go to the train station. The lobby is always open, and they keep a fire burning in the stove. We can wait there until it gets light. There are plenty of strangers coming through the station, so we shouldn't attract any attention."

"I guess you know how to find it."

"They tore it down before I was born, but I know where it used to be from my studies of Fort Collins history. We go up Linden to Walnut Street, turn right and walk to College Avenue, which we cross and go to Laporte Avenue. The station is only a block from there."

"No doubt about your memory, honey. Let's go before I freeze to death."

When the three got to the train station, they found it open, and the passenger terminal had a low fire burning in a pot-bellied stove. "Not blazing hot, but the oven sure takes the chill off." She sat down on the bench closest to the heat.

"You two relax. I'll be right back."

Missy took off her overcoat and wrapped it around her from the front. Ben walked over to the stove and spread his hands in front of the burner. On an impulse he picked up two or three logs and threw them into the stove, stirring the coals with a poker.

Chips returned in short order. "We're in luck. A train is due at 6:00 a.m. We can mix with anyone getting off and act like we've just arrived. Guess we'll have to step outside before the stationmaster gets here, so we don't have to answer any questions."

He pulled out his watch from his vest pocket and checked the time. "Almost 5:00 a.m., why don't you relax a little. I'll step outside and look for whoever comes."

Chips had barely gone out the front door when he saw a buckboard with several people, rolling up Laporte Ave. He ducked back inside. "Someone's coming. We need to get out of sight."

The three quickly gathered their things and went out the back door closest to the tracks. Chips spotted a small shed across the street and they hurried to get behind it as the buckboard pulled up to the station. Several men jumped down, along with a woman and young boy. One of the men had on a railroad uniform and conductor's hat. "Thanks for the ride, Charlie. Saved me from walking all the way in the cold."

Chips watched as the stationmaster went inside with the others, lighting oil lamps. He went to the stove and found it already warm and blazing. With a shrug, he threw in another couple of logs and went on to the ticket office.

Chips, Missy, and Ben huddled together behind the shed and stamped their feet to stay warm, hoping the train would be on time.

It wasn't. Chips didn't hear the whistle until after 6:15. It was starting to get light as the train finally rolled to a stop at the station. "Now's our time. Slip back across the street to the corner of the building. I'll go up to the platform first, when the coast is clear, I'll signal you."

Some people got off the train, mostly men. They paid no attention to anything except getting inside, out of the cold. Chips saw the opening and waved his hand. Missy came up the stairs with Ben behind, carrying all three bags. Chips retrieved his bag, and the three went inside.

"Howdy," said the stationmaster, coming out of his office, which also served as the ticket window. "Welcome to Fort Collins. You folks look about to freeze."

The three followed the man into the lobby and gratefully stood next to the stove.

"Are you coming to town to stay, or are you just passing through?"

"I had business in Denver. Our final destination will be San Francisco, but we'll be here a few days before we take the train to Cheyenne."

"Well, welcome anyway."

"Can you help us find a hotel and a place to have breakfast?"

110

"The best place in town is the brand new Tedmon House. Has all the conveniences. For me, I think the place for the best food is The Silver Grill, across College and down Walnut Street. I 'spect they'll be open now."

"Many thanks. We could use a filling breakfast."

They gathered their bags and went out the front door. They found the restaurant two blocks away. It was open, and the three went in and sat down at a table.

"Believe it or not, this place was still open and running as I grew up. I've eaten here before, and it was about the same then as now. They always had good food."

The breakfast turned out to be better than good, despite having to pay for it in advance, at fifty cents per person. Chips gave the server two silver dollars and received change. He left the change on the table, and they headed out.

"I think you should be more careful with your tipping," said Missy as they walked down the boarded walkway in front of the stores. "Even a twenty percent tip would have only been thirty cents, you left a half dollar. Nothing attracts attention faster than someone who's over-generous with their money."

"You're right, of course. I'll remember from now on."

The sun now shone brightly and made it seem warmer as they walked the short distance to the Tedmon House Hotel. It had all the marks of being new and elegant. A man waited behind the front desk.

"You folks are coming in early. Did you arrive on the train?"

"We did. I hope you have rooms available?"

"Matter of fact, we do. How long are you staying?"

"Three days. Do you have two adjoining rooms, close to the bath?

The clerk checked his register. "We have rooms open on the second floor. They're a little more expensive, being right next to the bath. It will be a dollar a day for each room. Will that be satisfactory?"

"Completely."

"Very well. If you'll just sign the register, I'll have our porter take the bags to your rooms."

"Should I pay for the rooms now?"

"You appear to be a respectable gentleman, but we always appreciate advance payment."

Chips opened his coat and took out his coin purse. He took out seven silver dollars and put them on the counter. "Could you give me change for a dollar? I don't have any, and I should have something to tip your porter for the bags."

"The porter is my son. He'll appreciate having something extra. He's saving to buy a horse."

The clerk handed over two quarters and five dimes, then rang a bell to summon the porter.

After they got to their rooms, Chips gave the young man a quarter for carrying the heavy bags up the stairs. He seemed happy with the tip, and Missy nodded her head as well, so Chips felt like he'd done the right thing all around.

When they were alone, Ben dropped his bag. "I peeked at the calendar on the wall at the front desk. It says today is February 1, 1880."

"Then we're in the right place at the right time. I haven't asked, Chips, but how do you propose to spend the next three days?"

"This is my hometown. I grew up here. I've also studied its history passionately. I would love to move around and meet, in person, some of the early founders of the town. To actually talk to them and learn their hopes and dreams of Fort Collins, would be a thrilling experience for sure."

He looked across the room at his companions. "Of course, that's not something of much interest to you. Maybe I could rent a wagon or a surrey and let you take yourself on a tour of the area."

Missy walked across the room and sat next to Chips on the bed. "Knowing the aspirations of people in this time is the kind of history I love the most." She patted Chips on the knee. "Besides, I'm supposed to be your wife. It will be easier to do what you want as a couple."

"Yeah, Colonel, oops, Chips. If this is the wild and wooly West you talked about, there have to be people my age to mix with and enjoy their company. I guess it's all right we aren't together every minute, huh Missy?"

"The risk is minimal given the circumstances. I think having different impressions is the type of research we're supposed to be doing."

Chips puffed his cheeks and then confided, "I can't tell you how much better that makes me feel. I didn't want to end up as a second-class tour guide."

Ben went off to his room, next door. Chips and Missy were alone for the first time. Chips stared doubtfully at the bed. "That dinky thing sure doesn't look like my bed at home, and the only one I share it with is my cat. This is another complication I hadn't considered. I guess I can manage over there on the couch."

"This is stupid. If we haven't figured out by this time in our lives how to manage awkward situations, we're sorry souls. How about we share this bed and cuddle through the night like honest to goodness grown-up people."

"Whatever you say, Missy, but I've got to say being with you makes me feel like a kid again."

Half an hour later Ben knocked on the door. Chips let him in.

"I'm all organized. I stuck my head out the front door. It's still cold, but the sun's shining. I'm getting antsy cooped up so long. Can we go out for a walk?"

"Tell you what. Let's drop Missy off at Welch's dry goods

113

store and let her shop while you and I find a barber and have a shave."

"Great, I'll spend some of this money we have."

"I've never had a shave in a barbershop. Let's go."

Missy dug in her valise and got some silver dollars and one Golden Eagle. She put the cash in her purse and said, "I suppose it's safe to leave our bags in the room."

"Property crime is rare at this time. Besides, the hotel keeps a sharp eye on people coming and going, and the only way up to our rooms is from the front desk."

Chips and Ben got their shaves. Missy spent more time talking to people than shopping but bought some small things she could fit in her bag.

That night they ate dinner at the Tedmon House. When they finished, Chips went to the front desk for some information. "Tell me, where would I go to find a lively poker game?"

"There's places for that all over town," said the front desk manager. "However, if you're looking for a game with more refined people, the best games are usually here at the hotel. I should also warn you, sir, they play for higher stakes at our table. The players are our leading citizens."

"That sounds interesting. Can you arrange an introduction for a visitor?"

"You can wait in the bar. When the regulars come in, I'll tell 'em you're an out of town businessman, looking for a game."

Chips returned to the table where his companions were finishing their desserts. He told them his idea.

"Are you sure about this, Chips? I've read terrible things about Western poker games."

"People are only mad when the stranger wins. I'm going to lose ... a lot. Meanwhile, I'll be capturing everything said. If some of the famous names in the history of the town are there, it'll give us an accurate record of actual history."

Ben took a sip of his water. "So, you intend to cheat so you can lose?"

"If I have to. I'm going to send out so many 'tells' everyone at the table will know what kind of hand I have."

"Are we allowed to watch? You must be extra careful not to get spotted jiggling the cards, Chips."

"Spectators are not generally allowed, Missy, and I don't plan to get caught."

Half an hour later the players for the night came into the bar. In Chips' life, these men were names of streets in Fort Collins. They introduced themselves one by one - Joseph Mason, Bill Stover, Benjamin Whedbee, and Franklin Avery. His heart skipped a beat as he shook hands with each of them.

"So, Mr. Gallant, Theodore, at the front desk, tells us you work for the railroad," said Joe Mason. "What do you do for them?"

"I'm a civil engineer, by education. These days, I manage construction crews and make sure they have what they need on a day by day basis."

"Headed on to San Francisco, are you?" asked Bill Stover.

"The Central Pacific offered me a better job than I have with the Union Pacific. My wife and I are on our way there now. We're looking forward to living in California. Speaking of my wife, may I introduce her to you gentlemen?"

"By all means," said Benjamin Whedbee. "Since I'm the old codger, I'm allowed to say it's always a pleasure to meet a lovely woman."

Missy laughed and stepped forward. "How do you do, Mr. Whedbee." She shook hands with the others as Chips introduced them.

"This is my brother, Ben. He'll be Robert's second in command on the new job."

Ben smiled and shook hands around with all.

"If you've a mind, Mrs. Gallant," offered Joe Mason, "my wife and some of the other town ladies are over in the tea parlor. Besides local gossip, they like to hear stories of far-away places. I'll introduce you if you like."

"How wonderful. Thank you very much."

Mason escorted Missy out the door and to the tea parlor across the lobby.

"You planning on sitting it, young man?"

"I'm not very interested in cards. I think I'll go out for a walk around town before I turn in."

"You be careful of all those intemperate, wild boys out there," said Bill Stover. "They're what you might call unpredictable."

"I've spent most of the past ten years in railroad boom towns. Not much I haven't seen."

Ben put on his overcoat and gloves and stepped into the cold night. Despite it being winter, many young men, and a few women strolled the boardwalks extending from the buildings. Bright lights shone out the windows and music from pianos, guitars and drums clashed for attention as Ben walked along past the open doors. The hitching posts in front of the abundant bars, bordellos, and restaurants were crowded with horses, stamping their feet to stay warm.

A group of three rowdy young men, fortified with heavy loads of alcohol, burst out of one of the noisy bars directly ahead of Ben. They pulled up and sneered at him. "Hey boys. We have a fancy dude in fancy clothes,"

"How 'bout buying us a drink?"

"Yeah, I bet you got lots of money," the third fellow leaned heavily against the biggest man of the group.

"Sorry boys, I'm only out for a short walk before I head back to the hotel." Ben used a pleasant and tolerant voice.

"Is that right?" blared the large man. "If we ain't good enough to drink with, maybe we ought to just take your poke."

Ben took a step back. "Come on, fellows. Don't do something you'll regret."

"You're the one who'll regret it." The big man reached into his coat and pulled out a knife with a six-inch blade. "I spect you don't want to argue with this." He waved it ominously in Ben's face.

Ben glanced calmly at the weapon, "That's not a knife." Opening his coat, he reached behind his back and pulled out his blade. He stepped forward quickly, grabbed the man by his coat and shoved the formidable, razor-sharp edge against the man's throat. "This is a knife."

All three of the men's eyes grew wide as they stared at the huge knife, but none of their eyes was wider or more terrified than the man with the knife. "Sorry, mister, don't want any trouble."

"No trouble. You boys run along and stop bothering gentle folks." He shoved the man back, and all three turned and ran away, rounding the corner at the end of the block and disappearing.

A small crowd gathered during the confrontation. A dusty cowboy observed, "You sure did handle those drunks. Biggest knife I ever saw."

Ben slipped his blade back into its sheath, "Nothing more to see." He touched his hand to his bowler and strolled away. The crowd gave him plenty of room.

Back at the Tedmon House, Chips had managed to lose sixty dollars, while laughing and engaging the others at the table in pleasant and light-hearted conversation. Using his extensive knowledge of the history of the West in this period, he accurately described life and events in places from Kansas City to Cheyenne.

The men were fascinated by the stories and descriptions. Chips played his hands just well enough to win about one pot out of ten. Twice, he smoothly dealt winning hands to Stover and Mason while giving himself a hand, which allowed him to bet seriously but still lose. He enjoyed himself immensely.

When the evening ended, Chips received an invitation to play again the following night.

"Can't say I don't like to come away a winner," Stover chuckled, "but I'm a little sorry for you, Mr. Gallant. You're a good loser and a crackerjack storyteller."

"Maybe I'll have better luck next time. Anyway, I enjoyed myself."

After a remarkable beginning, the 21st Century travelers relaxed as they mixed socially with a growing circle of new friends. Missy spent time with the women and families of the town, shopping, having tea, or simply conversing. In this day and age, extensive discussion on a variety of subjects represented a major component of how people entertained themselves. Without radio, television, movies, computers, the internet and everything else still in the far future, reading, writing, talking, and attending live theater dominated the social order.

Following his confrontation, the first night, Ben found himself talked about, and recognized. On the second day, he received an invitation to ride into the foothills with wranglers from a nearby ranch and hunt for deer. Ben's reputation grew larger after he downed a buck from two-hundred yards. The years of training and military exercises paid dividends, although he surprised himself by hitting a target so far away with no scope.

The second night, the team accepted an invitation by Franklin Avery to have dinner at his home. Chips jumped at the chance. The Avery home in his time was preserved as a local, historical site. Seeing it as it originally looked, with the man who'd built the home, seemed too good to be true.

The Avery's also invited the Stover, Mason and Whedbee families to come for dessert and a continuation of the perpetual poker game. The home rang with happy noise of children playing and adults visiting. The poker game convened in the parlor. Missy and the women retired to the living room. Ben became an even bigger sensation with his demonstrations of simple martial arts moves with the older boys, watched with glistening eyes by all the girls. The three walked back to the Tedmon House. Chips lost another fifty dollars.

The final day, February 3, 1880, the team slept a little later, knowing they would have to stay alert that night when the fire at the Welch dry goods store broke out, and use the confusion to slip away quietly for their recall at four a.m.

Comfortable in their surroundings, Missy spent the day helping Bill Stover's wife put up curtains. Ben went off to the ranch he visited the day before and tried his luck at riding a wild horse. Chips rented a buckboard, and he and Franklin Avery went up and down the streets of the town as Avery had laid them out. Most of the blocks had no houses. But Chips got a guided tour of the entire imagined city from top to bottom.

After dinner at the hotel that night, Ben excused himself and went up to the rooms to pack their luggage and prepare to leave. Missy joined the ladies who came with their husbands for the poker game. Chips sat down to make it a memorable evening giving the Fort Collins' leaders a run of luck they would talk about for weeks. He'd stopped at Stover's bank earlier that day and cashed in two, fifty-dollar golden eagles for silver dollars and handfuls of change.

Not knowing the exact time of the fire, Chips started the game at a brisk clip. He dealt himself great hands, but someone else at the table always had a better one. He bemoaned his misfortune with every hand, while the others laughed and promised him his luck was sure to change. The pots got progressively bigger. Nobody paid attention to Chips' hands as he dealt. Why would they? A dealer with losing hands wasn't scrutinized very carefully.

Two hours later, Chips began to wonder if he had enough money to continue when someone burst into the bar and called out, "Jacob Welch's building is on fire!"

The bar emptied immediately. Everyone ran to join in the effort to fight the fire. Chips went along, as did Missy. Ben followed shortly when he heard the commotion downstairs. A bucket brigade formed from the well in the center of College and Mountain Avenues, and adjacent to the Welch building on the corner. Chips and Ben worked passing buckets. Everyone labored desperately for half an hour before the fire completely consumed the building. After that, the concern centered on the people in the building when the fire broke out.

Chips knew from history two employees of the store, a man and a woman, did not survive. The entire community would mourn the loss of these young people who all expected to marry one day.

As the flames subsided and thick black smoke rose into the winter air, Missy joined Chips and Ben. "It's past midnight. If we expect to make a clean break, now's the time."

"Before I left the hotel, I brought all our bags down to the lobby."

"Okay, let's go."

The three hurried back to the hotel. No one was at the front desk or in sight. They grabbed their bags and made a return to the bluff over the river. Chips used the light to help see and pick their way down to the cottonwood grove. Then the three huddled up and waited the long hours. At exactly four a.m. a sphere of blue energy flicked out and snatched the explorers' home.

# Chapter 10
## The Unmasked Conspiracy

Jonas Cisco stood in the transmission center. His face, tight with anxiety.

The column of blue energy sizzled on the Gateway platform. Three figures appeared inside the column and took shape as the core completed its cycle.

Chips, Missy and Ben, hugged each other and then turned to wave and grin at the crowd surrounding the platform. Ben raised his arm, clenched his fist and jerked it down in triumph. Shouts and applause rang through the laboratory. Even the directors of the Academy and their wives stood and applauded.

Cisco and his officers rushed onto the platform hugging Missy and high-fiving Chips and Ben. Scott and Lino followed right behind. The entire group celebrated, laughing, shaking hands and dancing in a circle with arms around each other.

Finally, Scott turned and faced the members of the Academy and raised his arms to quiet the cadre of scientists. "We've done it. We've transported a team, 150 years into the past, 2000 miles away, for three days, and returned them safely. You can all be proud our years of work have given us this moment. We have pried open the secrets of the timestream."

Wild cheering reverberated through the building.

Scott raised his arms again to speak. "We are honored and grateful the directors of the Academy are here today. Without their support and belief this day would come, we could never have achieved our triumph. Let's thank them now."

When the commotion died out, the Horizon scientists disbursed. Fisk turned. "Very exciting, Dr. Hauser, what's next?"

"We're going to run our team through a medical examination and then let them have some rest. Meanwhile, we will be downloading and editing all the video footage we got from the jump. Later this afternoon, we will get together again and watch the videos of the mission and let you interview the team and get their impressions of what they experienced."

Cisco joined the Horizon leaders and his command staff as Scott spoke. "I know the last few days have been hectic. We've tried to give you a complete picture of how the recommendations I made to the Academy became a reality. Maybe you'd like to relax."

Fisk admitted. "You've certainly kept us busy. I think I could use a recess."

Cisco smiled. "Fine, we'll get you back to your rooms, see to it you have a big breakfast, and then leave you on your own until the after-action briefing this afternoon."

Cisco and Scott escorted the Academy out of the laboratory and into the waiting carts and watched them drive off. "Well, Jonas, think we impressed them?"

"Sure impressed me. The sight of Chips and Ben as well as Missy, back safe and sound took a huge load off my mind. I can't wait to hear all about their adventures in the Wild West."

"The medical doctors are checking them out from stem to stern right now. Owing to their high spirits on the Gateway platform, I don't foresee any side-effects from the time jump. When I came back from New York, I got a thorough examination, and they found nothing unusual. We don't expect anything now."

"I think we can count the visit of our VIPs a success. My guys and I showed them everything we've done to create an independent, self-sustaining, and viable community. There's still work to do, but we've stockpiled every conceivable part, piece, resource, and raw material imaginable from research gathered from hundreds of survival databases. Even stuffy old Fisk warmed up as time went by and got interested in the rationale of our planning and innovative ways we applied it to practical applications. All the directors of the Academy liked what they saw and agreed the money was well spent. Only Mr. Ahmed Al Aswira seemed strangely detached throughout all our tours and briefings. I got the feeling he thought what we're doing is a huge waste of time and money."

"Did he say anything to you?"

"Nothing directly. In fact, now I think of it, he didn't say much at all. The other men asked questions concerning the necessity of spending money on some, apparently obscure, element of our overall community designs. Once we explained the reasons to them, they would shrug their shoulders and grudgingly admit our planning was sound. I don't recall Aswira ever asking a single question."

"That is strange. Aswira's financial group is the single biggest contributor to the entire project."

"I've got enough on my mind. I'm not going to start making up things to worry about."

Ten hours later, the Academy and Sanctuary teams reassembled in the secure conference room at Cisco's headquarters building. Chips, Missy and Ben, looked relaxed and rested. After their medical examination, they went home, showered, ate some brunch, and then had six solid hours of sleep. The command team gathered around Chips and Ben, eager to hear anything. Scott and Lino exchanged small talk with Missy. The Academy directors filed in, dressed more formally than they had at six in the morning. Cisco invited everyone to take their seats. Missy moved down the table and sat next to Chips.

Cisco began. "We've come to the end of a long road and are about to embark on a new journey of stupendous proportions. As it stands, fewer than a hundred people in the world know what we know today. Obviously, the details and scope of this entire project must continue to be limited to people with a need to know. I rely on the members of the Academy to maintain secrecy."

"We don't need you to tell us to keep our fucking mouths shut, Admiral."

"Of course, Mr. Fisk. I apologize for my implying anything to the contrary."

"If I may," suggested Scott. "I think we're all eager to see the videos our team brought back. My technical crew worked on the raw footage for hours and has assembled a truly amazing account of our visit to the past."

There were no objections, so Scott turned. "Computer, playback video record, 'Western Expedition'. The lights in the room went down, and the video screen came to life. The first image was that of the three travelers standing on the transmission platform, the energy curtain enveloping them before they disappeared.

For the next thirty minutes, the audience saw highlights of three days of history, beginning with the team's arrival at the train station. They saw the Tedmon House Hotel, inside and out. Scenes unfolded with Chips playing poker and conversing with Fort Collins pioneers; Missy having tea with their wives; Ben applying just the correct amount of violence with the drunks; a detailed look at the city as it looked in 1880; and the dramatic finale of the fire burning the dry goods store. Missy stood back so the camera could catch pictures of Chips and Ben working the bucket lines. The cameras gave sharp, clear, full-color images.

When the screen went dark, and the lights came up, an eerie silence filled the room. People looked at each other with expressions of wonder. Fisk finally broke the silence. "Remarkable. Nothing will ever be the same again."

Everyone spoke at once, laughing, applauding, and thumping the table with their hands. Wyatt got out of his chair and walked over to Lino, hugging him so hard he lifted the startled man off his feet. Lino broke into a broad grin and

124

bounced a couple of light-hearted body blows off Wyatt's mid-section.

Cisco, smiling with everyone else, let the pandemonium go on for a few minutes before signaling for order. When the group returned to their chairs, he said, "Quite a show. A sure bet for an Oscar if anyone saw it. How about we hear from our jump team to summarize their impressions?"

Missy stood up. "We needed to establish methods in which we could blend smoothly with people from another time, to interact with them in ways that didn't produce any glaring paradoxes. I believe we have accomplished this. With good preparation, there's no reason we can't expand our visits along the timestream, leave no fingerprints, and gather tremendously valuable information."

Chips joined in. "After our return this morning we underwent another extensive medical examination. I have the results of the tests with me. I'm not a doctor, but I can tell you the medical folks who did the tests say we are all in great shape. Perhaps more significant, there's no difference in the medical baseline established from the identical exam we took before we jumped."

Cisco continued. "At the outset of this enterprise, we addressed the issue of how to prepare for the eventuality of a major interruption in the timestream causing a dramatic change in the present time. Over the past three days, the Academy has seen the results. For a summarization of where we are as of today, I've asked Colonel Duval to prepare a report. Go ahead, Wyatt."

"Computer, display infrastructure project standards."

The image showed a detailed graph. "You can see, we are at self-sufficiency in food, housing, medical, education, transportation, and public safety. Our models are based on self-sufficiency for a hundred years. As of now, we can grow, replace, or build anything in these areas. What remains, chiefly, is our inability to acquire new sources of energy, beyond electricity, to operate our petroleum-based fleets of vehicles, airplanes, and ships. Currently, our reserves don't extend beyond fifteen years."

"Thanks, Wyatt. You've seen the revolutionary city we've built in our tours. The last thing I want to say is we have imported thousands of specialists, farmers, computer techs, teachers, doctors, skilled laborers, and a dozen other categories of workers to fill the positions in Sanctuary. These people represent the cream of the crop. Our standards were stringent and fewer that one application in fifty made the grade. The current number of people within the perimeter of the secondary power dome is close to 30,000, roughly 10,000 families. This would become the core population in the event we became a real Sanctuary."

"Very well, Admiral. I get it now. My compliments to you." Fisk looked around the table. "Do any of the other members of the Academy have anything to add?"

Ahmed Al Aswira cleared his throat, breaking almost three days of remaining quietly in the background. "I have a question, for Doctor Hauser. Doctor, are you prepared to announce the full spectrum of time travel is now operational?"

Scott paused a few seconds before answering. "We've lived with this for so many years it's difficult for me to mark when I knew we had reached our goal. I guess this is the moment. So yes, mankind can sail the rivers of time. From now on, the possibilities are endless."

"Very dramatic," ridiculed Aswira. "One last question. Do you foresee any limitations on exploring any time in recorded history?"

"No. The work is finished. The question is meaningless. If you get in a car, you don't need to know how to make it run. All you have to do is decide where you're going, across town, or cross-country. It's the same with our Gateway. We've already figured out how to make it work. All anyone needs to do is select the time destination, last week or the Last Supper."

Aswira smiled. "Thank you. I have no further questions."

On that note, the meeting adjourned.

A week later, three men in expensive business suits entered a fifty-story office building in New York City. Two had well-trimmed beards, one was clean-shaven. They attracted scant attention as they went to the elevators and punched a button for the penthouse.

A guard met them as they stepped out of the elevator, smiled, bowed, and placed his hand to his heart. "This way, gentlemen, Mr. Aswira is expecting you." He led them through doublewide, ornate wooden doors. A huge room opened before them, like an entry pavilion to a luxury hotel. A house servant greeted them and led them across the room to broad steps leading down into an expansive inside arboretum. Glass panels sloped down across the garden from ceiling-to-floor. The sun shone in brightly.

Ahmed Al Aswira turned from one of the flowerbeds. He smiled as he took off his gloves and laid his garden trowel aside. "Welcome my friends. It has been too long since we were together."

He shook hands with each of the men and escorted them from the garden to a grouping of couches surrounding a coffee table with inlaid gold. When they sat down, Aswira ordered espresso, and sweet tarts then turned to the men. "When I returned from Charleston, I sent word and asked you to meet with me. I've been eagerly awaiting your arrival, there is much to discuss."

"Your message only said your endless research project achieved a breakthrough. I assume you have further details to add."

"Yes indeed. The Horizon scientists have discovered a way to travel in time."

Reaction among the three ranged from shock to open annoyance.

The senior of the three frowned. "Excuse me, Aswira, when we began this long range and costly operation of yours over ten years ago, you assured us we would capture the technology of matter transference. Now you present us with something else completely, this fairy tale of time travel."

Aswira leaned forward. "I can assure this is not a fairy tale, but an exciting reality, which I believe will produce an even greater victory for the true faith."

"I've no idea what that means," said another of the bearded men. "You'll need to provide a much better explanation of why you have deceived us."

"It was never my intention to deceive you. Matter transference was the initial goal of this research team. However, upon achieving an apparent breakthrough they found they had stumbled onto this entirely new discovery. During the past two years, they've concentrated on nothing else. I did not apprise you of this wonder because I needed to make sure the technology was not only real, but could be applied, controlled, used, and developed to a point in which travel in time might be regarded as routine."

"Are you telling us, you believe this fantasy?"

"I have seen it with my own eyes. I've never experienced such an unparalleled and revolutionary event in my life."

"Tell us, exactly how this will be of use to us."

"Because the Horizon scientists believe history will be altered if a significant enough change is made to the timestream. None of my other colleagues in the Academy believes that. I supported the Academy's position and then offered to fund the Horizon project plan to build a city. It was the only means by which practical time travel could be accomplished. More importantly, the Charleston researchers are correct. History can be changed. I plan to introduce such a variation in history, which I believe will produce an entirely different historical reality than we have today."

"This is becoming more unbelievable by the minute. You're going to have to provide a more extensive explanation."

"That is the principal reason I asked you to come today. Let me give you the fundamentals of time travel and the theories of branching universes."

Aswira went on to demonstrate his own extensive knowledge of the concepts involved in the practical application of time travel. Lino Arnett would have been impressed. He explained how his understanding of these radical ideas had grown. While the scientists in Charleston were devising safeguards for preventing any ripples in the timestream, he engaged in an extensive study to find singular events in history in which the revision of such an event would produce dramatic historical changes in the succeeding pages of history. After exhaustive research, he believed he'd found it.

"Following the death of the Prophet, Muslim armies swept across the Middle East, North Africa, and into Spain, conquering, subjugating, and converting populations of people as they moved. In the year 732, an Umayyad army commanded by Abdul Rahmad fought the Franks at the Battle of Tours. Despite outnumbering the Franks two to one, the Muslim army was defeated, and Rahmad killed. Most historians believe this was the high-water mark for Muslim expansion in Europe. However, if the battle had ended with victory for Islam, they also agree the history of Europe would have unfolded much differently. I intend to deliver such a victory."

The room was quiet for several moments while the partners processed and considered the thunderous revelations of all they'd heard.

"From what you've told us, you believe we are on the verge

of giving Islam its greatest triumph. Can you tell me how you will do it?"

Aswira opened his laptop and pulled up an image. "This is a special vehicle I've had custom made. It's a heavy-duty ATV capable of transporting men, plus several hundred pounds of weapons. This compact, mobile weapons platform would be a formidable presence on a modern battlefield. Can you imagine what impact and shock value it would have on a primitive culture with weapons no more advanced than bows and arrows? It will kill hundreds or thousands of soldiers in minutes and terrify the survivors into complete capitulation."

"And how do you intend to align yourself with the Umayyad army?"

"This battle was not fought in a single day. The Muslim army jockeyed about for ten days trying to devise a means of penetrating the compacted Frankish phalanx. I plan for us to arrive in the midst of this struggle at the main camp, with the flag of Islam flying from our ATV. We will be dressed in the same manner as the other soldiers. We will drive directly to the command center of Abdul Rahmad and present ourselves as a gift of Allah to destroy the army of the Franks. I can assure you our arrival will cause panic and abject fear until we have made our intentions known. After that, we shall be treated like royalty, and after the battle is won, we will be given whatever we desire."

The senior conspirator, scratched his grayish beard, "Do you really expect us to join you in this phenomenal scheme?"

"You have no choice. If everything transpires as I have outlined, our present day will be changed and distorted unimaginably. In all likelihood, none of us would be who we are or even exist. The only place on Earth not affected will be the city of Sanctuary within the secondary power dome, and according to my plan, it will be neutralized, at least in its ability to conduct further time travel missions.

"On the other hand, we will hold dominion following our victory. We will be able to command events throughout Europe. Each of us will be able to establish countries of our own and rule them by Sharia Law, and in the manner in which our beloved Prophet would admire. How could anyone ask more of their lives than that?"

"So, we essentially martyr our lives today, for a glorious existence in a new world," said a smiling conspirator.

Aswira nodded indulgently and enjoyed seeing the eyes of his fellow collaborators widen and glow.

A servant served a new round of espresso. As the men sat sipping their coffee and smoking cigarettes, Aswira outlined his plan.

"Following the demonstration of practical time travel, which I witnessed along with the other members of the Academy, I stayed a few days in Charleston. I became familiar with the operation of the Gateway systems. The scientists have made the process ridiculously simple. I also learned the schedules and routines of those who work there. In about two months, work will be completed on the independent city of Sanctuary. Taken by itself, it is a remarkable and thoroughly revolutionary achievement. The planners started with essentially a blank slate and built this new city from the ground up. You may have seen news reports of it. It's causing quite a sensation. Even more so, because it's still a restricted military base and public access is strictly limited."

The Gateway Center, the facility housing the transmission platform, is located at the geographical center of a twelve-mile-wide circle, with Sanctuary constructed around it. The Center itself is more secure than a Swiss bank. Anyone with thoughts of sabotage or a terrorist attack would have to first penetrate the outer security perimeter then work six miles to the Center through an elaborate labyrinth of connecting roads and past a sentinel master computer with several thousand surveillance cameras at its disposal. Fortunately, we will not have to face such a gauntlet."

"You have a better way in?"

"Yes indeed. Because I am a senior member of the Academy and was present for the first practical demonstration on the time machine, I will not be questioned at all when I return. My credentials and clearances have already been made known to all security personnel, and more importantly to the central computer. Since I stayed behind, for several days, after the other members of the Academy departed, I am known to the personnel inside the Gateway Center. My return will not be cause for any alarm.

One of the men snuffed out a cigarette. "Go on."

"As I said, in two months Sanctuary will be substantially completed. A major celebration is being planned to coincide with the Fourth of July holiday. It will be a historic event for the whole country. Media coverage will be extensive. With the population and the senior officials involved with their jubilee, and with a minimum of security personnel on-duty, we will use this moment of weakness to strike."

Three hours later Aswira finished telling his fellow conspirators the details of his plans, the schedule, and the awesome redirection of history that would be the result. The ashtrays were full, and a number of empty cups sat on the gold inlay of the coffee table.

"That meddlesome Navy admiral succeeded in building this city at great cost to us. He believes his planning will result in continuity despite any major changes in the time stream. He's right about that, but with the Gateway destroyed Sanctuary will be alone in an alien and hostile world. The rest of us will march into the past for the glory of Allah."

The four men stood and formed a circle with their hands

132

stacked together. Aswira spoke with triumph. "There is a saying," 'Time is the fire, in which we burn'. This fire will utterly consume Christianity."

# Chapter 11
# Assault on the Gateway

The long Fourth of July weekend had arrived. The holiday coincided with the celebration of the official chartering of Sanctuary as an independent community. Events filled the calendar with parties, public demonstrations, a grand parade, and an extensive fireworks display, culminating the festival, to serve as an exclamation point. Then, of course, the whole country, indeed, much of the world, intended to witness everything through the glaring lens of the media. Even Jonas Cisco felt caught up in the excitement despite being the one who had worked the hardest planning the jamboree.

He glanced at his watch. Almost time for the broadcast of the interview he and Scott had done the day before. "Computer, main screen, Fox News."

*Fox News Alert*

*Good morning, this is a Fox News Alert. I'm Carmen Minnick. For the past two years, the whole country has watched as the remarkable, even revolutionary, city of Sanctuary emerged from the drawing boards to this sparkling reality. Everything about Sanctuary is new, with innovations and cutting-edge technology everywhere you look.*

*We spoke earlier with the two leaders of this amazing creation. Admiral Jonas Cisco, commanding officer of the military base which has become Sanctuary, and Doctor Scott Hauser, the senior scientist of Project Horizon. Here's part of that interview."*

*"Admiral Cisco you've directed the construction activities of Sanctuary from the beginning. What sticks out in your mind as the biggest achievement?"*

*"I couldn't even begin to give you a good answer. When I look out at the city from my office in the headquarters building, now renamed City Hall by popular demand, I can see most of the public buildings surrounding Enterprise Plaza, and all the way to the Gateway Center. Practically nothing of the old Charleston Joint Operations Command Base remains. In its place, my team has built the most technologically advanced, unique, innovative, beautiful, and thoroughly livable community in the country."*

*"No arguments there, Admiral."*

*"However, Carmen, the glue that makes all this work, what makes it possible for an integrated connection between buildings, machines, systems and people, is our almost, life-like, master computer, which monitors and operates everything from the power to run the city, to the traffic lights, and the temperature in every home. The computer is able to intuitively distinguish, not only the information requested of it, but also the underlying motivation of why the question was asked. It works for everyone from the top scientists to a third-grade student. The computer is part of our lives. None of us consider it intrusive, more like a trusted partner. And it can be accessed by voice command anywhere in Sanctuary."*

*"Other experts say your computer is the best in the world."*

*"They are right."*

*"Doctor Hauser, something not as often discussed is the unimaginable possibilities of matter transference. This is the research mission which created the need for the city in the first place. Can you give us some insight on that?"*

*"I think everyone in the world has seen Star Trek movies where people and things are routinely transferred from one place to another. Displaying the technology on a motion picture screen is different from making it happen for real. The scientific geniuses who have worked for a dozen years to crack the puzzle have produced striking breakthroughs."*

*"I understand, Doctor, the energy field associated with this research is miles across."*

*"It is, twelve miles in diameter to be exact. Which is the reason Sanctuary is a circular city. We needed a static control zone. Although the energy transmission is not detectable except with delicate instruments. In any case, that's how extensive the matter transference field is. What we are trying to do is to reduce its size so it can become a practical tool capable of transporting something as small as a person."*

*"Is it possible the entire city of Sanctuary could be transported somewhere else?"*

*"Oh my, no. The field is far too weak for anything like that. The whole thrust of our research is to learn how to concentrate the field into a space twelve-feet, not twelve miles, wide."*

*"In any case, the official launch of Sanctuary will give the entire country an opportunity to see all the new advances and creative pinnacles you have reached. Thank you, Gentlemen, for taking the time to talk with us today."*

Cisco smiled. "Computer, cancel broadcast." The screen went dark. *I did that whole interview with a straight face. There's nothing like a fool-proof cover story. Scott did his part perfectly as well.*

There came a knock at the door, and Scott poked his head

inside, "Is it okay if I bother you, Jonas."

"Sure, come on in. I just watched our interview on Fox News. You did your piece like it was gospel and you believed every word."

"I sure liked doing it. I think between the two of us, we won the Oscar."

"I hope nothing happens to rock the boat. What's up?"

"Cameron Fisk texted me. He's bringing down the Academy directors on Thursday night to be here for the official dedication of Sanctuary on Friday. I don't think many of them will hang around for the party on Fourth of July Saturday, and the two days of hoopla through the weekend."

"They probably wouldn't be here for the dedication at all if Sanctuary hadn't become such front-page news as the magical city of tomorrow to paraphrase what I see on television. The only thing they were interested in, to begin with, was the reality of the Gateway and our access to the timestream."

"No doubt. Anyway, I'm glad they won't be underfoot to interfere with our celebration. They don't appreciate living here like the rest of us. For me, this is home."

"Why, Scott, are you developing a sentimental side?"

"If I am, then the whole country has puppy love. Ben told me the other day applications for employment have skyrocketed."

"I know it. A huge problem I never anticipated is the number of tourists wanting to 'visit.' Riley tells me they are turning away hundreds of people every day at the entry gates, and that he's had to boost security all around the perimeter. No matter how many ways we say it, people don't realize this is still a military base and not an amusement park. We hardly have room for the people who live here."

"Well anyway, I know all our residents are churning themselves into a fever looking forward to a fabulous holiday. I'll bet hardly a single person is planning on being out of town. The real show is right here."

"If you're finished. I've still got a few more hours of work to do on this super show."

"No, I'm done. I could have called or had the computer deliver the message. I wanted to make sure you're okay. Molly tells me you've been putting in long days without a break since she doesn't know when."

"Thanks, I'm hoping things will calm down around here after this weekend. I promised Wyatt we'd get out for a round of golf next week."

When Scott left, Cisco sat back down at his desk. He puffed his cheeks and said out loud, "I really will be glad to have a break."

On Thursday afternoon, three private jets landed bringing the senior Academy officials for the dedication ceremonies. Cameron Fisk came with his wife Shannon and Ahmed Al Aswira in one plane. Frank Williams and his wife Gloria were in another. Elton Kingsley came alone, but in a commercial jet chartered especially for the occasion. This aircraft contained a full complement of press.

Almost no press had been permitted inside the perimeter of the city throughout the entire period of construction. Now, the reporters and news anchors were overwhelmed with talking computers, self-guided golf carts, speedy light rail trains, the stunning Enterprise Plaza, and a garden-like landscape with beautiful buildings sprinkled amidst the greenery.

With Cisco now on the scene instead of in a TV studio, he found he couldn't go anywhere without having a microphone, or a camera stuck in his face, and lights flashing endlessly. He managed it all with grace, polish, and the smooth demeanor of a career officer.

One of the gala parades rolled out Friday afternoon, down

Inner Band Boulevard. Thousands of people lined the route of the motorcade. A military honor guard led the way, followed by two companies of elite troops, and a military band. Admiral Cisco and the command team came next. Wyatt came up with the ingenious idea of decorating a lowboy trailer pulled by one of the muscular little electric forklifts, with the forks removed, and covered with a bright green canopy shaped like a globe of the world. It gave the crowd a close view of Cisco and his officers, something they seldom saw since Cisco maintained a very modest public profile for him and his staff.

Then came the combined high schools' marching band. The hundreds of musicians made a mighty sound and the perfect set-up for the people of Horizon following on another lowboy. Along with Scott Hauser, Lino Arnett, and Missy Long were the shadowy members of the Academy. People didn't know who they were, but certainly recognized their local heroes and cheered enthusiastically. The Academy men and women had no idea the cheering was not for them and bought into Cisco's carefully laid plan with friendly ignorance.

The motorcade turned off Inner Band Boulevard and onto the roadway leading to Cooper River Stadium, named for the river flowing toward Charleston Harbor. The oval stadium was open-aired and seated 36,000 people. The busy venue hosted soccer matches, track and field competitions, concerts and community flea markets. Today it welcomed the dedication ceremonies for the city.

A broad stage was erected on one end of the stadium. The motorcade drove into the arena, around the track and up to the stage, while the honor guard went to center field to be joined by the combined bands. The bands entertained the mostly full stadium of people who hadn't lined the parade route. The parade watchers hopped trolleys, crowded into the light rail cars, or walked into the stadium. As the bands played, the stadium filled completely.

Wyatt Duval served as the master of ceremonies for the program. He introduced the principal leaders of Horizon. Scott gave a brief speech, long on honorifics and short on details, of anything relating to the hidden secrets of the Gateway Center. Next, Wyatt introduced the members of the Academy and their wives. Cameron Fisk gave a speech congratulating both the Horizon team for their exciting advances in science and the military staff for their conception, creation, and construction of Sanctuary.

Finally, Wyatt introduced Cisco. "Ladies and Gentlemen, as you look around today, you see what is being called the miracle of the modern age. There were choices made when this gigantic project began. We could have built a conventional city with conventional features. We took a different path because one man dreamed of something else, something better, something profoundly unique, something that would set an example of what could be achieved merely by not settling for the common or ordinary.

"For two years this man has labored in the background, never seeking more than the very best each of us could accomplish. On this occasion, it is my distinct honor to draw this man from the quiet path he much prefers and into the spotlight, he richly deserves. My fellow citizens, join me now in this salute to the real creator of our Sanctuary, Admiral Jonas Cisco."

The standing ovation went on for over five minutes. Cisco had written a few simple remarks. Now he sat riveted to his seat, totally unprepared for the outpouring of the crowd, and the chants of "Cisco, Cisco, Cisco!" His knees were weak as he stepped to the rostrum and raised his arms trying to quiet the cheering people. After several more minutes of arm waving and saying thank you into the microphone, the people finally blew themselves out and took their seats.

"A couple of years ago, I thought the job of overseeing the many missions of the Charleston Joint Command gave me as much work as I could handle. Then came Horizon and their electrifying explorations into new worlds of science and technology. After that, nothing was routine. We began building a foundation from which even more innovations could be brought to life.

"Some of you have been with us from the beginning. You went to work with the rest of us, drawn up in the vision we saw for an extraordinary place to live. As more of you arrived, you were also caught up in the excitement of our dreams.

"What we have today is because of your dedication, your commitment, your devotion. Our incredible new city did not happen because of anything done by me. It is the design of your own hearts. From this day on, you can say, 'We are the architects of the future, and we shall continue to cherish our creation and make it even more beautiful.'

"Remember this day, as we summon the future and celebrate our exceptional home, Sanctuary, the city of tomorrow."

Cisco spoke the true sentiments of his soul spontaneously. He raised his arms as he stepped away from the rostrum, and the citizens of Sanctuary stood with him. The stadium rocked.

With the completion of the dedication ceremony, Cisco led the official party off the stage to make way for a band. Soon, music filled the stadium, and the crowd danced and sang into the night.

As the entire population of Sanctuary enjoyed the concert and festivities in Cooper River Stadium, a medium-sized rental truck drove up to the checkpoint at the city perimeter routinely used for heavy equipment passing to the storage warehouses and the industrial section of the city.

A sleepy sentry stepped out of the guardhouse and

approached the driver of the truck, "Evening, sir, may I see your identification and cargo manifest?"

"Certainly," said a smiling Ahmed Al Aswira, handing the papers and his identification card to the guard.

The guard swiped the card through the terminal mounted near the guardhouse door. Instantly the grill on the terminal flashed a green light, and the computer voice said, ***"Entry granted. All access, all areas, good evening, Mister Aswira."***

The sentry read the manifest, "Another load of party supplies for the holiday?"

"Yes, indeed. I think it will be a very exciting Fourth of July."

"The computer says you're okay to go. Do you need any directions?"

"I know where I'm going."

The guard pushed a button and the steel posts across the entry recessed into the ground. He handed the manifest and ID card back to Aswira. "Have a happy holiday, sir."

Aswira drove through the gate and down Inner Band Boulevard past rows of warehouses. He pulled into a lot where other trucks were parked and located an empty space. He got out, went to the rear door, and unlocked it. The door swung open and Aswira shined a light inside. His custom-made ATV sat strapped securely to the floor covered with a heavy tarp. Satisfied his cargo had made the long trip from New York safely; he relocked the door and walked away. No one noticed his absence as he returned to his rooms at the Embassy Suites.

On Saturday morning, the Fourth of July dawned with a clear, deep blue sky. A cool coastal breeze blew in from the ocean. Jonas Cisco rose early. This morning he went to the Embassy Suites for breakfast with members of the Academy. Most of them were leaving following their attendance at the dedication ceremony. Apparently, few had any interest in the list of activities planned for the weekend.

"I've seen fireworks display before," said Cameron Fisk, sipping his coffee. "However, Aswira is staying behind as our representative. Shannon and Gloria Williams are also staying. Gloria says this is probably the only time she'll see any life in this city, and Shannon seems to have developed an attachment to your little town."

"They're all welcome. I'll make sure they enjoy themselves."

After breakfast, Cisco went to the airport with Fisk and the others. He breathed a sigh of relief as the jets taxied away for takeoff. He just had time to get to the assembly area for the gala Holiday Parade of which he was the Grand Marshall.

This parade dwarfed the one from the day before. Every department in the city had labored for days building elaborate floats. All four of the high school bands now marched separately between floats and other parade entries. Cisco rode on the lowboy at the front, behind the honor guard and platoons of marching soldiers, airmen, and Marines.

Following the parade, people disbursed for different activities including, a two-day soccer tournament at Cooper River stadium, a sprawling flea market in Enterprise Plaza, open houses at all the recreation centers, volleyball games at the beach along the river, plus family cookouts throughout the community.

Cisco made a point of visiting as many places as possible, joining in on the fun, and welcomed by all. The day passed pleasantly.

That night, everyone went back to the stadium, filling the bleachers and spilling out onto the field with lawn chairs, if they had arrived early enough to find a place to sit, to view the fireworks show. The Sanctuary Philharmonic Orchestra rehearsed for weeks preparing a program of music choreographed with the fireworks. Cisco found himself thrilled, with everyone else, as the colorful display of rockets went off above the stadium, and a sky-filling finale with a vocalist doing a spectacular job singing "God Bless the U.S.A".

As the last notes of the music ended with the final burst of fireworks, Cisco exchanged looks with the others who sat with him in the VIP section of the stadium. Wyatt Duval, Will Judd, Riley Marquis and their families, Chips Gallant and Missy Long together as a couple, Ben Crenshaw sat between Shannon and Gloria so they could say they had an escort, and finally Scott and Lino. All had tears in their eyes.

Cisco stood with the whole group. "It's been a wonderful but exhausting day. I'll be glad to finally head for home. What about you, Ben?"

"We have an after fireworks party at the Harbor Recreation Center with a bunch of the Coast Guard guys. I thought I'd stop by there for a while."

Gloria jumped on that. "Wow! A real, honest to goodness party? Mind if I tag along?"

"Sure, it's informal, nothing special, some socializing, dancing, a drink or two, like that."

"Sounds like fun. How about you, Shannon, you coming?"

Shannon looked straight at Ben. She and Gloria spent most of the day with him, as he represented city leadership. She found herself liking the mostly formal man and guessed they were about the same age. Still, this additional and informal event seemed, to her, a bit beyond his serving as a polite escort. "This sounds like something more personal to you. You shouldn't feel obligated to drag us along."

Ben looked back at her. Their eyes locked for a few seconds. Then Ben smiled. "No obligation, I'll be glad for the company."

"Wonderful," Gloria was oblivious to the chemistry cooking two feet away, "Do we get there in one of your little do-jiggers?"

"We can hop on the strasse. It's only a few stops away."

"What's a strasse?"

Ben laughed. "That's what we call our trolleys, the streetcars. When we put them in, somebody said it reminded them of the strassenbahns in Germany. The word means the same as streetcar in German, but the nickname stuck, and so that's what everyone calls them."

"Cute," said Gloria. "Let's go hop the strasse."

Cisco watched them go. "I wish I had the energy of the young again."

"My tribe keeps me young enough. Lino likes them because they never stop playing."

"I like 'em for more reasons than that, Wysenheimer. They're terrific kids."

"Okay, Uncle Lino. You coming home with me? With you around, Magda and I can catch a breath."

"Not tonight, Bud, I've got some work I need to do in my office."

"You must be kidding. Did you forget this is a Holiday? You're actually allowed to relax a little."

"I know that. But I have a theorem bubbling in my head, and it will bug me if I don't work it out."

"Don't work all night. You promised to take the boys fishing tomorrow."

"Looking forward to that as much as I am solving this problem. See you in the morning."

Lino headed out of the stadium.

Cisco enjoyed all the successful socialization of the once-feuding groups, and waved in cheer, "I'm still going home. See you all tomorrow."

Ahmed Al Aswira stared at his watch. It was past one a.m. He and his three fellow conspirators made their way to the truck parked in the lot. All four were dressed in ancient-looking Arab clothing. Something like the cartoon character Aladdin. However, they all had guns in shoulder holsters across their chests. They climbed into the truck, and Aswira drove on the Inner Band to the margin of Enterprise Plaza where they took a smaller road leading directly to the Gateway Center. They rolled up to the guardhouse at the entrance of the Center and were met by an armed and clearly alert guard.

"Manifest and identification."

Aswira handed them over.

The guard swiped the card, got the same "all-access" approval from the computer as before. However, this guard did not automatically open the gate. He looked at Aswira. "The computer says you have 'all access' but I have orders not to admit anyone after midnight without approval from one of the directors. Wait here while I make a call."

The guard turned his back to step into the guardhouse, and Aswira shot him twice with his silenced weapon.

Quickly Aswira jumped out of the truck and went into the guardhouse to lower the steel barricades. Then he climbed back into the truck and drove it to the rear of the complex, housing the transmission platform. He backed the truck close to the huge bay doors and got back out to swipe his identification card through the terminal. The door opened.

The men went to the rear of the truck and opened the doors. One of them pushed a lever. A heavy ramp augered from the rear. They clamored up the ramp and ripped the tarp off the ATV.

It sat there, looking deadlier than what the men had seen on the laptop in New York. Extending on both sides were six tubes containing rocket-propelled missiles. In the front, a mount next to the driver, supported an M-134 Gatling gun, capable of firing 3,000 rounds a minute. Additionally, there were conventional single barrel machine guns mounted on each side of the vehicle to be operated by the two men sitting in the rear of the ATV.

Aswira motioned to the men, and all four climbed in. The engine rumbled to life, Aswira drove it down the ramp and into the big room with the transmission platform circle in the center. The room was silent. The lights were dim, creating shadows of men and machinery.

A ramp led up to the platform. Aswira knew it. He asked Scott Hauser about it before when he'd stayed behind after the other Academy directors departed. Hauser told him they built the ramp to accommodate small vehicles in the event it might be needed for time jumps in which they existed. Aswira smirked to himself at the time. Vehicles such as the one he imagined certainly did not exist in the time he planned to use it. All the better. The shock value would give him more leverage.

Carefully, he drove the heavily armed ATV onto the transmission platform, parking it in the center of the red band marking the bullseye for the energy dome above.

He sprang for the control center facing the platform and began activating the system.

"It will take five minutes for the energy dome to build up enough power to transmit us. Prepare yourselves."

The men pulled out banded headdresses with cloth on the side and back to complete their masquerade as eighth-century Islamic warriors.

Aswira set the controls to October 9, 732 A.D., and pushed the master button to engage. Then from the bag he carried, he pulled out a bundle of Centex explosives with the detonator connected to a timer. He set the charge to go off five minutes after he and his partners departed and shoved it under the control board. He waited impatiently for the lights on the board to turn green. When all but the last light flickered from red to orange, Aswira knew he had a minute to get onto the platform and into the ATV before the energy curtain fired. He walked almost nonchalantly up the stairs and took his seat behind the steering wheel. He smiled at his fellow conspirators.

Lino Arnett stood in his office before a large whiteboard filled with mathematical equations. He had patiently worked and reworked these formulas for days. He'd returned to his office tonight because a promising new approach had emerged.

He was deep in concentration when a foreign sound interrupted him. *Where's that coming from?* Then it dawned on him. Thousands of relays were clicking on and off. This meant only one thing. The Gateway system had begun to cycle. Lino jerked with alarm. He'd always felt guilty about releasing this monster on the world. From the beginning, he'd feared his original discoveries could be commandeered by people with dangerous motives. He'd promised himself to keep that from ever happening.

He went to his desk, took out a lockbox, and grabbed a loaded Glock. He chambered a round expertly. Months of practice with Wyatt on the firing range made him deadly. He raced for the Gateway Chamber.

He rushed down the central corridor and swiped his card to unlock the double doors. He entered the room. An oversized ATV sat in the center of the transmission platform. He shuddered to see the machine guns sticking out its sides and the front. Four men, in strange clothing, sat in the vehicle.

A glance at the control board told Lino the energy curtain would engage in a few seconds. He crouched and fired at the men. The bullets found their mark and all three of Aswira's co-conspirators fell to Lino's sure aim. Crouching low, Aswira used the dead man in the passenger seat next to him as a shield. One of the men in the back seat fell forward, the other died trying to jump out of the ATV. When the Glock fired its last round, Lino sprinted for the control board to abort the transmission. Lino looked behind as he ran and recognized the driver of the ATV. He shouted in rage. "You're not going anywhere, Aswira!"

Lino reached the control board. Before he could punch the abort switch, Aswira stood up and fired his weapon. Two bullets hit Lino, knocking him to the floor.

The transmission cones came to life, sending a blue curtain of energy down to the transmission platform. Seconds later, the ATV, and Aswira with two dead conspirators cycled to the past. The remaining conspirator lifeless on the platform.

Blood dripped steadily from Lino's side and chest as he lay on the floor. He groaned and grabbed the chair to pull himself up. Then he saw the bomb under the control board and heard it ticking relentlessly. Wiping his eyes, Lino looked at the timer. Only two minutes remained before it reached zero. He gasped as he screamed into the speaker grill on the control board, "Computer, emergency alert! Assault on the Gateway Center. Send help."

Lino knew the explosives would destroy the transmission platform, making it impossible for the Horizon team to conduct any other time jumps. Holding the explosive package tightly, he struggled to his feet and staggered around the platform toward the open bay door at the rear of the room. The Gateway energy curtain continued to crackle.

Outside, Lino bent over in pain and moved slowly. He reached the grassy area, which ran up to the enclosure wall surrounding the Center. Balancing the bomb in his hand, he threw it at the top of the wall. It bounced off and fell back down close to his feet. Desperate, he picked it up, summoned the last ounce of strength in his body, and threw the bomb. This time it skipped on top of the wall and fell to the other side. Lino collapsed and waited quietly on the grass for a moment. The explosion shattered the night. A few feet away, a large section of the wall gave way and crashed into the enclosure. Lino smiled. Smelling the grass, as he lay on the ground, he whispered.

"You're beautiful." Then he closed his eyes and breathed his last.

❖

The Emergency Alarm had not gone off in Jonas Cisco's house since they tested it. It hooted as loud as he remembered. He switched on a light and sat up in bed. "Computer, what is the emergency?"

*"An emergency alert was sent from the Gateway Center."*

"Playback."

*"Emergency alert! Assault on the Gateway Center. Send help."*

Cisco immediately recognized Lino's voice. Before he could say anything else, there was a thundering explosion.

"Computer, Red Alert, city-wide. Seal the perimeter to all incoming or outgoing traffic. Send a 'Ready Team' to the Gateway Center with full arms and secure the enclosure. Notify the command team and Dr. Hauser, to meet me at the Gateway Center ASAP."

Cisco threw on some clothes, rushed out of his house to his personal transportation, and roared away. Less than ten minutes later, he arrived at the Center. The red lights of half a dozen emergency vehicles were flashing. Sirens blaring in the distance signaled more were on the way.

As he jumped out of his vehicle, a Marine sergeant rushed up and saluted, "Sir, an explosive went off at the Center, but on the plaza side of the wall. The guard on duty at the entrance is dead, shot twice in the back. I've deployed the Ready Team and called for more men to secure the enclosure. We are waiting your order to broach the Center."

"Send in the team. Radio me as soon as you clear the building."

The sergeant hurried off.

Cisco tapped his comm badge. "Computer, report."

*"The perimeter has been closed. Additional personnel are being disbursed to all gates, according to emergency plan alpha. Approximately, twenty feet of the Gateway Center exterior wall is down at the rear of the compound. A thirty-foot crater in the Enterprise Plaza is visible in the same location. Probable cause is an explosive device of unknown origin. There is one fatality at the entry guardhouse, and another person is lying in the grass near the site of the exterior wall collapse. There are no persons, other than Ready Team personnel, inside the Gateway Center building. No apparent damage inside is visible."*

Cisco nodded and then went on. "Computer, display the video record of all activity inside the Gateway Center in the past hour to my tablet."

The video began to play. Cisco saw Lino working in his office and Ahmed Al Aswira's entry through the rear bay door. The rest of the grisly scene unfolded as it happened. The surveillance cameras recorded Lino carrying the bomb away from the transmission platform, out of the building and throwing it over the wall. Cisco caught his breath as he saw Lino's body lying in the grass.

He screamed into his tablet, "Computer, send medical to the last shown location without delay! Embargo all records of the previous scene and all traffic relating to this incident to personnel with 'all access' clearance only. Revoke clearances to all directors of the Academy."

Then he picked up his radio. "Ready Team, report."

The Marine sergeant came back. "The only unlocked room we've found is Dr. Arnett's office, Admiral. But, there's a real strange energy field of some kind in the big room at the end of the building, up on a round platform. I think we have a body up there."

"Touch nothing. Do not get on the platform or allow any of your men to do so. Proceed immediately through the open bay door and locate Dr. Arnett near where the wall is down."

"Roger."

Cisco sat in his ATV trying to piece everything together. Simultaneously, Wyatt, Missy, and Chips came screeching to a stop in their ATV's next to Cisco. Scott arrived a few seconds later.

"What's happened, Jonas?" pleaded Missy.

"We've been attacked. Ahmed Al Aswira broke into the Center, shot the guard, and drove what looked like a heavily armed ATV onto the transmission platform. Lino tried to stop him, and Aswira shot him. Then he transported to wherever he set the controls. He left behind a bomb, presumably to destroy the power dome, but Lino managed to get it outside and over the wall before it went off. Lino is lying outside on the grass. He's not moving. The power dome is still running, and the energy curtain is still on."

"We gotta get to Lino," said a frantic Scott.

The radio crackled, "Sorry to tell you, Admiral, but we've found Dr. Arnett. He's dead. We've cleared the building unless you think we need to sweep for more explosives."

Cisco considered that. "I don't think they had time to plant more bombs. Have your Ready Team stand down. I'm on my way in."

Everyone listened to the report on the radio. The shock and agony on their faces matched the way Cisco felt. "We can't do anything for Lino now. However, we need to know if the Gateway is damaged in any way, evaluate what's happened, and help decide what to do next. Try to focus on that. I'll take care of Lino. Let's meet again, in an hour."

Cisco didn't give anyone time to think. He knew his command team would be busy cinching down the perimeter, making it secure and getting work crews started hauling away the rubble from the Center wall and the plaza. The civilians were in shock. They had no experience dealing with this kind of violence or the treachery of this assault. He forced himself to concentrate on practical matters, hoping it would keep the others from becoming hysterical, irrational, and of no help to him. He climbed back in his ATV and drove into the compound without another word.

The medics were on the scene when Cisco arrived. He walked over to them. They had put Lino in a body bag and were about to zip it up.

"He was shot twice, Admiral. Either round likely fatal. I've no idea how he managed to pick up the bomb and bring it out here. Even more surprising is how he found the strength to throw it over the wall."

Cisco stooped down and looked at the face of this brilliant, explosive, but gentle, sweet man. Tears filled his eyes. "Goodbye, my friend. The world will always be better because of you."

He nodded to the medic, who zipped the bag shut. Then he took hold of one of the straps. Three other medics helped him carry the body to a waiting ambulance.

# Chapter 12
# Marooned

Cisco followed the ambulance to the morgue. After giving orders to ensure proper preparations for Lino's funeral and burial, he drove back to the Gateway Center. He found the command staff, along with Scott and Missy gathered in the conference room. Everyone stood as he came in.

"Take your seats." When everyone had, he looked around the table. "Alright. Let's take this one step at a time. First, what is our current security posture?"

Riley flipped open his tablet. "As you ordered, the perimeter is closed. No traffic of any kind is moving in or out. A search of all surveillance logs for the past twenty-four hours shows nothing out of the ordinary, except for the truck that brought the armed ATV inside the city. The computer confirms the driver was Ahmed Al Aswira. He got through the security gate because he had an all-access clearance. The computer didn't report it because it wasn't actionable."

"What about public reaction?"

Ben gave his report. "I've notified the department heads of our alert status. All I told them was an explosive device detonated near the Gateway Center in Enterprise Plaza. I said we are trying to find out what happened, but they should assume terrorism, sabotage, or both. Your embargo of anyone but us having access to the computer record will keep the real truth from getting out until you're ready. However, Admiral, you need to make some kind of public statement soon, or we could have a panic on our hands."

"I can't make any public statements until we know what Aswira was planning, and what it means to us." Cisco turned to Scott. "Do you know anything about Aswira's intentions?"

"The controls were set to October 9, 732 AD. That doesn't

154

mean anything to me. Maybe Missy can tell us something."

At the other end of the table, Missy's head hung down. She sobbed. Chips attempted to console her. Cisco felt sincerely sorry for her and looked at Missy sympathetically. This moment needed a firm and rational approach.

"I know how you feel. We are shocked, angry, and overcome with grief. You want to strike back at this treachery, and we will, but not here, not now. What we need to do is find out the motives behind this attack on the Gateway. That includes you, Missy. Does Scott need to repeat what he said?"

Missy sat up, took a Kleenex, blew her nose and wiped her eyes. Then she took a deep breath and stammered, "No, I heard what he said." She seemed to collect herself and then went on. "That date corresponds to the Battle of Tours, in which a Muslim army was defeated by the Franks. It was the turning point for Islamic expansion in Europe."

"Of course," blared Scott. "That explains the armed ATV. Aswira is going back to change the outcome of that battle. He can do it too. With all those modern weapons, the Franks won't stand a chance."

"Why are the results of one battle so important?"

"Because, an Islamic victory would likely change the future of Europe. It could mean the entire continent might fall to the Muslims. If that were to happen, we would almost surely see a disastrous change in the timestream."

"How long before we would see a change in our time?"

Missy shook her head. "There's no way of knowing. It could be gradual over a long time, or the change could be abrupt and almost immediate. None of us has a clue. Even Lino didn't know. He'd begun to work on the problem, but admitted he was only nibbling around the edges."

"What are the chances of Aswira coming back through the Gateway?"

"I'm only guessing. But I don't think he intends on returning at all. He knows as much about branching universe theories as we do, and probably thinks the future will be so different he shouldn't bother. And besides, if he did come back through the Gateway, I'd blow his brains out."

Cisco smiled. "My sentiments, exactly."

"We have another problem."

"Go ahead."

"The Gateway is still engaged. There's been no one to turn it off, except me, and I've got a strange feeling I shouldn't."

"Why not?"

"We won't be affected by anything that happens in the past as long as the Gateway is running. My gut tells me we should wait until Aswira is finished with his grand plan. If the future is changed because of what he does, we might see the effects ripple down through time rather quickly."

Missy spoke up. "That makes sense to me. It will take at least another day for Aswira to establish himself with the Muslim commander and then turn his firepower on the Franks. History says the battle ended on October 10th."

Scott scratched his head. "I don't know if the Gateway can operate that long. It was designed to work in short bursts to send and recall our teams. It's risky putting that much strain on the system."

"Is there any other choice?" asked Cisco.

"I guess not. It's the only thing that sounds remotely like a deterrent when nothing is certain. I hope the power dome doesn't blow up."

A few hours later, Wyatt sat in the Admiral's office with the sun coming up. "Sure is a good thing it's Sunday. None of the civilians who drive into work at the federal agencies, still operating, will come to work. Tomorrow either, being a national holiday."

"Anybody complaining about not being able to leave the city?"

"Nothing serious, we're turning away a larger than usual number of lookie-loos. Most of our people are just getting out of bed. They went back to sleep when we made the announcement the explosion in the Plaza didn't injure anyone and that we believed it was an isolated incident. Do you still intend to not make a public announcement?"

"As long as everything stays quiet, people will go out this morning and do the things they were going to do for the holiday. We shouldn't call any more attention to the situation, at least until we get a better idea of what comes next."

"Did you report everything to the Academy?"

"The single satisfying pushback so far. First, I got to haul Cameron Fisk out of bed to tell him we'd been attacked. Then I told him, rather forcefully, it was a sorry thing one of his own inner circle turned out to be the biggest security risk of them all. He was appalled. I agreed."

"What does he think of Missy's bleak appraisal we might be in for a major shift in the time stream?"

"He doesn't know what to think. Neither do I. The only thing we can do right now is hunker down and try to ride out the storm. He did say he and Frank Williams would be flying in early this evening to pick up their wives to, as he put it, 'move them out of harm's way.' It shows how little he really understands the threat we could face. If our time is suddenly changed by the past, the safest place in the world to be is here at Sanctuary."

"Anything else I need to do?

"No need for both of us to mind the fort, Wyatt. Why don't you go home, get some rest, and spend time with your family? They probably want to enjoy the holiday like everyone else."

"I'll do that. Call me if anything new comes up."

After Wyatt left, Cisco had another cup of coffee while he thought through the scenes of the terrible night. During the meeting in the Gateway Center, he'd dispatched a team into the transmission chamber to fish the body off the platform. Riley got that job. He told Cisco later, he never saw men so frightened, working right up to the crackling, blue energy curtain. "I was scared too and I knew what I was looking at."

"Any idea who this guy is?"

"We ran face recognition on him and found out he's a filthy rich Arab, by the name of Saleh Ali Baghdadi. He has no known connection to the Academy but was one of Aswira's principal investors."

"Well, he's dead now. Find a discreet place to bury him. Keep it as quiet as you can."

"Roger that, Admiral, "I'll plant him in a pasture out in the country."

Cisco couldn't think of anything else to do to manage the crisis. The sun was well up now. The weight of command rested heavily on him. He stretched his shoulders and moved his head back and forth on his neck as if to shift the load. Then he got up, grabbed a day-old doughnut from a box, put on his hat, and went out to be with the people who would count on him to keep it all together.

As Cisco predicted, the people of Sanctuary almost went back to normal. Families went to church, friends gathered for barbecues and picnics, the soccer tournament at Cooper River Stadium attracted a huge crowd, and security men had to work hard to stay calm and friendly with all the people who wanted look at the giant crater in Enterprise Plaza.

Throughout the day, Cisco popped into as many places and events as he could. He had to repeat the prepared statement many times.

"Hey Admiral, what's the story on that explosion last night?"

"We don't know much yet. An explosive charge went off close to the Gateway Center, damaging the wall of the compound and a fifty-foot hunk of Enterprise Plaza. Nobody got hurt by the blast. We're investigating the cause, but we aren't ruling out sabotage. Because of that, we've locked down the perimeter. I hope it doesn't ruin your day."

"Nah, we're going to the stadium for the soccer matches. The only thing about last night is it woke up the kids and scared them to death. We told them it was just some fireworks going off in the wrong place."

"And maybe that's what it was. Thinking the worst is not a very good idea. Let me do the worrying."

"We'll do that, Admiral. Have a great day."

Cisco hated not being entirely forthcoming. He made a point not to say anything that was an outright lie. He would need the trust of the people in the days to come if any of the doomsday theories circulating among the command team and the Horizon brain trust began to happen.

All day long Cisco kept waiting for the other shoe to drop. He got annoyed with himself for constantly looking into the sky, or across the horizon, expecting something to happen. As it got closer to evening, he relaxed, telling himself he should take the advice he'd been passing out all day.

Besides, it was almost time for the jet with Cameron Fisk and Frank Williams to arrive and take away their wives. *Good one less thing for me to worry about.*

Saying goodbye to Gloria Williams took no effort. She reminded him of one of those women on the reality TV shows. All glitter and drama, and nothing much else. Shannon Fisk proved to be different. She genuinely liked Sanctuary and all it represented. She also had a sharp mind and seemed to understand full well the unique nature of the city even though she hadn't been told why it existed. In other circumstances, she

159

would be a good candidate for residency.

"Computer, have Mrs. Fisk, and Williams departed for the airport?"

***"Negative. They are still in their quarters at the Embassy Suites."***

"Give them a call and find out if they want me to pick them up."

A few minutes later the computer came back, ***"Mrs. Fisk and Williams are currently leaving the Embassy Suites. They do not require an escort and will take their own transportation to the airport."***

"Computer, call Dr. Hauser." Shortly, he answered. "Scott, I'm leaving for the airport to meet the Academy jet. Cameron Fisk is flying in with Frank Williams to pick up their wives. Do you want to meet me?"

"I've been nursing this power dome along all day. It wasn't designed to run this way. I'm trying to keep the system from heating up and overloading by switching back and forth through the redundant circuitry. We are drawing a tremendous amount of energy from the city grid. Kind of a balancing act. Can you manage without me?"

"I can handle Fisk. Let's hope he doesn't decide he wants a meeting about all this. We're long on questions and short on answers. Anyway, I'm going. If anything changes call me."

Cisco rang off and drove to the airport.

When he arrived, he found Will and Riley waiting for him on the tarmac.

"How come you guys look fresher than I feel?"

"Because we went home and took a nap this afternoon," said Will, "while you ran around all day holding everyone's hand."

"People will mostly return to their routines in the absence of any new threats. My showing up in as many places as I could, helped them do just that."

"Is Wyatt coming?" asked Riley. "I haven't seen him lately."

"I gave him the day off. After we finish here, I'm going home to bed. If anything comes up, he's on-call."

As they talked, three golf carts came through the gate and toward them on the tarmac. Shannon Fisk and Gloria Williams were in one, Ben Crenshaw and a Coast Guard Seaman in the second, and the third one bulged full of bags.

"Here come the Academy wives," said Riley. "Ever wonder why women always pack so much?"

"Most of those bags belong to Gloria Williams," said Will. "I think Shannon only brought one. She's a good one. I can't imagine how she got hooked up with Cameron Fisk. When I took her on the tour of all our power and energy sources, she asked a bunch of questions. She wanted to know why we built an oil refinery here and had such a deep fuel reserve. I had to do some fancy talking to skip around that. I don't think she believed me."

"Ben is as worn out as you. I'll bet he'll be glad to finish being the official escort of those girls."

Cisco didn't say anything. He wasn't so sure Ben would be glad Shannon was leaving. He'd seen them engaged in spirited conversations, and the expressions they exchanged were more than escort and guest.

The golf carts came rolling up. Shannon hopped out. "I love these super carts of yours Admiral. They drive themselves and the computer takes you anywhere you want to go. I'll miss them the next time I'm stuck in New York traffic. In fact, this whole city is a fantastic place.

"I'm glad you enjoyed your visit, Mrs. Fisk."

"I'm glad to be leaving," blared Gloria. "This place is so lame."

"Not much longer to wait. The jet should be along in a few minutes if they're on their flight plan."

Shannon looked up. "I wonder if we can see them coming?"

Cisco glanced at the sky. The sun had set, and the haze of twilight was giving way to the gathering night. A few stars began to twinkle. "They'll have their running lights on. When they are closer, they'll switch on the landing lights. On a clear night like this, you can spot airplane lights from as far away as thirty miles."

"Where will they be coming from?"

"Due north," Cisco pointed the direction. "Here, I've got some binoculars. You can spot the jet yourself." He reached into his ATV and pulled out a pair of binoculars, handing them to Shannon. "Measure about two feet up from the horizon from where you're standing."

Shannon took the binoculars and started searching the sky. Almost immediately, she sang out, "There it is."

Cisco looked himself. Without the benefit of the binoculars, it took him a few seconds to see the blinking lights of the jet. "Yep, around 10,000 feet and about twenty miles."

He turned around to say something to Ben, but before he could speak, Shannon said, "Admiral, the lights on the plane went out."

"Probably behind a cloud."

As soon as he said it, Cisco knew something was very wrong. He looked again into the sky. It had turned from a pale glow to a deep black. Now many stars twinkled. He kept looking, confused at the abrupt change. His eyes flashed down to the horizon, and he shuddered at the sight. The bright lights of Charleston, visible every night from here to the coast, were gone. He turned all the way around, slowly. The lights of the airport and the runway lights were still on, but beyond, as far as Cisco could see, the land was dark.

"Somebody pull the plug?" asked Riley. "I think they have a blackout all over Charleston."

The speaker in Cisco's ATV clicked. "Admiral, Lieutenant Jenkins here from the Comm Center. We just lost our upload to every one of the satellites. We also lost our external broadband link to cable, cell towers, and all internet connections. All the broadcast television signals are gone, and none of us can connect any calls outside of the city."

"Are our communication systems working inside the perimeter?"

"Yes sir, everything of ours is working fine. I called my wife at home on my cell phone, and the connection was loud and clear. Everywhere else beyond the city suddenly stopped transmitting."

"Lieutenant, I want you to begin scanning all broadcast bands from one kilowatt to a million megawatts. Listen for anything. Use the directional antennas and scan 360 degrees. Concentrate on signals which might be coming from anywhere to the east. Listen only, Lieutenant. If you should be hailed by anyone outside Sanctuary, do not respond. Keep a running recording of any signals you detect. I want this search to go on a wartime basis. Make arrangements to begin operating around the clock."

"Yes sir," said the surprised officer. The urgency in Cisco's voice got his complete attention.

Cisco tapped the comm tab on his shirt. "Computer, issue a battle alert for all military personnel. Run a level one diagnostic of all vital services within the perimeter. Initiate the 'Beachhead' protocols. Embargo any response to all inquiries regarding the loss of external communications, internet and broadcast signals. Do not issue any warnings to the public. Record the following message and broadcast it in response to inquiries on any of the orders just given."

Cisco took a deep breath and faced a surveillance camera with a smile on his face. "Hello everyone, this is Admiral Cisco. We've issued a precautionary alert for all military personnel assigned to Sanctuary. At this time, there will be no disruption to your normal routines or schedules. We are aware of the loss of all your external communications. This was not a result of a breakdown in any city systems. All community communications are operating normally. We are evaluating the causes of this developing situation and will keep you informed as soon as more is learned. We believe there is no danger or threat of any kind to you or your families. Please stay calm and let us try and sort out what's happened. I'll be back to you as soon as I have something new to report. Have a blessed day."

"Wow," said Will. "That was a mouthful. What do you want us to do now?"

"We can't do anything here. I want you two to call your wives and meet me in my office."

"Wait a minute, buster," spouted Gloria Williams, "what about the jet and getting us on our way home?"

Cisco looked at both women with real sympathy. "The jet is gone, and I don't think it will be coming."

"What the Hell is that supposed to mean? I want out of here."

Cisco would be forever grateful to Shannon for stepping in at that moment. He was about to speak some very harsh and uncomplimentary things to the painted lady with the red face.

"Gloria, some kind of an emergency has happened. I don't think the Admiral or any of the rest of these officers can tell you anything. The best thing for us is to not make it more difficult for them."

"How about me, Admiral?"

"You can escort these ladies back to their rooms at the Embassy Suites, and then I want you to go home and get some sleep. You look like you're running on fumes."

"Okay, Admiral, but what about you? You've been going even harder than I have, and for just as long."

"There's nothing for that now. I've got to get us through these next few hours. Move out."

Ben gave a snappy salute, then motioned for the Seaman to

reload the bags. "Come on, Shannon, I'll take you back to your rooms."

He walked briskly to the golf cart and waited for Shannon and a very vocal and abusive Gloria to climb in theirs. Then he tapped his comm tab. "Computer, three vehicles to the Embassy Suites, engage."

The golf carts took off in a rush.

While Cisco dealt with Ben and the Academy women, both Will and Riley called home to say they would be busy for quite a while, and for their wives not to wait up for them.

"I'll call Wyatt and Scott," said Cisco. "I imagine Chips is at the Gateway Center with Missy. Have the computer roust the kitchen and have sandwiches and coffee delivered to my office. I'll see you there in a few minutes."

On the way back to the headquarters, Cisco called Wyatt. He was already alert and ready, and said he'd be there right away. Then Cisco called Scott. When the scientist answered, he spoke immediately, "What's going on? I have people coming into the transmission chamber telling me they've lost their internet connections or can't get anything on their TV's."

"I think you can shut down the Gateway now. No question to me a massive interruption in the timestream has happened."

"Oh my God."

"Are Chips and Missy in the building?"

"Yeah. They've been feeding me doughnuts, coffee, and encouragement while I wrestled with this power dome."

"Well, gather them up and meet me in the conference room as fast as you can. I think we have a long night ahead of us."

"I thought last night was a long night, but okay, we'll be there as soon as I can get this baby shut down, and have the techs start checking for damage." He rang off.

Cisco was surprised to find the kitchen had rustled up platters of sandwiches, and a large coffee maker by the time he got to the meeting room. It looked like his orders to put the entire military cadre on alert were being followed like clockwork. He thanked the staff for their fast work and told them to go on home. He didn't believe any of them would.

One by one, the command staff came into the room and sat down at the long conference table. Scott, along with Missy and Chips came in together, looking worn and tired. Cisco could only guess at the tension and strain of keeping the Gateway running.

Ben rushed in last. Cisco raised an eyebrow. "I thought I told you to go home?"

"I got the girls back to the Embassy Suites. Gloria was a bitch. Shannon was a real trooper. As for me, Admiral, I guess you're going to have to list me as insubordinate, but if you believe I'm going to sleep through this, you must think I'm an idiot."

Cisco laughed at that. "Okay, Ben, we'll hold the corporal punishment in abeyance for now. Have a seat and help us think through this."

He stood and addressed the group. "I know you all were a little shocked I took such drastic steps. The truth is, I've been running these 'what if' scenarios through my mind since we first got a peek inside the old laboratory two years ago."

"I wasn't at the airport," said Wyatt, "but Will told me you rattled off orders like you had rehearsed them."

"In a way, I had. When that jet disappeared, then all the lights went out in Charleston, I knew we were probably on our way to a real crisis. When the comm center called and said all communications to the outside world were gone, I was certain."

Wyatt nibbled on a sandwich. "I hope what we have is not as bad as I think it is."

"We're going to find out right now." Cisco tapped his comm tab. "Computer, launch two surveillance drones. Direct them to fly at two hundred feet and five hundred yards beyond the eastern perimeter boundary in a half-mile arc. Activate all emergency perimeter lighting and intruder probe searchlights. Direct lights away from city boundaries. Re-task all surveillance cameras to record images of terrain outside the city perimeter."

*"Working,"* spoke the computer, *"Estimated time for drones to be on-station, and re-tasking of surveillance cameras, ten minutes."*

"While we're waiting, fix yourselves a sandwich and another cup of coffee."

"This is like a countdown to a missile launch," groaned Riley.

"More like having your last meal before execution," grumbled Wyatt.

Missy Long didn't say anything, but raised her eyes as if she were praying, and reached over and took Chips' hand in hers.

In less than ten minutes, the LED monitor on the wall came to life, and everyone stared in wonder.

The drones started sending images of the terrain outside of the city perimeter. The lights from the towers along the boundary shone brightly, illuminating the landscape.

The Cooper River flowed toward the ocean. Trees lined the banks marking the edge of a much bigger forest. There were marshes, swampland and several inland lakes. As the drones passed overhead, and their lights played on the water's edge, alligators splashed in sudden fright.

The main screen broke into multiple boxes showing other images of the land surrounding the city. They were much the same. The startled assembly in the conference room saw a panorama of pristine, untouched, undeveloped wilderness.

Charleston had not just gone dark. It had disappeared completely, along with all other evidence of human existence for a far as the eye could see.

Sanctuary was alone.

# Chapter 13
# Breaking the News

Cisco sat quietly and listened. He let the discussion go on for half an hour, then rapped on the table for order. "We don't know much. Let's start with what we do know. Obviously, a catastrophic change has occurred in the timestream. That's a given since everything we can see of the countryside surrounding Sanctuary shows nothing but wilderness.

"We also lost all our links to the satellites and nothing appears to be broadcasting outside the city. This means these conditions extend beyond the immediate vicinity.'

Wyatt sat back in his chair. "Pardon my ignorance, but I'm lost. Why are we seeing a wilderness? Have we been transported to a different timeline as well?"

"I don't think anything like that has happened," said Missy

"Do you want to explain?"

"I'll try. Understand this is all speculation on my part, but it fits with the facts.

"First, Ahmed Aswira assaulted the Gateway and was transported with a heavily armed ATV to October 9, 732, the eve of the final day of the Battle of Tours south of Paris. His goal was to change the outcome of that battle from a crushing defeat of the Muslim army to an overwhelming victory. If the Muslims were able to gain control of the continent, the history of Europe would evolve in a completely different way.

"Next you need to understand a basic tenant of Islam. From their perspective the words and writing of Mohammad represented the final word of God. Nothing needs to be added. The final chapter of human development has been written. We can see how this plays out in our own time. The Muslims are willing to use technology, but not to create it. In all history there has been only one Muslim Nobel Prize winner. Islamic religious leaders do not encourage innovation and creative thinking.

"If no new research is done in the sciences; physics, biology, mathematics, astronomy, medicine, engineering, through the next several centuries, after the Battle of Tours, which means no Reformation, no Renaissance, and almost no progress.

"Therefore, with no interest in exploration by the Muslims, it's entirely possible the new world was never discovered.

"What you see outside the perimeter is not a new timeline, but a continuation of the old one, sixteen hundred years later. Our 'now' is the same as it was before the interruption of the timestream. We have just transitioned to the current present where the United States does not exist and has never existed in the world given us by this singular, horrible event."

Cisco nodded his head. "You might be speculating, Missy, but everything you said sounds right."

"All this scares the hell out of me," said Chips."

Wyatt shook his head. "I can't imagine how frightened my wife and kids will be when they find out Charleston has disappeared."

"I would guess, the entire population will react that way. We need to decide how to prevent a widespread panic."

"None of our citizens know a particle about the real truth of Horizon," said Scott. "You're not thinking about telling them, are you?"

"Why not? If we're as isolated as I think most of us believe, we must start living, thinking, planning, and acting as a coordinated community."

Scott slapped his hands on the table. "But Jonas, what we're doing is science fiction to most people. How can you possibly predict how they'll act?"

A chair at the other end of the table scooted. Cisco waved a hand. "Got something to say, Ben?"

"I guess I don't know for sure how our people will react to

such a disclosure. However, I'm the one who evaluated and hired applicants for work and living in Sanctuary, and I can tell you I've been able to be very picky.

"What you have here, Admiral, is the absolute cream of the crop. Not only are our people overqualified in the skills and qualifications for the jobs we hired them to do, but I went beyond their resumes and looked into their characters. In my interviews, I told the applicants we were as interested in their approach to life as we were their talents, simply because Sanctuary is not like other places and their lives here would be unique and different."

"So, you're saying they'll think all this is some kind of an adventure?" Scott shot back.

"Of course not. What I'm saying is this group of people will adapt more easily to the new realities before them. Furthermore, I think they have a right to know what's happened."

"I'm with Ben on that," said Will. "If you have a crisis onboard a ship, the Captain always tells the crew everything he knows about the emergency and exactly what they need to do."

"If I could add something," said Wyatt. "In a situation like you just mentioned, you think about the lives of your fellow crew members. That's not what we have here. There are wives, husbands, and children involved. I have my own family to think of and, as I said before, when they wake up tomorrow they'll be truly alarmed. I'd better have some really good answers to their questions."

A soft voice whispered across the table, "Tragically, tomorrow will be a day of mourning."

Cisco turned to Missy. "I sorry. In the turbulence of the moment, I forgot about your—our loss."

"Yes, losing Lino is a tragedy. I will miss him terribly. However, the mourning is yours, Jonas —yours and everyone else in this room and every home in Sanctuary."

"Am I not thinking clearly enough here, Missy?"

"Your initial analysis is correct for as far as it goes, but you haven't yet closed the loop." Missy turned to address the entire table. "This fracture in the timestream is echoing down through the centuries—and is global. Has it occurred to you the reason why you don't have uplinks to satellites is because there are no satellites? Is the reason no one is broadcasting out there is because there's no one to broadcast to?

"My guess is there is no advanced civilization in the Western Hemisphere. Indigenous Native Americans likely inhabit it, and that is all. This means, all your extended families, your mothers, fathers, brothers, sisters, and all your children, who were alive in an alternate universe yesterday, are gone today in this alternate universe. When that reality sinks in, you will hear a cry of agony shrieking from every household."

Silence filled the room. Seconds stretched into minutes. Ben Crenshaw broke first. He pounded his fists on the table. Tears squirted from his eyes. "My mom, my dad, my little sister in Wisconsin, I can't believe it."

Riley, sitting next to him, was doing no better. He hugged Ben, and then both bawled in each other's face. The scene repeated itself, more or less, around the table.

Cisco felt crushing loss of his own. His sons and his grandchildren lived in California. He bowed his head, wondering how to weather this storm, or how anyone could find any fragment of comfort in the enormity of the moment.

Scott spoke first. "There shall never be grief this profound ever again. I'm so sorry for us all. I wish I could say Missy is wrong, but I can't. Somehow, until this moment, it was only theory, conjecture and supposition. Now, it's so real I feel it gnawing at my soul. Maybe we should break for a while until the sharp edge of this hateful hour stops slicing at our hearts."

The room grew silent again.

Eventually, Cisco cleared his throat. "As much as I hurt, as

171

bad as I feel, there are 10,000 families out there who need us now the most. We led them into this mousetrap. They won't thank us because they are the survivors. They're going to cry and grieve, and when they stop crying, they'll want someone to pay."

"I'm afraid he's right," said Wyatt. "If we're not careful, we could be ones holding the bag. We need to put the spotlight on the true criminals."

Hauser gave a sharp snort. "I wasn't thinking any clearer than the rest of us until Missy brought us to our senses. I apologize to you all; Jonas is right. We no longer have any choice. We need to make immediate plans for a full disclosure of everything. No more worries about changing history, it's already happened. We need to start thinking about how we're going to manage the future from the moment of the fracture. We will need full public support for that."

Cisco would be forever grateful to Scott for bringing the leaders of the now isolated, community back into a problem-solving mode. He thrust his own bitter feelings into a deep recess of his mind. "Does anyone disagree with what you just heard?"

No one spoke.

"Very well, here is what I propose we do."

Cisco opened his eyes and glanced at the time, three a.m. He dozed off after calling for a break. He shook his head to clear his mind. Over thirty-six hours had passed since the alarm went off in his home. Since then, every moment was flooded with tragedy, crisis, and disaster. He felt mortally exhausted. Around the room, the others had also drifted off.

The officers of the command and Horizon teams learned long ago to grab fragments of sleep whenever they could in times of adversities and trials. Scott slept in his chair, while Missy had retired to a couch and slept with her head in Chips lap. Chips had his head back on the couch and snored. Ben had his arms on the table with his head nested in them.

Cisco broke the silence. "Computer, status report."

*"Your last recorded message to the general population in response to inquiries regarding the loss of electronic media and conditions beyond the perimeter has played three thousand, three hundred and forty-six times. The studio personnel for your planned citywide broadcast at nine hundred hours, report all preparations complete.*

*"Aircrews are on alert. Reconnaissance aircraft are on the flight line, fueled, fully equipped and ready for scheduled takeoff at oh-four hundred hours.*

*"The 'Beachhead' protocol is in place. Work crews are installing pre-fabricated guard towers at one-half mile intervals around the perimeter boundary. Security is on station at all city egress gates. All traffic, in and out of the city is restricted to authorized personnel.*

*"Level one diagnostic is complete. All systems are fully operational. 'Beachhead' protocol is now monitoring all expendable assets. Inventory regulation and control have been initiated."*

The computer voice roused everyone in the conference room. Wyatt sat up and rubbed his face. "Did you sleep at all, Jonas?"

"A little bit. We all needed a break."

"That's for sure. Letting the department directors carry the ball after your public address is a good one. From now on these people will have to shoulder a lot more responsibility and feel the weight of command."

Cisco nodded. "Time to start waking them up and bringing them in for the 'full story' briefing. I hope none of them lose it."

"Let's hope Ben's right about the character of these people.

What's coming at them now could frazzle the bravest soul."

Ben came to life at the end of the table at the mention of his name. "Did you get any sleep, Admiral?"

"How come everyone keeps asking me that?"

"Because, Admiral," said Wyatt formally, "you're the one person we can't afford to lose. You represent the true heart and soul of our city, and from now on, everyone is going to count on you even more. I want you to promise me, after you've recorded your speech to the city; you will go home and get some sleep."

"I'm sure glad he said that Sir," said Ben. "He's right you know."

"Don't you think I should be out among our people after the broadcast?"

"After the broadcast, I doubt very many people will feel like leaving their homes at all," said Wyatt.

"I guess you're right. Okay, another few hours and I'll hit the sack. For the moment, Ben, do you have the list of directors we need to call?"

"Right here, Admiral."

Cisco glanced around. "Let's go over the plan one more time. Then we'll start waking people up."

Two hours later, Ben made his final call to the Director of Inventories, Logan Richards. He answered it on the third ring.

"Hello, Logan, this is Ben Crenshaw. Sorry to wake you so early, but something has come up. The Admiral is bringing in all department heads for a seven o'clock meeting at City Hall."

Ben listened for a moment and then said, "I couldn't even begin to tell you, but you'll never have a more important meeting in your life than this one. It'll be sunrise in a few minutes. Step out onto your balcony and try not to be alarmed at what you see. After that, don't wake your wife, throw on some clothes and beat it over here." He hung up. "That's the last of them, Admiral; I'll bet we have company pretty quick."

❖

Cisco wasn't surprised when an aide came into his office to report department heads were arriving in the conference room on the top floor of City Hall. It wasn't even six-thirty. He and the command team had slipped into his office with its bigger bathroom to freshen up before the meeting. Now they went back to the conference room. Logan Richards walked in right behind them looking confused, disoriented, and baffled. Several other department heads were already there. All of them seemed equally dazed.

"Have you guys seen the sudden change in the landscape?" asked Logan.

"We've seen it. Charleston has somehow disappeared. Craziest thing I ever saw."

As more of the department heads came in, they all had the same puzzled looks.

"After Ben woke me," Logan told one of the other directors, "I made myself a cup of coffee and went out on my balcony. Kind of a ritual with me, I like to look at our city. On clear mornings I can see the ocean. This morning I looked out and instead of the familiar buildings, bridges and landmarks of Charleston, I only saw heavy forest and a few small lakes."

Servers came in with doughnuts, pastries, and several carafes of coffee. Cisco could see the confused and somewhat frightened on the faces of all the directors. None of the command or Horizon teams were confused, but they all had worn, tired, and haggard faces.

"Help yourself to coffee and rolls, and take your seats, ladies and gentlemen. Let's get started."

Logan poured himself a mug. "I started the day about half a cup short," He grabbed a sweet roll and sat down. The others did the same. When all were seated, mixed in with the command and

Horizon teams, Cisco went to the head of the table.

"One of the continuing questions about Sanctuary, has always been the single-minded pre-occupation our city be a self-sustaining community. The official explanation given is we wanted to build a new kind of city. One to serve as a model for other cities to achieve a level of superiority and independence giving their residents the kind of lifestyle you all enjoy.

"It did not explain why we were stockpiling huge reserves of every conceivable product, equipment, instrument, device, tool, or spare part imaginable in multiple levels of redundancy. If you want to know how comprehensive this stockpile is, you can ask our inventory director, Logan Richards, who keeps track of all this stuff."

"It's incredibly extensive and complex. The computer does much of the work, but it's a never-ending job logging in all the tons of supplies coming in every day. It takes me and a staff of about two dozen others to keep track of it all."

"That ends today. From now on, nothing will come into the city we didn't grow, build, fabricate, manufacture, or invent ourselves."

The admiral took a deep breath and raised his arms to the people around the table. "So now we come down to it. All of you believe the Gateway Center is engaged in attempting to solve the riddles of matter transference. That is the official line. Of itself, this would be a revolutionary achievement. What you don't know is the Horizon team discovered how to do this several years ago."

Logan shook his head in surprise at this unexpected announcement. As he glanced around the conference table, the other directors appeared equally surprised. The command team stared straight ahead.

"I'll ask Doctor Hauser to explain the outcome of this discovery."

Scott stood up. "There's no easy way to tell this, so I'm just going to give you the bottom line. When we successfully began transferring living organisms from one place to another, something else happened. Our live animals were also moving through time. You can imagine the shock of the premier scientists in the world to see this phenomenon suddenly appear. The very idea time travel is possible, terrified us so much, we almost abandoned the entire project. Ultimately, we did continue and wrapped our work in a blanket of security. This is the reason the Gateway Center is locked tight and shrouded in secrecy. We call it the Gateway because we are sending people backward in time and then recalling them to the present."

This time the uproar in the room went on for over a minute. Before anyone could speak, Scott raised his hand for order. "We discovered another thing. An enormous secondary energy field extends outward from the primary transmission cone. This has the effect of preventing any changes in our time within the secondary field while the primary field is operating. We regarded this as a true blessing because it meant we could build a self-sufficient survival beachhead in the event any action by people travelling from the present, caused a major disruption in the timestream and altered the past so radically it changed our current world to something entirely different."

With that, Scott sat back down, amidst another bubble of conversation.

Cisco rose again. "This is why we built Sanctuary, and the reason for the extensive stockpiling of critical reserves. We wanted to make it possible for a population of highly skilled experts in a variety of fields with the right temperament, discipline, and sheer guts to find a way into the future. We hoped it would never happen."

Cisco paused, took a sip of his orange juice, and faced the flood of intense stares around the table.

"Two nights ago, a small group of conspirators from our host consortium of supporters, used their 'all access' security clearance to penetrate Gateway Center security. They killed one security guard getting in. They then shot and killed our leading scientist, Doctor Lino Arnett, before being transported back in time, heavily armed with modern weapons.

"Their purpose was to alter history by delivering a Muslim victory in a battle historically lost to the Franks in the early eighth century and paving the way for the domination of Europe by the Islamic Caliphate.

"What you saw beyond the borders of Sanctuary this morning is the undeniable proof these twenty-first century terrorists succeeded. We are alone, and nobody is coming to help us."

Cisco remained standing, surveying the white faces before him. This briefing was the worst of his entire life.

Missy got up from her seat and came to stand next to Cisco. He smiled briefly at her. She turned to the group. "Unfortunately, this is not the worst of it. Last night we lost our uplinks to every orbiting satellite. We also lost broadband communications for everything outside of the city. No internet, no cable TV, no long-distance cell phone communications, nothing."

"Before dawn this morning," said Cisco, "I dispatched long-range reconnaissance aircraft to the north, south, and west. They have been in the air for about two hours. That's long enough for them to cover an arc about four hundred miles in all directions. The crews report no city lights, no heat signatures, and no other aircraft. They do report settlements scattered here and there. Mostly likely, these are Native American settlements. A few of them are of some size, perhaps a few thousand inhabitants."

"What we are seeing from these preliminary reports," said Missy, "confirms our worst suspicions. The United States has ceased to exist. This means your families, relatives, and friends outside of Sanctuary are no longer alive in this version of history.

It is the most repulsive act of terrorism ever committed."

Just as before, when the Horizon leadership reeled from the death of Lino Arnett, Cisco did not give anyone time to think. "You men and women represent the key leadership for our city. This community will need your strength and resolve in the difficult days ahead. You must join the command and Horizon teams, all of whom have lost as much as you, and somehow find a way through this avalanche of problems and challenges so we can preserve what we have built and make a new life."

As a senior department director, Logan felt he had to speak. "This is one hand I wish we could pass, Admiral. It doesn't look like that's going to happen, so we have no choice but live with the grief and move on. I hope you're going to tell us what we do next?"

"We've given it a good deal of thought over the past two years. In general, there are two primary points of view. Some of us believe we should extend Sanctuary's control over as much of the land adjacent to the city as possible. This will allow us to begin the process of acquiring natural resources to augment and replenish the finite supplies we have.

"Others have a more global approach. The say the breach in the timestream should be explored and steps taken to restore as much of our past history as possible, perhaps even reverse the changes facing us at the borders of our city right now.

"We are going to do both. However, the singular priority, the fundamental necessity, is the preservation of Sanctuary for today and for the distant future. Without a functional, viable, productive and pro-active city, none of our other goals and strategies, mean anything. In the end, the debate is a circle. The city comes first."

# Chapter 14
# Together or Nothing

Logan Richards went home after the meeting with the other city directors and the command staff. Learning the Gateway Center's true purpose and capabilities had a greater impact on him than the loss of loved ones. Logan was an orphan and raised in foster homes, so he didn't have anyone to mourn. His wife was a different matter. Laurie had a mother and father. Even though she was an only child, she had more of an extended family. Richards could only guess how she would take the news they no longer existed. In any case, he needed to be with her and their two children when the Admiral gave his address. When he arrived, he found everyone awake.

"Oh honey, I'm so glad you're here," cried Laurie as he came in. "I woke up when the phone rang and couldn't go back to sleep after you rushed out. I got up, made my coffee and went out on the balcony. Everything, except our city is different. There's nothing but trees out there. I asked the computer for information and got Admiral Cisco's recorded message saying he was aware of the situation and would have a complete report at nine a.m. I called your cell and it went to voice mail. What's happened?"

"It's nearly time for the broadcast. The Admiral and some others from the Gateway Center are going to tell the whole town what I heard. Gather up the kids and we'll watch this together."

"Why do we need the kids?"

"This concerns them too. They might not understand everything, but they should see this."

"Logan, you're scaring me to death."

"I'm sorry, sweetie." He took her in his arms, "The most important thing to me is you and the kids are safe."

Laurie got up and went to the children's bedrooms. They came back to the family room with their mother and sat down on the floor.

"What's happening, Daddy?" cried ten-year-old Penelope.

"The Admiral and some others are going to come on TV in a few minutes, Penny. He will tell us why Charleston has disappeared, but Sanctuary hasn't.

"Is this a big deal, Dad?" asked eight-year-old Adam.

"The biggest deal you'll ever see. The biggest deal anyone has ever seen."

The large monitor screen across the room came to life. Soothing music and pictures of mountains, forests and abundant wildlife flowed across the screen. The pictures and music faded to a serious news announcer on the Sanctuary station. "We've interrupted all other broadcast channels to bring you the following important announcement from Admiral Jonas Cisco, commanding officer of Sanctuary."

The picture cut to the admiral standing at a lectern. He smiled. "Good morning, my fellow citizens of Sanctuary. I'm sorry to come into your homes so early, but, if you've looked outside, you already know the world outside the city is much different. We are going to tell you what it is, what it means, and what we have to do next. Joining me this morning are the two senior scientists at the Gateway Center.

"Before we begin, you need to know nothing has changed within the city. Everything is exactly as it was yesterday. There is no danger whatsoever to anyone within the city perimeter. I'll start by telling you the real reason Sanctuary was built."

Cisco went on to explain the history of Sanctuary, beginning with the first contact the old Charleston Joint Command had with the scientists of Horizon. As he spoke, images of the vast construction project, along with the storage of titanic reserves, filled his narrative. He concluded, "Now I hope you fully understand the unique and unconventional way in which Sanctuary was designed and built. It's time to tell you why. For that, may I introduce the senior scientist of Project Horizon at the Gateway Center, Doctor Scott Hauser."

Scott then stepped forward to explain the results of Horizon research. "Over a decade ago, we made the unexpected discovery people could be sent back in time." He illustrated the breakthrough with footage of the jump to Fort Collins in 1880.

Laurie turned to her husband. "This is unbelievable. Actual time travel. No wonder there are so many secrets around here. Several times I asked Doctor Arnett to talk to my advanced physics students on the theories of matter transference. He's the real brains at the Gateway Center. Now I know why he wouldn't ever come."

Logan put his arm around his wife. "Wait until you hear the rest of it."

Scott went on to explain the nature of the secondary energy field generated by opening the Gateway. "Whatever was inside the zone of the field would not be affected if an event in the past altered the present. This is why we built Sanctuary. It represented the only step we could take to preserve the present, as we know it. All of us hoped such a terrible thing would never happen. However, it has. All you have to do is look out your window. Sanctuary is untouched, but nothing beyond the boundary of the city is the same. Sadly, the past has been changed. Even worse, this was a deliberate act by people with self-absorbed, hateful motives."

Logan pulled his wife closer. "What he just told us is the reason why everything beyond the city boundaries has changed."

Penny turned to her father. "Daddy, what that man said scares me."

"Me too, honey. This is the beginning of some huge changes in our lives, from now on we have to be brave."

Missy came to the lectern and explained, in simple terms, how the alteration of a single event from the past could disastrously alter the future. She described this event in detail, both from the way it originally occurred, to the way the intervention from the present changed the outcome, and the succeeding history of Europe and ultimately the United States.

The Richards family's eyes froze to the screen as Admiral Cisco returned and gave an account of exactly what had happened. He left nothing out. Cisco believed the citizens of the city had a right to know everything. Beyond that, he didn't present any details of how the 10,000 families, a total of 30,000 people, would have to live from then on. That would be for another day.

Finally, Missy came back to the podium and spoke the terrible words Logan heard in his early morning meeting. Missy spoke with compassion and empathy, but the shadow in her eyes only made the tragedy even more sad.

"Does that mean Grandpa and Gramma are gone?"

"I'm afraid it does, son."

Cisco came back on the screen. This time his voice choked with emotion, and his face showed true marks of near exhaustion. He spoke as a man whose loss was more than he could bear. "All of us grieve for the loss of our loved ones. All of us have had our hearts ripped out. All of us are victims today. We are in a state of shock. Perhaps you are wondering how you can go on—if you can go on. Let me tell you, we will go on, even if there are no words I can speak to you, or even myself, to tell us how we shall endure this tragedy. All we can do is to carry the memories of those we cherished in our minds as we go forth from this terrible day.

"We will do some things. The directors of each of your departments are organizing public gatherings and prayer vigils. Counseling beginning at noon today will continue around the clock for as long as it takes for us to heal. Symbolically, all our flags shall fly at half-mast for the next month. Finally, in two nights we shall conduct a community memorial service at Cooper River Stadium as the last rites for two members of our community who have fallen in the new age we face...one being a dedicated soldier standing his post, and the other an honored colleague, our greatest mind, who died giving his life to save our vital portal to the timestream.

"May the eternal God of the universe, by any name He has among us, bless our community, and each of us. May His face shine on us as we pick up our torches and march into this day and go forth to a better tomorrow."

The Richards family looked at the blank screen and sobbed. They were not alone.

Sanctuary wept.

The studio lights went down, and the cameramen signaled they were clear. Cisco, Scott and Missy looked at each other as they unclipped their microphones.

"Very nice speech, Jonas," said Missy. "I can't imagine you saying it any better."

"Thanks, I only hope our people can work through this, somehow."

"I don't think they have any choice," said Scott. "The sooner they realize it, the sooner we can begin to take steps to manage the carnage of the rotten, horrific mess we're in."

Cisco stood up. "On that subject, I want you two to meet with your bright people and come up with some recommendations on how to manage this new timeline. Wyatt and the rest of the command team are meeting right now, hammering out the protocols we'll need to function as a city. The directors are busy bringing the people in their departments and their families together at recreation centers around town. They'll be the frontline to deal with the panic, sorrow, anger, confusion, and everything else. I hope we gave them enough information to answer most of the initial questions they'll encounter.

"Then tonight, when some of the shock has died down a little, we'll have a combined meeting with everybody. That's when we implement all the contingency plans we hoped we'd never have to use and start living by them day-by-day.

"Right now. Go home and catch up on your sleep. Don't call me until you wake up."

Missy made a little smile. "Are you going to obey your own orders?"

"I'm cooked. I have to rest. If I don't, I'll start making mistakes, and that's something we can't afford right now. Beat it."

At midafternoon Cisco returned to his office, freshly shaven, showered, and in a clean uniform. He felt considerably better, despite getting only six hours sleep. He wasn't sure he could say the same for his command team. They'd started working before Cisco's television address. When Cisco came into the conference room, he found it littered with cups, trays with half-eaten food, maps, notebooks, photographs, and several untidy piles of papers.

Wyatt seemed alert enough. "Ah Jonas, hope you got some rest. We've got a good start in half a dozen areas."

"Tell me."

Chips stood up. "Our long-range reconnaissance planes have completed overlapping arcs out to a thousand miles north, south, and west. They've been transmitting video signals throughout the day. After the sun came up, we got a detailed picture of the entire eastern United States—or what used to be the United States. Computer, show composite footage of reconnaissance sweeps."

The LED monitor went on. Cisco watched as video from each plane displayed images of the ground below. As far as the lens of the cameras could see, an endless forest marched off to the horizon. The images were broken by rivers running in ever increasing widths draining into the Mississippi.

That was not all. Carved out of the woodland, were wide, cultivated fields surrounding settlements. Some of them were quite large with thousands, even tens of thousands of people.

"Native Americans?"

"So it seems. They are numerous concentrations throughout the eastern half of the continent. We have located at least four major cities. We estimate the population of these to be over a hundred thousand. There is plenty of stone masonry, buildings or monuments several stories high. The agriculture is also fairly advanced. The principal beast of burden seems to be llamas. What we're looking at is a civilization well beyond the stone age."

"Anything close to us?"

"There's a major city about seven hundred miles west and south, about where New Orleans would be. Otherwise, there are all sorts of smaller settlements sprinkled throughout the southeast. We've had several drones in the air since sunup. Closer is a village with perhaps five hundred natives three miles east on Cooper River."

"Any sign they've noticed us yet?"

"Our guards on duty at the outer boundary spotted several men fishing in the river a couple of hours ago, about a mile from the perimeter. They're coming this way. I doubt it will very long before they come downstream far enough to be able to see the city."

"You can bet they'll take one look at our skyline and beat it back to their village. The next bunch that comes this way won't be fishing."

"What do you want to do, Jonas?"

Cisco sat back in his chair for a moment and then said, "Computer, how many Native Americans in our military complement?"

*"There are eleven men and four women who are*

*recorded as Native American."*

"Contact the men and have them report to me ASAP."

Chips ventured. "Birds of a feather?"

"Something like that."

"While we're waiting, I've instructed the computer to continue monitoring the feeds from the drone and notify us if anything like a delegation or a war party heads this way."

"Okay, how about perimeter security?"

"Well underway," said Riley. "We planned for this in our original Sanctuary design. Concrete pads were poured every half mile, and towers constructed to go on them. We've pulled the towers out of mothballs and are assembling them now. We'll have manned towers every mile, with surveillance cameras in between. Figure about two weeks to finish the whole system finished and make it operational.

"Excellent. Anything else?"

"Well, the forest comes almost right up to the perimeter we ought to clear an open space so we can see if anything's coming."

"Can you get a crew out there sometime soon?"

"I guess I can see if I can recruit some of the farming people to do the job. That brings up a different issue."

"What's that?"

"No problem with the perimeter security. I'm using regular military people for that, but civilians will be needed for the open space project. They're not so easy to order around."

Cisco sat quietly for a moment before answering. "This is something we need to face right away. From now on we have to work together to sustain our lives. Nobody's coming to help us. From what I've seen we're the only advanced island of civilization for thousands of miles. Unless we decide from the outset, to join together and hold on to what we have, Sanctuary will fail. Let me show you how fragile our situation is. Computer, based on our current usage of current stores, equipment, and supplies, how long before critical shortages will occur, excluding food production?"

*"Critical shortages in household goods will occur in five years. Current supplies of petroleum products will be depleted in ten years. General construction, maintenance equipment, and supplies will fall below current replacement levels in twenty years. Transportation and personal vehicle levels cannot be sustained beyond fifty years. City infrastructure useful life, before general reconstruction, can be estimated at one hundred years."*

"Now, let's put these numbers into human terms. Computer, estimate the current ability of the city to replenish critical supplies and equipment, and determine the employment index needed to maintain this standard."

*"That index is minus fourteen-point seven percent, assuming a labor participation at eighty-six percent."*

"We're used to seeing unemployment statistics at four or five percent, with a labor participation level at about sixty percent. The grim facts are, to keep our heads above water, we need to produce about fifteen percent more work with our existing workforce and our labor participation rate has to go up twenty-five points. About the only people not working every day will be the youngest kids in school, and women having babies in the hospital."

"All hands, on deck," said Will.

"And then some," echoed Wyatt. "I don't think I'll be getting in any golf anytime soon."

"Even if you had the time, my friend, it would be a short game," interjected Riley. "We only have seven and a half holes left. The rest went off into temporal never-never-land."

"Ah shit. A completely shitty ending to an already shitty day."

A couple of aides came through and cleared out the clutter from the conference room. The command team went back to their offices to carry out Cisco's string of orders. Cisco returned to his office. He didn't start working immediately, leaning back in his chair and looking out the window. The sun had nearly fallen, the last of the light shining across the forest, which marched down to the ocean.

*A beautiful view. So much different from the urban landscape of yesterday I could grow used to this.*

Of course, the circumstances which had caused the altered scenery to appear would now require the most inspired leadership of his life. His shoulders slumped with the thought of how much depended on him making the right decisions and inspiring others to do the same.

His heart ached for the loss of his sons and his grandchildren in a city which no longer existed. Ever since the crushing, tragic news was delivered to everyone else in Sanctuary, nobody asked him how he felt, of offered soft words to ease his pain. Cisco hadn't expected any, but it still hurt.

While he was still gazing, glassy-eyed, toward the ocean, Molly, walked into his office

"Admiral, the men you ordered to report, have arrived."

"Who?" asked Cisco, trying to sort out which one of his orders she meant.

"The men who are Native Americans."

"Oh, right. We've spotted some people close to the boundary, probably from the village three miles up Cooper River. I'm hoping these men can make a peaceful first contact."

"This on top of everything else you're doing?"

"We need peaceful relations with our new neighbors. I can't worry about having to defend ourselves. Besides, we're going to need these true Native Americans to help us with any number of things."

Molly came around the desk and put her hand on Cisco's shoulder, "Are you okay, Jonas?"

His secretary almost never called him by his first name and never in earshot of anyone else, so he shook his head and forced himself to focus his concentration. "Yeah, I'm alright. I guess I feel a little sorry for myself."

"Your boys in California? And the grandchildren?"

"I'm like everyone else in Sanctuary. I know they're not dead, but they are most definitely gone, whisked away to some other version of time. It amounts to the same thing. It hurts as much. What about you, Molly?"

"Not much of a family for me to mourn. All the people I care about are right here."

"In that case, we'll be the best family we can."

"You've always been that, Jonas." She patted him on the cheek.

"Thanks, Molly. Being able to break down a little to anyone makes it easier."

"Your welcome. Now, what do you want to do with these men?

"How many are there?"

"I counted eleven."

Too many to meet in here. Send them down to the main conference room. I'll be along in a few minutes."

"You got it. By the way, Admiral, straighten your tie."

When Molly left, Cisco rummaged through the stacks of papers on his desk. He found what he wanted, an aerial picture from the drone of the nearby native village. As he headed out of his office, he stopped in front of a mirror and straightened his tie.

When he entered the conference room, one of the men shouted, "Atten-shun!" Cisco could hear heels clicking as the eleven men rose from their chairs.

"At ease. Everybody sit down, and we'll get started."

Cisco showed the men some footage recovered from the drones of the nearby neighborhood. He then briefed them on the current situation, emphasizing how important it would be to establish peaceful relations with the Native American population. "What we want is to begin active trading with these people. As far as I'm concerned, information is a commodity. We need to know if they have affiliations with other native peoples. How they contact them. Are they currently at war with anyone? What kind of a social structure do they have? In return, there are lots of things we can give them. I want you to make a list of what you can carry to trade or give them as a token of our goodwill. Under no circumstances are you to provoke them in any way. If you find yourselves in a situation where some kind of force is necessary, you will employ defensive tactics only and then beat a hasty retreat. Questions or comments?"

"Yes sir," said an Marine sergeant at the end of the table. "I'm full-blooded Navaho, raised on the reservation. We used a lot of the same tactics in our dealings with other tribes or clans. I think I can remember most of the common signs we used to use to speak to people with a different language. I was also student of history in my years at the university. I think we should go in on horseback."

"Tell me why?"

"From what you've told us with the aerial sweeps, there are no horses anywhere. This is not surprising since the horse is not native to North America. They came with the Spanish in the 16th Century. The sight of men on horses terrified the Aztec of Mexico and made Cortez's job of conquering them a snap. I realize we aren't going in for gold and plunder, but I imagine men on horses will still scare the natives to bits. It might make it easier to establish a working relationship if we have a little leverage."

191

"You know, sergeant, that's a very good idea. It's such a good idea I think all of you should be mounted, with a pack horse to carry all the free stuff you're going to pass out. I assume you know how to ride a horse?"

"From the time I was a little boy, Admiral."

"What about the rest of you?"

Three of the men said they had ridden much of their lives. The others said they would be glad to learn.

"Great. Get the group together and make up a list of things you think a tribe like this might need or want and upload it to the computer tonight. I want you to be able to leave by sunup tomorrow."

"Why the rush, sir?"

"Because the men fishing along the Cooper River today saw the city. You can bet they ran home and told everyone what they saw. If we don't get ahead of this, we'll have all sorts of 'tourists' coming for a look themselves. We sure can't have these people wandering around inside Sanctuary. It would scare them more than the Aztecs ever were. Got it?"

"Absolutely, sir. We'll have a pow-wow with each other and be ready to leave tomorrow morning."

"Fine. And sergeant, I'm counting on you to make sure you don't go to that village with better weapons than they have."

"I understand, sir."

As the men filed out of the room, Cisco watched them gabbing eagerly to each other, planning for the mission, and soaking up the sheer adventure of what lay ahead of them. *Can't say I blame them for being excited. If I were twenty years younger, I'd lead the way.*

He gave orders to the computer to have horses brought in from the pastures, and to release the list of trade goods, and gifts to offer to the natives of the village. A drone would monitor the men and signal in the event something went wrong. With that

Cisco went back to his office to make notes for the bigger meeting with all the department heads.

❖

A palpable tension filled the air when the thirteen senior directors of each department in the city came into the conference room at six o'clock. They had grim faces. Cisco knew them and had confidence in each of them. However, the circumstances would test them all. The command team came in with the directors and found places sprinkled around the long conference table.

None of the good-natured jabs and jokes, common with a general meeting, circulated the table tonight. Meetings of this type were not held often and were always something of an event. They usually were called to announce the completion of a major project in the city. Everyone enjoyed them. Tonight, everything was different.

Cisco tried to bring a semblance of normality, stability, and calm to the anxious faces. "Nothing in Sanctuary has changed. Everything we had yesterday, we have today. There is no reason to fear for the safety of our families. Also, even though we hoped this day would never come, we prepared for it. We are capable of sustaining the city and its people at our current levels indefinitely, even if that means beyond the lives of all of us. Our children will enjoy the same services, education, access to medical treatment, opportunities for excellence in any number of fields, and even the same recreational and social programs we have today.

"We selected each of you to be the heads of your departments because your education, training, and experience qualified you to excel in your fields of expertise. However, this is only part of the reason you were chosen. Political gridlock, social turbulence, and civic irresponsibility were producing a crisis in the country endangering the stability of our union. You were selected because our very sophisticated vetting process determined you were committed to put an end to this spiraling chaos. I imagined the example we set, by the way we lived. could serve as a model for others to follow our lead."

"Excuse me, Admiral," said Edward Watkins, Director of Education. "What you are saying is all well and fine for polite discussion, but it hardly applies to the situation facing us today."

"Wrong. It applies even more intensely now than ever, particularly in your department, the education of our children. If we do not leave behind the incoherent wishful thinking of the pseudo-scientific class claiming to be social workers or behavioral psychologists we will never return to the traditional methods of imparting respect for law and social integrity in the minds of the young."

"And what would those traditional methods be, Admiral?"

"The same way you housebreak a dog. When they make a mess, you rub their noses in it to show them what you're talking about, and then you paddle them to make the point."

Director Watkins chuckled, and looked around the room. "I've often thought exactly that technique would go a long way in restoring order to the classroom. But it doesn't apply to our students. We have the most hard-working, dedicated group of young people any of us educators have ever seen. Do you believe such drastic steps will be necessary?"

"Not only will they be necessary, but you will inevitably have to employ them. With the entire student body disconnected from Facebook, YouTube, endless texting on cell phones to people all over the country, and the rest of the computer-generated diversions they've grown up with, your bright young people will begin to manufacture new ones. Most of them won't mean anything, but some of them will be destructive to the best interests of the city. You have to be ready, and willing to make graphic examples."

"I'm sure you're right, Admiral. As I see it, we need to construct a whole new mosaic of recreational and educational activities. Do you have any ideas?"

Cisco thought for a moment. "We are surrounded by wilderness and a whole population of natives with whom we must interact and live in peaceful co-existence. How about you put your staff to work thinking of ways to involve our young people in those areas? Sort of like the Boy Scouts on steroids."

Everyone laughed. Cisco hadn't intended to make a joke but was glad he did. When the laughter petered out, he smiled. "I'm so glad we can find something to laugh about today. We need to find ways to keep our sunny sides up and to approach problems with enthusiasm and a spirit of adventure. Think about that as we go forward. From now on its together or nothing."

# Chapter 15
## Setting the Pace

The pace of life in Sanctuary went from busy to super-charged. Every day, sometimes every hour, new things emerged in the lives of the city residents. Jonas Cisco had the satisfaction of knowing Ben Crenshaw's vetting process led to finding industrious people with a will to work and little fear about the future.

This day hadn't started with the best news. Scott and Missy came to Cisco's office the morning after the meeting with the department heads.

"Jonas, we have a problem,"

Cisco flipped his hand. "Why of course you do. Everyone has a problem, and they all end up on my desk."

"We are truly sorry, Jonas," said Missy. "I know the past few days have been a real strain for you. We would handle this on our own if possible, but we need your help."

"Oh well, this is the place to bring problems. That's my job. What's up?"

"It's the Gateway transmission core. When we ran it continuously waiting for the ripple in the timestream to take effect, we burned out several of the cones and most of the electrical bundles feeding them."

"How long before you can get back up and running?"

"A month, maybe longer. It's not only replacing the burned-out parts; the entire system has to be recalibrated."

"What do you need from me?"

"The replacement parts are in the strategic equipment reserves. Nobody but you can direct the computer to release them."

"Computer, Doctor Hauser has to rebuild the Gateway. Give him whatever parts and equipment he needs."

*"Acknowledged."*

"Anything else?

"Rebuilding the system is only the start," said Missy. "We need to start thinking about what to do when we begin making jumps. History as we know it has been thoroughly scrambled."

"Believe it or not, I've given that subject some thought. Why don't we just send a team of snipers back to right before Aswira slaughters the Franks and shoot the conspirators dead? If the Muslims never win, then why wouldn't history go on like it is supposed to?"

"If you're asking me about interfering with an event that's already been interfered with, I don't know what will happen. It sounds like an easy fix to a terrible problem. Maybe doing what you say would have the effect of changing history back to the original timeline."

"I guess you don't think the idea is so hot?"

"Look at the disastrous effects we got from a single change in history. That is now the actual reality of our world. If we introduce another cataclysmic event, even one designed to change it back to the way it was, we might end up with something worse."

"I thought it sounded too simple. Tell me, Missy, do you really think a significant risk exists to the safety of the people of Sanctuary if we were to try an operation as I suggested?"

"That's the problem, Jonas. I don't know. At best I'd be guessing. If it were me having to make the decision, based on the uncertainties, I wouldn't do it."

"If that is the case, then neither will I. We have to think of something else. If we can. You go ahead and get the Gateway operational again. In the meantime, let's all study this from every angle and try and find a way to proceed."

In the month, since what had come to be known as "The

Blackout", the people of Sanctuary dried their tears, spent time with their neighbors, discussed practical issues with department directors, searched their hearts, and moved on with their lives. For most people, not much changed. The interconnected web of life within the city made it easy for people to go about their work as usual. Teachers were still teachers. Doctors were still doctors. The maintenance crews still cut the grass.

What did change was the inescapable fact the vast inventories of supplies, were now slowly dripping away, like sand through an hourglass. The computer ran projections for what kinds of supplies would be used up first, and the department directors formed committees and study groups to devise ways to replace everything from crude oil to toilet paper. Any number of cottage industries were founded, not to make a profit, but to produce practical means of restocking the shelves.

Admiral Cisco applauded these efforts and made sure significant contributions were recognized and rewarded in the daily newspaper and TV with stories on these "Welfare of the City" entrepreneurs. They still called it a newspaper, despite the fact it was distributed electronically on everyone's computer pads. The idea of wasting paper in such a manner jarred the frugal sensitivities of the public.

The half dozen television channels operating in the city could no longer call up hundreds of networks with an avalanche of material, which no longer existed, from around the world. So, the channels were devoted to daily city news, weather, and a sports channel, now reporting only local sporting events. Also, a popular educational channel with excellent presentations on a wide range of subjects. However, the channel everyone loved devoted itself to pure entertainment of a home-grown variety, everything from karaoke, to magic acts, to productions from a blossoming theatrical company. The channels didn't operate all the time, but every night the people of Sanctuary could watch somebody on the entertainment channel hamming it up for all they were worth or settle in with a favorite movie called from the computer archives which stored thousands of them.

In general, Cisco felt very satisfied with the overall mental, spiritual, and physical health of the people. Not that there weren't still problems. He had to deal with one in particular early on.

"Admiral," said Molly on the intercom. "Gloria Williams is demanding to see you."

"I suppose she's standing right in front of your desk?"

"You got it."

"Okay, send her in."

Gloria Williams came storming into Cisco's office. "When are you going to do something about getting me back to New York?"

"I beg your pardon?"

"You know, New York City, the Big Apple."

"Mrs. Williams, is it possible you haven't been paying attention to the news lately?"

"Well, mister, I don't believe the shit you feed the masses. You have something else going on, and I want to go home."

Cisco sat back in his chair in bewilderment. The longer he sat there, staring at this drama queen, the madder he got. Finally, he said. "We aren't concealing any secret 'stuff'. We've told the people the complete and total truth about everything. Somehow you have chosen to ignore it. Let me spell it out for you. There is no New York City, no United States, and your husband no longer exists in this time. You are marooned here in Sanctuary like the rest of us. All of us have jobs and work to do. That goes for you too, Mrs. Williams. We do not have the luxury of unemployed, unproductive people. As of today, your lounging around at the Embassy Suites is over. The computer will assign you quarters with another single woman in one of the condominium buildings.

Tomorrow you will report to Commander Crenshaw. He will determine your skills and aptitudes, if any, and assign you a job."

"That's outrageous bullshit! I will do no such thing."

"Oh yes you will, and you will make the best of it. Computer, as of now, the woman in my office is on probationary status in the city. She will be permitted one hour to remove her personal items from her room at the Embassy Suites. After that, her key card will be invalid for any city services whatsoever, including transportation, until such time she is given a job by personnel and assigned living quarters."

**_"Acknowledged. Probationary status confirmed for Gloria Williams."_**

"You may not realize it, Mrs. Williams, but right now you are the only unemployed person in this city. You have an hour to pack your things. I advise you not to take more than you can carry because you're on your feet with nothing to eat or a place to sleep until Ben Crenshaw finds you a job. And I'd better not hear any complaints about your behavior, Mrs. Williams because I won't tolerate it. Now get out of here."

Gloria Williams glared at Cisco and then stormed out of his office. When she left, Molly came in.

"I heard most of that, Admiral. Anything out of you louder than normal conversation is a complete novelty. Are you really going to make her sleep on the streets with no food?"

"One night of going without everything won't kill her, and she'll be a lot readier to be reasonable when she sees Ben for an assignment. I'll call him and make sure he gets her in first thing in the morning."

"I can't say I feel very sorry for her. She probably hasn't had a chewing out like that in her whole life. Good for you."

"I'm glad we have only one of her."

"You have two loose ends. What are you going to do with Shannon Fisk?

"Shannon is a different person entirely. In the first place, she genuinely likes Sanctuary. Next, she's better educated. She has a degree in strategic planning. I was thinking of hooking her up with Missy. We're going to need all the help we can, figuring out how to manage the timeline to our advantage. Besides, now that Cameron Fisk is no longer in the picture, Ben is making sure she has plenty of company."

"You aren't thinking of bunking her with Gloria Williams?"

"For heaven's sake, that's the last thing Shannon needs. No, I'm going to make sure Gloria is put with a tough old school teacher or nurse—something like that—Gloria might turn out all right if she has the right kind of tutoring."

"Not bad you, old schemer. Before I forget Hank Winterhawk is waiting to talk to you."

"Who?"

"The Navajo sergeant you sent out to contact the native tribe."

"Oh, right, right. Send him in."

Sergeant Winterhawk marched into Cisco's office and rendered a snappy salute.

Cisco returned the salute. "Have a seat Sergeant and tell me all about our neighbors. I'm sorry I haven't been able to see you before now. After your first contact mission report said you'd established a working relationship with these people, and I didn't need to worry about them laying siege to Sanctuary, I sort of shelved the matter to work on more pressing business. So, tell me the whole story now."

"Well, sir, we went out the morning after meeting with you. We had to wait for dispatch to gather up all the supplies we requisitioned to use as trade goods. We loaded it all on a pack horse, then we mounted up and rode out. We kept in contact with headquarters through the drone. We could sense we were being watched from the time we left the perimeter. Pretty scary. We worried about getting an arrow in our backs. But nothing happened. When we got to the village, it was deserted. Not a soul around, except for one man. It turned out he was the chief and had sent everyone into the bushes while he faced us alone. Meanwhile, he stood in the middle of the village trying to pretend men on horses didn't scare him."

"Your idea to go out with the horses was right on target. Go on."

"I climbed down and made a peace sign to the chief. He got the idea, and we started to talk. I used every sign I could remember and learned a bunch of new ones in the next hour. You would be surprised how well you can communicate this way. Anyway, after a while, people started coming back to the village after they saw we weren't there to kill their chief."

"How did you pass out all the things you took with you?"

"I didn't."

"Maybe you should explain."

"By this time, most of the people had sifted back into the village. With the threat of violence gone, they got real curious about everything. We let the people pet the horses. They were a major topic as the people jabbered on about them."

"You were telling me about not handing out all the trade goods."

"Excuse me, sir; I got distracted. We made an elaborate ceremony of unloading the pack horse. We showed the people every item, from iron cooking pots to blankets, knives, axes, rakes, hoes and so forth. Our slick, recurved bows and deadly arrows got the most attention. The people recognized what they were and you could see them itching to get their hands on them.

"We didn't pass everything out indiscriminately. That would have undermined the chief's authority. We showed the people everything, but we gave them to the chief. It will be up to him to decide who gets what. We did pass out candy to the kids and gave lipstick to the women."

"Very wise, Sergeant. I couldn't have thought of a better way to handle it. Are you of the opinion we have established a strong relationship with the natives?"

"Absolutely, Admiral, I think we can come and go to the village whenever we like. And every time we go, we'll have new things to dazzle them."

"So far, so good, now tell me the downside to this, if any."

"This village is not a single isolated settlement but interacts with other villages. There is active trading between other tribes, plus I think periods of conflict and war. When word gets out about the windfall our neighbors have received, it will spread fast. I've no idea if there are even bigger and more advanced villages in North America, but if there is, you can bet they will come running."

Cisco sat back in his chair. Sergeant Winterhawk hit a nerve. Cisco knew larger cities did exist and not all that far away. He'd seen them from the surveillance flights videos. If word reached one of them, it could mean major trouble. So far, nothing of the military capability of Sanctuary had been revealed. *What if one of those cities decided to mount an armed expedition against the city, believing its most advanced weapons were better bows and arrows?*

He turned back to the sergeant. "Do you have any recommendations?"

"Thanks for asking, sir. I discussed it with the rest of the team, and what comes next. We agree we should not bring any of these people into Sanctuary. The shock of our being a couple thousand years advanced would only frighten them. Still, we need a way to maintain contact and continue to broaden our relationship."

"How do you propose we do that?"

"We think we should establish some kind of buffer outpost,

sort of like a halfway house. It would be open to anybody who wants to visit, or possibly seek medical treatment. We can control the environment completely, building what will be the least frightening and selectively stocking it with materials to offer as trade. In return, the natives can supply us with things they can easily acquire like wild game, tobacco, sugar cane, and most importantly, intelligence regarding any threats or dangers they should learn about from their contacts with other tribes."

"You've done a lot of smart thinking on this. I appreciate it. I'm going to do exactly as you recommend. I'll talk to Colonel Marquis and see about detaching you from your current duties so you can design, build, supply, and then take charge of this trading post. Can you prepare a report detailing everything you will need including building materials, manpower, inventory, and able people to work with you as ambassadors of the city?"

Winterhawk looked dumfounded then smiled. "Damn, Admiral, I guess the scuttlebutt about you is right on. You think smart and don't waste time taking action. Sorry for spouting off like that, sir, I promise to give you my very best effort."

"Make sure the people you recruit have the same attitude." Cisco stood up and came around his desk, reaching out to shake Winterhawk's hand. "Thank you very much for the fine work, Sergeant. I'm looking forward to reading your report."

"I'll start preparing it right away..." Winterhawk paused as if he wasn't finished.

"Is there something else, Sergeant?"

"Just this, sir. These people are not stupid. The fact they have a primitive lifestyle is irrelevant. They are strong, seemingly in good health, and very wise about living off the land. If we were to bring young boys, into the city, and educate and train them, by the time they were grown up, we would have formidable Marines."

"Something to consider."

# Chapter 16
## Another Revolutionary Idea

Exasperated, Missy struggled to crystallize her thoughts to the two men at the table. Hoping for a home-field advantage, she asked for the meeting to be in her office. She sat at her conference table with Scott and Cisco.

"Let me put this another way. We all agree, regardless of the current conditions in the timeline, the safety of Sanctuary comes first?"

"No question about that, Missy, but what you're proposing may be as dangerous as doing nothing. "

"Okay, let's rule that out first. Are either of you in favor of doing nothing and taking our chances?"

Neither, Cisco or Scott said anything.

"Do the three of us have the right to speak for 30,000 people and all their descendants?"

"Computer, what is your analysis of the last minute's conversation?"

*"The most recent poll indicates a substantial majority of the city's population would risk anything for the chance of recovering any part of their previous lives. Additionally, an even higher majority have the opinion all those responsible for producing their current situation be held to account."*

Scott shook his head. "Sounds like we do have the right."

"So, let's take it from the beginning. Managing the past is safer than risking the unknown outcome if we attempt to prevent the original breach in the timeline."

"Is that a question?"

"If you like."

"I'm with you on taking the safer approach. But look at all the many moving, and unpredictable, parts you propose to put in motion. I'm also not comfortable about trying to reform or restrain an entire religion."

Missy flipped her hand. "Islam is not a religion, it's a lifestyle. If we limit its scope and put out the fires of conquest we may prevent a very long list of terrible events from happening."

"Look, I'm all for finding a way to wipe out the damage Aswira did in Europe, and I'd like to see us capture him and snuff his army. The problem comes when we attempt to field a fully-equipped modern military force. Even if we can do it, and it works, how do you know the Muslim leaders will believe us when we threaten to invade the heart of their empire and do the same thing we plan to do with Aswira's army?"

Missy went on without any hesitation. "There are many, many instances in history where military leaders were given a demonstration of what kind of fury was about to be released on them by an opposing army and chose to negotiate the best terms available. Frankly, I think the leaders of Islam will rethink its philosophy of conquest if they face the extermination of its religion."

Scott spoke up. "This is purely technical, but your plan would involve doubling the size of the Gateway. That kind of modification could take years to finish."

"To say nothing of the manpower needed. Where would we find the men?"

"All good points. I don't have any answers. All I'm saying is we have the best chance of restoring some of the fractured timeline if we follow the blueprint I'm suggesting."

Cisco thought a minute then spoke with the voice of decision. "Very well. We'll start working on Missy's plan. I like it better than no plan at all. As we move deeper into it, we may find other avenues to follow which will improve our chances of neutralizing the blackout."

"I'll continue working, Jonas."

"Keep on it."

"I have some better news," announced Scott. "We've finished our final checks. The Gateway is now operational again. Sorry about being so optimistic about the repair time."

Cisco laughed. "As I recall, you said a month."

"Or more."

"Okay, six weeks qualifies as more. Not that I haven't been paying attention, but I've had my hands full getting Sanctuary settled down and running smoothly again."

"I haven't paid much attention to your problems either. How are things going...really?"

"Surprisingly good. Right now, everyone's talking about our relations with the native village up the river. The whole city wants to volunteer to help at the trading post since that's the only way to meet them in person. I have a meeting later today with Hank Winterhawk on that very subject. You're welcome to attend if you're interested."

"I am interested."

"Me too, Jonas."

Cisco poured himself another cup of coffee and offered some to Hank when he came into his office.

He picked up a mug, "Thanks, Admiral, I never seem to have enough."

"That's because you're like me, Lieutenant, always too much to do and not enough time to do it."

"I'm sure having trouble adjusting to my sudden promotion to an officer."

"What did you expect? It was your idea to create an outpost for the natives. I thought it was a great idea. Now the trading post is up and running, and you're overwhelmed with interested people on both sides, which proves, we were both right. We couldn't have such an important addition run by a non-com, so I consulted with the review board, meaning me, and promoted the best man, meaning you, to the job."

"Ha, Ha, Admiral, you're right about being overwhelmed."

Missy and Scott were an interested audience to the little scene. Missy giggled. "If it makes you feel any better, Lieutenant, he pulls the same stunts on us."

"I was about to introduce you to our senior Horizon scientists. The pretty lady is Dr. Missy Long, and the one with the dumb-looking face is Dr. Scott Hauser. By the way, don't tell Missy anything you don't want her to remember, she doesn't forget anything."

"How do you do," said Hank formally. "I've seen both of you on TV, I'm honored to meet you in person."

"Have a seat, Hank, and tell us all the latest about our contact mission." Cisco waved at the conference table.

Hank wasted no time. He sat down and opened his laptop. "Computer, give the statistics on traffic at the trading post since it began operations."

*"The trading post has registered 8,178 visitors since operations began. Many of the individuals have multiple visits. Currently, there are three separate villages in regular contact.*

*Would you like to know the numbers and types of trade items distributed to the native people?"*

"No, thanks, I only needed the basic numbers. The trading post is a busy place. Not only are people gobbling up the tools we give them, but they are loaded with curiosity about us. The natives, known as the Cusabo, can see the skyline of the city and some of the traffic on the roads and trains. They were frightened in the beginning but are growing bolder and more curious every day.

"The absolute best thing I did was to open a dispensary with doctors and nurses. Cusabo mothers have no trouble bringing their children in for treatments of all kinds, from broken bones to influenza. Things that could have killed these kids from not getting treatment get fixed lickety-split. Easily our number one goodwill enterprise.

"I also started a kind of school to teach English. I currently have fifty students on a daily basis. I'd like to expand our learning center and start teaching things beyond language. Sooner or later, these people will want to come into the city, and I think we should start giving them some fundamental education in more advanced subjects."

"Have there been any incidents of anger, hostility, or aggression?" asked Missy.

"Not to us. Some people from other villages have issues with each other. One of the things we made very clear from the beginning was the trading post represented neutral ground—a place of peace, where no one needs fear for their safety. I had to enforce that rule a couple of times in the beginning. You would be surprised to watch some of my martial arts experts at work."

"No, I wouldn't." Cisco turned to the scientists. "I've seen some of the footage of his boys in action. The slickest thing you ever saw. They waded into the fighting and got the natives separated and under control in less than a minute. I don't think they seriously injured anybody."

"How is it you thought of all these things to do, Lieutenant?" wondered Scott.

Hank looked sideways at Cisco, who nodded encouragingly, and then went on. "Sir and ma'am, I'm a Navajo Indian. I grew up on the reservation. Every day, my people asked, or demanded, tools, services, and medical treatment from the government. Sometimes we got it, and sometimes we didn't. It only got better for me after I went to college. When the Admiral gave me this job, I knew from my own life what the natives would need. I made sure we had a peaceful beginning and then kept my word about

209

giving them more than they ever had through fair trade and a spirit of cooperation."

"Very noble, Hank," said Missy. "I have a question. I've read your original report where you outlined your evaluation for all this. I see one point in your report you haven't mentioned. You told the admiral you believed we could recruit the best young boys, about twelve or so, and in ten years turn them into veteran Marines. Is that still your opinion?"

"Yes ma'am, our Cusabo boys would come with the experience of living off the land built-in. Plus, their ability to tolerate hunger, cold, heat and dangers all about them, would make those boys very able for sure."

"Excellent," said Missy tapping her fingers on the table. "Could you do this on a large scale, say three brigades?"

Hank pinched his eyebrows together and then said, "To what purpose, ma'am? That would be over 10,000 men. I can't imagine Sanctuary ever needing such an army."

"You asked me earlier where we would find the men for my plan, Jonas. I think you have an answer."

Cisco blinked and then shook his head from the sudden shift to an entirely different subject. "It might be an answer, Missy, but the logistics of such an operation are mind-boggling."

"We've got all the time we need to do everything we want."

Hank also didn't understand. "Did I miss something here? I think my trading post is an overwhelming job. Hearing even a piece of some conversation you've apparently already had, makes me agree with the Admiral. If you wanted to assemble three brigades, you'd have to recruit from all over North America."

"Exactly," more to Missy than Winterhawk, "Hank would have to repeat his trading post strategy in a dozen places."

"Not if you recruited out of those major cities the recon planes have spotted."

Cisco winced. He had not intended to reveal the existence of significant city complexes to Hank. He hoped the young lieutenant could establish his trading post and strong relations with the nearby native villages without giving him more to worry about until the time came. Apparently, this was the time.

Hank didn't show any surprise. "Our natives speak of a great city to the west. The way they talk is too specific to be idle chatter. That's why I wanted to bring it up today."

"Go ahead, Lieutenant, we might as well thrash this out right now."

"We are already trading with five villages as far away as twenty miles. An exciting and valuable discovery like Sanctuary is going to attract attention on a huge scale. Can you imagine how the story will have grown by the time it reaches one of those big urban centers? I think you need to start planning on a visit from the nearest one of these super villages, and they might not come with peaceful intentions in mind."

"We can't recruit from people we're fighting," said Missy. "We have to buy them off or scare them to death."

Cisco had an immediate opinion. "I vote for intimidation. There aren't enough reserves in the city to maintain some system of tributes."

"How would you do that?" asked Scott.

"Frankly, I don't know. We have a lot of footage of the advanced city closest to us. Maybe you can study it, Missy, and come up with an approach that will work."

"I'll do that, Jonas."

"Meanwhile, Lieutenant, you must have developed an intelligence network among the Cusabo. Make sure they tell you if they hear of any newcomers headed our way."

"Yes sir."

Two days later, Missy knocked on Jonas Cisco's office door, coming into the room at the same time. She plopped down in a chair in front of Cisco's desk.

Cisco turned away from his computer screen. "Maybe I should hire a Chief of Staff to run interference and be the gatekeeper to keep people from barging into my office."

"You already have a Chief of Staff with Molly. She keeps a lot of people out of your office and routine papers off your computer."

"True. You must be on very solid terms with her. Anyway, never mind the interruption. I'd finished what I was doing. What's up?"

"I've been studying the videos from the drone over that city near the mouth of the Mississippi River. I've also done some fairly deep research. I know who these people are. They're Toltecs."

"Excuse my ignorance."

"In our history, the Toltecs were a Mesoamerican civilization predating the Aztec and Mayans, who disappeared sometime in the eighth century. In this version of history, they didn't disappear but continued to expand from Central Mexico. That city to the west is a smaller version of what must be a much bigger Capital city in central Mexico. Even so, I estimate the population at 100,000 plus."

"I'll take your word for it."

Missy plowed on. "According to archaeological records, the Toltecs were a fiercely militaristic culture. They regularly conducted public human sacrifices. Boys were taken from their families at age ten and trained in warfare, religion and associated studies. Sort of like the Spartans in Greece."

"And you are telling me all this, why?"

"A Mexican archaeologist wrote a book about the Toltec culture including what he called 'The Four Agreements'. It represented what is believed to be the basis for their philosophy on life. Here's a short synopsis of what they say." Missy handed some papers over to Cisco.

It took several minutes for Cisco to read the entire synopsis. Then he sat back in his chair and reread it. Missy waited quietly.

"When you read this, it sounds like The Ten Commandments in a wordier way. Tell me why this is important?"

"This is the way to conquer these people without having to fight a war."

"You're going to have to help me out here, Missy."

"If their entire society is based on a deeply spiritual viewpoint, as crazy as it sounds to us, all we have to do is tell them we worship the same deity. Of course, our mutual God rewards our devotion and loyalty, which is why we have so much more than they do. So, if they want the same benefits, they should adopt our beliefs. You can drive the point home graphically. Announce that our common God thinks human sacrifice is wrong. The next time they have a slaughter at the top of their pyramid find a way to blow it up. After that, suggest selected twelve-year-old's come to Sanctuary for training. Keep that up for ten years, and you will have a completely peaceful continent, and an army of veterans to defeat anything we put in front of them."

Cisco shook his head in wonder. "You figured all this out in two days?"

"Not counting time out for lunches."

"Okay, I'm still not convinced of the bigger scope of your plan to revise the Islamic religion, but we sure will need an army to draw out Aswira, which we don't have. At this point we only have the basic outline of a plan. If we're able to start recruiting and training Toltec boys to build this fighting force, the education, and training facility can't be inside the city. We don't have space for it. So, you and Scott need to meet with all your smart people and figure out a way to expand the secondary power dome, so our army doesn't suddenly disappear because of any

213

further ripples in the time stream, by us or anyone else in the past."

"We've already begun that. Scott says it will be a big job and require a major overhaul of our entire system. However, he believes it can be done."

Cisco nodded. "Computer, begin a new file titled 'Recovery Project'. The purpose is to determine means in which changes in time affecting Sanctuary can be reversed. Measure impacts on city reserves and analyze how current city capabilities can reduce them. Also access records relating to Project Horizon capabilities, review data correlating to Toltec interaction, and project all possible outcomes."

*"Acknowledged. File 'Recovery Project' is created. Stated parameters are established. Review of pertinent records is in progress."*

"This is very complex stuff, even for our supercomputer," said Cisco, 'but I don't know any other way to study the data and correlate it into conclusions while maintaining the integrity of Sanctuary."

Missy collected her papers and stood up. "We'll also feed everything into the computer all the equipment we'll need to shove through the Gateway when the time comes to transport our army."

"I'll have the computer break down all the pieces of this wild scheme of yours and ship it off to the command team and the department directors. After they've had a chance to chew on it awhile, I'll call a general meeting, and we'll see where all the booby traps are."

# Chapter 17
# Assembling the Plan

Admiral Cisco glanced up at the clock on the wall of the conference room. The meeting of the combined command team, Project Horizon scientists and the senior department directors started after breakfast, continued through lunch, and now approached dinnertime with no sign of stopping or even slowing down. It had not been without controversy and some heated exchanges.

Currently, Riley led a discussion on military capabilities. "In terms of mounting a major operation, Sanctuary is a lightweight. We can't use our most lethal weapons because they're too large to fit into the Gateway. That rules out all our ships, submarines, fighter aircraft, in fact, any aircraft, except for drones. We have one battery of 105-millimeter howitzers, a couple dozen Humvees, and I guess we can arm some of our bigger ATVs. We have enough small arms and equipment to field three reinforced brigades, about 10,000 men."

"We may be lightweights in modern terms," said Director of Research Lea Solonga, "but based on the scenarios, projections and operational guidelines we've all been studying, what we have can flatten anything in the eighth century without breaking a sweat."

"Sure," said Will Judd, "if your operation is short. What if you have to maintain this army for months? How are you going to feed it, clothe it, rearm it, and provide fuel for the vehicles?"

"We can push supplies through the Gateway in sufficient quantities to handle our resupply," said Scott.

Wyatt hit a nerve. "Who's gonna resupply Sanctuary? None of our planning included attempting anything like this."

"Computer," said Cisco, "display remaining city reserves following an operation of ninety days."

The screen flashed the numbers in each category.

Will whistled, "An offensive running that long would bring us to critical shortages in several areas."

"Looks like food supplies are not one of them, assuming you Horizon guys are successful in doubling the size of the secondary power dome, so we can put more land into agricultural production," said Chips.

"We can do that," said Scott, "if we invade our strategic reserve and bring three more SMRs online."

Chips wasn't satisfied. "Have you also allowed for the power requirements when we have a military camp to house and feed 10,000 soldiers?"

"The added SMRs will cover that easily."

"Speaking of the camp," added Chips, "we don't have enough lumber to construct all the buildings for the troops. How are we going to get that?"

"When we clear the land for farming and pastures for our horses and livestock, we should cut enough timber to supply the sawmill," said Will.

"Let's go back to the combined operation of building an army and then transporting it to eighth-century Europe to trap and defeat the Muslim forces. Computer, factoring in our discussions today, what will be required of the people of Sanctuary to support this enterprise, and how long will it take to get ready?"

*"Based on all new data introduced today, ninety-two percent of all Sanctuary citizens will need to contribute twelve additional hours per week to satisfy the increased workload. Assuming other factors do not further delay the project, we can complete it in ten point six years."*

Cisco spread out his hands like a question. "This is not something we can just announce and expect people to line up to do. What the computer says means everyone shoulders a fifty-two-hour work week for ten years. That's a huge commitment, and people must voluntarily agree to it."

"Tell me you aren't thinking about putting this to a vote?" asked Wyatt.

"Worse than that. This has to be agreed to by a supermajority."

"If it makes you feel any better, Admiral," said Ben. "I don't think the vote will even be close."

"You're closer to the personnel temperature than anyone. You hired all these people. Tell us all why you think the people will support this?"

"Sheer rage. You can compare it to public sentiment following 9-11. Somebody has to pay for marooning us and wiping out all our friends and relatives. This plan gives us a chance to settle the score. Maybe even bring back the man who did this and put him on trial.

"Next, is the sense of purpose, the work toward a goal, even the excitement, and adventure this plan offers. Our people will understand from the beginning we will have to fight hard, and even then, might not succeed. The important thing is everyone works together, leaving everything on the field. Our people have a built-in winning attitude. Put it in the terms I just said, and you will have an almost unanimous mandate."

"Computer, evaluate Commander Crenshaw's analysis."

***"The Commander's summation has a ninety-five percent chance of being correct."***

Cisco stretched his arms above his head and yawned. "It's been a long day. It's been a long week. All of you have worked on your parts of the plan for days. If there are no objections, let's close the meeting and adjourn to a lavish dinner at the O Club."

"Sounds good to me," said Wyatt. "When do you plan to give your speech to the city?"

"Give me a couple days to write it and have all you look it

over to make sure I have included everything. By the way, don't talk about this to anyone. We don't want any wild speculation before I address the entire population. As a matter of fact, what do you think about delivering this speech to everyone at Cooper River Stadium? If Ben's right, the synergy of the entire population of Sanctuary might be infectious."

Cisco had to smile at the synergy among his senior staff. They hooted and pounded the table enthusiastically. The dinner that night was as sumptuous as he promised.

"The TV guys did a great job of getting the entire community fired up for your speech," said Wyatt. "I hope you're up to the hype."

Cisco smacked his fist into Wyatt's ample arm, "Very funny you clown, the last thing I need right now is somebody jiggling my elbow and making me more nervous than I am."

Wyatt gave no quarter, "Look out there. A full house—30,000 people—all ready to hang on your every word, and you could hear a pin drop. They're walking in like it was a funeral."

"Knock it off!"

Wyatt grinned and slapped Cisco on the back. "Relax Jonas. I just said everything you're thinking. Now the worst is over. All you have to do is go out there and tell 'em what you're gonna tell 'em. Those people love you. They trust you. Nobody has captured their hearts like you. If you don't already know that, then you're a bigger dummy than me."

Cisco turned to his friend. "Thanks, Wyatt. You're right of course. I'm not too sure about the love part, but I know they trust me to tell them the truth."

The two looked out the portico. The lights of the stadium burned away the dark of the night. The stage at the end of the stadium held a lectern in the center at the front. Behind were two short rows of chairs with members of the command team, and

Project Horizon seated on one side, and the department directors on the other. Bright spotlights lit the stage.

"Everybody is waiting for the main event. Try not to trip on the stairs when I introduce you."

He didn't give Cisco a chance to say anything and walked out across the track and up the stairs. He went directly to the rostrum. "Ladies and gentlemen, boys and girls, thank you for coming tonight. These last three months have tested us all. Every person here has lost loved ones. This tragedy came from the actions of men who sought to change history for the glory of their religion. I know each of you is burning to strike back. The leadership of our community has worked very hard to evaluate the options we have and to devise a way of giving us a way forward. We believe we have such a plan.

"This is why you are here. The commanding officer of Sanctuary has asked you to come tonight, so he can speak to you face to face and give you the facts as we see them and the future as we see it. Ladies and gentlemen, I'm proud to present your leader, and my friend, Admiral Jonas Cisco."

Wearing his dress whites, Cisco walked slowly from the portico toward the stage. The applause washed over him like a blanket. There was no cheering, only applause. It continued as he climbed the steps and came to the podium. He stood for a brief moment, then raised a hand. The crowd went silent almost immediately, settling into their seats.

"My sons in California and my grandchildren are gone, dead in this version of time. I don't think I will ever see them again. I think of them every day, and I grieve so much it hurts."

The people of Sanctuary had never heard Cisco speak of his family. Most of them didn't know he even had a family. Now, this outpouring of sadness from the man whose steady grip had led them through months of uncertainty and doubt came as a shock. Nevertheless, the community would never have guessed what came next.

Cisco took off his hat and grasped the podium with both hands. The giant screen above him showed the crowd the boiling rage building in his face. At last, Cisco raised a fist in the air and bellowed, "I'm gonna catch the miserable excuse of a man responsible for this abomination and make him PAY!"

A roar began to rumble through the stadium, growing in intensity with each passing second. The memorial service held in the arena three months before had been a time of weeping, and the agony of loss. Since then there had been no occasion to release the profound anger all felt. Now the entire population stood together, drumming their fury along with their leader. The stadium rocked with outrage and cries for retribution.

As the crowd roared, Cisco looked over his shoulder to Missy. She sat next to Chips, who had an arm around her, their hands locked together. She nodded at Cisco, smiling as she winked. It did not matter what he asked of his fellow citizens now. They would do anything he asked, pay any price, make any sacrifice.

Cisco looked back and faced the crowd. Now the jumbotron screen showed them the Admiral everyone knew, rational, measured and charismatic. Cisco saw them as part of a gigantic team with everyone having a role in the life of the city.

The Admiral looked around and began again. "Everyone, including me, must learn to keep our emotions under control.

"We have a plan, based on everything we know about this world, in which we live, and the world of the past, which we will attempt to change. The principal goal is to draw out and trap a Muslim army led by Ahmed Al Aswira, the man who assaulted our Gateway and changed the past for his personal gain. We hope to capture him and return him to Sanctuary to stand trial.

"This isn't going to be easy. It will require a maximum effort by each of you. We think it will take ten years to prepare. Here are the major points."

Cisco went on to explain the plan, in detail. As he spoke, the computer flashed information, graphics, and videos. The people of the city watched intently, many of them taking notes. When he finished nearly an hour later, Cisco concluded by saying, "Now you know as much as we do. For day to day life, I run the city in an orderly manner and keep the trains running on time. This is different. I'm asking you to take on a heavy burden. Everyone has to work overtime for ten years. We think this plan gives us the best shot, but I can't promise you it will work.

"This is not the kind of decision I can make myself for the simple reason I couldn't make the plan work by myself. So, we're going to vote 'yes or no'. If we are going to do this, it will take a lot more than half of us being willing. It has to be almost unanimous.

"Do you want to tell the computer how you'll vote, or are there enough here who've already made up their minds?" Cisco raised his arms. "What'll it be? Shall we go forward?"

Like a bowl of water suddenly disturbed, a wave of people flowed to their feet. Within seconds, Cisco could not tell if anyone remained seated. The rumble of a chant began somewhere and then filled the stadium. The people shouted, "go, go, go, Go, GO!"

❖

At the end of a lengthy conversation with Missy, Riley, and the computer, Cisco made a call. An hour later his office door opened. Molly stepped in. "Ben is here, says you called him."

"I did," Cisco got up from his desk, "send him in." He walked over and had a seat at one the end of the couch.

Ben came into the office. "I always suspect something I don't like is coming when we sit on the couch."

Cisco chuckled. "I guess you have me pegged awfully well. Have a seat."

Ben detoured to the service center and poured himself a cup

of coffee. "If this is going to be longer than a two-cup conference, you need to make another pot." He sat down and sipped his coffee.

"We have started pushing forward on a broad base. We need to begin thinking about how and where we're going to send a task force. To do that, we have to collect a bunch of intelligence. We need to learn how we can move around freely in eighth-century France. Missy and I have thought of a way to do that."

Ben seemed content to wait for more, so he said nothing, and sipped.

"We think we should drop a small team into France a full half century after the fracture in the timestream. Almost surely, Aswira will have died. Other people will be in charge, people with no knowledge of us. If we send in a team disguised as traveling merchants, they should be able to travel freely peddling their wares. Men like that learn a great deal and have general access to nearly every place they go. Also, people don't mind if they're different and eccentric. This disguise will cover up a multitude of sins. After you've gotten the lay of the land, we can start transporting you to a time closer to the fracture."

"You can't outfit a wagon with things not existing at the time."

"Right," agreed Cisco. "Missy is busy researching that very subject. Her idea is to offer merchandise which is sold in other places in Europe, but probably not in northern France. This will make our peddlers popular and increase our chances of collecting valuable intelligence because of blabby customers."

"So, what's the bottom line?"

"We fed the necessary skills for this team into the computer. They include fluency in languages, especially Arabic, and Greek. We need men with combat experience, and razor-sharp in martial arts. They have to have proven ability to think on their feet, adapt to all kinds of conditions, and recognize what kind of intelligence is valuable. Unfortunately, that list is pretty short."

"Besides me, who else do you have?"

Cisco handed over a piece of paper to Ben. "Here are the two officers who grade out the best. They are young, like you, and will become Sanctuary's future corps of leadership. If they do as well as I think, we can bring them back after a few years in the field with you. Then Riley can groom them as brigade commanders. Hank Winterhawk is already serving as Riley's second in command. He and I have already decided to give him one of the brigades. Never mind they don't yet exist."

"Talk about thinking ten moves ahead," said Ben shaking his head. "I can't imagine how you do it, Admiral."

"Keep this quiet. I want you three to concentrate on the mission in front of you."

"How soon do you want us to jump?"

"There's no rush. What is important is to pay extra careful attention to the history lessons Missy is going to give you. Our knowledge of his period is not very complete. Missy will be doing a lot of guessing on what life was really like. Also, we don't know what changes in society have come as the result of our presumed Islamic Caliphate. Don't get me wrong; you will be the best-prepared team in history, so to speak."

Ben smirked at the pun. "I'll talk with the men."

"That's fine. One final point, Ben, I didn't want to send you on this mission at all. You are far too valuable to risk. But the computer says you're the best man for the job, and Missy speaks highly of you from the jump to Fort Collins. Reluctantly, I'm overruled. Be careful and think twice about everything you do. Sanctuary is going to need you when the rest of the command team has moved on."

# Chapter 18
# Reconnaissance

Two weeks later, Ben and his two teammates were sure they'd absorbed more history than all their formal schooling. Day after day, Missy poured it on. Ben and his companions found the information fascinating, but there was so much of it they got overwhelmed and confused.

One afternoon, after a two-hour examination, which Ben was certain he would fail, he led a house revolt.

"Missy, I appreciate all you've done to prepare us for this jump, but I'm certain we're going to have enough trouble just trying to communicate. My French is worthless because the language hasn't evolved. I have serious doubts my Arabic is going to be in common usage at all. In any case, you are preparing us for a world which may have changed drastically by the rise of an Islamic Caliphate. Why are we learning all this stuff about how the ordinary people live?"

"Because life for those ordinary people will not have changed much, no matter who's calling the shots. You will need to be able to mix and interact with the general public as a base from which you can operate."

Dusty Rhoades spoke up. "So, we're wandering vendors. Tell me how the commoners are going to be able to buy anything we have for sale?"

"There are things for which you can barter, fresh food, even labor to help you. Even if most of the lower class cannot buy your goods, you will still need their patronage as a way of protecting you from hostile actions. I'm still not sure vending from a wagon as a cover isn't a dangerous idea."

"I think being traveling salesmen is a great cover," said Jack Kepler. "How come you think the cover is so dangerous?"

"Because, France at this time is barely civilized. You'll have a wagon and a horse. That makes you susceptible to attacks around the clock. You will have to be on guard all the time. I just hope you don't run into a force you can't beat. However, we are going to chance it. I believe the land around Paris will be somewhat more peaceful, and prosperous."

Crenshaw changed the subject. "What makes you so sure Aswira will establish his capital in Paris?"

"I'm not sure. However, Aswira is a 21st Century man. I think he will take what he knows of modern times and decide Paris is the right place for his headquarters. Paris is on the navigable Seine River. The island where Notre Dame is, was, today is a natural place to build a defendable fortress. After his magical display of power at the Battle of Tours, Aswira will be able to demand his capital be wherever he says, and he will be able to conscript the labor to build it."

"Let's hope we don't get swept up in the conscription and forced into work away from the Gateway," said Ben.

"Your cover as merchants probably moves you up the social class enough to avoid that," said Missy. "That's why your training is so broadly based."

As they were speaking, Admiral Cisco came into the room and sat down at the table. Missy smiled at him, and the others started to stand up.

"As you were. I dropped by to hear the latest on your preparations."

"I think I've told these boys about all I know. I was getting ready to start the final planning."

"You mean you're going to send us on summer vacation, teacher?" drawled Dusty.

"It won't be much of a vacation, but at least you'll be going in the summer, or close to it."

"If that's the case, why don't I hang around while you wrap it up?"

"An excellent idea. Ben, why don't you tell Jonas how we intend to proceed?"

Ben picked up a notebook and began speaking as if he were reciting homework. "We decided early on to use the flexibility of the Gateway as an aide. We don't have to slip back to the eighth century and rough it until we find out what we want to know. What we can, and will do, is to come back here as we reach each new step, rest, refit, resupply what we'll need, and then jump back. We can do this as many times as it takes to gather the information we need."

Jack Kepler spoke up. "Initially, we are going to drop into as deserted a place as we can, set up camp, and do nothing, waiting for someone to notice us."

Dusty added. "If the first people who discover us are poor farmers we will invite them to dinner and be generous with gifts. If the first people we see are Muslims, we will be merchant Muslims, and be equally as generous."

"The whole idea is to adapt to the conditions and match them," said Ben. As we learn more and our knowledge of the people grows we can jump back, add the things we need to adapt better and keep going."

"I'm going to place them about ten miles from Paris," said Missy. "Far enough to not attract the wrong kind of attention but close enough to be able to walk to the city and back in a day. If I'm wrong about Aswira establishing his capital in Paris, we can find out where it is, jump back, and then have the Gateway put us in the right spot."

"We can move as often as we like," said Ben. "No one will notice our absence since we'll have the Gateway return us within hours, or even minutes of when we left in the first place. Bit by bit, we will be able to learn the local language, make friends, bribe officials, and gradually settle in. One of us will always be close to the Gateway to make an emergency recall and bring back help if we run into something we can't handle."

"I hope you boys don't grow old and gray getting what we need."

"It certainly won't be a short mission, Jonas, but this way will give our team the most flexibility and protection."

"I agree with that. Any idea when you're going to pull the trigger on this operation?"

"I was thinking of the day after tomorrow."

"Whoa there, ma'am," said Dusty. "When I talked about leaving school for the summer, I was only kidding."

"You men have gotten everything I can give you. These are my best guesses on what you will face and how to weather any storm. There's such a thing as being too prepared. I think we should begin the operation."

"A strange collection," said Logan Richards. "We built it as you ordered, but most of this stuff is junk."

"Junk for us," said Ben. "But several grades better than anything the people on the other side of the Gateway have. We want them to admire our merchandise and equipment, but not enough to set off a mob of looters."

"These bows and arrows you had us make are real old fashioned. I doubt you will be accurate to more than a hundred yards. These cooking utensils are hardly better than wood."

"That's the whole idea. We want them to look like wood," said Jack.

"At least you let us make up serviceable backpacks, even though they give the appearance of being dirty and shabby."

"Believe it or not, we had a long discussion on whether to use backpacks at all. We think they will stick out and cause suspicion. But we couldn't think of a better way to pack supplies when we're exploring the territory near Paris," said Dusty.

"Speaking of supplies," said Logan. "Are you planning on

living off the land? Because you aren't taking any MREs at all."

"That would really attract attention. Better for us if we carry bags of salt, sugar, flour, some coffee, and spices. We can do some hunting and scare up enough to keep from starving."

"Is it true you were all Eagle Scouts?"

"Not me," said Dusty. "I learned all about camping, hunting, fishing, from my dad on the ranch in Montana."

Ben laughed and clapped Logan on the shoulder. "You shouldn't believe all the scuttlebutt."

"Well, maybe, but sending you guys off to the distant past with only a wagon, one horse, and a load of stuff I couldn't give away at a garage sale hardly seems like enough to do the job."

"Everybody is under the misconception this has to be a big operation," said Jack. "We don't want a big operation. The whole idea is to blend in as much as possible. Besides, you all think because we are going back in time almost 1500 years, we intend to stay there. You can expect to see us around here a lot. We plan to come back every few days for more supplies and new equipment to meet the mission."

"Yeah," said Dusty. "We need to come back to take a bath, wash our clothes, and brush our teeth."

Cisco watched the exchange with interest and some amusement. He was glad about one thing. His team didn't seem to be nervous. "If you've got everything you need, I suppose we ought to head for the Gateway"

The conversation, outside the bay doors of the Gateway, went on around the wagon, bulging with standard inventory for an eighth-century traveling vendor. It looked dilapidated, old, shabby and nearly worn out, but had been carefully designed to ride comfortably, carry a heavy load, and contain several hidden spaces for some of the more advanced equipment. The horse came from the herd of draft horses in the pastures of Sanctuary and trained to pull the wagon with ease. At the moment, the horse was not hitched to the wagon, since that would make it too long to fit on the transmission platform.

The team shouldered their backpacks and the rest of their equipment and headed inside to the Gateway They were dressed very simply but didn't appear starving or impoverished. Cisco thought all the preparations and planning had produced an excellent plan.

Despite the late hour, people lined the walls of the transmission center and cheered the men as they entered. The entire command staff waited as well. Scott got up from the control board and walked over.

"You will be arriving before dawn on Tuesday, May 15th, 792 A.D. fifty years following the timestream fracture. We want you to do a quick reconnaissance of the area. If everything is not right, for whatever reason, signal on your bracelets and we'll recall you."

Ben gave him a snappy salute. "Got it, Doc."

All three men turned to Missy, standing behind them. "You fellows are as ready as we can make you. Godspeed."

Ben gave Missy a hug. Dusty and Jack did the same. Then without another word, they took positions around the wagon and horse in the middle of the red circle at the center.

Scott went back to the control panel and operated the controls. Shortly, the crackling blue column enveloped them and they were gone.

Cisco went over to a service board and poured himself a cup of coffee. Then he settled into a comfortable chair. "I think I'll stay for a while."

Chips poured a cup for himself and sat down with Missy. The rest of the command team did the same. Chips glanced at his watch, ten p.m. Sanctuary time, five a.m. in France.

Sometime before dawn, Cisco closed his eyes and slept lightly.

The sound of people coming into the transmission center to relieve those on duty jarred him, and he opened his eyes. During the night, most of the command team headed for home. Chips and Missy were the only ones left. Chips slumped in his chair, snoring softly. Missy had her head in his lap. Cisco thought, *I'm so glad Chips has found happiness again. He and Missy are a sweet couple.*

As if his thoughts were an alarm, Chips snorted and tried to sit up without disturbing Missy, but she stirred when Chips moved. She sat up, smiling at him and patting his cheek.

"Did you sleep at all, Jonas?" asked Chips.

"Just now, and only for a few minutes."

"I suppose no news is good news. The boys didn't jump back right away, so they must have found a place that's safe."

"Happy morning to you, Missy," said Cisco. "Are you awake enough to tell me the protocol for the team to initiate a recall?"

"We've set midnight every night in France as the time for a routine recall. So, at four p.m. every day we will be on alert for their signal. They plan to jump back every four days to start. After they become more involved with people and situations that could stretch out considerably. In any case, there will be someone at the control board 24/7 in the event an emergency makes them have to scoot in a hurry."

"Okay then. I think I've earned some time in a real bed. You two should do the same. The techs will have the computer wake us if something comes up."

"Pleasant dreams, Jonas."

A full house jammed the transmission center four days later. No one knew if the team would signal a recall but nervously waited for it anyway. The clock clicked the hour. Ten minutes passed. Cisco could see tension and anxiety building in the faces about him. He tried to maintain an even and relaxed expression on his face.

A bell rang on the control board. Scott quickly cycled the Gateway. The cascade of energy in a blue column splashed on the transmission platform. The figures of three men, plus their horse and wagon appeared in the cone and sharpened to full resolution. When Hauser switched off the power, the men smiled and raised their arms in triumph. Cisco breathed a deep sigh of relief as the others in the room applauded the returning time travelers.

The first person on the platform was Shannon Fisk, who threw her arms around Ben, obviously not caring her man had filthy clothes, dirt on his face, needed a shave, and smelled. Other friends, comrades, and colleagues also crowded onto the platform welcoming all three. The horse stood placidly.

Cisco sat back and enjoyed the reunion, saying a prayer for the safe return of the team. This first jump had the most uncertainty and peril. There were so many unknowns. The smallest misstep could have been disastrous. Having the men back safely gave him hope future jumps would be the same. Of course, he would soon learn what issues faced them with the debrief. He could wait. The team needed time to decompress, eat well, and sleep soundly. Anyway, all the video footage from their body cams needed to be compiled, analyzed, and edited by the computer.

After breakfast the following morning, the team gathered with the senior leaders to give their report. Ben led the way. "We dropped at the edge of the forest next to a nice meadow. It had a pond and a stream flowing in and out of it. Very handy for us, and also likely to be used by residents of the area."

"We didn't have to wait long," said Jack. "In only an hour or so a couple of men, hunting, walked into our camp. They were real surprised to see our traveling road show. I got my bow and quiver of arrows and went with them. We tracked down a deer, and I made a lucky shot."

"We brought the deer back to the camp, and I dressed it out," said Dusty. "I've done it before when I hunted with my dad, so it went fast. Having a sharp steel knife helps. The natives were impressed and awfully pleased I gave them all the meat."

"All the time, I tried to communicate," said Ben. "I spoke some French and got nowhere. About the only words they understood were 'Paris and Muslims', neither of which got a positive reaction."

"Since we were so generous with the meat from the deer, we got invited for dinner," said Jack.

"How did that go?" asked Cisco.

"It turned out to be a small village," said Ben. "A couple dozen homes, and a separate building used as a gathering place, or a church. The horse got petted a lot, and our wagon got looked over. After everyone had seen enough, we had dinner and felt welcome."

The jump team went on to describe their experiences in the village. The crude tent they'd brought to sleep in, turned out to be several orders better than anything the people had seen before. They pitched it next to the wagon and tethered the horse. The team took turns watching all night to make sure nothing turned up missing, but nothing did.

No matter how hard they tried, the team succeeded in amazing the simple people with each little thing they did or had. "One village woman complained about a headache," said Ben. "I gave her a couple of aspirin. The effect stunned both her and us. She bounced around joyously, gabbling to all the others about how wonderful she felt. A translation would have only confirmed what we saw."

Cisco and the rest of the leadership team listened with rapt attention, as Ben described the next days. His team lived happily with the people, helping with the hard work of farming with crude tools and ingratiating themselves with better tools, and especially when they lent their horse for some of the heavy jobs.

Throughout their time in the village, Ben and the others, would point to things or ask a question with a gesture. They repeated, in English, everything said to them. The discreet body cams soaked it all up, recording it for analysis by the core computer.

After two hours of listening, Cisco sat back in his chair. "Computer, how long to edit the video footage recorded by the jump team and give us a one-hour presentation, showing the important events of their visit to France?"

*"Limiting the recordings from three men over four days to a single hour-long video will require input from the team to make selections on what content to delete."*

"I think I can help with that, Admiral," said Ben. "Computer, what is the current length of your edit?"

*"Approximately four hours."*

"When we finish up here, I'll start working on the final edit. Why do you want it limited to only an hour?"

Cisco took another sip of his coffee. "I thought we might show the people of Sanctuary an insight into medieval France."

"You know, Jonas," said Missy, "that's such a marvelous idea, I think you should do the introduction."

"I rather think Ben ought to do that."

"Oh, he can fill in with narration as the video plays to describe what's happening. Dusty and Jack can join in too, but since you're the one who began our policy of 'maximum disclosure with minimum delay' for the community of Sanctuary, you should start off the program with appropriate remarks."

Cisco looked around the room. The looks on everyone's faces made it obvious he needn't bother to argue. "Thanks a lot, Missy."

# Chapter 19
## Locking Down

Cisco shouted over the clamor rolling through the packed conference room. "Come on people. Settle down here. We've got a lot to do."

The noise abated only a little. Cisco had to chuckle to himself. He couldn't really blame the gushing and bubbling by his hard-working teams. They had labored endlessly these last few months. With all preliminary work complete, it was time to begin the implementation of the primary strategies and campaigns. The teams could not help exchanging overlapping particulars of each part of the master plan.

"I said settle down." This time the command team, seniors of Project Horizon and the directors of the major city departments sat down and began opening the crowded files before them. When the room grew quieter, and people focused on the matters at hand Cisco took a place behind a desk podium.

"A few months ago, the people of our city gave us a mandate. We were told to attempt to restore as much of the past as possible to something recognizable. Nobody wants Sanctuary to continue to be an island in the wilderness with no past and an uncertain future. Further, our citizens demand the people responsible for putting us in this pickle be captured and brought to the city to stand trial. To accomplish this, I talked to the community about the four major things we had to do.

"First, we must devise a way to alter the timeline, so history can evolve predictably. To do this, the subjugation of Europe by Islam must be eliminated.

"Second, we have to build a military force of 10,000 men to do the job. We believe three brigades will be deadly enough to defeat any Muslim armies we will encounter in the past.

"Third, a significant expansion of facilities, and resources, not currently within the perimeter of the city, must be built to house, feed, educate and train this fighting force.

"Fourth, the Horizon team must develop a means of expanding the Gateway field to double the size of the existing secondary field.

"We've had a while to work our big plan. Let's see where we are today."

"If you don't mind, Jonas," said Scott, "I'll go first and get that part of the discussion out of the way."

"Of course. By all means, lead us off."

Scott came to the podium and spoke without notes, "Essentially, expanding the secondary field is a question of sheer power. We've brought three more SMRs out of strategic reserve and attached them to our existing power grid. We already know how to construct the field, so we will use that as a reference point and begin the process of slowly expanding the field. As we go along, there is an incredible amount of work to calibrate the power and adapt it to our existing system. The original idea was not to build a secondary field at all but to produce the transmission core to beam matter. Working the problem backward, especially without Lino to help us, is going to take some time. The outcome of our work will also increase the size of the transmission core so more, and bigger things can be transmitted. We believe we will be able to complete this work within the timeframe already established for the remainder of the goals." Scott stepped away from the podium and took his seat.

"Short and sweet, thanks, Scott. Let's move now to the manpower portion of our plan. For that, Riley will be the commander of our army."

Riley took his place at the podium. Unlike Scott, he had a thick folder of notes. "The manpower for our army has to come from the Toltec Empire. For the past several months we've learned their language from local Cusabo natives who speak

Toltec. We first had to teach them English and then translate that into Toltec. "We started running surveillance flights with drones over the big city to the west. We've learned from the Cusabo, the name of this city is Chitza. It took three months for news of our existence to gain serious interest by Chitzan leadership. Subsequently, they dispatched an armed reconnaissance force of several hundred for a raid on Sanctuary.

"We intercepted this force a hundred miles from here and drew them into an ambush. We killed all but the officers, taking them prisoners. I'm sure they expected to be sacrificed according to their own practices. Instead, we sat them down, fed them lavishly, and then proceeded to give them our prepared statement, acknowledging the sovereignty of their principal god, Quetzalcoatl, claiming it as our own. We then explained how our people had grown in the shadow of this god, whom we call God, and had learned many new things. We talked about how our 'mutual' God led us into a new and glorious life and said the Toltec nation could have the same experience if they were to follow our lead. Then we gave them some pretty slick things, like a bunch of Bic lighters, and sent them on their way back to Chitza."

"It didn't bother you that the introduction of modern technology into this culture could alter their future?" asked Research Director Lea Solonga.

"The lighters, along with all the other gifts we gave them, will soon wear out and be discarded. As modern artifacts, these do not fundamentally change the culture of the Toltecs."

"And also," added Missy, "we can presume our own efforts to recover much or most of our past, will result in a new timeline including us, but excluding the Toltecs. None of their civilization is inside the secondary field. We don't care how much their civilization is changed by the introduction of modern technology since they won't come with us when we alter the old timeline. We hope."

Riley continued his briefing, "The plan is for us to repeat the process with any more expeditionary forces they send out. Then we send in our own delegation, mounted on the biggest horses we've got, plus a company of my Marines, to open talks with their leaders. We hope our presence doesn't set them off. If we get past that, we begin the process of telling them all the things our mutual God does not approve of, including human sacrifice. Then we wait for their next big public sacrifice ceremony on top of one of their pyramids and put on a show of power which should scare them to bits. After that shock sinks in, our team we'll inform their leadership we can bless and reform their society to the true reverence of the Deity, by taking thousands of their carefully selected young boys, ten to twelve years old, to raise in the proper ways. After that, it's just logistics to transport these kids to our facility outside the perimeter and start training and educating them. By the time these boys are men, we'll have the army we need to transport to France and snuff the Muslims."

A general rumble of conversation began as Riley closed his folder and went to his seat. Cisco let it go on for a minute or so, and then returned to the podium.

"Assuming all you've heard so far goes as planned, we have the problem of how to handle as many as ten thousand men. For insight on that, we have, Will, my chief of logistics, and the architect of Sanctuary, Chips Gallant."

Will and Chips stepped up and took their places sharing the podium. "Crews will clear the land," said Chips, "and workers will build facilities to house the recruits. The training center will have barracks, classrooms, a medical center, mess hall, and plenty of room for training and recreation."

As he spoke the screen showed visuals of the nine-square-mile complex. Chips clicked to another image. "Located adjacent to the open areas will be a transient camp of equal size. When the young Toltecs first arrive, they will go there. It's much more rustic and similar to the kind of housing and lifestyles they're accustomed to. This is where they'll learn English and the basics of how life will change when they move to the permanent barracks. It will be a major shock when they do. Nevertheless, this training center will still seem dated to us ... about the level of the 1950s. None of these soldiers will be permitted inside Sanctuary until they are fully grown, trained and acclimated to advanced technology. We estimate two months for construction of both facilities."

Chips stepped aside for Will, who clicked to a different view on the screen. "We will plow an additional 5,000 acres and put it into agricultural production. We have to prepare for 10,000 more mouths to feed. The added strain on inventories beyond that includes clothing, weapons, medical services, and schools, and a long list of other disposable items which we must take from reserves or manufacture ourselves. The computer has run a number of scenarios. The bottom line is the entire population of Sanctuary is going to be very busy for a very long time. I am sending all the data and numbers to your iPads. I suggest you study them thoroughly and be prepared to give me input on ways you can implement each component that applies to your department."

Cisco went back to the podium. "Now we come to the main event. After we raise and train an army, labor for ten years, and devote all our waking hours to getting prepared, we have to take the field and defeat an army which will likely outnumber us five or six to one."

He paused to let those facts sink in. The grim and intense faces around the room told him he had everyone's undivided attention. "The two most critical elements of a successful military engagement are intelligence and surprise. We expect to have both. Let us bring you up to date on what we've done so far. For that, we will hear from Ben Crenshaw. He and his team have already lived and worked in eighth-century France for the last four months.

Ben came to the podium. Dusty Rhoades and Jake Kepler joined him. Even though they were wearing uniforms, they hardly looked like servicemen. Their hair was long, and they had full beards.

Ben smiled at the people in the crowded conference room. "We began our mission a full fifty years after the original time fracture. We believed this would be long enough for the initial conspirators to have died and left their caliphate to others. We wanted to know how extensive the occupation of Europe by Islam was, and get a grounding on their principal strongpoints.

"We went originally as traveling merchants," said Dusty. "This gave us natural cover, and people expected us to be kind of odd and different in the first place, so we didn't attract undue attention.

"We were at a great disadvantage when we first arrived," said Ben. "We didn't know the country, the customs, the laws, the disposition of the military, and worst of all, we couldn't speak the language. It took us weeks to become fluent enough in the local dialect to carry on a conversation. It would have taken much longer if we hadn't made regular jumps back here and had the computer translate the language from our video logs and build us a vocabulary."

"Fortunately for us," added Jack, "we dropped near a small village whose people loved and appreciated what we did for them, and absolutely despised the Muslims. We made that our headquarters while we spread out to gain what information we could."

Ben picked up the narrative, "Eventually we felt comfortable enough to make some individual visits to Paris. Missy had it right when she said Aswira would pick that for his capital. In fifty years it had grown to be an important city, filled with merchants, travelers and a considerable number of Arabs who had migrated to France to snatch everything resulting from the Muslim victory over the Franks."

"Ben wouldn't let us take the time today to describe what life is like for the non-Muslim population," said Dusty. "I will only say it is terrible in every possible way. I have written a long report and made it available to all you if you'd care to read it."

"Aswira had indeed died, some years before we arrived," said Ben. "He left the caliphate to two sons from women he married after arriving in France. Conditions for the common people went from bad to worse. About the only way to get some small relief was to convert to Islam, and a great many people have done so."

"In our village, there is a general nod to Islam in public and to government officials," said Dusty. "Privately, they continue to worship God in the traditional Catholic manner. Once we convinced them we weren't spies and were Christian ourselves, we were even more accepted."

"The people in the village do not own their land," said Ben. "They are tenants on extensive lands owned by the Martel family. Charles Martel was killed at the Battle of Tours, but his son, Pepin, took over and continues to manage the family holdings. He began an active trading business with the Muslim caliphate supplying grain, wood, fresh vegetables and laborers to the palace in Paris. When we first met him, he was quite old, and could barely pay his taxes. Fifty years of being drained by the Muslims depleted almost all his resources."

"We used a drone to map the land," said Jack. "Pepin's lands are extensive, hundreds of square miles, enough to conceal our brigades of soldiers when we transport them, and we've picked a place to mount an offensive against a Muslim army."

"After we got a better picture of the conditions in France," said Ben, "we changed our tactics and started jumping to the time

240

shortly after the fracture. We have to be extremely careful. Aswira is still consolidating his conquest, and we can't attract any attention at all for fear of being discovered. We are back at Pepin's large land holdings. He's a much younger man now. We are giving him some strategic assistance in the form of salt, which he is using to buy off the Muslims and maintain his position."

"Excuse me, Ben," asked Ed Watkins, the Education Director. "Tell me why you are using salt?"

Ben smiled. "These days we don't think about salt at all since it's so plentiful. Not so in medieval times. Salt doesn't come easily to most people. It has to be mined and carried long distances. It has the same value as money. Pepin can't pay his taxes in gold. The Muslims will think he has more of it and sack his chateau. With salt, he can say he has a steady supply, and his means of obtaining it is none of their business."

"That's very resourceful, Ben," said Watkins.

"It's not my idea. Missy used her extensive knowledge of history to figure it out."

"In any case," said Dusty, "in return for the salt we got a grant of land of our own. We picked a spot, several miles from the estate's chateau. Computer, show the location."

A video flashed on the screen. A ridge of densely forested hills surrounded a valley in a U-shape. At the open end, a small river flowed out; at the other end, a waterfall poured into the valley.

"This is ideal for us," continued Dusty. "We tapped the waterfall to run a turbine connected to a generator to give us power. A crew of workers and materials made jumps through the Gateway to build an oversized barn. We even put solar panels on the roof to generate more power. This gives us a fundamental infrastructure where we can live and work in private, and safely jump back and forth to conduct our expanding operations."

"The barn looks very ordinary from the outside," said Ben.

241

"Inside is a much different story. All the comforts of home, so to speak."

"Even though we are Pepin's trusted confidants and loved by the common people, we're still a mysterious and scary lot," said Jack. "We don't have to worry about people being curious. Our headquarters is given a wide berth by everyone, including the Mayor. However, we still have intruder sensors located throughout the area, and one of us is always on guard."

"Every day we learn more," said Ben. "During the next ten years, while Riley is growing an army, we intend to flood the area with spies. When the time comes to begin our major operation, we'll know what Aswira has for breakfast."

"Aren't you afraid of being ratted out by one of your spies looking for personal gain?" asked Logan Richards.

"None of our spies will be Franks. We'll use volunteers from Sanctuary."

"But that means asking our people to live in a primitive society, maybe for years. If they get caught they might be tortured or killed."

"Sounds risky, doesn't it? And it is. I've chatted around with my Coast Guard compatriots on the subject. They recognize the hazards and were highly annoyed when I said few of them will be picked for the assignment."

A titter of amusement drifted through the room.

Cisco came back to the podium. "So that's the plan. If any of you have a better idea, now's the time."

The room was silent.

"Okay. You don't have to come up with anything right now. I'm going to let you study the details, especially as they relate to your own areas of responsibility. The computer will help a lot with this. It has all the numbers, production capabilities, and available personnel. In a week we'll meet again, and I'll ask the same question. After we've finalized the entire undertaking, we'll put it into a video package we can show to the entire population. Don't be surprised if a lot of people are able to add new, better, more efficient ways for us to proceed. I've always thought having a hundred or a thousand people thinking about a problem is better than one person. I hope the smart citizens of Sanctuary can think of many better ways to carry out this over-sized job."

❖

And that's the way it turned out. A week later, the city leaders convened again, and made numerous additions to the master plan. The video production techs edited the results into a two-hour special, which was then aired on television to the entire community. Cisco introduced the production, and each of the senior leaders narrated their own sections of the plan with pictures, graphics, and video inserts to highlight each important part.

When the program finished, Cisco, seated at his desk at the headquarters building, came back on camera. "Six months ago, you asked us to come up with a plan to restore as much of our history as possible and extract justice from the people responsible who illegally stole our past, our families and our lives. What you've just seen is the result of your call to action. None of us who devised this plan, believe it is complete. I think each of you may have something valuable to contribute. I urge you to review those sections of the plan which fall into your areas of skills and talents. Look more deeply, with the aid of the computer, to examine the project in greater detail. Come up with new ideas. I can assure you, every department head has an open mind and open door. Don't be shy about expressing your opinion.

"Finally, let me emphasize what this means. We are about to embark on a dangerous, unpredictable and long journey. I can assure you, your command team will work steadily, purposefully, and relentlessly to accomplish our goal. Join me now and do the same."

# Chapter 20
# Into the Future

So, "Operation Recovery" began. All four of the major parts of the plan moved forward.

Riley continued to gather intelligence on the Toltec Empire. He and everyone else in his company-sized strike force were learning the Toltec language while sharpening their skills in tactical operations. They got a chance to put their training to use a month later when a larger force of Toltecs was intercepted a hundred miles from Chitza. As before, only the senior leaders survived the ambush and were treated the same as the previous war party. They were fed a lavish meal, loaded with presents, and sent back to the urban metropolis with assurance the strange people to the east, armed with powerful weapons, were not enemies, but wished to establish peaceful relations.

Scott and the Horizon team struggled to devise a way of doubling the size of the secondary field. The work was complicated because while the research progressed, the Gateway transmission center had to remain operational.

Ben hadn't waited while other planning went on. His mission had already begun. He wasted no time putting new elements into the Frankish operation. With a base established from which more extensive ventures could be launched, Ben started recruiting people to serve as spies and informants.

Ten men and two women were seated at desks in a room watching a special video presentation showing footage, previously unseen by the people of Sanctuary, of life in the eighth century. The pictures showed how primitively most of the population lived. Those who thought it would be thrilling to jump back in time fifteen hundred years were seeing the stark reality of what to expect, and how they would have to live. There was nothing adventurous about it.

When the video finished, Ben came to the front of the room. "Grim and ugly, isn't it? Every day will be a struggle. Not only will you have to live in these shoddy, unclean and dingy conditions but you will also have the added burden of concealing everything connected to modern times, while still carrying on an active intelligence-gathering mission. We'll take every possible step to ensure your safety. However, this work will be unpredictable and always very hazardous and dangerous. I thank you all for volunteering, but now that you've seen what it will really be like, you may have second thoughts.

"This is your first opportunity to drop out. In fact, you can change your mind any time before the transfer jumps begin. The training will tax you to your limits, both physically and mentally. As we proceed and you see the full scope of your involvement, you may decide this is not for you. Or we may find you don't meet the physical, mental and emotional standards necessary. In such case, we will drop you from the program, no matter how much you object. We know what's ahead better than you. Trust us when we tell you it's for your own good to find other ways to contribute to Operation Recovery.

"Now, I'm going to leave you alone for a few minutes. While I'm gone search your hearts and minds. If you can't bring yourself to shoulder this commitment, leave. No one will think less of you."

When Ben came back ten minutes later, there were three fewer people in the room. He started a dozen groups in this way.

The training covered a wide range of studies, including learning a new language, physical exercise, self-defense, comprehensive first-aid, and the fundamentals of tradecraft in espionage. Two months later, he had fifty men and women who survived the challenging program.

Bit by bit, he cycled these people into the past and set them

245

up as traveling traders, merchants with small shops in the urban areas surrounding Paris, soldiers with advanced skills, and several other trades. Their jobs were to maintain the masquerade and still be in a position to gather intelligence of all kinds. He supplied them from the base, inside the lands of Pepin, the Mayor of the House, using an intricate system of rendezvous and drop points scattered around the countryside so not to attract attention to the base itself.

As time passed, this network become deeply entrenched, and blended into the daily lives of the unsuspecting Frankish people. The conducted business would be done, and a steady stream of intelligence flowed to the Frankish headquarters and ultimately into the Sanctuary database.

Chips began construction on the two centers they would use to train and educate a flood of young boys to mold into a fighting force, ten years in the future. Working on the assumption the Horizon team would find a way to expand the secondary field, he and Will began the job of building the camps to train and house an army.

"I haven't asked," said Chips, "but what does all my ordering of equipment and supplies to build this mini-Sanctuary do to our strategic reserves?

"Well, that depends. If, when we finish rejiggering the timeline, we end up with something close to the 21st-century world we had, then we can probably expect to replace and restock everything. If not, then I would say future Sanctuary two or three generations down the road are in serious trouble."

"That sounds like everything around here. We don't know much about nuthin'. I suppose we have to go ahead and do the best we can. Okay, the computer says we need to build a post for our soldiers three miles square, and a transient camp for the kids the same size. For each camp, I need to build quarters designed for two men per room in two-story buildings. That will mean over a hundred buildings. Each building needs a common area, toilet, and shower rooms. Then we have to build classrooms, mess halls, and an advanced infirmary. Add to that a training center and recreation area and the rest of the service buildings. I'm gonna start with the transient camp since that's where our first bunch will come. Anyway, I've got to build that part of the project in two or three months."

"Can you do that?"

"If we recruit every man and woman in the city who can swing a hammer."

"I think I can help take off some of the pressure on available manpower to clear and plant all the new fields for crops and pastures using the Cusabo. Hank Winterhawk told me the other day that these people really want more of our better tools, household goods, hunting equipment and so forth, and are willing to work to get them."

"With our reputation, we should attract a lot of men from a long way off. How are we going to feed them?"

"Food is the least of our worries. I can handle as many as show up."

"Then tell Hank to spread the word, and we'll put 'em to work."

A month passed quickly. Every day for Cisco went by with a stream of people in and out of his office with reports, issues, complaints, challenges and surprises. This day brought something unexpected.

His intercom buzzed and Molly said, "Admiral, there's someone here to see you."

"Who?"

"Maybe I should just bring her in."

"Okay."

The office door opened and Molly came in followed by a much-changed Gloria Williams. Gone were the fancy clothes, the heavy makeup, and the perfectly styled hair. In its place was still a very attractive woman who looked like she spent a lot of time outdoors with a natural tan, a pair of rumpled shorts and a clean, but somewhat faded T-shirt.

Molly stood away, and Gloria walked up to Cisco's desk. "I've come to see you, Admiral, because I want to give you my most sincere apology."

Cisco glanced at Molly, who gave him a grin and a nod.

"I don't think you need to apologize. But you sure look a lot different from the last time I saw you. Why don't you have a seat and tell me what's been happening in your life." He got up and came around to one of the couches waving a hand to invite Gloria to sit next to him.

"When I came here the last time, you delivered some awfully tough love. I resented it at the time, but you didn't give me a lot of choices. I hated sleeping on a park bench and going without anything to eat for a day. When I went to see Ben Crenshaw the next morning, he asked me what I could do. I'd thought about that a lot while I sat on the bench, so I told him, honestly, the only thing I really knew a lot about was gardening. I was ashamed to say I didn't have much to offer."

"I'll bet Ben didn't see it that way."

"No, he didn't. He said having pretty growing things in Sanctuary made people happy, and he was glad to find someone who could contribute in that way. So, I went to work with the crews who spend their time taking care of the extensive landscaping in our city. I found myself drawn to the work. I made friends ... real friends. Before I knew it, I found myself getting up before dawn every day, and looking forward to work. All I do to get ready is comb my hair and put on a little lipstick."

"You look great to me, Gloria. Good work outdoors in the

sunshine agrees with you. I'm happy you found something you like."

"As time has passed, I've thought a lot about my life. The last few days we've been working around City Hall, and I remembered everything you said to me. I felt like it was time for me to tell you in person how sorry I am for what I used to be."

"I've noticed all the new flower beds out front. Is that your handiwork?"

"Me and a couple others. The design is something I saw once in a magazine. Do you like it?"

"It's beautiful. You've found a way to make a real contribution. I'm proud of you."

Gloria dabbed her eyes with her T-shirt. "That means more to me than anything. Thank you very much, Admiral. You're like the dad I always wished I had."

Cisco got to his feet and put out his hand to Gloria. It surprised him when she threw her arms around his neck and hugged him warmly. Then she sniffed and wiped her eyes again. "I gotta go. I told the guys I wouldn't be long. We've got a lot to do today." She rushed out of the office.

Molly lagged behind, "Not much comes into your office that isn't a major issue or a crisis. It's good to see something wholesome and rewarding."

"Amen to that. I'm glad Gloria has found some meaning and purpose to her life."

Cisco worked in his office the rest of the day, teleconferencing with several department directors. He had dinner delivered and munched a sandwich as he worked. He jerked in surprise when his intercom buzzed. "Molly, why didn't you go home hours ago?"

"Who's going to hold your hand if I'm not here? Chips and Hank Winterhawk are waiting to talk with you."

"Let's have them."

Cisco headed to his conference table as Chips and Hank came in. "Howdy, let's sit here."

Hank opened a thick file. He'd learned not to waste any of the Admiral's precious time. "We jumped the gun on bringing recruits in for training at the transient camp. I've spent a lot of time talking with the Cusabo. They aren't huge believers in the gods of the Toltecs, but they sure are interested in ours. They don't care if we call Him Quetzalcoatl or Donald Duck. They want to be included in what we're doing with our construction projects. We've gathered up a couple hundred young boys from tribes throughout the area and started them on the training project."

"No kidding? So how are the boys adjusting to their first smattering of an advanced civilization?"

"Remarkably well. After they got over the shock of living about fifteen grades higher than they're used to, they settled in and are gobbling up the learning, despite the training being demanding both physically and mentally. Quite a few had some understanding of English which helped a lot. I have to say, Admiral, the Cusabo have absorbed a tremendous amount after six months of rubbing shoulders with us."

"Are you of the opinion it'll be the same with the Toltecs?"

"Most likely. Boys that age are all about the same. We are introducing them to complicated battle tactics, but they regard them as exciting games."

"How do suppose the Cusabo will get along with the Toltec boys?"

"Probably all right. All of them will be forced to deal with the same demanding drill instructors. That environment will likely make allies of them against a common opponent."

"What do you estimate our wash-out rate will be?"

"Maybe twenty or thirty percent."

"Computer, what contingencies are there to deal with

individuals not measuring up to our standards?"

*"Some of the personnel may have mental skills allowing us to train them in different areas. The majority who are dropped from the program will be returned to their homes without a sense of failure."*

"Explain."

*"The training is unique and specialized. With such a narrow band of qualifications, those without the skills to complete the training regimen will be grateful for the experience and consider themselves better because of it. Further, what they do learn will be of value to their own culture."*

"Something like not completing Seal training. Men are sorry they didn't make it to the end but happy for the opportunity."

"That sounds right to me too, Admiral."

"Construction continues all over the camp," said Chips. "We have most of it finished. Certainly, enough to handle the Cusabo recruits. We have all the basic structures up, the barracks, classroom building, medical center, and admin headquarters. My carpenters are working on the interiors now. I expect another six weeks or so to finish."

"What about personnel for training, teaching, doctoring and so forth?"

"Everything would go smoother if we had Ben, but he's a little busy in France right now. It will help if Riley assigns us some drill instructors. I hope he can give us a hand."

Cisco sat back in his chair. "Wyatt has picked up the slack in a lot of the areas when guys on the command team are not around. I'll see what he can do about getting the right people into the transient camp."

# Chapter 21
# Taming the Toltecs

Some months after the initiation of Operation Recovery, Admiral Cisco gathered those who remained from his command team in the operations center. Ben and his team were back in France. Will was commanding a small task force with a destroyer and a cargo ship in the Gulf of Mexico.

Cisco wanted his commanders to gather in front of the computer screen and watch the end of a delicate campaign led by Riley. The operation began with the defeat of a new, much larger force of Toltecs, on their way to Sanctuary, quite near the city of Chitza. Cisco believed if they smashed this war party almost on the suburbs it would be possible for his troops to accompany the survivors back to the city and engage in negotiations with city leadership. Doing this might prove disastrous to the Sanctuary strike team.

They were a small group to begin with, only a company-sized force. Walking, or in the case of the Marine officers, riding in on horseback at the lead of the column followed by the captured Toltec leaders with the Marines in formation behind, might result in the Chtizan leaders ordering an attack on the foreigners. Even armed with modern weapons, the Marines would be heavily outnumbered. It would be a bloody battle but they would still lose.

Cisco knew this but reasoned the two previous encounters of shock and awe by expeditions sent to raid Sanctuary would make the sovereign of the city think twice before ordering such an action. Particularly if the surviving Toltec officers were mixed in with Riley's seasoned veterans. It was still a gamble. Everything Sanctuary did on a daily basis was an equal challenge.

An overhead drone sent a live feed. Hank had a camera focused on Riley to give updates. The computer had a choice of many other body cams to fill in the entire picture.

Riley gave a running report as the company came to the edge of the city. "I think it's a good sign we haven't seen any organized resistance. There sure are a lot of people watching us as we pass. I'm using military precision combined with a little Hollywood. I've got the company marching and horses carrying speakers on the sides playing loud music."

 Pictures, provided by the drones, showed Marines marching smartly, despite being dressed in battle armor and wearing full packs. The music blared, and people covered their ears or ran away as the company passed. The faces of the people ranged from curiosity to terror.

"What's that music Riley's playing?"

Cisco sat back in his seat and grinned at Wyatt. "That is the fight song of the University of Southern California Trojans."

"You're kidding"

Cisco chuckled. "Perhaps much more appropriately, the music came from an old movie called 'Captains from Castille' when Cortez entered the capital of the Aztecs."

Everyone watched as the tiny army of Sanctuary marched into Chitza.

The formation moved down the stone street and into the central plaza of the city. Pyramids rose hundreds of feet high on both sides. Directly ahead a palace stretched across the end of the plaza. In the center stood a broad platform. Several hundred men were crowded onto it, many wearing colorful costumes and jewelry that glittered with gold. A massive throne stood in the center. Its sole occupant, a regal looking man. The sleeves of his jewel-crusted garment flowing over the sides of what appeared to be solid gold armrests.

Riley looked into the camera "I'm not going to give this head honcho time to think."

As soon as he said it, he started shouting orders. A squad of

Marines escorted the captives off to the side. Riley, Hank, and the other officers rode their horses almost to the platform and formed a line of five men on five colossal horses. Their faces stern. Their posture erect. The company of Marines behind them began marching in the precise formations of a crack drill team.

Chips leaned closer to Cisco. "Isn't that the same show they put on at the 4th of July Jubilee?"

"The very same. I think the effect on the crowd will be somewhat different."

Cisco was right. Thousands of people had poured into the plaza with the Marines and looked at them with awe and wonder. All were accustomed to seeing their own soldiers gathered in semi-symmetrical formations for ceremonies and public events. None of them had ever seen soldiers such as these. They were gigantic men, moving gracefully, without a hint of hesitation.

The ceremony finished with all the Marines shouldering their rifles and firing a three-round volley into the air with three sharp, ear-splitting cracks. The entire mob of thousands took a collective several steps back, as did all the men on the platform.

"Watch this. Riley is about to make a speech."

The horses carrying the speakers divided into an expanded circle around the company of Marines, facing partly toward the crowd, but mostly at the broad platform.

Riley got off his horse, walked up the stairs, and stood facing the sovereign of the city. He spoke to him, but his voice boomed from the speakers. He spoke in fluent Toltec. "Greetings to the people of Chitza. We salute you, noble master of the city. Only recently, we have discovered people of our own kind living in this land. We are happy to know we share the same god, known to you and us as Quetzalcoatl. For many, many years we have followed the teachings of our god, and he has blessed our people. We have learned much, and have much we can teach you, so your people will also be blessed. We come today to offer ourselves as your friends, companions, and partners in trade and commerce. How say you, great Master? Will you open your doors and your hearts to us in fellowship?"

"Nice speech," said Wyatt, listening to the computer's translation. "Didn't know Riley had it in him."

"He didn't. The Computer wrote the speech for him. She sifted through a million facts and came up with the words. It's designed to influence these people at their most vulnerable spot, their religion, and to produce the highest probability of a positive outcome. I hope she's right. Otherwise, we are about to lose a hundred of our best men and be back at square one."

"Hold it," said Chips. "Looks like the mayor, or whatever he's called, is gonna say something."

The chief of Chitza rose from his chair. He walked regally forward toward Riley. He was not an old man but one in his prime. He gave every impression to Cisco's practiced eye of having no trouble being in charge. Cisco could also see he was forcing himself to appear calm as he stood half a foot shorter in front of this tall and stern stranger.

Riley broke into a measured smile and put out his hand. The chief looked at it, and then put out his hand as well. Riley gasped it in a firm handshake.

"This is very good," said Cisco. "This head of state for Chitza is likely used to people bowing and scraping. Riley is meeting him on equal terms, and the man accepts that."

The chief smiled now as well and turned to speak to the assembled men behind him. His voice came out deep and clear. Nobody in the room understood what he said until the computer began a translation. The gist of the words was that the people of Chitza welcomed their new friends and looked forward to knowing them better and learning the lessons of Quetzalcoatl which had given them such wondrous things.

When the chief finished speaking, the crowd of officials on

255

the platform began to gather around Riley more closely. Riley spoke into his mike. "So far, so good, Admiral. After I get the men settled, I'll begin hauling these people out of the Dark Ages. Should be interesting. When something new happens, I'll report in."

"The show is over for the moment. Likely, the mayor of Chitza will throw open the doors of hospitality, and there will be lots of celebrating and posturing by the natives. The computer will keep track of what goes on and alert us when we get to the next phase of the plan."

Missy acted as Cisco's tripwire to manage the changes to the timestream created in the present by the introduction of new and frightening revelations to a continent of people a thousand years behind Sanctuary's advanced technology.

"It's disturbing to me, Jonas," she said during an evening conference and dinner in his office. "On one hand, we're doing everything we can to restore events in the past, so we might have a more predictable present. On the other hand, we are exposing people in this present to any manner of modern technologies, which will change history for them."

"That's undoubtedly true. But since we expect to get our own past back by patching the fracture in the timestream created by Aswira, won't that mean we will leave this present behind? Why should we care about this new branching timestream?"

"I wish I had an answer for that. Everything we are doing represents a long list of unknown variables. What if pieces from the civilizations we are changing, bleeds into the reality we are seeking to restore? What if our meddling in the timestream from our own past produces a different outcome then the 'old' present we want to engineer? All it will take to distort the new timestream, in France, is the introduction of even the most trivial of any of our technology to the people of the past."

Cisco rubbed his brow as if he were attempting to wipe away the discomfort. "Just listening to you switch back and forth from old history to new history gives me a headache. Marching along and implementing all the events we've set in motion, gives the illusion of development and progress. I wonder every day if we are doing the right thing, ... taking the right steps."

"We all agreed a long time ago that doing nothing was not acceptable. For better or worse, the pathway we are following seems the most logical and least damaging of anything I can imagine."

Both sat bolt upright when the Computer announced, ***"Admiral, there is an emergency transmission from Colonel Marquis."***

"On screen."

The screen flickered and then Riley's face appeared. "Admiral, our civilians were attacked. We have five dead."

"What's happened?"

"I'm trying to get a better picture. The specialists we brought ashore from the cargo ship, were attacked at dinner in an open-air plaza tonight by a bunch of men armed with war clubs. I had Hank with a squad of Marines escorting them, or we would have lost the lot. By the time the shooting stopped, we had five fatalities, and a dozen wounded. On top of that, we have two missing men."

"Did they get lost in the dark?"

"Unlikely. I'm suspect they got hauled off when we were breaking up the mob."

"What about the injured?"

"Evacuated to the cargo ship. The medical staff is working on them."

"If you have the immediate situation under control, you need to start searching for our people."

"Already underway. I've got the whole company sweeping

the city."

"I thought everything was going all right."

"Me too. In the last month, we've been wined and dined here in Chitza. The local leadership is obviously anxious to please such advanced and deadly visitors. We've taken advantage of that."

"Then why this outbreak of violence?"

"Two days ago, a contingent of officials and many soldiers arrived here from Tula, the Toltec capital, down in Mexico. Since then conditions with the local government have cooled. I get the feeling these new people don't believe the story they hear from Zontamuza, the sovereign of Chitza. The civilians we brought in to start sessions on science, technology, and religion were already here. We thought it was safe to bring them ashore. When relations began to go south, I had Hank take some Marines and guard the unarmed civilians."

"That was smart. How many Toltecs did your guys shoot?"

"Twenty dead. A number of others ran away."

"What's your plan?"

"At first light tomorrow, I'm going to storm into Zontamuza's throne room and demand to know where our missing men are, and why my people were attacked. I figure the top brass from Tula will be there as well. I'm not going to very cordial. Meanwhile, I've got my Marines back in body armor and on full alert."

"Call me back when you learn anything."

"Will do, Admiral." The screen went dark.

At first light, Riley and Hank went directly, with a squad of Marines, to the palace of Zontamuza. All were dressed in full battle gear. The men carried rifles. Riley pushed past the guards at the entrance and weren't stopped until he got to the doors of the Hall of Kings.

"You may not enter the chambers of Zontamuza without his

permission," said a gaudily dressed gate-keeper.

Hank shoved the man against the wall, the point of his knife against his throat, "We are going in. If you want to live you will stand aside."

Riley's Marines overpowered the three other guards, leaving them in bloody pools on the floor. Riley pushed open the doors, shoving the guard in front of him.

Zontamuza broke away from the group he was with, and walked quickly over to Riley, his hands out to the side. "Please Konel, this was not my doing. The Grand Minister of the Great Natchala has come from Tula. Natchala does not believe you are the sons of Quetzalcoatl. Neither does he believe you possess better weapons and have much power."

"Where are my men?"

"They were taken by warriors of the House of War. In all the realm of the Toltec, there are no greater fighters. The Grand Minister will sacrifice your men today as an example of the power of Quetzalcoatl, over your boasts."

"I will speak with this Minister,"

"He will not speak to you."

"Are you not the sovereign of Chitza? Order the release of my men."

"Natchala is my brother but is still my master. I must obey his command."

"Zontamuza, if Natchala doubts we are the true expression of the will of Quetzalcoatl, he will see for himself this day in Tula, as will your Grand Minister, here in Chitza. Death and destruction will come to your city. My people will not be sacrificed and will be returned to me unharmed."

"I wish it were otherwise, Konel, but when the sun has risen to its highest, the grand pyramid will run with the blood of your comrades."

Riley turned on his heels and stomped out of the chambers.

Moments later he was on the radio, speaking urgently to Cisco in Sanctuary.

❖

Jonas Cisco sat at his desk with his hands cupped over his face. *Five good people dead. Two more facing a public execution. If I were my commanding officer, I'd relieve me for dereliction of duty. There's nothing for it now. I've done all I can.*

His dark thoughts and fears were interrupted by Molly on the intercom. "Admiral, they are ready for you in the ops center."

"On my way." Cisco wondered why he hadn't been notified by the computer.

"If you want to know why it's me telling you this instead of the computer. I told her to send the message to me first. This is one time when you needed to hear flesh and blood."

"Thanks, Molly, you read my mind."

"That's why they pay me the big bucks. Better get moving."

Cisco took the elevator down to the ops center. As he walked in, the big screen covering the back wall displayed multiple pictures from the body cams of the Marines in Chitza, plus another set of images showing the bridge of the destroyer Alamo anchored off the delta of the Mississippi in the Caribbean. Chips was standing in front of the screen.

Cisco ordered sharply, "Report."

"Riley has his company formed, and they are ready to march into the plaza," said Chips.

Cisco watched the signal from the drone. It looked like the entire population of Chitza filled the plaza. The sun had reached its zenith. The Grand Minister came striding out of the palace. No less than two hundred soldiers came with him along with the other members of the official delegation from Tula.

In the center of the formation of soldiers were the two civilians. Cisco could see they were terrified but otherwise uninjured. The soldiers came down the stairs from the palace

260

pushing people aside as they made a corridor for the Grand Minister. The two men were driven by another squad of soldiers behind the Minister. The entire contingent moved steadily to the base of the central pyramid.

Cisco sat down in a chair facing the screen. "Riley says his informants inside Zontamuza's inner circle told him the Grand Minister will climb to the top of the pyramid with a few of their holy men and speak to the people of Chitza. He will tell everyone we are frauds and prove it by executing our people. I hope the intelligence is right about that."

He picked up a headset and put it on. "Start your men moving, Riley". The camera focused on Riley who nodded and turned in the saddle of his horse and barked out some orders.

Cisco watched the formation begin to move forward. He spoke again into his mic. "Will, are you seeing this?"

"I am. Waiting for your command."

"Stand by."

The five Clydesdales with Riley and his officers saddled moved forward. Behind them, the company of Marines marched in an open formation, their rifles in their hands. On the flanks, were the horses carrying speakers. On this day, there was no triumphant music. Instead, the steady booming of huge drums filled the air.

The Grand Minister turned at the sound of the approaching drums, but arrogantly climbed the steep stairs of the pyramid. He turned and raised his arms. "People of the mighty Toltec Empire! Natchala, our sacred master, has spoken. These trespassers into our land are not who they say they are. They are demons from deep in the ground who have come with lies. Now, we shall prove they are nothing to fear. We have taken two of their number and will sacrifice them to the true God of the Earth, here on our cleansing alter."

"Fire."

Riley pointed to the sky. The crowd looked up in horror as a howling missile shattered the air and blew the entire top of the pyramid to pieces in a thundering explosion. Riley's company of Marines scattered the crowd like a ship parting the seas. They surrounded the Grand Minister's Toltec warriors and mowed them down to the last man. The only people standing when the smoke cleared were the two men from Sanctuary, looking terrified, grateful to be alive.

"Give your men a well done. After you march them the hell out of there and into a safe place."

"Roger. I sort of doubt anybody is going to be very interested in tangling with us now."

Cisco turned back to Will on the Alamo. "Dead center, perfect. What about the cruise missile?"

"I launched on your order, Admiral. Time on target in Tula, three minutes."

"Let's hope it does the same to the grand pyramid in Tula as I just saw in Chitza."

"We sent a lot less ordinance to Chitza, so's not to injure any of our people. What we sent to Tula will do considerably more damage."

"And will have the same effect. From now on, nobody will doubt the God of Sanctuary is the mightiest of them all."

# Chapter 22
# Midway

The sun hung low in the sky, still several hours before setting. Today was the summer solstice. Jonas Cisco sat on a couch on the balcony of his office. The top of City Hall gave him a clear vision of the ocean to the east. Inner Band Boulevard curved off to the left and right. Enterprise Plaza spread out below. The usual crowds of people strolled across it, moving in an out of the alcoves of parks and gardens. Cisco enjoyed spending time here every day, relaxing from the stacks of work always piled on his desk. He sipped at his cold sweet tea.

Besides it being the solstice, nothing much separated this day from all the others. The difference was in Cisco himself. He felt mortally tired. The continuously changing optics of the major projects, he himself began, these five years dragged at his mind and body. He sagged back and wished Project Horizon had never driven him to put this colossal cauldron in motion. He recalled the first meeting with the command team when Lino said, "The technology we're working on is not just advanced; it's revolutionary. So far beyond your scale of understanding it will terrify you to the core."

*Lino, bless his soul, was right.*

He'd felt sorry for himself long enough and was about to go back to his desk when Molly came out onto the balcony.

"If I knew you were going to loaf out here. I'd have come out sooner. I needed a break two hours ago."

Cisco smiled and poured Molly a glass of tea. "Have a seat, fellow slave. We shall conserve our strength until the evil King drives us back into brutal service."

Molly sat and sipped her tea. "Nice day. Looks like things are hopping on the plaza. Everyone's enjoying their day off."

"Is it Sunday?"

"It is. The only person in Sanctuary who doesn't remember that is you."

"How come you're here? You should be relaxing with everyone else."

"This place would fall apart if I wasn't in the office."

Cisco turned and looked at his office manager. "That's the stupidest thing you've ever said. Nobody is that indispensable."

"Funny. That's what I was going to say."

"What's the Hell is that supposed to mean?"

Molly turned to the video monitor at the edge of the balcony. "Computer, play Admiral package."

The screen showed a recent meeting of the command council including some of the original command team, Project Horizon, and the three top department directors. Cisco drummed his pen on the table and burst out. "Why are we going over the same ground? I already have all this stuff from the reports you send to the computer."

"Who says, you are paying about as much attention to her, as you are us," said Wyatt.

"I think I'll stop paying any more attention to you, starting right now." He gathered his papers from the table and stormed out of the room.

Molly looked away from the screen. "My, my, just plain cranky. Less like a commanding officer, and more like a three-year-old."

Cisco's face turned red with anger. He fumed, about to say something loud and highly uncomplimentary. Before he could say a word, Molly glared at him and raised a halting finger in his face.

Cisco flopped back on the couch. Slowly, his face blanched with remorse and regret. "What's wrong with me?"

"Do you see those people down there? They're working as hard as you. The difference between them and you are they know to grab a little downtime ... whenever and however they can and enjoy it for all it's worth. These hours, half days, and stolen nights are all they have. They're still able to function in this super-charged world of ours only because they have the sense to relax, let off some steam, and think about something besides the mountains of work we all have.

"You, on the other hand," Molly pointed, "haven't spent a night at home for a month. You sleep in your office, eat in your office, and work sixteen hours a day. You haven't socialized with people since any of us can remember. When was the last time you took a walk through that plaza down there?

"You're closer to the edge than I've ever seen, Jonas. Worse, you are a perfect example of the edge your entire city is creeping toward. You'd better do something, and do it quick, or you'll have an entire population burned out and as worthless as you are becoming. In case you haven't figured it out, you are the reason we work so hard. You gave us hope when we got stranded in this impossible timeline. You gave us purpose. We need you now more than ever."

Cisco knew she was right. He'd let himself fall into the trap of managing details and forgotten to serve as the inspirational driving force toward an unknown future for all Sanctuary. *I'm failing everyone, including myself.*

Molly put an arm around his shoulder. "Admitting you have a problem is always the first step. Next comes doing something about it."

"I've no idea how to start."

"I do. The first thing you're going to do is go home, have a good shot or six of your favorite cognac, then go to bed and sleep. When you wake up, take a shower, put on your best whites, and spend some time with the people who love you. Mix with them, tell them they're doing a good job and everything is going to be all right. Show up at every recreation center in town, wander

265

through the plaza, feed the birds, and relax. You are banned from your office I see the spring in your step, and the smile on your face comes back. Now vamoose and let the team you trained handle the load."

Cisco went home and drank half a bottle of cognac. In the last moments, before he sagged into bed, he thought *Tomorrow, I'll figure out what to do.*

Cisco came to the rostrum in the big meeting room of City Hall. The buzz among the department directors, command staff and Horizon team stopped at once. The presence of their sure-handed, resourceful leader commanded the honor and respect of all.

Meetings of this kind were rare. The managers of Sanctuary video conferenced each other every day, and Cisco met with senior officials frequently. However, everyone sitting down together was a novelty.

"I've asked you to join me this morning, to thank you for your endless work and incredible achievements. The computer helps me keep track of our primary indexes. We have maintained our supplies and inventory at pre-blackout levels. In medicine, computer science, and manufacturing we are in even better shape. What's more, the training of our Toltec brigades is right on schedule. We have a solid network of spies and informants operating in eighth-century France. Ahmed Al Aswira has no idea we exist and won't until it's too late.

"Two weeks from now we'll mark the sixth anniversary of both the founding of Sanctuary and the blackout. During this time, the people of our city have worked hard, very hard, without complaint. Since we are past the midpoint in reaching our goals, we deserve a vacation."

A chorus of applause and cheering rang from all in attendance. Cisco let his hard-working partners celebrate for a few minutes. He lifted his arms for order and once again the room grew quiet.

Cisco grinned. "I admit, I've been on furlough the last few days, something I haven't done for a long time. I had a chance to wander through the city and visit with many people. I learned something. Despite our heavy schedules of work, life goes on. To my surprise; I learned our symphony orchestra is rehearsing for a fabulous concert on the 4th of July; our theatre group is preparing to present a play; dances are planned at every recreation center; and a spectacular flea market will have a three-day-run in Enterprise Plaza. Maybe best of all, there's a wedding coming up. I'm not sure how Ben Crenshaw managed to carry on a courtship spending so much time in France, but he's convinced Shannon Fisk to marry him.

"My dear friends and companions, a good friend of mine reminded me that all work and no play makes for a grumpy Admiral. I offer my sincere apologies."

Bigger applause filled the room and this time Cisco saw a lot more smiles.

"Here's what I'm thinking. We'll we spend a couple days of reorganizing our grand social schedule. Then, I'll make an address on television announcing a general holiday for every possible person in Sanctuary beginning the 4th of July weekend and continuing for three weeks. We'll sprinkle fun events through that time, so something is going on every day."

"Not to throw cold water on something so welcome as this, Admiral," said Riley, down the table. "What are we going to do with our Toltecs?"

"I'm glad you mentioned that. Currently, we have 8,000 soldiers inside the training center, ranging from fifteen to nineteen years old, and 2,000 new twelve-year-old recruits in the transient center. Our policy has always been to offer relaxed freedom of movement for the brigades, except inside the perimeter of the city; reasoning our advanced levels of technology was more than they could absorb. You work with these boys every day. Do you still believe that?"

"Not for the older boys. Their education system is pretty high-tech even for our own kids. Remember we were every bit as selective in picking recruits as we were to fill the complement of the city. With four or five years of intensive education and training, the Toltecs are about at the same level as students their own age in Sanctuary. Even the younger boys don't regard our advanced technology as magic."

"I propose we march the brigades, minus the kids in the transient center, into Sanctuary across town to Cooper River Stadium and let them enjoy the 4th of July festivities with the rest of us. Most of our people have had little or no contact with our soldiers. The Toltecs have had limited contact with the population of Sanctuary. I think we should let them celebrate together."

"That will be a huge morale builder. We damn sure need to restrict the Toltec view of the city to the basic infrastructure."

"You work out the details."

Each department added their ideas of ways to make the general city furlough an exciting and thoroughly enjoyable time. Cisco sat back and let them bubble on about what to do with this and that.

As the meeting broke up, Molly, came wandering up from the back of the room, and whispered. "Welcome back, Jonas."

Tupac and Chakala were sixth-year senior student soldiers. Both commanded companies of their own and were promoted to Captains. They didn't know it, but they were on their way to higher ranks with more responsibility. When the word came down the brigades would be allowed inside Sanctuary for a holiday celebration, they couldn't contain their excitement. The idea of entering the magical city overwhelmed them. As the day grew closer, they drilled their companies relentlessly to ensure they would not disgrace themselves.

The night before the grand march, the two were in their shared quarters.

"Do you ever miss your life in Chitza?" asked Tupac.

"Sure. I miss my family," said Chakala. "What I don't miss are the clouds of mystery spread by the priests in the temples, or the gory public executions. I hated watching those when I was a little boy."

"That came to an end when the Eastmen blew the top off the temples in Chitza and Tula."

"And killed Natchala, presiding over more executions in Tula. Zontamuza is a far better leader of our people. His willingness to grasp the potential offered by the Eastmen have proved a godsend to the entire Toltec Empire. My father's last letter contained a long description of the infrastructure improvements. New technologies are being introduced into every part of city life. He says keeping up with it is challenging. Nobody is complaining."

Chakala finished buffing the brass buttons of his new dress blue uniform and gave them an appraising look. "If the Eastmen had not sent teachers to teach English to the people, we would still be using our own clumsy alphabet."

Tupac took the buffing cloth. "As it is, what we've learned here is so far beyond the daily lives of the people of Chitza I'm not surprised when my father writes to say he's overwhelmed with new things there. Things which you and I learned years ago."

Perhaps more surprising to the families of the young men would be the changes in them. A nutritious diet and excellent medical care gave both a length of bone and superior physical condition. They were already several inches taller than nearly everyone in Chitza. They spoke perfect English, were skilled at operating computers. They knew more about the world around them than even the most learned Toltecs. They adopted the religion of the Eastmen entirely. They guessed their living quarters, despite having hot and cold running water, private baths, heating, air conditioning and electricity, were still several steps down from the gleaming city.

They had never seen more than the very tops of the tallest, futuristic buildings because Riley installed vinyl slats in the ten-foot-high fence separating Sanctuary from the training camp. He did this to forestall any curiosity by the young men in the camp and prevent speculation on what wonders lay beyond the wall. Nevertheless, the soldiers in training still knew Sanctuary was beyond anything they could imagine. Every man dreamed of seeing it in person someday.

That day had come.

The world around Cisco glowed. He sat comfortably in a soft chair with a crystal goblet of cognac at Chips Gallant's house. "I have to say, Chips. This place is so much better with a woman's touch. I should have expected Missy would be as good at decorating as she is with everything else."

"I think I'm the luckiest fellow in all creation. This used to be a plain old house till Missy put her touch on it, and on me."

"For your information, Bub, this is the first time you've been here."

Cisco thought about that a minute. "How long have you two been married?"

"Almost four years."

"Really? I can't believe that."

Chips smirked. "Sad but true. You've been so busy trying to conquer the world, you forgot you have friends."

"A fact another dear friend of mine reminded me of lately."

"Anyway, Molly jarred you back to the land of the living in the nick of time."

"We wouldn't have wanted you to miss Shannon and Ben's wedding."

"Especially since you got to walk Shannon down the aisle."

"It was my honor. She looked beautiful. They're a perfect couple. I still can't imagine how Ben managed to pull it off."

"You can be sure Shannon did a lot of the work," said Missy. "All Ben needed to do was fall in love."

"Too bad they can't fly off to some beach resort for a proper honeymoon."

"It comes with the times, so to speak," said Missy. "Anyway, they'll have lots of togetherness for the next few weeks, while we kick off our shoes and relax."

"Maybe I can convince them the concert and fireworks show are their special wedding gift."

Chips sipped at his brandy. "As a matter of fact, tomorrow is a very large deal. Not only will everyone celebrate a bang-up Fourth of July, the whole town will have a first look at the army we've been raising. I think Sanctuary is more excited about that than anything else."

Tupac and Chakala enjoyed sleeping late. They had a leisurely breakfast with the other Toltec officers. The brigades would not form until late in the day for their march into the city, so the two found some time on their hands. No training, no school, no drilling were themselves a holiday. They strolled out of the training complex to the Trading Post. This facility had grown from the single building built by Hank Winterhawk. Today it featured stores, shops and entertainment centers catering, not only to the Cusabo tribes and the soldiers of the brigade but also to other native American tribes from far and wide. The people of the sprawling Cherokee nation made regular pilgrimages to trade and acquire a wide variety of tools and specialty items. Hank's original edict the entire Trading Post perimeter be neutral ground for all people was still strictly enforced. On this day, Tupac and Chakala did some shopping to send gifts home to their families, then went to a movie at the expansive theater with the widescreen.

Late that afternoon, the two returned to their quarters to change into their dress blues for the march into the city. They joined their companies, conducting an inspection of the men, in advance of another one by higher-ranking Eastmen officers.

The loudspeakers sounded assembly. The companies formed into battalions, which formed into brigades until the entire division stood in even ranks across the grass field. At the front, General Riley Marquis, the commanding officer, climbed the stairs of the reviewing platform. His voice boomed through loudspeakers. "Division! Attention!" The sound of 8,000 pairs of heels clicking together rang across the parade ground.

"At ease. Men, this is the day for which you have waited. Today, you will march into Sanctuary, then on to Cooper River Stadium for a grand celebration of the Fourth of July with the everyone who lives in the city.

"The entire population will turn out to line the parade route cheering as you march past. You will maintain discipline at all times. When we reach the stadium, a feast will be served and you will have time to relax. Then, as night falls, you will reform, march into the arena, hear beautiful music and watch a grand celebration of fireworks. When the program is over, you will march back to the training center.

"You should know, the Admiral will be at the stadium. You have seen the Admiral on television before, but none of you have ever seen him in person. Remember, he is your supreme commander and the leader of Sanctuary. We honor and respect him. I've no idea of his plans. He may join you at dinner. Try not to embarrass yourself if he should speak to you."

Late that night Tupac and Chakala could relax in their rooms, after witnessing and experiencing the most magnificent spectacle of their lives.

"I guess," said Chakala, "after the years of education we've received on so many new concepts, I thought entering Sanctuary would be a little more of the same. I sure was wrong about that. What I saw today went beyond anything I could have ever imagined. Somehow, I thought the ATV's we see here are all there were. Today I saw thousands of them."

Tupac hung his dress blues in the closet. "I could hardly keep myself marching in order looking at the sights. I know now how much more we have to learn. Tall buildings, huge machines running on tracks, and Cooper River stadium itself."

"I felt filled with pride and gratitude as we were cheered by the people of Sanctuary. I haven't any idea what awaits us in the future, but I am dedicated to the Eastmen. I will serve them with honor and valor."

Chakala grinned. "You almost fainted when the Admiral walked up behind you and asked if you were enjoying your meal. You spilled your tray jumping to attention."

"I shall never forget it. He filled me with warmth and a feeling of pride. He spoke to me in such a gentle manner, still his voice was filled with strength and purpose. I believe we are blessed to be commanded by such a noble Master."

"Maybe I got the best of it all. While you were busy being overwhelmed meeting the Admiral, I lined up for the lots to be chosen to return to Chitza. I got picked to go on one of the transports to visit my family during our two-week furlough. Can't say I'm going to miss you much."

# Chapter 23
## Stirring the Pot

### *Year Ten*

Cisco waited for the red light to blink on. When it did, he smiled into the camera. "Greetings. I don't often speak to you as I am tonight. I haven't needed to, simply because the leadership of our city has been so efficient in moving us forward to our final goal. However, this evening is different. I want to summarize our planning and tell you how we expect to proceed.

"We are coming to the end of ten long years of work. We have built an army, infiltrated the headquarters of the enemy, marshaled our resources and prepared in every way possible to attempt to return as much of our past as possible to the present.

"Tonight, we include in this broadcast the men of our combat forces. I speak directly to you soldiers now. You deserve to know what comes next and how it will profoundly change your lives. For ten years of your young lives, you have learned a common language, been introduced to an accelerated learning program in the sciences, mathematics, engineering, medicine, philosophy, and, of course, the true word of God which guides us all.

"During the past four years, you have concentrated on training in weapons, combat strategies, with complex field maneuvers to sharpen your skills and harden your bodies. We believe you are best soldiers in the world. I hope so because we are about to lead you into war. In fact, elements of the division are already in the field. Fighting has begun."

Cisco paused, seeming to collect his thoughts before continuing. "What you haven't heard is the reason for this war. We have prepared a program to disclose our desperate situation. Everyone in Sanctuary knows the story. Now you will too. After you see this presentation, I hope you can forgive us for what we have done.

274

"For the rest of you, the people of Sanctuary, I think it's important to remind ourselves why we fight and what we hope to achieve. Thank you."

With that, the discovery of time travel, the complete story of why Sanctuary was built, the assault on the Gateway, and the terrible consequences, as a result, began to replay. Cisco could not bring himself to look at it again.

Chakala sat in an empty room. The entire presentation astonished him. When it finished, he sat quietly for long moments trying to comprehend the magnitude of what he witnessed. As a grown man, he had learned more than he thought possible since coming to the world of the Eastmen. Knowing they were themselves the victims of a sinister plot which totally altered their lives, filled him with compassion and sympathy. The more he turned the facts over in his mind, the more he realized he and his compatriots were the solution. He also knew why Tupac and his company of soldiers were gone. They weren't only in a far-off land, they were in a far-off time.

"Frankly, this training program would not have worked if we didn't get a jump start from people like you with existing skills in the critical areas," said Ben to the man seated in his office. "You speak Arabic, understand the culture of the Middle East, and a combat veteran."

"Maybe. The rest of the training took everything in me to keep up. Missy Long is one tough taskmaster. I think I've crammed ten years of history into a couple months."

"You have to know the era in which we will place you. Missy concentrated your training on the history of the caliphs of the Umayyad rulers of the eighth century, so we could insert you into Aswira's court without arousing any suspicions. From this point on your name is Hassan."

"Common enough name. What's my job?"

"You will arrive at the palace of Aswira bearing documents identifying you as a member of the court of Hisham, leader of the Umayyad Clan. This particular Caliph enjoyed a relatively long and successful rule. He was Caliph at the time of the original Battle of Tours and continued until he died of diphtheria in 743 A.D."

"What if Aswira checks my credentials?"

"He won't, or can't, in time to do him any good. Anyway, the government in this period is so chaotic and turbulent, the bureaucracy is hardly reliable. Aswira will be pleased the Caliph recognizes him as a power in Europe. You will arrive with as much pomp and circumstance as we can muster. Aswira will mark you as a man of substance and influence."

"Then I keep track of everything he does."

"Right. We hope you will become a trusted advisor, serving him in helping make France a model of Sharia law and life according to the word of the Prophet."

"That's not going to make me very popular with the people."

"No, it isn't. What's worse, to sustain Aswira's confidence in you, you may have to do things contrary to everything you believe. However, if everything goes according to plan, in only a few months the people being persecuted will be set free, our army will wipe out Muslim influence in Europe and history may unfold in a manner more like the way we remember it. I'm hoping Aswira can be brought back to Sanctuary to face justice."

"Missy says I have the most dangerous job."

Ben closed his notebook. "No doubt about that. You'll be operating at the mouth of the dragon. You'll have to forget you know even a word of the English language. One false step, you'll be exposed and killed. Our entire operation could fail.

"At least I'll have a cushier life, living in the court of the Caliph."

"Andre, am I not one of your best customers?"

"You are indeed sire, and I appreciate your business."

"Then when am I to receive the merchandise I ordered four months ago?"

"You must understand, sire, the tableware, dishes, and plates you ordered, along with the better metal pots and pans, must all come from merchants far to the south. I sent wagons and men to purchase these things on the day you ordered them. I expect my men to return any day. As soon as the goods arrive, I will send word to you immediately."

"See to it. You do remember I have paid for this merchandise?"

"And you should remember, sire, I have always delivered everything I promised, and what you have received is superior to anything in all the caliphate."

"That may be so, but my patience is not endless, especially with an infidel."

"May Allah speed my men home soon."

"I hope it is soon. We are expecting some important visitors any day. I wish to entertain them in the manner they deserve."

"I will send a man to search for the shipment. Who are your visitors?"

"Several important imams are making the journey, though Spain, all the way from Mecca, to help the Caliph of France correctly apply Sharia Law."

"It is important to understand the will of Allah."

"Perhaps you shall find the pathway to paradise yet."

When the Muslim official left the shop, Andre turned back to his partner and said quietly, "That dude is going nuts waiting for his stuff. I love watching them squirm for the supposed overland delivery. Radio the barn and tell them they can send the order through the Gateway. Find out which drop point they want us to use. Don't forget to tell Ben about the arrival of those VIPs."

"Think he'll bushwhack them?"

"Ben's been looking for a chance to make a statement. Something to show there is serious opposition to Muslim rule in France. This could be that opportunity."

"What do you think he'll do?"

"Something shocking and arbitrary, like having the entire party found dead with their throats slit. I expect that will grab Aswira's attention."

Ben sat back in a chair. Andre's personal report had, indeed, given him the opportunity he'd waited for to begin clandestine operations against Aswira. Hank Winterhawk, Jack Kepler, and Dusty Rhoades had all cycled in with Captain Tupac's company. They waited for Ben to issue orders.

"Our Muslim friend didn't happen to mention how large an escort was coming with these Imams?"

"He didn't say, and I didn't want to press him for details. I imagine these are important enough church people to command a fair-sized bodyguard."

"Well, we won't take any chances. Captain Tupac, I want you to move your company south and intercept this bunch. You need to let them get about twenty miles from Paris before you ambush them. Pick off enough of this force with snipers to reduce them to a small group. Then move in with your men and finish the job. I want this to be as bloody as possible."

"We won't let you down, Commander."

"I'm sure you won't. Prepare and brief your men. You should leave on horseback by tomorrow morning."

"Aye, Aye, Sir." Tupac saluted and rushed out of the building.

Ben turned to the officers. "I think you guys should go along. The Admiral picked you to command brigades when we begin the major operation. You've spent almost ten years proving that was the right choice. I want you to see Tupac's men in action. Even though this will be their first actual combat, they are well trained and ready for a fight. Try not to get in their way. Just make sure there are no survivors or any trace we used modern weapons."

"Roger."

"Andre, I want you to start a whisper campaign. We want Aswira's informants to think the people have had enough of this Muslim tyranny. Say there could be an uprising of the Franks. When the news reaches Aswira of the massacre of the imams and their entire escort, he'll lose sleep over the trouble brewing but won't have any idea who and what is doing it. After he sits and stews for a while, we'll launch the next part of the plan."

Tupac's company shadowed the Muslim entourage for three days. His scouts contacted the party fifty miles south of Paris. There were three wagons and fifty mounted soldiers. As they moved slowly along on the poor roads, the Toltecs moved with them and waited. When Tupac's drone showed the force twenty miles from Paris, he set up his ambush between two wooded hills.

Toltec sharpshooters started shooting from the rear of the formation, and the Muslims began to die. Soon men and horses were in disarray, turning from side to side, trying to figure out from where the attack was coming. More men fell from their horses. The imams in the wagon cowered in fear.

When only a few of the Muslim riders remained, Tupac dispatched his troops, swooping down with machetes flashing. Men in the underbrush shot the horses out from beneath the men, who jumped up to face the attacking Toltecs. With almost no real fighting, the Sanctuary soldiers moved in and killed the remaining guard. Tupac smiled as he saw his men parry the swords of the Muslims and use martial arts skills never seen in Europe before this moment. When it was over, none of the foreign soldiers were on their feet, and the Toltecs began to systematically slaughter all still living. The imams were dragged screaming to nearby trees and hung from the limbs, their eyes cut out, throats slit, and intestines hanging from their stomachs. Similar treatment was given to the soldiers. Tupac made sure no signs remained of any of men or horses being shot. The road between the hills ran with blood.

As quickly as they had come, the Toltecs melted into the forest. Hank, Dusty and Jack were only spectators to the grisly battle. They grimly reported Ben's orders were followed to the last detail.

News of the massacre spread quickly to the outskirts of Paris. Andre listened to the story being told by more than one horrified witness who had stumbled onto the scene. He began his string of rumors. Only hours passed before Ahmed Aswira got the entire account from his trusted counselor Hassan.

Aswira raged. "How can this have happened? How can I explain this tragedy to Caliph Hisham? What can I say?"

"Many questions with no answers, sire. The Caliph will ask many more. What is most disturbing is these accounts say the entire party was struck down by an unknown enemy. Surely, not the work of farmers with pitchforks. A more lethal force of trained soldiers must be operating in the land."

"But who? Certainly not anyone in the service of Pepin. His house is the only family remaining in France who might challenge my authority. Yet I have kept a close watch on him. There has never been any sign he is training or housing fighting men. He trades freely with me and would have much to lose if his lucrative business stopped."

"I agree, sire. The attack occurred many miles from Paris. Perhaps another of the major infidel landowners are responsible. What are your plans, my lord?"

"I'm going to send my cavalry riders on raiding quests to the south and east of Paris. They will go willingly. They are eager to plunder the remaining Christian churches. I'll tell my captains to be prepared to leave in a week."

❖

When Hassan reported the results of his meeting, Ben shook his head. "I'll say one thing about Aswira. He's predictable. Time to transport Chakala's company through the Gateway."

"Better tell him to come prepared. Word of the massacre has spread through Paris. You can be sure Aswira's soldiers have heard about it. They'll be on guard from the time they leave the castle keep."

"Our boys are the best at guerilla tactics. I've seen it. Last year when I went back to Sanctuary, Riley took me out on one of their exercises. We started walking on a trail with five of his soldiers. One by one they all disappeared. I figured the point was to show me how these guys could slip into the forest without me seeing them. Riley and I kept walking on the trail for a couple of miles. When he stopped, he whistled. One by one all five guys came oozing out of the forest. I never saw anything the whole time we walked. They followed us every step. One of the men even handed me a candy bar wrapper I'd thrown away. All Riley said was I shouldn't litter."

"How are going to cover up these Muslims have been shot?"

"Shooting with rifles is not all they can do. They're just as deadly with bow and arrow, crossbows, machetes, knives, spears, blowguns, slings, or their bare hands. They can also set up traps that make it look like the victim died from an accident."

"I'll take your word for it. What's the plan?"

"My guess is the Muslims will go out in platoon-sized units, maybe twenty or thirty armed men each. They'll figure a cavalry unit of that size won't have to worry much about being attacked, and the smaller the unit, the less loot they have to share.

Generally, we scouted out where the most tempting targets of opportunity are so I'm going to send Tupac's company out tomorrow and have Chakala's company deploy when they arrive. Between the two of them, we'll bag the whole lot."

"Losing a couple hundred men is not going to deplete Aswira's force much. He has a standing army of several thousand men."

Ben tossed another log into the fireplace. "And every single one of those men will be scared to death to leave the castle after none of the others come back. We might even set it up so a few make it alive back to Paris. First-hand horror stories always have the greatest effect."

"Why do I have the idea you and your team have thought this through forwards and backward?"

"We have. We plugged every possible scenario we could imagine into the computer and asked her to figure the probabilities for every one of them. Then we took the dozen most likely events and had her crunch every possible tactic we could use. The result was a thick manual of plans within plans within plans. I've probably absorbed more of the book than Dusty or Jack, or Hank, but we all can rattle off page after page without even thinking. This action by Aswira was at the top of the probability list after we ran the first operation."

"I think I'll head back to the castle for the easy job of giving bad advice to our prime victim."

"This isn't an easy job, Hassan, and it is vital. We wouldn't have known which way to jump if you hadn't told us. Plus, you misdirected him away from Pepin's estate. We don't want Aswira thinking much about him till we're ready." Ben got to his feet and pulled Hassan up with a handshake. "Thanks a lot."

Colonel Winterhawk waited to greet Chakala as he ushered his men to meet the rest of the company in the open area outside the barn. No matter how many briefings were held, the men still could not help but be a little daunted as they crowded onto the platform in the Gateway center and found themselves suddenly transported to a different hour, different place, different part of the world, and a different time.

"Everything okay?" asked Hank as he exchanged salutes with Chakala.

"It went well. None of my guys flinched an inch. But I have to tell you, Colonel, I caught my breath when the first platoon disappeared in that blue curtain. Can't say I got used to it when it came my turn."

"Everyone thinks the same thing. I've been through the Gateway a dozen times. I'm always jittery about jumping to another time. I'll be glad when this is all over, and I can forget time travel ever happened."

Chakala looked around and sniffed the air. "I think the weather here is cooler and less humid."

"This is the end of spring; warmer weather is coming."

"What comes next, sir."

"Settle your men in the courtyard. Then round up your platoon leaders and senior non-coms and meet me inside. Commander Crenshaw will tell you his plans for the company."

Half an hour later Captain Chakala came back inside the barn with his leadership team. Ben stood waiting in front of an easel. "Take your seats."

He turned over the first page showing a map. "We are here at our headquarters on land owned by the principal surviving Frankish noble from the Battle of Tours. Ten miles to the north is Paris, the capital of the caliphate."

He pointed at a spot, twenty miles south. "Two weeks ago, Captain Tupac's company ambushed a party of officials and their escort. They came all the way from Mecca to help Ahmed Aswira further his control of this country and enforce Sharia Law. They never made it. They were slaughtered in a very public and bloody way.

"As a result, Aswira is sending Muslim cavalry in five groups to ravage in the south. His idea is to make an example to anyone he can and permit his soldiers to plunder and loot Christian churches. The first of these groups departed this morning. They are headed to the nearest of their intended targets. Other forces will leave over the next few days to push farther east."

Crenshaw pointed to each of the expected places where the Muslims would go. Then he turned over the next panel on the easel, showing a more detailed look at the lands to the south and east. "Captain Tupac's company left two days ago. They will intercept the first two of these cavalry units at places well beyond the lands of our host Frankish noble and ambush them. A few will be allowed to escape to come back to Paris screaming how their comrades were chopped to pieces by unknown enemy forces.

"Your company will leave on horseback tomorrow, Captain. You are to move east and prepare a very unwelcome arrival for the other three Muslim cavalries. Begin by having your snipers shoot enough of their force so your men can move in and fight hand to hand with the survivors after you shoot their horses out from under them. Make sure you send in your best men. The Muslims will be desperate and armed with very sharp swords."

"We have trained to fight in this manner, Colonel. How graphic a demonstration do you want us to make?"

"Absolutely devastating. We want as bloody a scene as you can make. Try and hold back a couple of men from each group to witness the gory ways you dispose of their comrades and then allow them to escape. Make sure these men never catch any of your people using modern weapons. That's the one thing we don't want Aswira to find out. When you are finished, leave the corpses scattered around, hung from trees, chopped to pieces, whatever you can manage, before you slip away leaving no signs."

Chakala looked grimly at his officers and sergeants and asked if there were any questions. There weren't. "We will be ready to depart at first light, commander."

"I'm sending along a couple of small drones for you to use to keep track of these people. Shadow them for as long as you need before you find a good spot to bushwhack 'em. If you have nothing else, I won't keep you. You have lots to do before you leave. My people will help you with the horses."

Chakala and all his men stood and gave Ben a snappy salute. Then they left the barn to gird for war.

# Chapter 24
# Cocking the Trigger

Ahmed Aswira sat and listened intently. He leaned forward on his throne, his knuckles white from gripping the arms. Before him were three soldiers, pouring out the account of the ambush of their comrades. Hassan lounged in a nearby chair.

"Arrows came flying from the hills on both sides of our mounted troops," said one man. They killed half of the horsemen before we could do anything. We bunched together to use our shields. But then our horses were shot with many more arrows, and our remaining men had to fight on the ground."

Another man continued. "Suddenly strange looking men came out of the trees. They moved so quickly and attacked so fiercely. We defended ourselves as best we could. These men had only knives or no weapons, yet they did things I could hardly imagine. They threw our men to the ground, they moved and struck quicker than snakes; we couldn't even use our swords."

The second soldier stood with his shoulders slumped. "I have never seen men move so fast,"

The first soldier extended his hands, his finders spread wide. "They fought in ways with their arms and legs and bodies, I could not believe."

"A few of us broke away and ran. Almost all were caught and killed. My comrade and I managed to get to two of the last horses and ride away."

Aswira scowled at man who had remained quiet. "What about you, dog?"

"I was at the rear of our formation with the pack horses. When the attack started, I saw the same thing as these two. I drove my horse into the trees and watched. These men looked like Mongols. Not like us at all. But, my lord, never have I seen such skillful fighters. They did things I can't even describe, and as my comrades said, they moved like lightning. When they were finished, they cut out the eyes, slit the throats and slashed my comrades in terrible ways. I left the pack horses and rode away. In my life, I have never been so frightened."

"Perhaps you men should have died with your companions." Aswira slumped back in his chair. "However, it's good some survived to return with this account of what happened. Go back to your quarters and have something to eat."

The three men left the room. Aswira turned to Hassan. "I have heard two other reports from survivors of these massacres. Every group I sent out has fallen to this unknown enemy. What can be happening?"

"I cannot say, sire. Only a few are left from the over two hundred soldiers you dispatched. I know these were skilled fighters, seasoned in other campaigns. Whoever attacked them must be very good soldiers, indeed."

Aswira nodded. "I will meet with my captains. I must reassure them losing a small number of our soldiers is not a threat to our army. Nothing in all this land is as mighty as us."

"If I may suggest, sire, there are many soldiers in the service of the Caliph in Spain eager to prove themselves in battle and have an opportunity for wealth in the spoils of war. You could also send riders to Hisham's court at Resafa in northern Syria. Say true valor and bravery can be shown, and great riches gained if they should come to Paris to join your service."

"An excellent idea. I will dispatch riders today with letters by my own hand offering the gains you suggest."

"I would add that a rebellion of Christians is endangering the principals of the true faith of Islam."

"There is no evidence such an uprising exists. All we have seen thus far are skilled mercenaries and brigands attacking by ambush. No army is rising to oppose me."

"That may be so, sire, but your call for many veteran fighters will be more enthusiastically received if they believe the words of the Prophet are being challenged."

"Once again you proved to be a wise and able advisor, Hassan. I shall write, most eloquently, in the manner you suggest."

❖

Two months passed. Every day the size of the Muslim army got bigger. Aswira's appeal had enthusiastic appeal throughout the Islamic world.

Chips and Missy came through the Gateway, along with Riley, for a conference with Ben. Chips went to survey the work being done to construct the refugee camps. Missy continued to monitor each site to ensure nothing was included that might reveal any modern equipment or supplies of any kind.

When they were settled around a table in their headquarters, Ben told them his latest news. "Muslim troops are pouring in. Aswira's urgent message got an immediate response from all over the Umayyad Caliphate. The first to arrive came from Spain. Then other units from North Africa took the short cruise across the Mediterranean. We are now seeing some heavy cavalry from as far away as Egypt and Syria."

Riley concentrated on the tactical situation. "How is Aswira explaining the fact no army is facing him?"

"He's playing on the theme of an unknown, but deadly, force of soldiers decimating his troops less than a three-day ride from Paris. The survivors of the massacres have retold their descriptions over and over. The stories are getting better every time they tell them. Tupac and Chakala's men did everything but fly."

"So how many soldiers are we going to end up having to fight?"

"Accounts vary. Anywhere from fifty to eighty thousand men. Over half of them are the vaunted Muslim cavalry."

"Having so many men coming from throughout the Umayyad Caliphate will only make our end game more real and convincing," said Missy.

"It's still a TREmendous army I've got to face out there. The slightest miscalculation and we could be in big trouble."

"Speaking of calculations. How is your planning going for the evacuation of fifty square miles of countryside?"

"You tell me. You're the one building refugee camps for 100,000 people."

"The sites you selected are remote enough. We have all the supplies assembled and waiting in Sanctuary. My people can set up the camp, including tents, kitchens to prepare meals and feed the Franks. All according to my slave driver wife who keeps making me remove anything which doesn't look like the mid-eighth century."

Missy summarized. "We won't have a problem making the people get out of the way of a war. What we can't do is introduce anything which does not exist in Europe at this time. The Franks need to believe they are being sent to safety by the benevolent Mayor of the House, as Pepin is known. Essentially, he is the king of the Franks, in the old timestream, and we hope, the new one as well."

Ben pointed at the map. "Timing is everything. We need to initiate a revolt by Pepin, evacuate the non-combatants, and transport the entire Toltec division, more or less simultaneously."

"May the Lord be with us."

The chateau of Pepin the Short smelled of elegance. Missy and her team conducted extensive research on the very best, most modern products available in the world in the middle of the eighth century. Ten years of importing them from Sanctuary factories gave the estate a genuinely imperial appearance. It also gave Ben a lot of leverage with the Frankish Mayor or the House. On this day he needed every bit of it.

Pepin got up from his desk in his private office. "Well, Master Benjamin, what new wonders do you bring today?"

"I bring a wonder, your majesty. But it is not something you can hold in your hand."

Pepin chuckled indulgently and waved Ben to a couch. "In that case, you should sit down and tell me all about it."

After a servant had poured both men a glass of wine, Ben waited for him to leave the room.

"On this day, I bring you the biggest prize of all."

Pepin chuckled again. "What would that be?"

"Freedom."

"From what?" Pepin sipped his wine.

"Freedom for all the Franks from the tyranny of the Islamic Caliphate.

Pepin put his glass on the table and glared at Ben. "That is not something to be spoken of, even in jest."

"I can assure you, sir, I have never been more serious in my life."

"In case you hadn't noticed, Aswira has increased the size of his army by ten times to put down, what he calls, rebellion in the far reaches of his realm. I have not seen any signs of this rebellion, and thus far, none of the Muslim devils have invaded my lands."

"The rebellion of which you speak was begun by me. Aswira sent out raiding parties in all directions. You must have heard all these forces were destroyed."

"So, my informants tell me. This is preposterous. How could *you* start any rebellion or command such savage men about whom everyone is talking? You are only a trader. A very good one, but still just a merchant."

"I am much more than a common trader, or even a common

man, Pepin. You say it, but I know you do not believe it. You know, full well, the luxuries you have prized all these years could not have been delivered by a hundred master traders. You have chosen to ignore this obvious fact."

"I do know it. I've said nothing and welcomed all the endless luxuries you have given. Yet it has always been a mystery to me. It's an even bigger mystery now when you say this rebellion is of your doing. This is all very upsetting and confusing. Are there even more secrets?"

Ben smiled. "Many more, my friend. It is by our design such a huge Muslim army is clogging the streets of Paris to battle an unknown enemy. Here is the plain truth. For the past ten years, my compatriots and I have plotted to destroy Aswira and remove the scar of Islam from all of Europe. We are now on the verge of springing our trap. When the Muslims are utterly defeated, you will take your place as the rightful king of the Franks."

"That would be something beyond my greatest hopes, or prayers. I cannot imagine how that could possibly happen."

"It will happen, exactly as I have said. However, to set matters in motion, you must play an important part."

Pepin scooted closer to Ben on the couch. "Tell me."

A grim-faced mayor of the large Frankish town close to Paris listened as Dusty Rhoades explained to him what he must do.

"These are the orders of Pepin himself?"

"They are, sir. There is no time to lose. You must call the entire population to the city plaza today and deliver the orders of the king. Then I will tell your people what they must do next."

"I cannot believe an entire army is waiting to challenge the Muslims. I've heard Aswira has assembled an army of his own numbering over 60,000 men."

"In any case, Pepin will defeat them and drive the Moors from our land."

"I'm not certain I can convince our people to leave."

"Perhaps they would prefer to stay and be trapped in the middle of a war."

The mayor shook his head and thought for a moment. "We shall obey the command of the king."

Later that day, the 5,000 citizens of the city crowded into the central plaza. Dusty pinned a microphone to the mayor's tunic, saying it was special gift of the king. The mayor raised his hands and spoke. Everyone looked about wondering how their soft-spoken mayor's voice could be so clear and reach to the farthest corner of the plaza.

"My people! I bring you glad tidings and important news. Lord Pepin, Mayor of the House for all the Franks is preparing a revolution. He has raised an army and very soon will meet the Muslim invaders in war. When the war is over, the Muslims will be dead, and we shall be free to worship our Lord Jesus Christ in freedom!"

A roar swept through the plaza. Dusty stood aside and smiled. These were the moments that made all the years of toil worthwhile.

The mayor raised his arms again. "Lord Pepin wants you to be safe during the fighting, so tomorrow we will leave the city for a place of refuge. My friend Dusty has come from Paris and will tell you what you must do."

Dusty stepped forward and spoke in a voice loud enough to rattle the windows. "Citizens! Fellow Franks! Your time of living under the heel of tyranny of Islam is over. Very soon you will be FREE!"

Another, even louder cheer, echoed across the plaza.

"As the mayor has said, you will all be taken to a place of safety where the sting of war cannot hurt you, your wives, your children. All preparations have been made. You will have places to sleep and hot meals every day. You need take nothing with you but clothing. Leave all else behind. I promise when you return everything will be as you left it. Men and boys will walk. Women, small children, the old and weak will ride on wagons. We leave at dawn tomorrow."

At first light the following morning, teams of horses hitched to large, flatbed wagons rolled into the town plaza. The people were there but milled around aimlessly until the mayor and Dusty took charge and loaded the women and children aboard. Then the wagons started moving, and the rest of the population followed them.

In villages and hamlets throughout the combat zone, the same scene was being repeated, by the other two brigade commanders as the people moved beyond harm's way.

Cisco strolled across Enterprise Plaza. He made a habit of doing this every day, regardless of the number of emails in his inbox, or the jabbering prompts from the computer for his attention. A favorite stop for him was a secluded grove of trees in a pocket park. Flowers filled the grove. It always gave Cisco a chance to relax, especially in these tumultuous last weeks. The people of Sanctuary had worked so hard. Cisco had never seen such single-minded dedication to a goal. Everyone knew their job and the part they played in Operation Recovery.

As he entered the grove, he pulled up short, surprised. Sitting on a bench, Chips and Missy were kissing each other.

"Excuse me. Guess this grove is not quite so empty today"

Missy giggled. "It's okay Jonas. We grab private moments whenever we can."

"I thought you guys were working in the refugee center."

"We are," said Chips. "Almost all the people are settled now, and we have thousands of people working double-time to make everything run smoothly. We grabbed a little time off. We're going back tonight."

"It sure is deserted around here."

Missy looked around and nodded. "So many of our people are in France, scattered all over. In addition to the thousands working in the refugee camp, we have support units clear down to company level throughout the division. They're doing the cooking, washing, and a dozen other jobs. Everything we can to let our soldiers focus on the task ahead."

Chips handed Cisco a glass of sweet tea. "I'm glad you broke away from the office to take some time for yourself. I know you worry about how things are going. This is your plan. But now you've done all you can. Take a breath and let us peons do the work."

Missy got up from the bench and hugged Cisco. "Nobody is going to forget you standing at the Gateway for two days straight as each company of soldiers made their jumps. It was a great morale booster. Almost none of the men have ever been so close to you. Having their hand shaken by the man they revere just a step or two under God, calmed their fears and filled them with deadly resolve."

"The next time we see you, will be in France when you come to personally to pull the trigger and confront Aswira."

# Chapter 25
# Defiance

Ahmed Aswira stormed around the throne room knocking dishes from tables, and scattering papers. His generals stood in a tight group waiting to receive their orders. Hassan lounged in a chair. His expression revealed nothing.

Aswira held a paper, shaking it over his head. "Have you read this letter from Pepin?"

"I have, sire."

"Are you not as outraged as me? He claims this rebellion is of his making. He claims I should have paid more attention to the enemy on his doorstep. He insists the Franks will no longer obey anyone but him. He threatens me, do you hear that, he threatens me, and will destroy any forces I send to attack his chateau"

"I read that, sire."

Aswira raged. "Pepin, the pipsqueak argues the Franks reject Islam. His people are Christian, he says, and that our faith is merely another expression of how people can worship Allah. That the words of the Prophet have been distorted by lesser men. He even includes a drawing of our Prophet. Not only is this forbidden, but the drawing itself shows Mohammad in a highly uncomplimentary way."

Aswira strode over to his senior general and held up the letter for him to see. The general's face went red. "This is blasphemous. Give the word, sire, and my men will squash this infidel like a bug."

"Pepin demands all Muslims leave Europe. He demands, he demands, just who the Hell does he think he is?" Aswira marched up the stairs to his throne, turned to face the men in the chamber, and continued reading the letter, "...you have invaded our land, looted our treasures, and defiled our people. If all Muslims do not begin a general withdrawal immediately, all will die."

Aswira threw the letter down grinding it with his heel. "General, take a thousand, no, two thousand, of your best men. Ride to the Chateau of Pepin and burn it to the ground. Kill everyone. We shall see who is the master after all."

"As you command, sire." the general struck a fist to his chest. He turned and tramped from the royal chamber, his other commanders following him.

When the soldiers were gone, Hassan commented. "Very inspiring. I'm sure the general will lead his cavalry himself."

"I want you to go with them, so you can report back to me."

Me! I'm not a soldier."

"No matter. You need only observe and let the army do the fighting."

Chakala radioed Tupac on the other side of the low ridge of hills leading to the chateau, "They're coming."

"Let's hope your platoons of soldiers with phony shields and spears, set up in front of the chateau, is enough to incite the Muslims to charge."

"Don't think we need to worry about that. As soon as they see there's somebody to fight, I'm sure they'll spur their horses at full speed. This is gonna happen fast."

"All my guys are ready. We'll start firing as soon as the claymores go off."

"Did you send men to cover their retreat?" We can't have any survivors go back and give Aswira some kind of garbled story. He has to know only what we tell him."

"I have three ATV's with machine guns ready to move in behind the Muslims as soon as they pass."

"Okay. Here we go."

As the lead elements of the Muslim cavalry rounded the rise and looked down the shallow valley leading to the chateau, the general could see a number of soldiers behind tall shields in a tight phalanx. Long spears faced toward the enemy.

"There is your rebellion. They should have brought more men," yelled the general. "Ride now and cut them to pieces."

The cavalry massed as a single force. The soldiers spurred their horses, lowered their spears, and screamed as one as they hurtled toward Chakala's men.

There was no order to the charge. Two thousand men galloped across the open ground. Chakala watched calmly until the lead elements of the cavalry were a bare two hundred yards from the phalanx then issued a single word command. "Fire."

Simultaneously, three dozen claymore mines set up in front of the phalanx detonated. From both sides of the ridge, the Toltecs began firing. Six miles away, a battery of howitzers recoiled as they sent rounds on their way.

The entire front of the Muslim cavalry was shredded by the claymores. More men and horses went down like dominoes from Toltec guns. In the center of the massed cavalry, artillery rounds exploded. In less than a minute, nearly two thousand Muslims lay dead or dying on the ground. A small number of riders turned to flee, leaving their comrades, to fight alone. Companies of Toltecs emerged from the trees and waded into the shaken and terrified Muslims. Brief fights dotted the battlefield, but it was soon over. Machine gun fire from Tupac's rear guard signaled the survivors didn't survive.

Riley sat back from the monitor sending pictures from the drone above the chateau and smiled. Then he pressed the transmission button on his radio. "Well done, men. Compress the perimeter. Make sure no one has escaped. Sweep the battlefield. None of the Muslims should be left alive."

Tupac acknowledged. "Roger."

"Hassan, are you listening?"

"Roger, I saw the entire thing. It still made my skin crawl."

"All the better. You won't have any trouble giving Aswira the planned report."

❖

Scott stared at the screen in his office. "Computer, analyze the current conditions of the Gateway transmission cones."

*"Transmission cones are operating nominally. Rotation of the transmission system through three levels of redundancy shows no current anomalies. Routine maintenance and repair, of each redundant component, during idle periods of operation, continues to provide ninety-seven-point nine percent reliability."*

"Are there any other issues requiring attention?"

*"The previously reported broken support beam under the transmission platform continues to have a three-inch depression when more than five hundred pounds of weight is placed on that area. Repairs are adequate, but we recommend an entire replacement of that section."*

"We can't take the time to tear up the platform. The system is cycling two or three hours a day, moving personnel and equipment back and forth to France."

While Scott talked to the computer, Missy came into the office and sat down quietly on a couch.

"Personnel evaluation."

*"Recent adjustment of work schedules has improved worker efficiency with an eight percent decrease in operator errors."*

Missy leaned forward. "I told you rotating the teams to four days on and three days off would make them work better. Everyone wants to be around the Gateway in the exciting times when its cycling soldiers and supplies, but our people get burned out without even knowing it. Mixing up the schedule gives the

298

whole team a feeling they are contributing and get more rest. Not that it slows them down much. They use their days off to teach school, coach soccer teams, take a shift or two in the workshops, or lend a hand at the Trading Post. I think they're happier."

"You were right again, Missy. I sort of forgot your schedule changes in all the clatter of men and women coming and going."

"I'll bet if you asked the computer, she would tell you about half of those operator errors are yours. Of everyone in Sanctuary, the one person that comes to mind the least is you. I've come to take you away from all this."

"Meaning what?"

"I'm taking you home for a family meal and a whole night away from the Gateway."

Scott scowled, then brightened. "Now you mention it, I'm getting tired of eating lukewarm meals in my office. When do you want me to come?"

"Right now. Drop what you're doing and walk away. I'll whisk you away in my super-charged golf cart."

"Your golf cart is the same as mine."

"Don't tell my husband that. He thinks all his tinkering makes a difference."

When Scott and Missy got to the Gallant home, Scott realized he hadn't been there since the two married. Now he thought of it, he'd never been to Chip's home. It filled him with regret and sadness knowing how insular and lonely his life had become. Project Horizon had changed everyone. Him the most. He slumped along behind Missy to the front door.

"Aha!" exclaimed Chips as the two entered. "It's about time you showed up. Missy and I think you have the slenderest social life in all Sanctuary."

"Except maybe Jonas."

"A thing of the past." Chips shoved a snifter of brandy into Scott's hand. "Jonas hit his wall five years ago, right before he gave us all three weeks off. He's much more mellow now. He and Molly come around for dinner and a game of bridge every week. They aren't a couple, but she makes for a handy fourth."

"Plus, we have the only hot tub in town that's not at a public pool. It's bubbly and fun. We'll have a dip after dinner."

Dinner turned out to be a tremendous pleasure for Scott. He complimented the chef and asked if Chips did all the cooking. Missy nodded. "I don't like cooking much, but Chips enjoys it. He's pretty good, don't you think?"

"Wonderful. It's another thing I learn about my friends, every day."

As the three settled into the hot tub, Scott's fatigue washed away as he finished his third brandy. Chips turned to a little business with his wife. "With all our activity in France, aren't you afraid we'll scramble the timestream even worse?"

"It's a problem. When we laid out the plans for Operation Recovery, I spent months devising procedures to minimize the risks. When we confined our interaction with the population of eighth-century France to trading, all we had to do was make sure we didn't introduce anything more modern than what they had or could acquire. Now that we've moved tens of thousands of people into a refugee camps and scattered them all over the combat zone, plus using modern weapons against the Muslims, the probability for making a mistake which alters the future is much higher."

"Does having thousands of our own Sanctuary personnel working the refugee camps make it worse?"

"I hope not. Heaven knows Jonas made them study long enough. They all know a few words and phrases in the current Frankish language to smooth the way in interactions with those nervous refugees."

"I'm more worried the Gateway keeps running."

"You and me both. Scott joined the conversation a trifle

muddled from the alcohol. "I've got triple backups on everything connected to running the cycles. We rotate the critical electronic relays daily, and the computer runs diagnostics on the idle systems when they're not in use. It wasn't originally constructed to function so often or so long, but when we remodeled the entire structure of the Gateway ten years ago, we built in a lot more durability. So far, we' haven't had a glitch."

The conversation went on for another half hour before Scott began to droop. Chips helped him out of the hot tub and down the hall to the guest room.

He slept for twelve hours.

Ahmed Aswira looked gloomily out the window. A black plume of smoke rose in the far distance.

*The attack on the chateau went badly.*

He turned back to his advisor. "You say, Hassan, these ghost soldiers emerged on all sides of my men and, even though they were on foot, managed to overpower the mounted cavalry in minutes?"

"It astonished me. These strange soldiers moved with incredible speed. They were armed with what looked like very long knives. Our men tried to strike them with spears and swords, but their weapons bounced off these fighters as if they were made of stone. They chopped at the horses and the men until none remained. The sounds of death were everywhere. Never have I seen such slaughter. What are you going to do, my lord? Three months of fighting, thousands of brave men dead, an army afraid to take the field, and this enemy still has no face."

"Pepin has a face. I'll squeeze the truth from him."

"Pepin has not been seen for days. He was not on the battlefield."

"Probably laughing at me from his chateau."

"I wouldn't know. Your cavalry never got closer than

301

shouting distance."

"We can't keep continuing to operate in the dark." He turned to his house steward, "Send word I wish to meet with all my generals immediately."

The generals were escorted to Aswira's private conference room and seated around a table. When Aswira entered, they all stood and bowed. He waved them to their seats. "I want the rebel leader Pepin found. I wish to know where his army is hidden. I want to know why we send raiding forces from Paris and have them killed by an unknown band of enemy forces who strike without warning and then disappear.

The senior general stirred from the end of the table, "We shall do as you command, sire. However, since the last battle when so many men were killed before they could attack Pepin's chateau, there is fear and uneasiness among the ranks. We must learn more about the rebel forces we face. I suggest we send small patrols of no more than two or three riders to scout the land within a two-day ride from the palace."

"Fine. Send out fifty such scouting parties if you can find enough brave men who are not afraid. Do whatever is necessary to locate this rabble."

"New units of men are arriving every day. Most of them from Spain, where they have no one to fight. They have not yet seen this phantom rebel force. I will assign these men to our reconnaissance mission."

A Toltec scout, hidden near the outskirts of Paris, radioed a message to the command center, "Muslim patrols are coming out of the city, two or three riders each. I counted forty of these small groups scattering in every direction."

The brigade commanders, and Ben sat ready. Riley answered "Roger." He turned to Ben. "Aswira has no military training or combat experience, but he knows enough to send out patrols to try and get a better picture. We've got the entire division in position. They've dug bunkers and built fortifications around our chosen battlefield, we'll let these patrols wander around wherever they like."

"What about the refugee camps?"

"We aren't going to allow any of the patrols within five miles of them. The rest of the cavalry scouts can thrash around, poke through the remains of the battle near the chateau and discover all the empty villages and cities. Eventually, they will stumble on our fortified positions and see we are getting ready for the main army to march out and face us. That's when Aswira himself will bring his heavy weapons out of mothballs and go with his combined forces to mow us down like he did ten years ago. This time, the outcome will be different."

# Chapter 26
## Setting the Trap

There wasn't a single empty seat in the small auditorium on the first floor of City Hall. Cisco brought all fifty of his Toltec company and brigade commanders back from France. The command team, the department heads and the seniors of Horizon were there as well.

The undercurrent of conversation went silent when Cisco strode to the rostrum in front of a large screen.

"It does not matter if you've been with me for ten years or twenty, we are all bound together now. We have worked, sacrificed, abandoned our personal lives, given all we had, to bring us to this moment. You have wondered if this day would ever come. I will tell you now ... it is here."

Cisco paused to let the magnitude of his announcement soak in.

"My trusted compatriots will tell you how we will succeed, beginning with the commander of our assault forces, General Riley Marquis."

Riley walked to the lectern, grasping its edges. "Computer, display the field of operations."

The image flashed onto the screen, Riley stepped up to it with a pointer. "Aswira has 60,000 men, 30,000 of which are mounted cavalry. He may have more. Reinforcements are arriving steadily from Spain. In any case, we will face this army with 10,000 men, a single, reinforced division of fifty companies. Despite being outnumbered six to one, surprise and superior firepower are our greatest strengths.

Riley pointed to the screen. "This is our battlefield. It is a broad plain surrounded by heavy forest. Near the end it pinches down to this series of hills with the highest point in the center. We plan to draw the Muslim army into this narrow stretch of land where we can engage it on three sides. Colonel Rhoades and Colonel Kepler's brigades will be on the flanks, with Colonel Winterhawk's brigade in the center.

"We have constructed an earthen wall at the top of this hill. It will look like the battleground at Tours in 732. Colonel Winterhawk's brigade will be at the top of this hill with a phalanx of dummy shields and long spears to give Aswira an enticing target for his rockets and Gatling gun."

Riley stood aside for Ben, the chief of intelligence. "For the past three months we have conducted flash raids on Muslim cavalry, the largest being the recent engagement when Aswira sent two thousand men to attack the chateau of Pepin the Short. We killed his entire force. This convinced Aswira a rebel army had been assembled under the command of Pepin, who sent a letter declaring his independence from Muslim rule.

"Now a second letter has been delivered to Aswira taunting him to take the field with his army. His patrols have reported they have discovered the whereabouts of the rebel army. Our belief is he will attack since he now has an actual rebel position.

"Our strategy is to draw Aswira with his armed ATV into the battle intent on destroying the uprising. It is vital we have both Aswira and his weapons exposed at the same time."

Both Riley and Ben sat down, and Cisco returned to the rostrum. "There are three principal goals to this operation. First, we will annihilate the Muslim army down to the last man and capture their generals. Don't feel remorse for the wholesale butchery of so many men, I don't. The removal of the Muslim army from France and Spain will clear the way for the Christian Europeans to resume the course of history as we remember it.

"Second, the Muslim generals will witness the destruction of their army with weapons beyond their wildest imagination. We intend to send these men back to the Capital of the Umayyad Caliphate demanding Muslims withdraw immediately from all

Europe, North Africa, Egypt, and Palestine. If they do not obey this command, we will threaten to assault the entire Middle East with even more terrible weapons, and Islam will be destroyed. We will emphasize to these generals we will respect the practice of their religion and expect them to do the same.

"Third, we hope to capture Ahmed Aswira alive and return him to Sanctuary to stand trial for his crimes."

Cisco looked across the room. "Are there any questions or comments?"

A Toltec officer stood. He gripped his hat in his hands and rocked back and forth on his feet, obviously overwhelmed by the presence of Admiral Cisco, but, nevertheless, compelled to speak.

"Yes, Major Tupac."

"Yes sir, Uh, what happens to us when the battle is over?"

Cisco paused a moment to let the depth and meaning of the question settle in the minds of all Toltec officers. He glanced at Missy and raised his eyebrows a fraction.

She got up from her chair in the front row and walked down the center aisle and stood in front of the Toltec officers. "In the last five years, all of you, and many more of your companions have become a part of Sanctuary. You come and go through the city as freely as the rest of us. You learned about us and our apparent magical ways. None of which are magical any longer.

"You have learned as much about timelines and time travel as us. You share with us the truth there is no assurance that all, part, or none of our past will be restored. We just don't know. We have hopes and dreams, but that is all they are. We also have no idea whether any changes in the timeline will be sharp and abrupt as before or occur over a more extended period of time.

"Having said that. We are about to fight a battle which we hope will be the catalyst to restore the fracture in the timeline. When the battle is won, we will transport the entire division back to Sanctuary as fast as possible in the event a change happens quickly. Then, every man will have a choice. You may stay in Sanctuary and journey to whatever future awaits us, or you may take a step beyond the influence of the secondary field and rejoin your friends and family in the Toltec Empire."

"Sorry you asked the question, Major?"

"No sir, I'm not. I believe it is better to let each of us search our heart and choose what is best for him."

Aswira stared hatefully at the letter. "This is even more offensive than before. Pepin dares me to take my army to the field and do battle with his rebel Franks. He boasts his men will strike down whoever comes to challenge him. He says this land is only for Christians, and Islam is a scar on the face of his country. He goes on to say many insulting things about the Prophet."

He turned to his senior general, who scowled in mutual outrage. "You are certain you've found the location of this rabble stronghold?"

"Yes, sire, our scouts have located their fortifications less than a two-day ride south of Paris."

"How strong are their defenses?"

"My scouts report a considerable number of rebels, perhaps several thousand, massed behind an earthen wall at the top of a hill. I will not be able to tell how strong it is until I've seen it for myself. But no matter, sire, we will erase this filth from the earth."

"Prepare the entire army to march. I will be in the vanguard carrying weapons of great power which will destroy the Franks and end this rebellion. Allah, Akbar!"

In the Division Command Center, Ben listened as the reports came in from lookouts watching from Paris and along the enormous Muslim army's route of march. Riley followed them from signals sent by drones high above.

"It looks like Aswira plans to move his army far enough on the first day to camp overnight so he can launch his assault early on the second day."

Ben looked at the drone images. "The litter carrying Aswira has his ATV mounted like the throne chair. I don't think anybody is paying much attention to the weapons."

"No reason they should. All that equipment looks like decorations to the Muslims." Riley adjusted the picture and got a closer look at the ATV. "I'm more interested in how much ammunition he has left. We have no idea how much of his original ammo he used at the Battle of Tours."

Both men studied the pictures for a few minutes. Finally, Ben looked away. "From what I can tell he has six rockets left."

Riley nodded. "He has at least two canisters for the Gatling gun in addition to the one loaded in the gun."

"That's a lot of firepower. I hope your troops dug nice deep holes to duck into when Aswira starts shooting."

"There's plenty of protection for the men in the bunkers. We need Aswira to shoot himself empty before the boys' pop up and start shooting back."

"By that time, the main force of Aswira's army will be on top of them. I hope Hank's guys stay steady."

Riley looked at Ben and gave him an evil grin. "Don't start getting a case of the nerves. Trust me partner, we've drilled this scenario to bits. That big, fat army doesn't stand a chance. Anyway, time for you to pick up Pepin at the refugee camp. Make sure he gives a good speech about how he's heading out to crush the Muslims and give his Franks a new life. Then hustle him off to safety with his personal guard. Plenty of time when this is over for Pepin and his troops to ride onto the battlefield and claim victory."

"Don't you get nervous either. The company you detached for our part have drilled this as much as you have."

The two men laughed and shook hands.

The Muslim army rode hard the whole day after leaving Paris. The litter carrying Aswira's litter, with his ATV on top, had eight men on each side, and Aswira changed the bearers every hour to not slow the army. By nightfall, they camped a mile from the edge of the plain. Aswira took out a pair of binoculars and looked at the hill where the enemy fortifications were built. He could see many men moving around on top of it. They carried tall shields and long spears. *Exactly the same as Martel's defenses. Too bad they haven't learned a thing.*

"General, after dawn tomorrow your cavalry will follow behind me onto the plain. Your foot soldiers will march behind the horses. I shall be at the head of my army. When I get close to those fortifications, I shall unleash the power of Allah on them. When I am finished, your cavalry will assault the hill and kill everyone. Leave no man standing. Take no prisoners. This rebellion ends tomorrow."

"May Allah bless your realm for a thousand years, sire."

"When I lead our charge tomorrow, all will behold why I am the master of this country and how I will make it larger and stronger. You and your senior officers may ride with me until I begin the slaughter of the Franks. Then move to the side, let the army pass, and be witnesses to my awesome power."

"As you command, sire."

On the hilltop fortification, Tupac watched as the Muslim horde filled the horizon for as far as he could see. Major Chakala stood next to him.

"Well, there they are, my friend. Even though we knew what was coming, it's still a fearsome sight."

"No time for worrying now. Think you can remember the plan?"

"Right. Your men will remain inside the bunkers while Aswira moves up and blasts away at the dummy shield and spear wall. When he runs out of ammo, the units on the flanks will tell us. Let's hope he doesn't get killed when we open fire."

Tupac cocked his head. "Let's hope you don't get killed when you take that select company of yours into the middle of all that and snatch Aswira. Our fields of fire exclude that section of the battlefield to keep us from shooting your guys. You'll have to handle whatever cavalry and infantry are inside that open corridor."

"Whether it's a little or a lot, my men will get the job done."

You have the most dangerous job in this entire operation, but you're the only one I would trust to pull it off."

"I hope my snipers and sharpshooters give us plenty of cover."

# Chapter 27
# The Final Battle

Ahmed Aswira put his hand up to shield his eyes from the morning sun. A sinister grin washed across his face. "General, our day of glory has come. We shall advance." He barked orders to his carriers and the men shouldered the litter and rushed out onto the plain. Behind him, ranks of cavalry, a quarter mile across, trotted their horses.

Riley watched images from the overhead drones. He spoke into the command radio communicating with his forces concealed in trenches along the series of hills at the end of the valley, "Everyone wait for my order to fire. We want Aswira to believe he has blown our shield wall to pieces."

The litter grew closer and closer to the earthen fortification at the top of the hill. When it was just out of arrow range, Aswira shouted. "Stop! Now you infidels shall taste the power of Allah."

He bent to the controls in the ATV and squeezed the trigger for the rocket pack. The first of the rockets went flying in a burst of flames toward the shield wall. It struck near the center and exploded in a fiery blast. Shields and spears flew in all directions. Aswira grinned and pulled the trigger again and again. More missiles flew, exploding along the shield wall with devastating results.

His missiles spent, Aswira pulled the bolt of his Gatling gun and began spraying the shield wall, back and forth with a hail of bullets, laughing all the time. The generals nearby watched, their eyes bulged, as they held their hands over their ears to cover the noise.

Aswira reloaded the Gatling gun twice with his spare canisters. When they were empty, he screamed. "Order the charge. Overrun that fortification. Kill all who remain alive."

The general waved, trumpets signaled the advance. Thirty

thousand men and horses sprang forward with wild shouts. The infantry followed closely behind.

The cavalry charged almost to the top of the hill, surprised it was covered with live soldiers. Riley waited until the last second. Calmly, he spoke into his microphone. "Fire."

A hundred claymore mines exploded, shredding the cavalry riders fifty feet deep into their ranks. A wall of bullets sprayed from the fortification, and a thousand more riders fell dead.

At the same time, Gatling guns opened fire from the flanks of the hills and onto the plain, now a death trap for the advancing army. Men and horses were mowed down by the thousands.

Behind the carnage, Chakala knew this was his moment to act. He said in his radio. "Take down the litter bearers on this side."

Snipers fired, and the eight men on one side of the litter collapsed in bloody gore, spilling the ATV and Aswira to the ground.

"Let's go." Chakala and two hundred men rose from their cover in a small grove of trees, racing at top speed across the plain, spraying death from their automatic rifles as they ran. Gunfire from Toltec sharpshooters covered them. Horses reared, dumping men. The ranks of the infantry nearby, broke in a wild rush to escape the sudden death of so many of their comrades to the front, sides and behind.

Chakala reached the litter first. He dropped to his knees squarely on the back of a dazed Aswira. He grabbed the Muslim's arms and pulled them behind his back, slapping handcuffs on his wrists. Then two of his men threw a blanket around Aswira, wrapping him tightly.

"Withdraw," screamed Chakala. The entire special force, with four men carrying Aswira, dashed away from the litter and toward the outcropping of trees. As they ran, the Toltecs continued firing. More men and horses fell.

The Muslim army was now in disarray and panic. But not all. The remaining veteran core of the Muslim force shot arrows at the fleeing company, others chopped at the Toltecs with their swords. Nearly all the arrows and swords bounced harmlessly off the fully-armored soldiers. But some found their marks on the arms and legs of the men. Some were slashed with Muslim swords as they ran. Their comrades picked them up or helped them hobble along. Two dozen Toltecs lay dead on the field, caught in the flight of arrows and the swinging swords.

Riley watched closely. When he saw Chakala's forces, and their captive, had reached safety, he keyed his mike again. "Artillery, open fire."

The exploding controlled fragmentation, anti-personnel rounds laid waste to entire sections of the battlefield. A trio of heavy-duty ATV's appeared on the plain behind the men and horses trying to flee. Toltec soldiers spit death from Gatling guns.

The charge of the cavalry and men turned into a rout. Men and horses sought the safety of the forest. Everywhere they ran, gunfire found them—the men died.

Some tried to find cover behind their fallen horses or the piled bodies of soldiers—the men died.

A brave charge of a company of Muslim cavalry trying to hurtle over the hill fortifications failed—the men died.

The remnants of the Muslim army were now trapped on all sides. Toltec soldiers advanced onto the plain killing all who faced them.

On a bluff just off the plain, the generals of the army mounted their horses to flee. Before they could ride away, a full platoon of men surrounded them. One general broke from the group and spurred his horse savagely. He fell dead, his head blown apart. Another drew his sword but a Toltec shot him in the head as well.

"Get off your horses," ordered a green-clad soldier. "You are our prisoners. Witness now the destruction of your army."

The generals dismounted and stood in a group, unable to take their eyes off the slaughter going on before them.

When the last of the Muslim army, only a few hundred men, retreated to a tight perimeter for a final stand, Riley spoke into his mike, "Ceasefire. Advance and surround those left alive."

The entire division walked purposefully forward. Now the Muslims had their first sight of the deadly soldiers who had killed tens of thousands. They were dressed in green, camouflaged uniforms. They wore strange helmets.

Chakala joined the platoon guarding the generals. He turned to them and said, "You shall now see how our soldiers can fight without the weapons they carry. They are better than any soldier in all Islam."

From the ranks of the surrounding Toltecs, a few hundred men stepped forward. They dropped their rifles and pulled out long razor-sharp machetes. Then they dashed forward into the crowd of soldiers, their blades flying. The Muslims fought furiously, but soon, most of them were dead. The remaining fifty stood, with eyes swinging wildly, as an equal number of Toltecs stepped forward, dropped their machetes and waved ominously at the Muslims, daring them to fight men with no weapons at all. The dust on the ground rose from the deadly struggles. The generals watched in horror as their men, still swinging their swords and knives, were systematically dropped to the ground, killed by unarmed men, who fought with moves quicker than their eyes could follow.

The generals knew this was the end. They expected nothing, except their execution as the final few left alive from 60,000 men. They stood straight, determined to meet their deaths with courage and dignity. Aswira stood defiantly with shackles on his arms and legs. He was dirty and disheveled, and his nose was bloody.

From across the plain, an ATV sped toward the knoll. The generals watched it approach in wonder and disbelief. Such a vehicle moving by itself could not be possible. It rolled to a stop, and a tall figure stepped out. He was dressed in white. Stars glittered on his shoulders and rows of colored ribbons adorned his chest. He wore a matching white hat, with a visor which shone so clearly it reflected the image of the nearby trees. He walked up to Aswira and stood before him.

"Cisco!" How can this be?"

"Did you imagine, Ahmed, we would let you kill our people, destroy our past, leave us stranded in the wilderness, and not do something about it?"

Aswira sputtered and cursed.

"Not much to say eh, Ahmed. Well, I have something to say. You are under arrest. You will be transported to Sanctuary to stand trial for your crimes. Take him away, Chakala."

Aswira shuffled off. Cisco watched him go. Then he turned to the generals. They had not understood the words just spoken since they were in English. Now Cisco spoke to them in Arabic.

"Aswira was not one of yours. He is one of ours. He is a Muslim, but the Islam he practices is hateful, destructive, and sinful."

Cisco stepped up to the commanding general of the Muslim army. "What did you witness today?"

The general looked up into the eyes of the tall admiral. "I have no words. We brought a powerful army onto the field to destroy a rebellion of the Franks. Now, all are dead. The field is covered with their bodies. They were destroyed by terrible weapons I cannot describe."

"Did you see the end when my soldiers faced yours with no weapons and still prevailed?"

"I did."

"Even without weapons, my soldiers can defeat any soldier from any army in the world."

"I do not doubt that."

"Now I give you my final word. The Islam you practice is also hateful and is not according to the will of Allah. You have been lied to by Caliphs whose only religion is one of conquest and the domination of innocent people who never meant you any harm.

"Your lives will be spared. You will return to your homes. You will tell Caliph Hisham what you have seen today. You will tell him Allah has placed weapons in the hands of the Christians to prove your ways are wrong. Your imams must re-read the words of the Prophet and discover he intended a world of peace, not war.

"Islam must withdraw immediately from all of Europe, North Africa, Egypt, and Palestine. You will disband your armies. We will respect your right to worship God in your own way and practice your faith in your own lands. We expect you to respect ours. Never again shall Islam take armies into war and conquest. This is the command of Allah. If you do not obey, He will not be understanding. Men such as myself will come to your own countries. They have weapons and soldiers of the kind you witnessed here today.

"Your task will be difficult. Your caliph may not believe you. When he speaks of jihad. When his imams say Islam is the final truth of Allah, show him this." Chakala handed Cisco a hand grenade. He took it, pulled the pin and threw it. Seconds later came a thunderous explosion. Every one of the Muslims jumped in fear. Cisco took another grenade and handed it to the general. He held it in his hands as if it were a hot rock. "This, is your proof I speak the truth."

"Who are you?"

"It does not matter who I am. What does matter is for you," Cisco turned to the rest of the men, "all of you, remember this day and know Allah gives you this warning."

Cisco turned and walked away. Chakala pushed Aswira to the ATV. Then they were gone.

# Chapter 28
# Mission Accomplished

Nobody celebrated in France. The Toltec division began jumping back to Sanctuary as soon as the battle ended. The citizens of Sanctuary who had worked in the refugee camps walked away to transfer points a mile away. Every spy, or informant disguised as traders, merchants, or advisors gathered every shred of 21st-century technology and departed. The Gateway cycled continuously.

Cisco had no idea if the new interruption in the timestream would occur rapidly as before, or take longer, or not happen at all. His sole mission was to evacuate everyone from eighth-century France as fast as possible. The transfers took two days. Cisco and the command team were the last to leave.

When he and the others stepped off the Gateway platform, they went at once to City Hall and the conference room at the top of the building. Scott and Missy came from the Gateway Center. Everyone was exhausted. They fell into comfortable chairs, munched from a plate of pastries, and poured themselves cups of strong coffee.

Riley looked around the table. "Well, we did it. We actually pulled it off."

Cisco nodded with a grim smile. "Yes, we did. I know you're all worn out, but we can't stop now. I feel like we're operating on borrowed time."

The others knew that and sat straighter in their chairs.

Chips spoke first. "I guess what we want to know, is when we can expect a change in the timeline, if any."

"Your wife is still the reigning expert on that. What about it Missy?"

"Nearly twenty-four hours passed for the change to occur ten years ago. We've already used up more than that getting everyone back from France. Despite all our efforts, we must have altered the past in many small ways. We also introduced a major and unpredictable variable with our forced intervention to the Islamic world. Maybe we'll get some extra time."

"I sure hope we didn't make it worse."

"We ran hundreds of 'what ifs' through the computer. The actions we took had the highest probability for an outcome favorable to a modern world."

"I'm not going to worry about it until it happens. Computer, battle report."

*"Toltec casualties are fifty-three dead, and two hundred seventy-six wounded. Twenty of the wounded remain in critical condition. All Toltec personal have returned to Sanctuary, including the dead and wounded.*

*Drone and body cam footage indicates that as many nine hundred Muslim soldiers survived the battle and were able to escape into the forest."*

Ben ventured. "I wonder if that means anything?"

Missy shook her head. "Unlikely, I doubt many of those men will survive retribution from the Franks. In any case, those who do manage to return home will retell the events of the battle. It only adds more credibility to the accounts of the generals."

"How did Pepin react when you showed him the battlefield, Ben?"

"He threw up. I almost did myself. You'll never see anything ghastlier than sixty thousand dead men and thirty thousand horses."

"No doubt. Did he finally realize what kind of a victory he'd been handed and the huge responsibility we've given him?"

"Time will tell. I had to leave, so I wasn't able to spend a lot of time talking to him."

Cisco looked at Scott. "If you hadn't done such a great job of keeping the Gateway running, we'd still be stuck in the eighth century. Give your crew a big thanks from me."

"Don't plan on making any jumps in the near future. We had some failures in the systems and were running on the third redundancy before we could power down. We're running deep diagnostics of every relay, circuit, power lines, everything. We contracted the secondary power dome to the original city perimeter. The Trading Post and the entire training center are now outside that power field."

"Speaking of which, there's the matter of our Toltecs. Computer, how many of the brigade are choosing to remain in Sanctuary?"

***"Two thousand, one hundred and sixty-four."***

Wyatt seemed surprised. "That many? I would have guessed almost all of them would choose to stay in their own time."

"Many of them have established personal attachments," said Ben. "A good number have started new careers of their own. We have teachers, engineers, computer techs, and several other specialty categories. We'll be able to fit them right in. They'll be welcome and valuable."

"Anything I've forgotten?"

Riley stared at Cisco. "You must be kidding. What about the guy who started all this, and we ran a ten-year operation to bring back to Sanctuary for trial?"

Cisco puts his hands to his face and shook his head. "Pretty dumb of me to let such an important thing slip my mind. I must be getting old. Anyway, Ahmed Aswira is currently in a special cell I built in the hopes we would be able to capture him alive. It's in the back of the building downstairs."

"I can't wait for him to face court-marshal. I hope you televise the whole thing."

"I'd probably get shot if I didn't. Anyway, everyone knows what's being decided. The people of Sanctuary have a right to see the final chapter of Operation Recovery. Besides, I don't want a circus going on around the trial. Let everyone stay at home and see it all."

"When are you planning on having the trial?"

"As soon as we finish our job. Right now, we need some sleep. I'll have the computer wake up the department directors and start everyone working to clean up the mess we made building up for the operation and our mass evacuation. Let the men and women who've been busy in France be reunited with their families. I want as much done as possible to return to normal in the event the timeline catches up with us. Meeting adjourned."

The people of Sanctuary didn't need to be told what to do. With only a hint of supervision, they rolled up their sleeves and went to work. They wanted their city back in the order it had before the final months of Operation Recovery jumbled everything. They worked with purpose, knowing any sudden change in the timeline could force them to face new or threatening challenges. They disregarded the danger of this possibility and sweated, day and night, for a week. Whenever Cisco took a break from his own work and walked out on his balcony to look out across the city, he marveled at the industry of his fellow citizens. It was time for the two remaining events of Operation Recovery.

"Computer, I have a message I want it broadcast on all Sanctuary channels."

The trial of Ahmed Aswira, with Cisco serving as the presiding judge, entered its second day. On the first day, the video evidence of Aswira assaulting the Gateway, shooting the guard on duty and killing Lino Arnett was shown. Additionally, motives for his actions were also presented.

The people of Sanctuary hung on every word.

The defense attorney argued Aswira acted from a dedication to his religion and should be spared execution on those grounds. Aswira made it worse by continually jumping up and interrupting. "This Christian court has no jurisdiction over me. I demand I be tried by a court of my own peers and by the tenants of Sharia Law."

"Objection overruled," said a calm and measured Admiral Cisco.

The military jury required only an hour to return with the verdict—guilty on all counts.

Now it remained for Cisco to pronounce his sentence. Sanctuary held its breath.

"Ahmed Aswira, this court has found you guilty on all charges. I will offer you a final choice. You may choose death by hanging or be imprisoned in solitary confinement with no human interaction whatsoever for the balance of your life."

"I will outlive your chains. I will have the comfort of Allah."

"So, you choose imprisonment?"

"Yes! May Allah curse you for your evil ways."

"Remove the prisoner."

Sanctuary was satisfied. There had been enough killing.

Following the trial, Cisco announced the final act of "Operation Recovery. A general assembly would be held in Cooper River Stadium that night to allow the Toltec division to pass in review so the entire community could salute their service and remember their fallen comrades.

Bursting with emotion, the people of Sanctuary packed the stadium. The Toltec soldiers, marched into the arena to a thunderous, standing ovation that went on for many minutes.

Finally, when everyone had taken their seats, Cisco came to the rostrum. His image shown large on the jumbotron.

"My fellow citizens, I welcome you here tonight. We honor our Toltec compatriots without whom we could never have prevailed in our mission to France. I wish to thank each of you men in arms, and also to pay honor and tribute to those of your ranks who fell during the struggle. May we all observe a moment of silence as a token of our respect."

The stadium went quiet and stayed that way until Cisco said, "Amen."

"Ten years ago, you gave me an order to devise a way to attempt to restore the timeline to recognizable forms and to bring the criminal, who left us alone in a hostile world, to justice. I am proud to say tonight—Mission Accomplished!"

The stadium rocked with cheering and applause. When the crowd screamed itself almost hoarse, Cisco continued. "None of what we did would have been remotely possible if every single one of you had not chosen to make the sacrifice, pay the price, and work as no other people have done for so long. I could not be prouder than I am tonight. May our future be as bright as our souls and may each of you remember this tremendous achievement for the rest of your lives."

If a major shift in the timestream was imminent, somebody had forgotten to tell the people of Sanctuary. With the return of so many thousands from France where they had worked at the refugee camps and many other places scattered around France, there were joyous reunions. The city had known little else but endless labor, late nights, and very few days off for many years. With the knowledge all the hard work had finally ended in triumph, public celebrations broke out spontaneously. Enterprise Plaza hummed with activities. The party continued for days.

Cisco let everyone enjoy themselves. He hadn't declared a public holiday. He hadn't needed to. The people of Sanctuary took it upon themselves to celebrate on their own. They knew what they'd done and were more than willing to take their feet off the gas.

Jonas Cisco slept a lot during the next week. Two days he didn't go into his office at all. One afternoon Molly stopped by his house, and the two of them sat on the patio, sipping sweet tea.

"I haven't told you, but you sure have beautiful landscaping and a garden full of flowers. How did you ever find the time?"

"I didn't. All this magic came to life under the green thumbs of the Mason couple."

As if summoned by pixie dust, the couple came around the corner of the house. Molly looked at them and laughed. "I should have known."

The Mason couple were Gloria and her tanned and smiling husband.

"Howdy, Admiral. Have you noticed all our new plantings?"

"I have, indeed. Can I offer you and Buddy a glass of sweet tea, as thanks?"

"Thanks a lot, Admiral. I'm parched."

Molly headed back inside. "I'll get some glasses and bring out a pitcher."

"I have the lushest landscaping in the whole neighborhood. It's too bad I haven't been home to enjoy it much."

"Oh, that's okay, Admiral. We knew the day would come when you would win the war and came home to smell the flowers. We took care of things till then."

Cisco had to marvel at the tanned, trim and naturally beautiful woman in front of him. Her marriage to Buddy a few years before seemed to suit them both. Cisco sat back and grinned broadly. "Don't you think it's about time you started calling me Jonas?"

"I could never do that, Admiral. I honor, respect and love you too much. To me, you will always be The Admiral...my Admiral."

Molly returned to the patio. "I heard that. I think you have

324

correctly summarized the general feeling of all Sanctuary, Gloria. I'm glad somebody finally said something to make the old iceberg melt a little."

Cisco blushed, and tears filled his eyes. "You folks give me a lot more credit than I deserve. I thank you. I promise to walk through my garden at least once a day and enjoy every new addition."

Gloria drained her glass and punched her husband in the stomach. "Come on, handsome. Now we know he's paying attention we can't afford to miss a single weed."

When the two were gone, Molly asked, "Do you plan to come to the office tomorrow?"

"Maybe I'll go fishing instead."

A week after the Gateway returned the 21st-century travelers to their homes, and housing found for the Toltecs choosing to remain in the city, Chips and Missy went out for a walk on Enterprise Plaza to take in some of the flavor of the jolly days, and festive nights.

"I'm not sure I understand all this," waved Chips as they strolled along. "People don't seem to care if the timestream changes or not."

"Is it really so surprising? Ten years ago, we were stranded, abandoned in a wilderness. We were angry, afraid, confused and without purpose. Jonas Cisco put us to work and gave us goals and hope for the future. The people of Sanctuary bought into his vision of a better tomorrow. Now, ten years later, we have accomplished what we set out to do. Along the way, the memories and heartbreak for loved ones lost, have faded. Today we are stronger than ever, independent, self-reliant, and proud of who we are. We have developed our own identity which we mutually share. I suspect people don't care much if our future changes a little, a lot, or not at all. Who we are is a lot more important to them than any unknown challenge around the corner."

Chips was about to tell his wife how smart he thought she was and how much he loved her when a group of party-goers swept her up and into a crowd singing, dancing, and barbequing hot dogs on a grill. Eventually, he got to dance with his wife.

The party came to an abrupt end, five days later.

# Chapter 29
# Timequake

Cisco was sleeping soundly when all the lights in his bedroom went on, and the video screen came to life.

Groggily he sat up in bed. "Computer, report."

*"Two minutes ago, a major alteration in our immediate environment beyond the perimeter was detected. All indications are a major shift in the timeline has occurred."*

"Summarize."

*"Multiple audio and video signals are being received, both from Earth-based transmitters and satellite communications. An urban center of some size now exists east of Sanctuary and continuing to the coast. Additionally, more suburban pockets can be seen in a 360-degree arc surrounding the city."*

"Any telephone communications?

*"There are no landline communications because no hardwire connections exist. However, intermittent cellular traffic is present."*

"Are they speaking English?"

*"Oh, yes sir. Standard colloquial American English. However, some of the entertainment channels contain unfamiliar idiomatic expressions."*

"No doubt. Do you have the capability to access an internet information source?"

*"Such a source is available. It is not the familiar Google but is known as Spyglass."*

"Begin a search starting with all American historical records and expansion to global records of the same kind. Start a log of significant differences in these records from recorded history before the Blackout."

*"Working."*

"Issue a city-wide emergency. Put armed guards at every city entry point. Allow no one to enter or leave the city until further notice. Alert all security personnel. Establish sentry points around the perimeter of the city at no less than two hundred-meter intervals. Wake all command staff, Horizon, and department directors. I want them in the main conference room at City Hall in one hour. Wake the kitchen staff and bring pastries and hot coffee to the conference room."

Cisco jumped out of bed and put on a uniform. He splashed cold water on his face to make him fully alert. Then he ran outside, jumped in his ATV and roared off to City Hall.

He wasn't the first to arrive. Chips and Missy were waiting for him.

"It looks like the timestream has changed, Jonas."

"It has. I locked down the perimeter and stopped any traffic in or out of the city. I don't want a bunch of visitors before we're ready to handle them."

*"Admiral, there is an urgent message for you from Major Jenkins in the Comm Center."*

"On screen."

Cisco remembered Jenkins, as a Lieutenant, from his original conversation with him ten years ago. He was older, but still as excited.

"Admiral, we've reacquired satellite communications, a lot of it. Most of the civilian traffic is normal, but the military frequencies are going nuts."

"What are they saying?"

Basically, a bunch of communications regarding the appearance of a previously unknown city in the vicinity of Charleston, South Carolina. We also have quite a few transmissions sent directly to us. The gist of the messages is 'Who are you?'. What do you want me to do?"

328

Cisco paused and poured himself a cup of coffee while he thought. "Stand by Major, I'll have the computer send you a message to transmit shortly." He broke the connection. "Computer, record this message. Broadcast it on every external source you can."

He strode to the rostrum at the front of the room, turned in the direction of one of the surveillance cameras, straightened his uniform and tie, and put a smile on his face. "Good morning, America. My name is Admiral Jonas Cisco. All this is as much of a surprise to us as it is you. The name of this city is Sanctuary. We have our own perimeter guard here, although we haven't used it for quite a while. I'm using it now to limit the number of non-resident visitors. The infrastructure of our city is quite fragile. A sudden influx of people would be difficult for our 12,000 American families and make all our kids late for school.

"Let me tell you what I can. Originally, Sanctuary was a military installation, which is why I'm sort of like the mayor. We were part of a major experiment in some advanced technology a number of years ago. It looks like the outcome of that experiment is hitting us all in the face this morning.

"I hope you will be patient while we sort this out. I'm not entirely sure what to do next, I hope some of you have some suggestions. If such is the case, we're wide open. Try contacting us by phone or your computers. I hope to be back to you soon. Have a wonderful day, and may the Lord bless you."

Cisco stepped away from the podium and sat back down. "Computer, how many factual mistakes did I make in that message?"

***"Based on the search parameters given by you earlier, there are no significant anomalies."***

"That's a relief. I was just winging it."

He looked up at the others at the table. Most of the department directors came in while he spoke. The room was now quite full. Everyone looked at him, mostly with strange expressions on their faces.

Missy broke the silence. "That was astonishing, Jonas. It's like you practiced what to say before you said it. The first thing you did established an immediate connection with us and the rest of the country. Then you went right on, as if you were apologizing, for limiting access to the city on the grounds of us being delicate and fragile and not wanting to upset our families and make the kids late for school. This is so informal and believable, I'll bet nobody is going to question your motives at all."

"I liked the part where you said we were an unmilitary, military installation," said Wyatt. "It conceals the fact, if push came to shove, it would take a couple divisions of troops and saturation bombing to knock out the best-trained, elite fighting force in the world. Never mind most of it disappeared with the shift of the timeline."

Scott chimed in. "Your hint of us being part of an exotic experiment will disarm a lot of people. People suspect all sorts of secret technology is always being tested, with unknown effects. Saying we were swept up by that same technology is a good way of making us victims and not mad scientists. You managed to say a lot without actually saying anything."

Chips finished. "Evoking God in your final statement puts a halo around you and us. People don't rush to judgment so quickly when they believe you have a spiritual base."

"Well, thanks for the book reports, boys and girls. You do realize all I did was buy us some time. From now on the questions will get a lot harder to answer."

"My guess is you appearing in uniform as a Navy Admiral will get an almost immediate response from the Pentagon, assuming there is such a place."

Chips pointed at one of the monitors. "That won't be very

330

long. I played back your instructions to the computer earlier and sent several work crews out to hook up some telephone land lines to our system."

"Fine, I want to communicate clearly."

The team spent the next two hours sorting through their options, based on the fragmentary information they had and formulating some basic strategies of what to do next.

When Cisco got back to his office the phones were ringing. Molly put down a receiver. "Everyone from the local Chief of Police, to the Mayor of Charleston, to the Governor of South Carolina has already called."

"What did you say?"

"I told them I couldn't add anything more to what they already knew, and any future statements would be released as conditions allowed."

"I'm sure that satisfied them completely."

"Of course not, but I had a fun time. There's one call you need to handle yourself."

"What's that?"

"It's from the Chief of Naval Operations in Washington. He's called twice. I told him you were in a meeting, but I'm sure he has you on speed dial."

"Okay, we might as well start the ball moving up the chain of command. Ring me when he calls back."

Cisco had an illuminating half hour looking at some very surprising facts on the computer about the history of the United States as it currently existed. It gave him a better foundation when Molly rang saying the CNO was on the line again. Cisco picked up the phone.

"Admiral Wilson, I sorry I haven't been available before now. I've had a busy morning working with my staff."

"If you think you've been busy, I can guarantee it's nothing compared to the madhouse around here."

"I'm sure. What can I do for you, Admiral."

"The first thing you can do, *Admiral,* is tell me exactly who you are."

"Lost track of me, did you?" He could hear the frosty tone in the voice on the other end of the phone and wanted to stay cordial as long as possible.

"We didn't lose track. You don't exist. There is absolutely no record of you in any Naval archives."

"Well, if I don't exist, and you are convinced I'm not an Admiral, then how come the Navy had you call me up?"

"Maybe we ought to drop a few tons of ordinance on your shitty little city and be done with it."

"I'm glad you aren't making the decisions. How would you like to take the blame for killing 30,000 innocent men, women and children? It would look bad on your record, to say nothing of how it would play on all the network television news hours."

"Now look you, miserable pipsqueak, I'm not..."

"No, you look, Admiral. Every other CNO I've known have been calm and rational men. You act like a shave tail out of Annapolis. This is what you're going to tell your superiors. My orders for everything connected to this entire situation came directly from the President of the United States. The current man may not be the same guy, but he's still the commander in chief, and I have specific orders not to discuss any details whatsoever with anyone else. You have the biggest event since the collapse of the San Andreas Fault fifteen years ago. I suggest you treat it the same." Cisco slammed the phone down, sat back and smiled.

Molly came into the office. "Was that you're pissed off for show voice, or you're pissed off for real voice?"

"Probably a little of both. That guy is a jerk. Anyway, I'm sure he got the message. Probably they recorded it. The next call *will* be from the President. I don't want to speak to anyone less, except for our own people."

332

"We have a dozen helicopters orbiting the city," reported Riley that afternoon. "After people figured out trying to sneak their way into the city wasn't going to work, they took the next best option."

"I hope they're taking lots of pretty pictures of our unique community."

"Wall to wall on every television network," said Chips.

Ben looked up from his computer screen. "Have you guys been studying the data coming out of the computer about this country?"

"That's supposed to be your job."

"I've been doing it. In addition to us being the big news, there are seventy-five states, and the United States is the largest country in the world. Somewhere in history, the United States managed to annex Canada, Mexico, Central America, and all the islands of the Caribbean."

"That is astonishing. Guess nobody is worried much about illegal aliens."

"Very funny, Admiral. Here's something you don't know. The date in the timeline is the same as when the blackout occurred, but the current state of technological advances in this country is way behind where our old country was when we got tossed into the time dumpster."

"No kidding? Where does the computer say the country is ... about?"

"The estimate is current technology in the United States is about at the mid-1970s level."

Chips picked up the thought. "That means, what we have here is fifty years ahead of anything they have."

"That will give you leverage with the President when he calls back," added Missy. "How are you going to use it?"

"I've gotten real partial looking out for the best interest of the people of Sanctuary. I expect I'll let that be my guide.

# Chapter 30
# The New, Old World

"Stand by for the President," said a White House operator.

Cisco took a deep breath as he sat at his conference table. Around the table were the members of the command team and the Horizon seniors. He decided to let his trusted team listen in on this call. Glancing around the table, Cisco saw the same apprehension on their faces he felt in his stomach.

"This is President Hardy," came a voice on the other end of the line.

"Good morning, Mr. President, I hope you're not as nervous as we are."

"No bets on that, Admiral." The President had a deep voice. "You've managed to upset and frighten the whole country. In the end, all this got dumped in my lap. Don't expect me to treat this as a social call."

"Of course not. I wish you had the capability to stream video so I could look you in the eye. How people look when they say things is often as important as them saying it."

"I gather two-way television is common for you?"

"Oh, yes sir, we routinely video conference with each other when we communicate."

The President sounded like he wasn't interested in small talk as he went on. "Very well, Admiral. I have a problem. Your city suddenly appears from nowhere. You haven't allowed anyone in there, but I have detailed footage of your city from our surveillance helicopters. Most of what we see shows a city with clearly advanced technology. Where did it come from? How did you acquire it? How much more am I not seeing?"

"All good questions, Mr. President. The answers would take hours to explain, and you would still only understand a tiny piece of the whole story."

"Well, somebody better start explaining something. I've got Congress screaming for answers, the entire military on alert, and an avalanche of Press beating on my door. To say nothing of the whole country being scared to death."

"I'm sure that's true. I'm also sure you've heard I told your senior chain of command I am specifically ordered to disclose nothing about Sanctuary and the details surrounding us to anyone except the commander in chief. I am fully prepared to do that."

"Start talking."

"The story of Sanctuary is so complex, so enormous, so sensitive, and so dangerous to our country and the entire world you need to start thinking about joining with me to find a way to handle it. I'm sure that only makes it worse for you but I do have a plan."

"What's your plan?"

"You have to come here as soon as possible."

"Are you out of your mind? The obvious risks of me stepping into a place with a thousand unknowns, like I'm some kind of explorer in the wilderness, will never be permitted by the secret service."

"Nevertheless, Mr. President, you have to come. After you hear and see the whole story you will have tremendous decisions to make. Not to add to your problems, but it will take a week for us to thoroughly brief you, and only you. I can promise you will be completely safe."

"So, you say."

"Sir, I am a loyal American citizen. I was born and raised in the United States. I have served in the Navy for over forty years. When you know everything, you'll be glad I maintained the confidentiality in this matter."

"Well, I...."

"Time is of the essence, Mr. President. You will not be able to keep the lid on this for long. I implore you, Sir, come to Sanctuary as quickly as you can."

"I'll get back to you."

The connection was broken. Cisco looked around the table. "Questions, comments, suggestions."

"Assuming he will come," said Wyatt, "how are you going to tell the story?"

"I'm not going to tell it, at least not right away. What I'm going to do is to give the President a glimpse of how advanced our technology is in every field. Once he realizes what a mammoth resource we are, he'll start thinking of how to exploit it for the good of the country, and probably for his political future. Having him hungry to cash in on what we have, will make explaining who we are and how we got here a lot easier."

"That sounds right," said Scott. How much are you going to tell him after he finds out how amazing we are?"

"Everything. All of it, from the beginning, when you were locked up in that warehouse, right up to the time three weeks ago, when we beat it out of medieval France."

Missy joined the conversation. "That might be the best course. I've had a chance to read the President's biography. He's not some party hack who got elected on charm and favorable press. He's quite intelligent, very visionary, and not afraid to make tough choices. Maybe we got lucky and had the right man come along at the right time."

It took two days to work out all the details. Riley had several heated conversations with both the military and the secret service about the President's security. Cisco thought he pulled a brilliant maneuver by getting the military to surround Sanctuary with troops ostensibly to protect the President. Riley got overwhelmed trying to guard the perimeter and keep a hungry public from breaking in and trashing the whole city. Now the Army did the job for him. The fact they were still excluded from entry into the city, didn't bother him one bit.

The command team, dressed in formal uniforms, the Horizon seniors, Scott chafing with an unfamiliar tie, and Missy with a long dress, stood on the tarmac with Cisco wearing his dress Navy whites. Several thousand of the population of Sanctuary stood behind security lines eager to greet the President's plane.

Cisco took a deep breath as the plane touched down. "Okay gang, here we go."

The President emerged from the plane smiling and waving. A band played 'Hail to the Chief' and Cisco stepped forward to greet the honorable William Hardy, and the First Lady.

The delicate protocols guiding this visit were hammered out in advance. The President shook hands with the Sanctuary officials and then was led to an enclosed golf cart. It was the same one used by Cameron Fisk years before. Cisco got in with him, and two secret service agents stuffed into the back. Missy escorted the First Lady to her own golf cart, also with secret service agents. The President raised his brows when he saw there was no steering wheel and Cisco spoke 'engage' to the computer. The entourage rolled away.

Cisco had to smile as the cavalcade followed a fairly lengthy course toward City Hall, the computer gave descriptions of the amazing, revolutionary architecture, blended into a parklike setting, and the intricate transportation infrastructure weaving through the city. He remembered how the Academy reacted when they first arrived in Sanctuary. They knew a good deal more about the city, and its many innovations than the President did today. They were still somewhat overwhelmed, just as much as the rest of the country had been. Sanctuary was built to impress, even in that more modern age. Cisco could see the President looking at everything with wondering, astonished eyes. If he had a hint he had done hardly more than scratch the surface of the

337

marvels awaiting him, he would have been speechless.

Exactly as Cisco said, it took a full week for the President to absorb the entire story of how Sanctuary came to be, how it became isolated and alone following the fracture of the original timeline, and what it did to claw its way back to the new present, and new world.

Both the President and First Lady were physically sick, just as Pepin, when they witnessed the slaughter of 60,000 Muslims in eighth-century France. Cisco had his doubts about including the First Lady in the full briefings. Missy told him, about the importance of her seeing and hearing everything her husband did.

"You have to include her, Jonas. She's every bit as smart as him. He counts on her to help him manage the affairs of this huge country. When they go home, he will need her to move forward. Besides, he'll want to be able to talk to someone. You couldn't expect him to keep this secret by himself."

Cisco agreed.

On the day before the final meeting, the First Couple explored the city on their own and wandered about Enterprise Plaza. The worries about their personal safety were long gone. The President relegated his secret service detail to discreet monitoring from a distance. The people of Sanctuary treated them with respect but refrained from invading their privacy unless invited to do so. The First Couple did engage a number of people at random. The grass-roots description of Sanctuary's history, if anything, was more compelling than the official version. Neither one of them could remember enjoying a day more.

The last day included a final meeting with the President. Cisco had to smile that when the two of them were alone, it was now 'Bill and Jonas'.

"The first thing I want to say, Jonas is thank you for keeping

338

this stupendous story from anyone but me. You certainly understood the correct way to proceed when I didn't. You were absolutely right. Having this information out in the open would be a disaster."

"True. Now we get down to it. What are we going to do next?"

"I suppose you've got a plan? After seeing the many brilliant decisions you've made over the years, I'm inclined to trust your judgment."

"Yes, I do. Initially, you need a credible story of how we got here. Computer, tell the President the result of our analysis."

*"After reviewing the complete history of the world and the United States as it evolved in this timeline, following the actions by Sanctuary in medieval France to correct the damage of the first fracture, the most plausible course of action is as follows.*

*The public should be told that a radical experiment into time travel was initiated approximately fifty years in the current future. The result of this experiment was Sanctuary and all its people were unexpectedly thrust into the past, appearing fourteen days ago. There are no explanations as to why this happened. None of the people in Sanctuary are qualified to repeat the experiment, and all data regarding how the original researchers achieved this breakthrough is lost. Sanctuary is an anomaly. Its advanced technology from a half-century in the future presents unexpected benefits for the United States and the world."*

The President took a sip of his sweet tea. "I think that will work. We can't explain anything because we don't know anything. Meanwhile, the United States makes a bundle on all your marvelous technology."

"Most of our Toltec soldiers are gone, transported to their

own branched universe. We can't maintain security on our own."

"I'll station troops around Sanctuary. Hell, I'll build a whole base around you. Nobody will have access to the city without your permission."

"Thanks, Bill. With your help and permanent discretion, the old history of the world will die, and the new history will unfold in its own way. In a few years, private enterprise, and the government will have mined all our secrets. Then Sanctuary can go on as a beautiful, unique, innovative city, special, but hardly mysterious."

"What are your plans for the future, Jonas?"

"Me? I should have retired years ago. I think I'll take my share of the loot we're going to make and buy myself a little ranch in Colorado."

The President made a big speech that night on nationwide TV, telling everyone the "true" story of Sanctuary. Afterward, Cisco had the satisfaction of knowing the public bought it hook, line, and sinker.

A month later, he had dinner with Chips and Missy at their home.

"Scott told me the other day not to expect any new jumps in the near future. The damage to the Gateway was extensive in the recall. Anyway, the work they're doing now is more academic than operational."

Missy sat back in her chair as if it was the first time she's relaxed in ten years. "That suits me. I've had enough time travel to last two lifetimes."

"I get the feeling the whole community feels the same."

"Are you really going to retire, Jonas? I'm not sure Sanctuary can get along without you."

"Poohey. It's time for all us old codgers to make an exit. Wyatt's going, so's Riley, and Will and Scott. Let Ben, take over and worry about everything with Hank, Dusty and Jack to help him. You should both buy the ranch next to me, and we can catch trout in our river."

Missy jabbed her husband with her elbow. "That's exactly what I told him last night."

"I think we made a difference, partner,"

"I know we did. The best thing I've seen since we arrived in this new, old world was a look I had of the skyline of New York the other day."

"What's so special about that?"

"The towers of the World Trade Center are still standing."

**Everything about Phil Walker, his books, his approach to writing and interesting blogs may be found at philwalkerbooks.com**

### Enjoy these books by Phil Walker on Kindle

Sanctuary In Time
The Black Angel
Crusade of The Black Angel
The Rangers are Coming
Lions and Tigers, and Bears, OH GOD!
Out of the Emerald Cathedral
The Magic and the Misery

### The Starlight Series

The Holy Mission
The Galilee Foundation
The Galilee Garden
Island of the Angels
Terra Rising
Heaven's Angels
The Galactic Quest

### Non-Fiction History

Visions Along the Poudre Valley
Modern Visions Along the Poudre Valley

### Order paperback books from Amazon

The Black Angel
Crusade of The Black Angel
The Rangers are Coming
Sanctuary in Time